None
but the
Dead

LIN ANDERSON

PAN BOOKS

First published 2016 by Macmillan

This paperback edition published 2017 by Pan Books
an imprint of Pan Macmillan
20 New Wharf Road, London N1 9RR
Associated companies throughout the world
www.panmacmillan.com

ISBN 978-1-5098-0700-0

1 3 5 7 9 8 6 4 2

A CIP catalogue record for this book is available from the British Library.

Typeset by Palimpsest Book Production Ltd, Falkirk, Stirlingshire
Printed and bound by CPI Group (UK) Ltd, Croydon, CR0 4YY

For DI Bill Mitchell

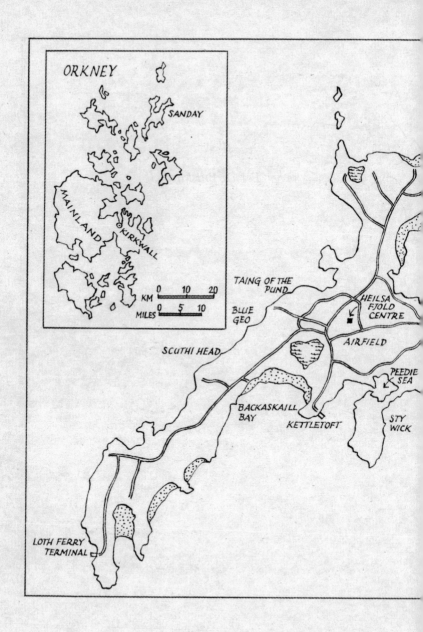

ORKNEY

MAINLAND

KIRKWALL

SANDAY

KM 0   10   20
MILES 0   5   10

TAING OF THE PUND

HEILSA FJOLD CENTRE

BLUE GEO

AIRFIELD

SCUTHI HEAD

PEEDIE SEA

BACKASKAILL BAY

KETTLETOFT

STY WICK

LOTH FERRY TERMINAL

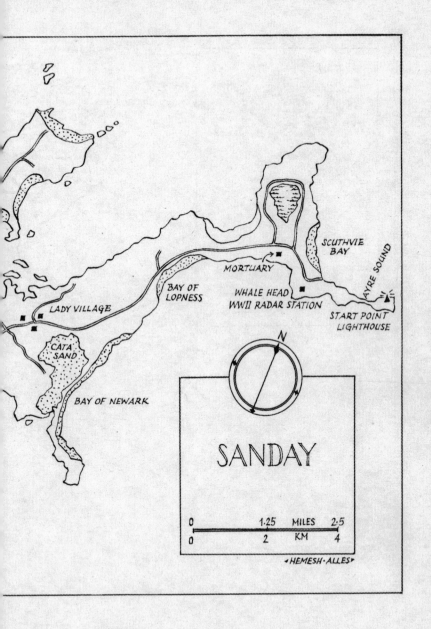

SCUTHVIE
BAY

MORTUARY

WHALE HEAD
WWII RADAR STATION

BAY OF
LOPNESS

AYRE SOUND

START POINT
LIGHTHOUSE

LADY VILLAGE

CATA
SAND

BAY OF NEWARK

N

SANDAY

| 0 | 1·25 | MILES | 2·5 |
| 0 | 2 | KM | 4 |

◄ HEMESH · ALLES ►

None but the dead are left to tell the tale.

Music, chatter and laughter spill from the Nissen hut to follow them. Her hand is hot in his as they run, her breath coming in small gasps. Reaching the top of the dune, he jumps down onto the beach. Turns and lifts her.

She is light as a bird in his hands. The smallness of her excites him as he lays her on the white sand. Pushing up her dress he finds the warm smooth skin of her inner thigh.

She halts his hand and anger sparks, though he strives to quench it.

'You do love me?' she says, her lovely eyes questioning.

In that moment, he does, as he loves everything he desires.

She releases his hand and offers up her mouth to him. It is soft and sweet and deep.

She smothers a cry as he enters her, and he knows now for definite that he is the first. This excites him even more. He has lost sight of her now, drowning in his own pleasure.

Realizing this, she suddenly shifts, emptying herself of him.

Her cry of 'No' is swallowed by his big hand.

'Yes,' he says and tries to re-enter.

But she fights. Oh, how she fights. His surprise at that gives her the chance to momentarily escape his clutches.

He cannot allow this.

His anger explodes, like the surge of water through the nearby channel.

1

When he surfaces it's still dark, his mouth is thick with whisky, the skin on his bare thighs rubbed raw by grains of sand. She lies beneath him, half buried. Her eyelids are veined blue, the smudged lipstick distorting the shape of her mouth.

Her eyes, which he thought beautiful, are now as glassy-eyed as a dead fish.

He stands up, adjusts his clothes. For a moment he feels pity. Then it becomes annoyance and anger at her for spoiling the moment.

The sand will shift, he thinks. I cannot bury her here.

1

He could definitely hear the sound of children's voices.

Mike threw open the kitchen door. The area which would have served as a playground was empty, the supposed cries of children replaced by the wail of the wind.

He'd read all about the gales that swept these northern isles before he'd decided to move here, and had thought himself immune. After all, he'd been brought up next to the North Sea.

But I didn't know an Orkney wind.

At this point the object of his thoughts tried to wrestle the door from his hands. Mike stepped back inside and closed it. The summer had been windy, but there had been occasional days when that wind had softened to a breeze and he'd been lulled into a false sense of security as he'd worked on the renovation of the hundred-year-old building.

Wait until winter, had been the most common response from the locals. Mike had smiled each time that had been said, indicating he wasn't afraid of bad weather. It wasn't as though the temperature dipped dramatically. Snow was almost unheard of. Frost too. What could be so bad about winter here on the island?

He stood for a moment, listening to the wind whistling through the eaves.

That was what I heard. Not children's voices.

'I was a teacher for too long,' he said out loud as though to convince himself.

Leaving the kitchen area he went to check on the stove, touching the wall behind, feeling the warmth absorbed by the stones. The conversion of the big room that had been the main classroom in the island primary school had created his living space. Open plan, it was his kitchen and sitting room combined. His bedroom was a smaller room off one end, which he thought had been the teacher's office. All this had been his spring and summertime task. Now autumn was here he was planning to break up the tarred area behind the house and prepare it for his garden, or more properly his vegetable patch, to be ready for next spring.

Mike put the kettle on. It would be dark soon. The nights had drawn in swiftly. That was the other warning he'd had. The long dark nights when day ended by mid-afternoon. That hadn't worried him either. If he was deep in a book, it didn't matter if it was night or day. He would read in the dark months of the year and work on his painting during the long summer days. And there were other jobs he could do when the weather was bad. Such as sorting out the loft.

Mike glanced upwards. The rafters above this room were exposed, so no loft here, but the yet-to-be-renovated half of the building, which had been the teacher's living quarters, had a sizable loft. He'd opened the trapdoor and stuck his head in to take a look. Even fitted a light, but he hadn't got round to checking the loft space out properly. Maybe now was the time to do that. After all, the digger wasn't coming to break up the playground until tomorrow.

*

There were thirteen of them. Placed at regular intervals among the rafters. Finding the first one had excited him. Flower-shaped, the intricately tied greyish strip of muslin resembling a rose – like something fallen from Miss Haversham's wedding veil. It was obvious by the colour and texture of the material how old it was – as old as the schoolhouse that stood resolute against the winds that stripped bare this northern isle.

Intrigued by one, Mike found himself disturbed by thirteen. All as intricately tied, all distinctively different as though each referred to someone or something unique. He had removed only one from the thick layer of dust and ash that lined the loft, carefully bagged it, and taken it to the tiny island heritage centre.

The curator, Sam Flett, who wasn't an incomer like himself, had welcomed Mike and asked what he could do for him. When Mike placed the muslin flower in its clear plastic bag on the desk, the result had been unexpected. The weather-beaten face had openly blanched, but worse was to come when Mike attempted to remove the flower from its bag.

'Don't handle it,' Sam had said sharply, causing Mike to let go of the bag in surprise.

Sam, who'd appeared to be avoiding even looking at the flower, had asked, 'Where did you find it?'

'In the loft at the schoolhouse.'

'Then my advice is to put it back,' he'd said. 'As soon as possible.'

'But what is it?' Mike had asked, apprehensive now.

Sam had hesitated, before saying, 'On death, the hem of a child's smock was torn off and fashioned into a magic flower.'

5

'Really? Why?'

'The flower represents the child's soul.'

Mike had expected him to add *of course, that's just superstitious nonsense*. He hadn't.

'There are another twelve of them in the loft,' Mike had told him.

'Leave them there, and put this one back.'

I didn't follow his advice.

He hadn't disturbed the others, but thinking to investigate further, he'd left the single flower in its bag on the kitchen table, where it still sat. After all, he'd reasoned, what harm could a muslin flower do him?

Hugh Clouston was an island man born and bred. Owning the only resident small digger had made him invaluable, a treasured part of the community, and oft required in all weathers. Hence his confident yet relaxed demeanour.

He gave Mike the thumbs-up as the metal teeth finally broke through the compacted surface and the bucket scooped at what lay beneath. The filled shovel rose, then swivelled to the right and released its load.

Low sunlight caught the cargo as it fell, a shower of sandy soil mixed with small stones, and something else – white, solid, shapely.

Mike didn't register what looked like a bone at first, not properly, but the next scoop brought something he couldn't ignore. The skull rose and, as the digger turned and the bucket released, it fell earthwards again, landing on top of the mound of displaced earth as though to watch its own grave being excavated.

Hugh, earplugs in place, didn't hear Mike's initial shout,

nor did he appear to register his frantically waving hands indicating something was wrong. The noise of the digger seemed to rise with Mike's distress, as though the sudden and obvious presence of death had resulted in a crescendo.

'Stop!' Mike screamed.

This time it worked. Hugh emerged from whatever daydream he'd been having. The engine was shut down. Mike dropped his waving arms and pointed at the white object sitting atop the pile of earth and stones.

Hugh Clouston hadn't seemed perturbed by what he'd unearthed.

'Orkney's covered with Neolithic graves, but we'll have to report it. The Kirkwall police will want to take a look.'

The call to the police station made, Mike watched as the digger and its unfazed driver departed, trundling out of the school gates. Back now in the kitchen he immediately went for the whisky, his hand shaking as he poured himself a glass.

I had no choice, he told himself again. *Not with Hugh here.*

Now the police would come to Sanday. They'd visit the schoolhouse. Ask him questions. They'd want to know who he was. And why he'd come here.

2

Detective Inspector Erling Flett had taken the rather garbled call as he sat in his office contemplating the fallout from the weekend in Kirkwall, which had included a couple of fights in the town centre and a domestic, all three fuelled by alcohol. Orkney wasn't a hotbed of crime, but it had its problems as all communities do, and consumption of alcohol and its related activities was one of them.

That wasn't to say that the islands had never featured in high-profile cases. Barely months had passed since mainland Orkney had formed part of a major murder enquiry when a young woman's body had been discovered in the Ring of Brodgar. Fortunately, the perpetrator had not proved to be local, although the notoriety of what became known as the Stonewarrior case had certainly put Orkney and its Neolithic stone circle even more prominently on the map than it had been before.

Tourists visiting the islands, either by their own volition or via the huge cruise liners regularly docking at Kirkwall, came to view the Neolithic sites, which were plentiful. That particular case, which had become an internet sensation, had merely added a little modern-day spice to Neolithic history.

Erling asked the man to repeat what he'd just said, a little more slowly this time.

'My name's Mike Jones. I'm doing up an old schoolhouse on the island of Sanday. I hired Hugh Clouston to break up the ground at the back of the building. He dug up a human skull.'

'Is Hugh there with you?'

'He is. Do you want to speak to him?'

Erling indicated he did. Unearthing the past in Orkney was an everyday occurrence and probably something Hugh, who he knew, had met before.

When Hugh came on the line, Erling asked him exactly what had happened.

After Hugh had said his piece, Erling asked, 'How far down was this?'

'Maybe three feet below the tar,' Hugh estimated. 'I stopped when I brought up the skull. There's another bone. Maybe a leg bone.'

'And you're sure it's human?'

'I'd say so. And small.'

'A child?' Erling said.

'Possibly.'

'Can you secure the area until I can get out to you?'

'Sure thing. I'll put a tarpaulin over it.'

Erling asked to speak to Mike again.

'How long have you been renovating?'

'Since spring.'

'Have you found anything else?'

The hesitant silence suggested he might have.

'Well?' Erling encouraged him.

'Nothing in the grounds, no.'

'Inside the building?'

Another hesitation. 'I found something in the loft. Strips of old muslin made into flowers. I took one to the museum and Sam Flett urged me to put it back where I'd found it. He was adamant about that.'

'Did Sam say why?'

'He said they represented the souls of dead children.'

Erling waited until the other passengers had climbed into the tiny island hopper, then took the last seat nearest the pilot. The woman with the fiddle case, who he recognized as a visiting music teacher, inserted her earplugs. The other passenger looked like a businessman with his briefcase and smart suit.

Dougie, the pilot, started the engine, indicating that earplugs weren't so much a luxury as a necessity. Particularly if you were island hopping all day like the music teacher. A few moments of loud revving saw them bumping along the tarmac past a 'proper'-sized plane bound shortly for Edinburgh. In moments they were up, rising into a clear sky like a seagull. From the ground that's exactly what they would look like.

Like most Orcadians, Erling was familiar with this mode of transport. By far the quickest method of reaching the outer isles, it was wholly dependent on the weather. Mist brought the service to a halt, as did strong winds. Often he'd arrived by plane, only to return by ferry because the weather had changed.

Today the late-October sky was clear, the wind only brisk.

Erling turned his attention to the view.

In truth he never tired or became blasé at this aerial sight of the archipelago he called home. Of the seventy islands, only twenty were inhabited. Sandstone formed their base, which was covered in rich fertile soil, as evidenced by the green pasture below. But mild winters didn't mean that the cattle for which Orkney was famous wintered outside. Erling knew that well enough. On his father's farm overlooking Scapa Flow, the kye had been housed in the big byre through the worst of the coarse winter, his job being to feed, water and clean them out. The meat they produced was second to none and world renowned. Meat, cheese and whisky, Orkney's original exports, supplemented more recently by oil and renewable energy. And now, of course, tourism.

Through the front window he caught sight of one of the huge liners heading out of the harbour north of Kirkwall, specially constructed to accommodate the eighty ships that called annually with 80,000 passengers and 25,000 crew. Kirkwall was now the most popular cruising port in the UK. An economic boon for the islands, but a headache at times for a mainland of only 202 square miles and its 11,000 inhabitants.

The island they were bound for was one of the most northern ones. Its name perfectly described it. As fertile as the mainland, it had by far the best beaches. Erling had spent holidays there as a boy, staying with a distant relative of the same name who he'd called Uncle, and whose cottage overlooked miles of white sand.

His 'adopted' uncle, a retired teacher and widower, now spent most of his time at the island museum, the same Sam Flett who had apparently urged Mike Jones to return the magic flower to the schoolhouse loft. Once off the phone with Mike, Erling had given Sam a call. Getting his answering service, he'd left a message to say he would be on the island today, and would try and call in at the museum.

Sam wasn't one for flights of fancy, so Mike's story about being warned to put the magic flower, as he'd called it, back in the loft, didn't sound like Sam Flett. Unless, of course, Sam had merely been teasing a gullible incomer.

As the plane dropped towards the small airfield at Hammerbrake, north of the strip of water called the Peedie Sea, Erling spotted the jeep parked alongside the hut that served as the waiting area. Then they were down and trundling along the hard-core runway. As the step arrived together with the fire safety equipment, Erling was first out to allow the others to escape the confined space behind him.

He exchanged pleasantries with the two fire crew, then headed for the jeep.

Erling was in little doubt that at least half the island would already know why he was here. There had been little point in asking Hugh Clouston to say nothing until he arrived. That would have had less chance of success than asking the tide not to come in. Besides, the more people who knew about the discovery, the more likely he was to acquire information.

The schoolhouse had probably stood there for a century and the police weren't interested in hundred-year-old remains. His intention was to confirm that they were human remains, then to bring in a team to establish just how old they were. He could have a murder enquiry on his hands, or simply another piece of Orkney's history to interpret.

Derek Muir, the resident Ranger, greeted him with a firm handshake. Employed to take visitors round all the island sites, he was an authority on the past and the present. He knew everyone, their forefathers, their children and grandchildren. Back in the fifties, Muir had been the most common surname in Orkney, and it still was.

Short in stature, bristle-chinned, his face chiselled from

granite, his eyes Viking blue, he could tell a tale, yet also keep his counsel when required.

'Long time no see.'

'That's because you're all so well behaved in the northern isles,' Erling countered.

'Or we police ourselves, with no need for interference from Kirkwall,' Derek said in his matter-of-fact manner.

Erling settled himself in the passenger seat.

'So we're off to view old bones?' Derek said as he reversed, then turned onto the main road.

'If that's what they are,' Erling said.

En route, he asked a few questions about the new owner of the schoolhouse.

'Keeps himself very busy with his renovations. Occasionally to be seen in the Kettletoft Hotel. Nice enough chap. Not sure if he'll survive the winter.'

'What did he do before coming to Sanday? Do you know?'

'He was an art teacher. Early retirement, I believe.'

'Why here?'

Derek shrugged. 'A house in the south can buy four up here. Fancied a chance to make a new life. Or escape.'

'Escape?'

'They all come here to escape something. Even folk from Kirkwall,' Derek said with a knowing smile. 'It's just you can never escape the weather.'

As if on cue, a sudden squall hit the side of the jeep.

'You won't be flying back,' Derek offered.

The schoolhouse looked like the one Erling had spent his primary-school days in. L-shaped, the backbone of it had housed the big classroom where they'd all sat at desks

13

according to age. A second room had served as a dining room and occasional second classroom where the bigger folk went for more grown-up lessons such as maths.

How Erling had envied the older pupils that privilege. He remembered going into the room after such a lesson and finding strange shapes on the blackboard, which seemed to symbolize a world he could not yet access. A world the younger Erling had wished to join as soon as possible.

Eventually he had, and the magic of the world of mathematics had lasted through secondary school in Kirkwall. Even as far as university. That the complexity of life might be depicted symbolically had fascinated him. One thing though had spoiled that concept.

Maths could describe the physical world, but it couldn't describe a human thought. There was no formula for that. Nor a formula to work out why people made the decisions they did. So he hadn't become a maths teacher after all, but a police officer. Quite why, he wasn't sure, although he was certain that he had made the right decision. Both in his profession and the fact that he had chosen to return to his native Orkney to live and work.

His mobile rang as they approached the schoolhouse. Erling glanced at the screen and was pleased to find Rory's name.

'Can you talk?'

'Not really,' Erling admitted.

'I'll be back tonight. Will you be there?'

'If I get back from Sanday.'

'I'll cook us something.'

'Good,' Erling said and hung up as Derek swung the jeep in between the old-style school gates and drew up at what had obviously been the main entrance. As Erling climbed out, a figure appeared in the doorway. Tall, sandy-haired, the man looked to be in his forties.

Erling introduced himself. The handclasp was firm and the man kept eye contact.

'Thank you for coming out, Inspector.'

'Is Hugh still here?'

'He had to go to another job. He says to give him a ring if you want him back.' He gestured that they should enter. 'It's quicker if we go through the house.'

Erling followed him inside.

The entrance fed on to a narrow hall. Mike immediately turned left and they were into the big room that Erling remembered from his own schooldays. High rafters, wooden wainscotting, big windows to let in the light. No school desks here, but a comfortable living space and heat radiating from a stove on one wall.

In his classroom there had also been a stove, fed by coal by the pupils. Everyone wanted a seat next to the heat, especially in the dark days of winter. It was worth working hard and getting good marks just to be awarded a desk next to it.

Mike led them out through a door at the rear area of the big room, which also housed his kitchen. Functional, organized, the man had, Erling thought, made a really good job of the conversion. The door open now, Mike ushered them outside, his expression worried by what lay before them.

Erling surveyed the scene.

This, he decided, had definitely been the playground, although the field beyond the fence had probably been used too. In Erling's schooldays on the Orkney mainland, the pupils hadn't been permitted to go beyond the perimeter fence. Despite the prospect of punishment, they'd all disobeyed. The fields and, in his case, a neighbouring shoreline were a much more enticing prospect than the confined tarred surface. The secret was always to be back before the bell rang for the end of break.

The tar here was pitted, weeds pushing up through cracks, the surface gradually attempting to return to soil. Several feet from the back door was a mound and what Erling assumed was the hole covered by a tarpaulin, weighted down by four stones. Mike stayed by the door, his expression suggesting he had no wish to view again what lay beneath that cover.

Erling indicated that Derek should free the corner nearest the door and together they set about folding back the tarpaulin. A gust of wind intervened as they lifted it, whipping it like a sail. A swift move on Derek's part saw it caught and secured behind the mound.

And there it was. The reason for Erling's visit.

The skull sat atop the loose earth, the empty eye sockets directed towards them. Erling heard an intake of breath as, behind them, Mike Jones revisited that image. It wasn't the first skull Erling had seen dug up, but the impact was always the same.

He recognized it as human, but was completely unable to picture the owner of the bony structure. From a skull it was impossible to tell if someone's nose turned up, or if they had tiny delicate ears, or dinner plates sticking out on either side. The area around the eyes was likewise lacking in bony structures, so that feature, the most expressive and individual of a real face, had to be estimated. Something only those artists who would aim to put a face on the skull staring at him now could imagine.

It wasn't large, nor was it very small.

Beside it lay a bone, which at a guess might have been

a shin bone, or maybe an upper arm. Erling wasn't familiar enough with the human skeleton to say which.

He took a step closer. As he did so, the topsoil shifted a little, sending a small shower of stones into the hole. Erling followed their path down and something caught his eye. Poking out from the soil was a shape that just might be part of a ribcage.

Derek had joined him.

'How long do you think it's been here?' Erling asked him.

'You'll have to get in a real expert to tell you that,' he said honestly.

Mike was standing at the door. The wind, chill now, seemed to meet his tall thin body with force. It was better not to be too tall on these islands. Those closer to the earth were less troubled by the wind.

Erling used his mobile to take a photograph, then pulled over the tarpaulin and secured it, adding another couple of stones.

They re-entered the house in silence.

'What will happen?' Mike said, once he'd shut the door.

'I'll get a forensic specialist to take a look. Then we should know how old the grave is. If it's a hundred years or more, the police won't be interested.'

'But someone else might?'

'This entire archipelago is a wonderland for archaeologists. What were your plans for the playground?'

'Vegetables, but not until spring.'

Erling nodded. 'Okay, now show me what you found in the loft.'

*

He had painted the image with a swiftness and sureness of hand he'd never experienced before. The intricacy of the magic flower still astonished him. He'd intended keeping the grey colour of the strip of muslin, but had found shades and hues dropping from his paintbrush. Even now, gazing on his attempts at painting one, Mike wanted to paint them all, although he would have to remove them from the loft to do that. A thought that made him uneasy.

Perhaps I could take photographs of them in situ and work from that.

The policeman's voice broke into his thoughts.

'Did you paint this?' He was observing the canvas with an appreciative eye.

'Yes,' Mike said, almost shyly, because he thought it was better work than he'd done for some time. 'The original is here.' He lifted the bagged flower from the table and offered it over.

The detective immediately tipped the flower into his hand, causing Mike's heart to speed up. He didn't regard himself as superstitious, but since he'd found out what the magic flowers represented, he hadn't handled them again.

The detective spent some moments examining it before passing it to the Ranger.

'What do you think?'

Derek whistled between his teeth.

'I've heard of these but never actually seen one.'

'What is it exactly?'

'The hem of a muslin smock torn off and made into what was known as a magic flower. The story goes they were fashioned to represent the soul of the child who'd worn the smock.'

The detective looked thoughtful at this explanation, but there appeared no unease at the Ranger's words.

He checked with Mike. 'And you said on the phone there were others?'

'Twelve,' Mike said, hearing a catch in his throat. 'In the loft of the unrenovated section.'

'Thirteen deaths in one school?' The detective posed this question to the Ranger.

'The deaths could have been over a long period. Maybe the flowers weren't all made for pupils at the school. Maybe they were for younger siblings or even for different parishes.'

'How long has this building been here?'

'The one-teacher schools were closed in the late forties and the pupils centralized. This building's been here for at least a century.'

'What about registering the deaths?' Erling said.

'Registration became compulsory on 1 January 1855. Before that, deaths may have been written in old parish records but not necessarily,' the Ranger explained.

'Could these have anything to do with what we found out there?'

'I couldn't see the children, whoever they were, being buried next to the schoolhouse. More likely they'd be laid to rest in a cemetery or on their own croft ground.'

Mike found himself momentarily relieved by that thought, then realized why he shouldn't be.

'Then who's buried out there?' he said worriedly.

3

The wind that had buffeted the cottage throughout the night had gone, although evidence of it was there on the salt-streaked windows. She'd been wakened by its howl in the dark middle of the night. Lying there in the warm cocoon of her bed, Rhona had watched the rain lash at the dormer window, a defiant moon forcing its way through the dark mass of cloud to gaze down on her as though in sympathy at the onslaught.

Last night, and the three that had gone before, had all brought back sweeping memories of her childhood. This had always been her room. The view to the stars, when they were visible, her window on the heavens. Back then, she'd taken comfort in the knowledge that her parents slept next door and there was nothing to fear from the sound and fury of the elements that beat at the three-foot-thick stone walls, at times as though some mad god wanted to sweep her, her parents and the stones that sheltered them off the face of the earth.

Now all was still, the silence broken only by the soft sound of waves on the nearby shore.

Rhona dressed and, grabbing her jacket, opened the front door and stepped outside.

Her breath caught in her throat as it always did as she took in the sight that lay before her. Some said that the view from the Gaelic college Sabhal Mòr Ostaig on the Sleat peninsula across to Knoydart on the mainland was one of the world's best.

Rhona was inclined to agree.

At moments like this, the idea that she should move back here and live in the family cottage always resurfaced. As it did when she was particularly stressed by work or emotional relationships. Then the recurring dream of opening this door to see what lay before her now was her brain's way of escape. But how to be a forensic expert resident on Skye? Rhona smiled at the thought, although her expertise had been required here on at least one occasion, or more particularly on the neighbouring island of Raasay.

Her survey of the bay was rewarded by the sight of two black silky heads bobbing on the surface, observing her.

They're back.

Rhona made an instant decision. It might be the last time this year she could do this without dying of hypothermia. She went inside, grabbed her wetsuit from where it hung in the back kitchen, stripped off and prepared for her swim.

The whiskered faces observed her with interest as she made her way across the strip of sandy shore. The touch of the water as it seeped into the legs of her wetsuit made her gasp. Determined, she pulled on the hood. *Five minutes. No more than ten.* After which she would have a very hot shower.

As she stepped deeper, the sand shifted to accommodate her weight, the ripples caused by waves reflected on the surface of the water. Her own image as she determinedly moved deeper was as clear as though she looked in a mirror.

In the hooded wetsuit I look like one of them, although maybe not so plump and thankfully minus the whiskers.

Rhona braced herself, then did a dive, the shock of the cold water on her head seeming momentarily to stop her heart. When she broke surface, gasping, she found the two seals watching her with avid interest. As Rhona approached them in a steady crawl, they parted company, to each take up a place alongside her, as they had done two days ago.

Then began the performance that had characterized their previous encounter. If she stopped, they stopped, and viewed her. If she didn't immediately begin swimming again, they ducked and dived as though to encourage her, or maybe simply to show off their skills. If she swam away from them, they followed, trying to keep her, it seemed, from going ashore. She was their plaything which they didn't want to relinquish.

But they had the layers of fat required to survive in a winter sea. She did not.

Ten minutes later, Rhona reluctantly turned and headed for shore. The rule of cold-water swimming was to stop when your skin went from bristling cold to downright painful, and she had now reached that point. She headed swiftly up the beach to the bright-blue kitchen door. By the time she reached it, she was chittering. Getting the wetsuit off with shivering hands was harder than putting it on. Eventually she succeeded and headed for the shower, turning it on at full power and as hot as she could manage without scalding herself. A glance in the mirror over the sink as she stepped in registered blue lips and pale skin.

I look like a mortuary specimen.

This time her gasp was more from pleasure than pain as the hot water met her head and shoulders. As a feeling other than cold took over her body, she laughed.

'That was great,' she shouted, as she soaped her tingling skin.

Dressed again, she checked on the fire in the small sitting room to find it had lasted the night banked up by peat. She stirred and replenished it, then set about making breakfast. Back in Glasgow, breakfast would have consisted of a couple of cups of coffee. Once at the lab, she would eat whatever Chrissy, her forensic assistant, had brought in for them, which could be anything from a traditional filled morning roll (egg, sausage, bacon or all three) to a simple croissant. Rhona always accepted whatever was on offer.

Here, things were different. No Chrissy to supply breakfast, no calling out for home delivery or Sean to cook an evening meal. On Skye she had to be self-sufficient. She had to shop and cook.

Rhona set up the frying pan and loaded it with square sausage, tattie scones, a slice of bacon and some mushrooms, then poured herself a coffee to warm her inside as well as out.

Scooping the cooked food onto a plate and slipping it in the oven, she fried two eggs from the supply left at her door by her nearest neighbour, Tam Evans, who had come to Skye from northern England to keep goats and hens.

Fifteen minutes later she had surprised herself by wolfing down everything she had cooked.

Chrissy and Sean would be proud of me.

The fire had re-caught and was bringing a warm glow to the room. It seemed a shame to leave it, but leave it she must. It was a long drive back to Glasgow, and she was keen to set out as soon now as possible. As she began her packing, the room darkened as a sudden squall came in from the west, splattering thick drops of rain on the window. The bay she'd swum in earlier and the distant outline of Knoydart were both shrouded in mist. Her playmates too had gone.

Packed and ready to leave, Rhona fetched her mobile and made a call. With luck she would be back in the city by early afternoon.

4

The cat was eyeing him with what McNab decided was a malicious green stare. It stood at the bedroom door, tail upright, the tip swishing the air in what looked like a warning. McNab wasn't fond of cats in general. This one he positively disliked.

And the feeling is definitely mutual.

Since Freya had brought the cat back to stay at her flat, there was now no avoiding it. Smart, it ignored McNab when Freya was about, lavishing its affection on her, so that it appeared docile and lovable. McNab knew the opposite to be the truth.

He had been the one to find the cat standing guard over the body of its former mistress, Leila Hardy. He had seen the cat defend her remains with the ferocity of a panther. He knew the cat's past and its true character. He also knew that it didn't want him around. It had made that quite plain, to McNab at least.

McNab had made a joke of it at first, then declared outright that the cat didn't like him.

Freya had observed him with those thoughtful eyes, then said, 'I owe it to Leila to give him a home.'

And she was right. Leila had been a colleague and a fellow Wiccan and she was dead.

McNab decided after that to keep his mouth shut regarding the cat. As long as Freya didn't invite it into the bedroom with them, he could live with its malevolent presence, although enticing Freya back to his own flat was now the preferable option for their nights together.

McNab turned from the cat as his mobile rang. The name on the screen was Rhona. McNab answered with a smile.

'Dr MacLeod. *Ciamar a tha thu?*'

There was a short silence as she digested his attempt at a Gaelic greeting. If she answered him back in the same language he was sunk.

'I'm fine. Thank you. And yourself?'

'Okay, although there is currently a large black cat considering whether to launch itself at my throat.'

'It's still there?'

'You bet it is and with no thoughts of leaving.'

'How's that working out?'

'It's not allowed in the bedroom, when I'm here at least.'

'You told Freya the reason why?'

'I did.'

'And how did she react?'

'I won't say she didn't look intrigued.'

'But you stood firm?'

'Stand firm, that's my motto,' McNab said.

There was a muffled sound from Rhona's end, which might have been smothered laughter.

'You sound happy,' McNab said.

'I am.'

'When is the island idyll over?'

'I'll be back early afternoon. Anything happened while I've been away?'

'A drugs bust at Excalibur. A six-car pile-up on the Kingston Bridge. Some trouble at the footie . . . Nothing that would interest you or we'd have called you back.' He paused.

'Sean there with you?' he asked, knowing full well from Chrissy that he wasn't. Something he took a perverse pleasure in, without wishing to examine the reason why.

'No.'

'See you soon then.'

She rang off, leaving McNab wondering what the phone call was really about. The fact that Rhona had contacted him at all was surprising. But he was glad that they were back on speaking terms.

The cat was still sitting in the bedroom doorway as though on sentry duty. The green eyes narrowed as they met his.

It's putting the evil eye on me, he thought and not for the first time.

The cat, who apparently went by the name of Styx, had been used in Leila Hardy's sex magick games. Having a big black moggy sitting on your face during sex, its claws raking your shoulder, had apparently been a turn-on for some of Leila's male companions. Or maybe it had been a turn-on for her.

Last night, when McNab had finally told Freya why he didn't want the cat in the bedroom with them, she'd seemed intrigued.

'I've never heard of a cat being used in sex magick before,' she'd said.

Having declared his aversion to the cat's presence, McNab had then made it obvious he didn't mind the other Wiccan practices that Freya indulged in during sex.

At that she had led him into the bedroom and closed the door firmly on the cat.

'So I'm still in charge here,' McNab told the watching cat. *But for how long?*

The cat swished its tail at him, then sprang past to meet Freya as she emerged from the box room that served as her Wiccan temple. McNab watched as his rival used all his feline powers on Freya. Rubbing himself between her legs, miaowing up at her with those green eyes. Freya responded by scooping the cat into her arms and nuzzling it.

McNab would have sworn that the cat grinned at him.

'Who was on the phone?' Freya said.

'Dr MacLeod. She's headed back from Skye and wondered if anything bad had happened in her absence.'

'And has it?'

'I'd better go to work and find out.'

As McNab approached to say his goodbyes, the cat sprang from Freya's arms with what sounded like a growl. When McNab gave her a long lingering kiss, he heard a distinct hiss from the floor area.

His mobile rang as he exited the main door from Freya's set of flats.

'DS McNab here?'

'Can you get along to . . .' The caller quoted an address in the East End. 'The body of an elderly IC1 male reported in flat 1F2.'

'Suspicious?'

'We need a detective to tell us that,' the voice said drily.

McNab swore a retort and hung up, finding himself hoping it was. Not that he welcomed murders per se. Just that murder was more in his line of expertise than a drugs bust at a Glasgow nightclub.

At this time of the morning, he had to join the rest of the commuter traffic snaking its way through central

Glasgow. Never patient, he contemplated a blue flashing light, but decided against it. There was nowhere for the traffic queue to get out of his way except to mount the pavement, which was thronged with pedestrians.

McNab made do with tapping the driving wheel and muttering under his breath.

Eventually the traffic thinned and he found himself approaching the red sandstone tenement block of the address. There was a squad car outside and a policeman stood at the entrance to the close, trying to look important.

'What have you got?' McNab flashed his ID.

At his arrival, the young constable looked less confident and stuttered a bit in his explanation.

'The neighbour said he wasn't answering and he hadn't been seen for a week. We forced the door and found him sitting in his chair, dead.'

'How, dead? Like old-age dead?'

'I couldn't tell, sir.'

'Who's been inside?'

'Myself and PC Dobson.' His face flushed red.

'Where's Dobson?' McNab said.

'She's on the first landing, guarding the door.'

McNab sprinted the stairs to find a small blonde wearing a determined expression, surrounded by the distinct smell of vomit. McNab didn't have to look far to find its source.

'Did you do that?' he said accusingly.

'No, sir.' She looked askance at the accusation.

'Your partner, then?'

'He went in first,' she explained. 'It was the heat and smell, sir.'

'He didn't vomit inside the flat?' McNab demanded.

'No, sir.'

McNab indicated she should stand aside, then opened the door. The stink in the close was nothing to what now enveloped him. But the blanket heat and noise was even worse. McNab knew that sound only too well. The song of feasting bluebottles.

He crossed the small hall, following the buzz. The door to the main room stood ajar, but none of the flies were keen to escape. McNab covered his nose and mouth with his sleeve and took a look inside.

The figure sat slumped back in a winged armchair in front of an electric fire with two bars beating out heat. As McNab stepped nearer for a closer look, the blowflies rose like a small threatening cloud, descending almost immediately again to continue their feast.

From where McNab stood, there was no obvious sign of a struggle, no blood, but the smell of defecation, stale urine and decomposition were unmistakable.

McNab retreated to the close where PC Dobson stood resolute, her nostrils pinched shut.

'Get some fresh air,' McNab told her.

She couldn't disguise her relief at the order. 'Yes, sir.'

McNab pulled out his mobile.

5

'Flypapers and an electronic swatter would be good.'

'A buzzer?'

'Definitely,' McNab said sarcastically.

'Great.' Chrissy sounded as though she relished the thought of a swarm of flies.

McNab was aware that Chrissy McInsh, Rhona's right-hand woman, had a strong stomach. He'd seen her order up a smoked sausage supper midway through examining a burnt-out body in a skip, but he was determined to be clear just how bad it was.

'There was a heater on full blast,' he added.

'Don't turn it off,' she ordered.

'Are you trying to tell me how to do my job?'

'Wouldn't dream of it,' Chrissy said sweetly, and rang off.

The two uniforms were standing either side of the main door like sentries, the bloke studiously avoiding McNab's eye.

'Your place is upstairs, officer,' McNab told him.

PC Williams wasn't happy about that, but didn't argue.

When he'd disappeared, McNab addressed his partner. 'The first one I saw like that, I was sick too, but I made sure I got outside first.' McNab fished out a fiver. 'Find the nearest coffee shop and bring me back a double espresso.'

Since he'd cut back on the booze, caffeine had become

his drug of choice, and he found himself craving it almost as much as the whisky. Still, it didn't come with the same hangover. McNab went back upstairs to find PC Williams on duty beside his own vomit, his expression determined. McNab wondered if he planned ever taking another breath.

'Which neighbour called the station?'

PC Williams nodded in the direction of the one other door on that landing.

'Name?'

'Mrs Connelly.'

McNab's rap was swiftly answered. He displayed his ID to the elderly woman who stood before him.

'What's that smell?' she demanded.

'Unfortunately my officer has a weak stomach.'

She thought about that for a moment. 'So Jock's dead then?'

'He is. May I come in?'

She stood back and let him pass, then immediately shut the door.

'How long?' she said.

'A while.' McNab didn't go into detail.

She shook her head. 'I was away a week at my son's place. I checked on Jock the day after I got back, but he didn't answer. Sometimes he just liked being on his own. Come through, detective,' she offered.

If next door smelt of decomposition, this flat assaulted his senses with lavender. Whether it was polish or air freshener, McNab had no idea.

Mrs Connelly took him into a kitchen, and offered him a cup of tea. McNab said yes, despite hankering after his coffee. From his experience, people talked more with a cup of tea in their hands.

As she busied herself with kettle and teapot – none of this teabag in a cup nonsense – McNab took in the surroundings.

The phrase, 'A place for everything and everything in its place', sprang to mind, much like the flat he'd called home as a child. For some reason, that made him relax, and he sat back in the chair. Even smiled as he was handed his cup and saucer.

'How did he die?' she finally asked, after allowing McNab time to savour the brew.

'We don't know yet.'

'He was about ninety, I think. He told me once that he'd been a Bevin Boy during the war. Worked in the mines. The miners called him Jock. That wasn't his real first name. Drever was his surname though. He came from up north somewhere by his voice.'

'From the Highlands?'

'He never said where exactly, but he did talk about collecting seaweed when he was a boy.'

'Lewis? Harris?' McNab tried.

Mrs Connelly didn't look as though she knew where he meant, but continued to ponder, so McNab changed the subject.

'Did he have any family?'

She shook her head. 'I don't think so. At least he never mentioned any.'

'Was there anything wrong with him?'

She gave him a wry look and McNab suddenly realized there was a twinkle in her eye.

'Apart from old age, you mean?'

'Apart from that.'

She gave a little laugh. 'He never talked about it if there

was, although the truth is, his mind was wandering a bit. He sometimes called me Ella. I assumed that was his late wife's name. He showed me a photograph of them once.' Her eyes misted over. 'I'll miss Jock. He was a real gentleman.' She rose and, taking her cup to the sink, started to wash it.

'Thanks for contacting us,' McNab said.

She turned. 'What'll happen to him?'

'We'll establish how he died.'

'Who'll bury him?'

'Maybe we'll find a relative,' McNab offered.

'If not?'

'I'll keep you informed,' McNab told her.

When McNab emerged, the mess on the landing had been sanitized. PC Williams's colour was back and his nostrils had re-opened, allowing him the luxury of breathing. He was holding McNab's double espresso. McNab accepted it and swallowed it down.

'Forensic's here, sir,' he said, indicating a bundle of boiler suits next to the door.

McNab pulled one on and, once encased, re-entered the flat.

Metal treads had been laid in the hall and as he pushed open the door he noted that the buzz of flies had dissipated, suggesting Chrissy had been busy with the fly swat. Entering, he saw she'd also netted a selection, which were now beating themselves against the sides of their individual jars, ready to be sent to entomology to ID, should this prove to be a suspicious death.

Chrissy sensed his entrance and turned.

'Before you ask, the duty pathologist's been. It's not obvious how he died. So you'll have to wait for the PM.' She read his disappointed look. 'What's up? Life not exciting enough for you?'

Knowing she was referring to Freya, McNab smiled in what he hoped was a self-satisfied manner. 'I wouldn't say that.'

Chrissy dismissed him with one of her looks and went back to work.

When McNab had first entered, his focus had been on the body and the smell. Now he checked the room out properly. It had obviously served as the kitchen and Jock's sleeping quarters, as McNab discovered when he opened a cupboard door and found a recess bed behind it.

The two-room flat, or room and kitchen in Glasgow parlance, was typical of these old tenement blocks. McNab had been brought up in a flat very like this one. They'd also, like Jock, had a bathroom, a luxury in the past, where a shared toilet on the landing had been par for the course.

The furniture in the sitting room was solid, well-crafted and not of this era. It also looked as though the room had rarely been used. There was an air of abandonment that went with the film of dust.

Three framed black-and-white photographs stood on a sideboard. The first was of a group of mixed-age primary children with a female teacher taken outside a stone building. The second image was of a black-faced lad in his teens, outside what looked like a colliery. In the third, Jock was older. Handsome, tall, straight-backed, with a pretty woman on his arm. It looked like a wedding photograph.

A search of the drawers produced a tin box. Inside was a marriage certificate. According to it, Jock's real name was James Drever. Born in January 1925, he'd married Grace Cummings in Newcastle in 1948. No birth certificates for any children they may have had, but a death certificate for his wife some twenty years before.

So who was Ella?

'McNab?'

He abandoned his search and answered Chrissy's call.

'Take a look at this.' She eased up the old man's right trouser leg.

McNab crouched for a closer view. There were pressure marks on the mottled skin that ran round the outside of the thin, veined leg.

'There's a matching one on the left leg,' Chrissy told him, pulling up the neighbouring trouser to let him see. 'And the arms.'

There was nothing obvious on the bony wrists, but when Chrissy pulled up the sleeves there was visible bruising halfway up each forearm.

McNab had seen such marks before. If rope or tie tags were used they looked like burn marks. Thin wire was worse, slicing through the skin. McNab had a sudden image of what might have happened to the old man prior to his death.

'Any other injuries?'

'None visible. Without stripping him, we won't know,' Chrissy said. 'I take it you've checked for a break-in?'

'We're three floors up. I can't see anyone climbing in a window, and the uniforms that found him had to break down the door.'

'If he opened the door to someone, they could easily have pushed their way in.'

'And his neighbour wasn't there to hear anything,' McNab said. 'Okay, we'll have the place checked for prints, although there are no signs that the flat's been searched. The dust next door is evidence of that.'

Chrissy produced a wallet. 'This was in his back pocket. There's money still inside and a cashline card.'

'If it was a robbery they would have had that,' McNab said, genuinely puzzled.

Old people did get robbed in their own homes. Too many of them. Some were killed for next to no reward. Tying up an old man but not stealing anything was weird.

'I'd like Rhona's take on this,' Chrissy said, matching McNab's own thoughts exactly.

'She's on her way back,' he told Chrissy.

Her eyes narrowed above the mask.

Before she could ask, McNab told her. 'She called me from her island idyll this morning.'

'Really?'

McNab smiled just to annoy her. 'You mean she didn't call *you*, her right-hand woman?'

By Chrissy's dismissive expression, he had no chance of pissing her off by suggesting he was the favourite.

'I'll text her,' was the response.

6

The five hours from Skye had passed in a blur of rain and wind, the majestic scenery she'd enjoyed on her way to the island lost in the downpour. Rhona had been lucky to get across the Skye Bridge, already shut now to high-sided vehicles.

The Minch had seethed below her like a cauldron, the wind whipping at the sides of the car as though in punishment for her leaving. Like life, the Scottish weather could change in an instant, which it did frequently. From an early-morning swim to this, she thought, as she turned her windscreen wipers up a notch.

The radio kept her company, when she could pick up a good enough signal, which was intermittent. Eventually she gave up and resigned herself to trying to make out the road and nursing her own thoughts.

Stopping at one of the few petrol stations to be found en route, she took the opportunity to check her mobile, and found two messages. One from Chrissy saying she'd been called out to a body, the other from the Orkney detective she'd worked with previously, asking her to give him a call.

Intrigued, Rhona did so.

He sounds so like Magnus, was her first thought, as they went through the relevant greetings. Erling Flett had gone to school with criminal psychologist Professor Magnus Pirie and they'd been firm friends too. Both tall, and built like Vikings, Rhona remembered the first time she'd seen the detective waiting for her as she'd arrived by helicopter near the Ring of Brodgar.

When a small silence followed their initial exchange, she said, 'I'm assuming this isn't a social call?'

'No,' he admitted. 'We've found something I believe is a speciality of yours.'

'A buried or concealed body?'

'A digger working in the grounds of an old schoolhouse unearthed a skull and a long bone. I've taken a look in the hole and it's definitely a grave.' He paused. 'I've informed the powers that be, so no doubt they'll be in touch with you officially. I just wanted to give you the heads-up on the find.'

'Is this somewhere on the mainland?' Rhona said.

'No. On one of the most northern isles. Sanday.'

Rhona knew about Sanday. Not because she'd been there, but because a forensic team from Aberdeen-based R2S, Return to Scene, had been involved in the forensic investigation of a murder case some years back on the remote island of around five hundred inhabitants. A love triangle gone wrong, the victim's body had been buried on one of the many white beaches that Sanday was renowned for.

'The remains may be too old for Police Scotland to be interested,' DI Flett added, 'but . . .'

'I'd be happy to take a look.'

'Let me know when you're coming and I'll take you out there.'

'Is there somewhere I can stay on Sanday? Or do I have to travel back and forward to Kirkwall?' she said, knowing that's what the R2S team had had to do.

'We're out of season now, but I'll see if I can sort something out.'

Rhona rang off, then gave Chrissy's mobile a call.

It rang out for a while before Chrissy finally answered. 'Where are you?'

'I'll be back in the lab in the next half hour,' Rhona told her. 'How's the body?'

'Fancy taking a look?'

The rain had followed her from the west, or alternatively Glasgow had sent its own version to meet her. The city was drenched, as were its inhabitants. The constant beat of the windscreen wipers did little to countermand the downpour. Sitting at another set of traffic lights, Rhona watched the blurred faces of the pedestrians, heads down against the wind, with the entertainment of an odd umbrella deciding it had a mind of its own.

Alongside her now weren't the choppy waters of the Minch, but the fast-flowing waters of the River Clyde, swollen with the rain that had obviously been falling heavily in its catchment area.

Despite this, her mood on re-entering the city had been upbeat. First DI Flett with his Orkney burial, now Chrissy wanting her opinion on another body had lifted her spirits. Holidays were all well and good, but, she decided, you only realized how much you enjoyed your work when you were away from it for a while.

Rhona smiled as a brolly detached itself from its owner and set off along the street. The young woman made no attempt to follow, mouthing what looked like, 'Fuck off, then,' instead.

Ten minutes later Rhona drew up outside a tenement block with a broken downpipe that was turning the front of the building into a mini waterfall. Three vehicles were parked outside. A patrol car, Chrissy's van and what looked like McNab's car.

An officer stood just inside the open doorway, sheltering from the rain and the leaking pipe. The young woman checked her ID and let her pass. Heading up the stairs, Rhona found a male officer manning the door with a supply of suits.

Kitted up, Rhona went inside.

The smell of decomposition and all the other odours that accompanied death were there, except the tell-tale metallic scent of blood. So whatever had happened here, it hadn't been a bloodbath.

Entering the flat was like stepping back in time. Linoleum flooring in the hall, with faded floral wallpaper. There were three doors off suggesting the layout of a typical room and kitchen, with a small bathroom.

Hearing movement behind one of the doors, Rhona pushed it open.

There were two suits in the room. One dusting for prints, the other definitely Chrissy.

Rhona stood for a moment surveying the scene.

This room too had an old-world feel to it. A central rug lay over linoleum that must have been put down half a century ago. Two winged-back chairs faced an old-fashioned two-barred electric fire. The room was overly warm, although the fire was turned off.

The body sat in the furthest-away armchair. The elderly man was dressed in a shirt and knitted cardigan with leather buttons, and wore plain trousers. On his feet were dark socks and well-worn checked slippers. His hands were open, sitting side by side on his lap.

Flies had obviously been feasting in the heat, more of them than she would have expected at this time of year. Blowflies were the insect family most associated with dead bodies because of their acute sense of smell – they could pick up the scent of blood at a hundred metres. The scent of decomposition brought them too, and they colonized a body more swiftly than any other insect form.

You couldn't hide blood or a body from blowflies, however hard you might try.

Chrissy had registered her, but had chosen not to interrupt Rhona's train of thought.

Rhona now approached the body and attempted to look on it with fresh eyes, aware that Chrissy thought something 'wasn't right'.

An elderly man dying in his armchair next to the fire wasn't unusual, perhaps even a good and peaceful way to go. So why wasn't her assistant happy? Chrissy, aware of Rhona's intention, motioned that she was heading out for something to eat and she would leave Rhona to it.

Which was just what Rhona wanted.

'You're going where?'

'Sanday,' Rhona repeated.

'It's one of the Orkney islands,' McNab offered knowledgeably. 'With lots of beaches.'

Chrissy turned on him. 'How do you know that?'

McNab merely raised an eyebrow and drank down the rest of his espresso.

After her brief examination of the body and scene, Rhona

had located the two of them in the nearest cafe, enjoying filled rolls. Rhona had ordered up one for herself, which she'd then attacked with gusto. The mug of tea that went with it was definitely builders'-brew strength, but hot and surprisingly delicious.

Eventually Chrissy could wait no longer on Rhona's findings and had asked her outright.

'The wounds on his legs and arms suggest he was restrained before his death,' Rhona had said. 'I'd be interested to see if there are marks elsewhere.'

At that point Chrissy had thrown McNab a look of triumph, so she obviously agreed.

'So someone duffed up the old boy. Maybe even caused his death?' McNab had said.

'We won't know how he died until the post-mortem,' Rhona had reminded him. 'But he was restrained with some force. By the nature of the marks, I'd say rope was used.'

'I picked up what might be a rope fibre from his sock,' Chrissy had intervened.

'Once we have full access to his clothing, we'll know more.' Rhona had turned to McNab. 'The place looks undisturbed, especially the other room. The dust layer was untouched apart from round one drawer.'

'That was me,' McNab had said. 'I found a marriage certificate and a death certificate inside for his wife.'

'Nothing was taken as far as you know?'

'Not even his wallet,' Chrissy had said.

'Which doesn't suggest the motive was robbery.'

It was in the brief silence that followed their discussion that Rhona had chosen to spring her news about going to Sanday.

'So you're off on a jolly,' Chrissy said with a haughty look.

Her forensic assistant might be a gallous Glaswegian lassie, but she had a wardrobe full of regal looks to select from in such circumstances.

Rhona tried to keep her face straight as she answered. 'I thought you might like to come with me.'

Whatever Chrissy had been expecting in reply, it hadn't been that.

The look dissolved. 'Really?'

'We'll excavate quicker with the two of us.'

'What about Jock?'

'You've processed the scene. It's up to the pathologist and DS McNab to find out what happened to him.'

Chrissy was definitely warming to the idea. Rhona watched as McNab registered that he alone wasn't going on this jolly.

'It's very windy up there, especially at this time of year,' he said in a discouraging fashion.

'I bet there's a nearby pub with live music and handsome farmers.' Chrissy smiled at the thought.

'The forensic tent won't stay up,' McNab warned.

'You don't like the countryside, remember?'

By his expression McNab was torn between imagining he was missing out on something in tandem with the fact that he disliked anything more rural than a Glasgow park. He shrugged as though he didn't care.

'So when do you two head off?'

'First thing tomorrow,' Rhona said.

Chrissy suddenly thought of something. 'How exactly do we get there?'

'That all depends on the weather.'

7

The wind had continued to rise, just as Derek had forecast. Now over the jeep radio, the Ranger confirmed that Erling wouldn't be catching the hopper back to the mainland.

'Can we make the next ferry?'

'We can,' Derek said confidently.

Leaving now meant Erling wouldn't get a chance to speak to Sam about the flowers in the schoolhouse loft, but that could keep. Erling was keen to get back to Kirkwall, especially after the call from Rory.

They'd been together for a few short months, yet it seemed much longer. Rory was an incomer, currently working as a diver, based on Flotta in Scapa Flow, the terminal that provided the landing for the Piper and Claymore fields pipeline system. Flotta, no longer solely a small farming community, was in fact home to the second largest oil terminal in the UK after Sullom Voe in Shetland.

They'd met when Rory had chosen to spend a week's leave in Stromness to dive for pleasure rather than work. Erling occasionally dived himself, and when he'd gone out with the local club, he'd found himself buddied up with an English bloke, who Erling suspected from the outset had a lot more experience in diving than he had.

When they got talking in the pub afterwards, he found out why.

'Don't you want to do something different on your days off?' Erling had asked.

'Diving for pleasure is something different,' Rory had assured him, with a smile. 'So, what do you do for a living?'

Since most of the people in the pub knew who he was and what he did, there had been little point in avoiding an answer. Rory's eyes had widened somewhat and he'd given a small whistle between his teeth.

'Well, well, well.' He glanced around the packed pub. 'In a place where everyone knows your name.'

A Liverpudlian, Rory was outspoken and not remotely reticent about his sexuality, although perhaps already aware that Orcadians rarely broadcast anything about themselves, he had chosen to take his time with Erling.

They'd done a second dive together, alone this time, taking in more of the sunken ships that Scapa Flow was famous for, after which Rory had given a potted history of his own life up to now.

'Married at twenty,' he'd declared with a shake of his head. 'I was trying to be what my father wanted me to be.' He'd paused then. 'Or maybe what I wanted to be.' At that point, he'd taken a couple of mouthfuls of his pint. 'My wife Gail knew before I did, or at least faced up to it before I did. We're on good terms and she's remarried now.'

His sad smile at that point had melted Erling's heart.

'What about you?' Rory had asked.

So Erling told him.

'My best friend at school, Magnus Pirie, was the one to tell me. He became a professor of psychology, so he was obviously good on the subject of people's behaviour. He also had and still has a very strong sense of smell. When I demanded to know how he knew, he said he could smell it.' Erling hesitated. 'Apparently pheromones do have a scent.'

'You had the hots for this guy?' Rory had laughed.

'I suppose I did.'

'Is he still around?'

'He has the house next to Houton Pier, where you catch the boat to Flotta, but he's not always there. He lectures at Strathclyde University. He also occasionally works with Police Scotland as a criminal profiler.'

'So,' Rory had said, suddenly serious. 'Everyone knows about you?'

'I suppose so. I never think about it any more. When I went off to university, I thought I wouldn't come back here to live, because I wouldn't be able to be myself. I was wrong. Orcadians are a very tolerant people. It's also pretty much a classless society. The incomers who get it wrong don't realize that. Orcadians aren't impressed by people who think they're somehow grander than others.'

Rory had grinned at that. 'Okay then, we're equal, but I can guarantee I'm the better cook.'

And that had proved to be the case. On leave and staying at Erling's place, Rory always did the cooking. As would be the case tonight, Erling hoped.

As they drove on to the long pier at the southern tip of the island, they found half a dozen vehicles waiting to board the ferry. Erling had chatted to Derek en route from the schoolhouse and asked if he'd check out somewhere for Dr MacLeod to stay.

'The hotel doesn't usually take guests in the winter months, but they might make an exception in the circumstances.

Otherwise, I could see if one of the self-catering cottages would be available. How long would it be for?'

'That depends on the age of the bones. If they're more recent, then it's likely to be a murder enquiry which won't just involve Dr MacLeod,' Erling told him.

'So we might need space?'

'An MIT, a major investigation team, would appear.'

Derek nodded. 'We've been here before.'

That was true.

There were a lot of words left unsaid in the Ranger's remark. The community of Sanday had been shaken by a previous murder committed on the island by, it had to be said, incomer on incomer. Yet it had brought the eyes of the world on this small island and had turned the eyes of the islanders on one another.

The arriving ferry was discharging its cargo and vehicles, the array of which signified the diversity of island life.

'I'll contact you once I know when to expect the forensic team,' Erling said. 'Can Mike Jones be trusted to leave the grave untouched?' Erling was aware that had the find been on the mainland, the site would already be cordoned off and a policeman on duty.

'I'll check in on him, but I assume you'll send an officer tomorrow?'

Erling said he would. There was a chap from Sanday working at the police station in Kirkwall. If he sent him, he could perhaps find accommodation with his family. He would also no doubt gather information more readily than a stranger. On the other hand, his loyalty might lie with his kith and kin, should it become a murder enquiry.

Ninety minutes of choppy crossing later, Erling was disembarking at Kirkwall harbour. Dark now, although only just late afternoon, the wind was driving rain across the frontage of the Kirkwall Hotel, where a few disconsolate oil workers stood around the door, smoking and wondering when they would get back to Flotta, or wherever else they were working.

Erling had a sudden image of the tarpaulin, and wondered if the six stones he'd loaded it down with would be sufficient. Even the shallow stretch of water that lay beyond the harbour was frothing in anger. Erling took shelter at the back of the Ayre Hotel and rang the old schoolhouse number.

'Mr Jones? DI Flett here. I hope to have a forensic team out to your place sometime tomorrow depending on the weather. Can you do your best to keep that tarpaulin secure until then?'

'It's wild here, but I'll try.'

'Thanks. I'll call you when I have word of their arrival.'

Erling rang off, dipped his head and stepped back out into the wind. The street ahead of him was empty, anyone with any sense staying inside. He began to wonder if Rory had made it back from Flotta. Depending on the time of day, the crossing might take between eighty minutes and an hour and a half. In bad weather it could take longer – if the ferry had ventured forth at all.

Erling remembered hitching a lift on a fishing boat to Flotta when a teenager. Stuck in the wheelhouse with the captain, who seemed unconcerned by the giant waves breaking over the boat, Erling had thought his end was nigh and that he was bound for a watery grave. Tight-lipped, both to control his fear and his heaving stomach, he'd realized in that moment that he wasn't invincible and that death courted everyone, including his teenage self.

When they'd finally docked, the captain had drawn him to one side and told him, 'It wasn't your turn today, son, and it wasn't mine, but that doesn't mean it won't be your turn tomorrow.' He'd laughed then. *Probably because of the look on my face*, Erling thought.

The police station loomed into view. Once he set things in motion for tomorrow, he would pick up his car and head for home, hoping Rory was already there. He could call and check, of course, but that felt like tempting fate.

The Orphir road was quiet. No one followed him out of town and he met only the headlights of a couple of cars heading into Kirkwall. On his left Scapa Flow was barely visible on the odd occasion that the moon escaped from behind the scuttling clouds. The darkest part of the year was approaching when an endless night would swallow most of the day. Nevertheless, the sky was rarely covered by a grey blanket the way it was in the southern cities. An Orkney sky was vast and varied, with sharp shafts of sunlight competing with fast-moving dark clouds. Locals said if you couldn't see Hoy then it was raining. If you could see Hoy then it was about to rain.

Passing Houton Bay on his left, Erling noted that the ferry was sitting at the jetty, which either meant it had made it back from Flotta or alternatively it hadn't gone across earlier. Erling noted too that the lights weren't on in Magnus's house, which didn't surprise him. Usually if Magnus planned to be back on the island, he would contact Erling and let him know.

Turning right onto the Scorradale road, he passed the old primary school and the building opposite which had once been home to the local shop, selling everything from wellie boots to bere bannocks.

Had he been heading into town, topping the hill he climbed now would have afforded what Erling regarded as the best view on mainland Orkney. When his grandmother had left him the croft house in her will, Erling had rejoiced in the fact that he would take in this view across Scapa Flow to Hoy from the highpoint of the island every morning on his way to work.

As he neared the white-painted croft house nestled below the road on the left-hand side, Erling noted with a rush of pleasure the light on in the single tiny window that faced the road.

Then again, maybe I left it on this morning?

He drew into the narrow parking space. As he headed down the flagstone steps, the wind trying to prevent his descent, he could see now that there was more than one light on in the cottage, signifying that Rory had indeed made it back.

Opening the door that led from the porch into the flag-stoned kitchen, Erling was greeted by a delicious smell of cooking. Rory stood facing the range, stirring a pot. The radio was on, giving out the Orkney news, which Rory was listening to intently.

Erling stood for a moment taking in this domestic scene and deciding he liked it.

As he was about to announce his arrival, Rory's mobile rang. Checking the screen, he immediately answered.

'Hey there.'

The soft tenor of Rory's voice halted Erling's greeting in his throat and made him step back into the porch. He found himself both suspicious and guilty at the same time, which seemed ridiculous.

He'd only known Rory for two months, and most of that time they'd spent apart. They weren't a couple, just an occasional item. Both free to go their own way. Even as Erling told himself that, he knew it wasn't true. It may have remained unspoken, but that hadn't been the arrangement. At least not for him.

Retreating outside, Erling took refuge in the homebrew shed, selecting a couple of bottles of beer to take back in with him. This time when he opened the door, the radio was off.

'I thought I heard the car a while back,' Rory said with a smile.

Erling brandished the bottles. 'I was in the shed. Good smells,' he indicated the pot. To cover his discomfort, he immediately set about opening a bottle and pouring the golden liquid into two glasses. 'God, it's wild out there.'

'You don't have to tell me,' Rory said. 'The ferry was pitching like a roller coaster.' He accepted the glass Erling handed him, put it down on the surface and drew Erling towards him.

'We have half an hour before the meal's ready.'

8

Mike eased his way along the support between the rafters. Above him the wind whistled, skimming the roof, puffs of it catching his face as it found its way below the slates. He was reminded of when he'd first arrived and had stayed in a caravan parked on site as he'd worked on the main room to make it watertight.

On the Ranger's first visit, Derek had warned Mike to build a wall round the caravan to stop the wind getting underneath.

'And weigh her down with rope and blocks.'

Mike had thought the man was exaggerating to make him feel, as an incomer, he knew nothing of the place he'd chosen to come and live. He'd been wrong, as he'd swiftly found out. At midsummer the wind could be as strong as at midwinter. Waking to the scream of it round the caravan, he'd finally taken refuge in the partly restored building, preferring stone walls round him, even if rain was coming through the roof.

It had been the dampness on the ceiling that had sent him up here in the first place. Checking the state of the loft, he'd found the layer of peat ash, and the flowers.

Which was why he was back.

His mobile in his right hand, Mike positioned himself to take a photograph. Even now, he recognized this one as quite different from the flower that still sat in its plastic bag on the kitchen table. He was no gardener, but to his mind this one resembled a budding rose. He took a selection of photographs, then began to crawl towards the next one.

The wind had dropped, or maybe it had only paused for breath.

And in that moment of stillness he heard it again. The sound of children's voices.

Mike froze, straining to hear, feeling if he moved at all the sound would cease.

For a moment he thought he heard a girl's voice now separate from the others and she was singing. A rhyme perhaps? A playground rhyme?

When he'd first come to the island, he'd listened intently to the locals talking to one another, only half understanding what was being said. Despite his incomprehension, he loved the musical sound of the voices, the cadences, the rhythms.

He'd purchased *Sanday Voices – An Oral History* from the heritage centre. Along with the small book came a CD which he'd played over and over again because he took pleasure in both the stories and the voices themselves.

Is that what was happening to him now?

Was he replaying those voices in the head? Matching them to the wind?

The other thought returned. The one he didn't like to contemplate.

What if removing the flower from the attic had been a mistake?

What if he had disturbed the soul of a child? A girl?

He began slithering backwards, keen now to get out of the loft. When he reached the trapdoor, he dropped down, his feet searching for the rungs of the ladder. A trick of the light seemed to him to pick up the row of flowers, six each side of the central plank like a path leading between tiny graves.

Then the light snapped off and all was darkness.

Later, having cooked and eaten his evening meal, Mike downloaded the photographs he'd taken in the loft. The second flower, he realized, was smaller than the first. Did the size of the flower have anything to do with the age of the child?

He went to view his original painting again and found himself imagining, if it did represent a child, what would he or she have looked like? Picking up his pad and charcoal, he began to draw.

A heart-shaped face, wide questioning blue eyes, a small nose, dark hair, cut straight at shoulder length. As he drew the mouth, he found himself giving it the hint of a smile.

He stood the drawing on the stand next to his painting of the flower. It had been a girl's voice he'd imagined he'd heard singing. He closed his eyes and tried to remember what the words had been, but couldn't.

The metal flue on the stove rattled suddenly as a further gust of wind hit the chimney.

I'd better check the grave before I go to bed.

Mike had no wish to open the back door again. Nor to gaze on that tarpaulin, knowing what lay beneath, but he didn't want the inspector to focus on him for any reason.

He opened the back door and stepped out, closing the door behind him. Immediately the sensor picked up his presence and switched on the outside light. Mike tried to focus in the sudden glare.

The tarpaulin had shifted, he realized. One of the stones was missing, with a corner now flapping.

'I should have checked sooner. The policeman won't be happy,' he said to himself.

As he tried to secure it again, he realized that the long bone now lay exposed on the broken tar. Swearing at both the wind and this discovery, he fetched it back and slipped it under the tarpaulin, moving the stone back into place.

'I can't be blamed for the fucking wind,' he muttered.

Shaken, he retreated indoors again.

The sooner they excavated and took the thing away, the better.

9

Tom the cat at her heels, Rhona walked around the flat, reclaiming her space. Sad to leave Skye, she found herself happy to be home again. Although it looked as though it was going to be a short stay. Arrangements had already been put in place for the trip to Orkney tomorrow. According to DI Flett, there was to be a lull in the weather for forty-eight hours at least, which would give her a window of opportunity to excavate. After that the situation was expected to deteriorate. A tent would probably be out of the question because a light wind Orkney style still amounted to a gale elsewhere. The hours of daylight would be short. Excavating a grave was a painstaking business, but she and Chrissy worked well as a team and, if given a full two days, it might be done.

Rhona called out for a pizza, then set to work unpacking from her Skye trip and repacking for the next one. In between times she called Mrs Harper one floor down, who kept Tom alive when Rhona wasn't there. Mrs Harper welcomed her home then immediately asked after Sean, who was even more of a favourite than the cat.

'He's playing in Paris for a week,' Rhona explained.

'I'll feed Tom, no problem. How long will you be away this time?'

'Hopefully a couple of days, depending on the weather.'

The pizza having arrived, Rhona settled down to eat.

The shriek of the alarm woke her at six. Having gone to bed at ten, in an effort to get a good night's sleep, Rhona had still been awake at midnight. Sleep had come after that but it had been an exhausting experience. Her entire dream time had consisted of trying to get to the excavation site with every possible obstacle preventing her. When she finally did arrive, she'd lost both her equipment and Chrissy on the way.

Showering quickly, Rhona turned the final blast of water to cool to waken her properly. By 6.45 a.m. she was heading west alongside the Clyde towards the helipad where the Air Support helicopter was based. Under a dark sky, the city appeared to slumber, its residents for the most part not yet ready to face the day. Overnight the wind had dropped, the rain had ceased and, Rhona thought, it had got colder.

That's all we need now – snow.

Chrissy had beaten her to it. Dressed in what looked like a cagoule for Arctic conditions, she peered out at Rhona from a fur-framed hood, an excited expression on her face.

'Neil says we're going to land on a beach,' she informed Rhona.

Rhona's first thought was that Chrissy had requested they land on a beach.

'There's a field right next to the site,' she said.

Chrissy shrugged, defeated for the moment. 'It was worth a try.'

'Did you bring supplies of food?' Rhona asked.

Chrissy patted her rucksack. 'Enough for today, at least. I take it we have transport and a place to stay tonight?'

'According to DI Flett, the resident Ranger is our transport and we have a place to stay.'

'With meals?' Chrissy checked.

'It's a self-catering cottage.'

Chrissy didn't like the sound of that. 'Who's doing the cooking?'

'You are.'

Ten minutes later, Glasgow dropped beneath them and Chrissy fell silent, registering that it was impossible even for her to be heard above the noise of the blades. As the sun rose, they headed north, the snow-dusted mountainous landscape of the Highlands extending out on all sides. Then they were crossing the flat peatland of Caithness and Sutherland with its scattering of deserted crofts and the ridges of abandoned peat banks.

After that came the Pentland Firth, the stretch of fast-moving tidal water between the Scottish mainland and the Orkney islands. Rhona had seen all this before. To her assistant, the sight of the dark humpback of Hoy, the golden curve of Rackwick Bay and the wide waters of Scapa Flow were fascinating and new. Chrissy, sensing Rhona's eyes on her, turned, grinned and gave her the thumbs-up, indicating what McNab had feared – this was in fact a jolly and one he wasn't party to.

As they flew over Scapa Flow, Rhona looked for Magnus's house next to the jetty at Houton, pointing it out to Chrissy. The grey stones of Kirkwall appeared below them with the majestic centrepiece of the red sandstone St Magnus Cathedral, then they were out over the harbour and heading north-east towards Sanday, passing the islands of Shapinsay, Stronsay and Eday on the way.

Seen from above, it was clear why Sanday was so named. It seemed that there was as much white sand to be seen as green fields, so Chrissy's desire to alight on a beach could certainly have been realized.

During the midnight hours she'd spent awake, Rhona had checked out the island in some detail. The location they were bound for lay in the remote northern part, where the World War Two radar station had been housed, and home too to the famous black-and-white-striped Stevenson lighthouse. It was also some six miles from the nearest shop, something Rhona hadn't mentioned to Chrissy.

The helicopter was hovering now like a big noisy bluebottle deciding where to land. A long sandy bay was visible on the southern side, a similar beach to the north. After a moment or two, the decision was made and they dropped steadily down, not on either of the beaches, but on the strip of grassland between.

As she climbed out of the helicopter, Rhona spotted a jeep parked a short distance away, a man standing either side of it. Then came a wave of recognition from the taller of the two and DI Erling Flett came striding towards them.

On the short drive to the schoolhouse, Erling explained that their driver, Derek Muir, was the resident Ranger and would be their transport while they were on the island.

'Derek knows everyone and everything about Sanday.'

At that point, Chrissy had brought up the subject of food.

'My assistant has a formidable appetite, which isn't diminished by digging up bodies,' Rhona explained.

Derek had smiled at that. 'I'll make sure there's plenty of provisions at the cottage,' he promised. 'And some Orkney ale.'

The schoolhouse stood alone, surrounded by grassland. Rhona could hear the sound of surf breaking, indicating how close it was to the sea.

The owner must have heard the jeep's arrival or perhaps had been watching for it, because he opened the front door as they entered through the old school gates.

He was tall and lean, with a shock of sandy hair. Rhona's first impression was that he was nervous about their visit, which was only to be expected. Finding a body buried in your garden was a disquieting business. What could prove to be an interesting forensic task for her was more of a nightmare for him.

But it seemed there was something more than just the presence of the remains that was worrying him, as they discovered when he led them round the side of the building and through a further gate.

'There was a problem last night with the wind,' he explained. 'I came out to check around midnight and found the cover had broken free and the bone was outside. I put it back, of course, and secured it again.'

Erling made some reassuring noises and thanked him, but that didn't seem to ease his worry.

Now at the rear of the building, a mound covered by a tarpaulin was visible just yards from Mike Jones's back door. When Erling indicated that he and Derek would lift off the cover, Rhona stopped him.

'It's better if Chrissy and I get kitted up first, then we'll take a look. I'll come and speak to you once the site's secure.'

Erling nodded, looking pleased that she'd taken charge.

Suited now, Rhona set up the time-lapse camera in the corner nearest the building where it couldn't be knocked down, then covered it to protect it from the rain. One image would be taken every ten minutes of excavation, then stitched together in an MP4 movie, which could be used in court if required.

Glancing at her watch, she estimated that they had maybe four good hours of daylight left, daylight being essential to see the soil layers. After which they would cover the grave with plastic tarp and peg it down with archaeological arrows every few feet.

Ready now to remove the current cover, she sent Chrissy round the other side and they both set about getting rid of the stones. Lifting the sheet back, they got their first sight of the grave. The single bone Mike had mentioned lay on the perimeter of the mound. The hole dug by the shovel was about three feet deep. On the opposite side Rhona could make out what might be a portion of exposed ribcage. All of this was as Erling had described and evidenced by the photograph he'd taken on his mobile.

Bar one thing.

There was no skull now atop the mound of earth.

'Where's the skull?' Chrissy said, echoing Rhona's own thoughts.

Assuming it had been dislodged when the tarpaulin had broken free, they checked both the hole and the surrounding playground.

Ten minutes later they were convinced it was nowhere to be found.

'Could someone have removed it?' Chrissy suggested, mystified.

At that moment, Rhona could think of no other solution to the mystery. The skull had been here yesterday and was now gone. She took her first time-lapse video, then instructing Chrissy to lay out an alphanumerical grid round the suspect area at 0.5m intervals for reference purposes, she went inside.

The three men were seated silently at the kitchen table, drinking coffee. Mike Jones, she thought, looked no more at ease than he had been outside. Rhona wondered if the missing skull was the reason for his discomfort.

'The skull's not there,' she told Erling.

'What?'

All three men were observing her with the same expression of mystification.

'It was on top of the mound,' Erling said. 'You saw the photograph.'

'It's not now.'

'Did it fall into the hole?'

'No.'

At that point everyone looked at Mike Jones.

'Mike?' Erling said.

He looked back at them, aghast. 'I didn't remove it. It must have been blown away when the tarpaulin came loose.'

'We've searched the area inside the fence. It's not there,' Rhona said.

Erling studied her expression. 'You think someone deliberately removed it?'

'Without another explanation, we have to consider that a possibility,' Rhona said. 'How many people know about the grave?'

Erling checked with Derek, who shrugged. 'By now, most of the island I would think.'

'I didn't tell anyone,' Mike protested.

'You didn't have to. From the moment Hugh Clouston left here, the word was out,' Derek said.

'Who might take it?' Erling said.

'Kids, maybe?' Rhona offered.

'Kids?' Mike looked taken aback by her suggestion.

'Have you seen any kids hanging about the place?' Erling asked.

It seemed to Rhona that Mike paled at the question. Erling noticed it too.

'Do local children come round here?' he asked.

Mike hesitated for a moment, then said, 'I thought I heard kids playing out here on a number of occasions, but I've never actually seen them.'

'Who lives nearby?' Erling asked Derek.

Derek rattled off a number of family names together with their offspring.

'You check with the parents,' Erling said, 'see if you can find out if a skull has turned up. If we can't locate it that way, I'll have to start a proper investigation.'

Rhona left them to their deliberations after checking that Derek would come back for them as soon as the light started to fade.

'How far is the cottage from here?' she asked.

'A five-minute walk. I'll pick up some provisions after I've checked about the skull, then come back for you. If you want to knock off earlier, just follow the track eastwards from the gate.'

'What about a key?'

'It won't be locked.'

Rhona didn't express her surprise at this, having just spent the previous few days on Skye where many people didn't lock their doors either.

Back outside, she found Chrissy taking surface soil samples and recording what little vegetation there was to be found in the tarred surface around the grave.

Putting aside the issue of the missing skull, they both got down to work.

10

McNab had made a point of observing the Air Support helicopter leaving its base by the Clyde, taking Rhona and Chrissy on what he had described as a jolly. Rising early from his own bed, which Freya had not shared the previous night, he'd gone up onto the roof and watched for the distinctive yellow and black shape heading north. After which he'd done fifty press-ups, had a shower, then cooked himself some breakfast.

His new regime, since he'd laid off the heavy drinking, had led to better health, although he acknowledged that at times the drinking had just been replaced by new but equally obsessive-compulsive behaviour.

When his time was spent with Freya he could channel his energies into sex. When that wasn't available, he had to expend them elsewhere. Normally work would help with his terrier-like tendencies, but with no major case to concentrate on, he was, without a doubt, bored. True, there were always the run of the mill messes to clear up, but a major crime investigation gave him something to really get his teeth into.

Even as he thought this, McNab poured another coffee and turned his attention to the subject of the old man, now lying in the mortuary awaiting his post-mortem, which was scheduled for this morning. At least today, he had something in prospect to occupy his thoughts.

A thorough search of Jock Drever's flat had produced

nothing more than a picture of a life without ornament and, apart from the photographs and what Mrs Connelly had told him, very little of the past. To live that length of time and not to have made any impact, or none to be seen, struck McNab as improbable as well as sad. Some of the bastards he'd locked up had affected countless lives and destroyed many in the process by the time they'd reached their mid twenties.

We are what we do and where we've been.

What had Jock done and where had he been? McNab found himself keen to know, despite the fact that it might have no bearing on his death. He glanced at his watch.

Well, let's see how he died, first.

Jock's clothes lay spread out on a white butcher's-paper surface to catch any transferable evidence such as fibres or hairs. The underwear soiled by death had been bagged. Dr Sissons, dressed for the job in surgical pyjamas and plastic apron, his shower cap and goggles already in place, acknowledged McNab's entry, his eyes glancing round as though expecting more than just him.

'No Dr MacLeod?'

'Sanday,' McNab said, 'digging up a body.'

'Recent?' Sissons said, looking interested.

McNab shrugged, indicating he had no idea.

'Okay, so now that you're finally here, Detective Sergeant,' Sissons said with special emphasis on *sergeant*, pointing up McNab's demotion, 'we'll begin.'

McNab had certainly been demoted, but he hadn't been late to these proceedings, so it was definitely a wind-up on the part of the pathologist; McNab managed to successfully ignore it.

McNab didn't like post-mortems although he'd attended many. He'd never grown used to the smell, the sight of folk's innards lifted out and weighed. He didn't like the noise of drills through bone. He wasn't fond of the sight of blood and the dissection of the human form like a piece of meat on a butcher's slab.

It had always seemed to him that attending a scene of crime, however gory, could in no way compare to what he was about to witness. Yet it was worth it, if it told him the one thing he really wanted to know. How the victim had died.

Jock Drever had been a tall man, well over six foot. Age didn't seem to have shrunk him as it did most people. The body was sinewy and his build looked much the same as it had in the photograph of his younger self taken on his wedding day. Lying naked, the rope marks on his shins and forearms appeared more prominent, or maybe the current state of decomposition had enhanced them.

It had been hot in the room, which normally sped up the putrification process. McNab knew his basics. Green after two to three days, marbled and bloating after a week or more. Heat sped up the process. Cold delayed it. Dryness mummified and maggots destroyed. Blowflies laid eggs in the mouth, nose and eyes, the groin and armpits if available. They normally hatched in twenty-four hours, grew half an inch in length feeding on the corpse for twelve days.

Chrissy had caught a selection of flies for the bug man, which according to her could be fed anything to keep them alive for study, and extracted some maggots which she'd fed good Scottish mince to. Others she'd blanched in boiling water and stored in vodka. Mince and vodka were trademarks of hers, inherited from Rhona.

Rigor mortis started around two hours after death. The

rigid stage developed eight to twelve hours in, after which the fixed stage might be there for eighteen hours. After thirty-six to forty-eight hours it had left the body in the same progression it had entered – small muscles were quickest to go either way, larger muscles longest.

Taking all these things into consideration, McNab had decided he thought Jock Drever had been dead for three days at least. What he was keener to know was how the old man had died. His own take on the proceedings featured an intruder threatening the victim by tying him up, which had unfortunately resulted in his death. Realizing this, the intruder had removed the rope to cover their tracks, and scarpered. The only part of the story that didn't work for McNab was the fact that nothing had been stolen, not even the old man's wallet. So what was the point of the break-in?

It seemed Dr Sissons was about to offer his own scenario. He motioned to McNab that they should go next door, where they both de-gowned. By this time McNab was ready to burst a blood vessel. Despite listening carefully to everything Sissons had said into the overhead microphone, he still had no idea why the old man had died.

'Coffee, Sergeant?' Sissons headed for the machine.

'Double espresso.'

Sissons chose a straight black for himself and waited as they were served up, while McNab champed at the bit and tried not to say, 'Well?'

Sissons took advantage of a nearby chair, sat down and began to sip his coffee in silence. McNab forced himself to drink his espresso and bite his tongue, hoping that by not asking outright, he was pissing off the pathologist just as much as he was himself. Eventually his not-so-patient silence was rewarded.

'As you heard from the recording, I believe the victim died in the chair where he was found.' Sissons took another sip of coffee.

Christ, the man drank coffee as slowly as he thought.

McNab headed for the machine and got himself another double shot to avoid shouting, 'Just tell me how the fuck he died.'

Eventually Sissons did.

'If I was to hazard a guess, I'd say he probably died of dehydration. In people over fifty, the body's thirst sensation reduces and continues diminishing with age. Many senior citizens suffer symptoms of dehydration without even realizing it. In this case, were he tied up in an overheated room for an extended period of time . . .'

'It would accelerate the process,' McNab said.

Sissons nodded.

'To try and establish dehydration as a factor we can test for urea in his blood – which would be high. We can also look for other electrolytes – sodium, potassium and chloride in the vitreous fluid I took from his eye, although these change after death and are more difficult to interpret.'

McNab was picking up the message that determining exactly who or what was responsible for Jock's death wasn't going to be easy.

'Were the bindings taken off after he died?' he asked.

'He'd been tied up, that we have established, but blisters in the periphery of skin marks can also be formed post-mortem. We can't say for definite that he was dead when the bindings were removed.'

McNab absorbed this. 'But if he was freed while still alive, wouldn't he have sought help?'

'Dehydration can cause hallucinations and confusion and

by then he may have been too weak to move from that chair.' Sissons met McNab's look. 'None of which conjures up a pleasant thought,' he said quietly.

'You're right. It doesn't.'

'Did he have a home help or any family member caring for him?'

'Not as far as we're aware.'

'Unfortunately, abuse of the elderly isn't uncommon. Even within the family.' Sissons threw his paper cup into the bin. 'A full report should be with you in a couple of days, Sergeant, and I'll pass the clothing on to forensics.'

McNab registered the bite of the wind as he exited the new Southern General Hospital and its £90-million state of the art mortuary and forensic facilities. Gone were the days of the old red-brick mortuary next to the Crown Court in the Saltmarket where the victims of Scottish serial killers such as Bible John and Peter Manuel had had their post-mortems. McNab regretted the old mortuary's passing, but was still impressed by the move to what Glasgow folk had, in their inimitable manner, christened 'The Death Star', because of its space-age design.

And at least you can park here, he thought as he located his car in the mammoth car park. Once inside, he checked his mobile. There was a message from DI Wilson requesting his presence and a text from Freya saying she was working on her thesis tonight and couldn't see him. Nothing from Chrissy and Rhona. It seemed Sanday was proving more interesting than the case they'd left behind.

McNab started up the engine, wondering why no message from Orkney was more disappointing than Freya's rejection.

11

The vastness of an Orkney sky was what Rhona remembered most about her last trip here. On Skye the mountains dominated, controlling where light and shadow fell.

Here the sky is bigger than the land or the sea.

Walking home now along the rough track that led to the cottage, the heavens a mass of purple and red, deep blue and black, even Chrissy appeared momentarily silenced by the sight. Either that or hunger and fatigue had taken over.

They had worked until the diminishing daylight no longer allowed them to distinguish the stratification of the soils. It had been a painstaking business. Working in from the grave cut, recovering fill longitudinally in spits or small sections no more than five to ten centimetres deep per grid square, bagging the samples of soil, dating and timing them.

Taking scene images throughout every single action as well as the time-lapse video had been crucial. Procurator Fiscals and Senior Investigating Officers were now extremely precious about who took what images during the recovery process of a body. Whereas in the past a specialist team from R2S might have been called in, now the 360-degree panel camera work was done by trained SOCOs and the PolScot imaging unit made up the court presentations. Cost had become an important factor now there was a single force, and outsiders that they would have to pay for weren't used unless there were extenuating circumstances. Rhona had always made her own personal recording of the scene alongside R2S, so for her things hadn't changed that much.

The weather had held, breezy but dry, as Erling had predicted. They'd worked continuously except for a short break, during which they'd made use of the schoolhouse toilet and gratefully accepted Mike's offer of coffee, which they'd had with the selection of sandwiches Chrissy had brought. Rhona had noted in the brief time they were with Mike that he seemed more relaxed when Erling wasn't about, although he was clearly worried about the missing skull.

'Could an animal have removed it?' he'd said as he served up the coffee.

'Animals do disturb graves, but it's normally the smaller bones that are taken,' Rhona had explained. 'The skull is heavy.'

'So a human being took it?'

'That's the most likely explanation.' She paused. 'You mentioned you've heard children playing nearby?'

He looked perturbed by this. 'Yes, but I've never seen them.'

'Could their voices have carried from the beach?'

'The dunes are in between, but I suppose that might have been what happened.' He didn't look convinced.

'The old playground could be a draw,' Rhona offered. 'The surface is ideal for football and other ball games.'

'Then why when I open the door is no one there?'

Rhona wondered if perhaps the local children were simply playing tricks on him. 'Have you met your nearest neighbours?'

'Not really, no.' He tried a smile. 'Everyone's been friendly enough, it's just I've been too busy with the renovations.'

Chrissy had said nothing during the interchange, but had plenty to say when they were back at work.

'It's like the *Wicker Man*,' she'd announced as she'd picked up her trowel.

'What?'

'An incomer on a small Scottish island discovers Pagan cult and is sacrificed to their gods.' Chrissy had paused for effect. 'Hey, wasn't the incomer a police officer come to investigate the disappearance of a young woman?' At this point Chrissy had given a knowing nod to the grave.

'That puts us in the firing line,' Rhona had reminded her, 'not Mike.'

'Oh my God.' Chrissy had adopted a terrified look. 'And we're alone tonight in an isolated cottage. We should have brought McNab along to protect us.'

By close of day they'd processed approximately half the fill. Rhona had drawn the section that could be seen, taken notes on the compaction, the stratigraphy of the side walls and some more soil samples, and dictated notes to Chrissy on the vegetation growth.

All being well, tomorrow would see the skeleton fully exposed.

They secured a plastic tarp over the area, and pegged it down.

With the disappearance of the skull, Rhona's concern wasn't for the wind to lift the tarp, but for a person to. It seemed that Erling had had the same thought, because shortly before they'd finished for the day, a young police officer had arrived via Derek's Land Rover and announced that he was on sentry duty for the night.

By his speech, Officer Tulloch was Orkney born and bred. He was also tall, handsome and immediately in Chrissy's sights. Rhona would have felt sorry for the bloke had he not looked so pleased by the attention. Chrissy had immediately extracted the fact that he was from Sanday, his family owned a farm a few miles distant and that there was a social evening in the local hotel a few nights from now.

'Will you still be around?' he'd asked Chrissy.

'It depends how long it takes to finish here.'

Rhona had forsaken their flirtatious conversation and sought out Derek.

'I've delivered food to the cottage for you,' he'd told her. 'I can run you there now.'

'It's fine, we'll walk,' Rhona had indicated the animated conversation still going on nearby, 'once Chrissy's finished her interrogation of Officer Tulloch. I've stored the equipment in Mike's shed. Did you have any luck with the skull?'

'Not yet, but I've done the groundwork. I think we'll know soon if one of the local kids took it. What about the rest of the remains?'

'We'll reach them tomorrow.'

Derek had wished her goodnight at that point, promising to be back the following morning. Having removed her boiler suit, Rhona quickly put on her jacket against the cold.

'You're not outside overnight?' she'd asked Officer Tulloch.

'I'm in Mike's kitchen with a clear view of the site.'

'Don't fall asleep,' had been Chrissy's final orders to him.

With the next turn in the track, their cottage came into view, the windows bright with light. Entering a small sitting room, the warmth from a solid-fuel stove hit them after the short but cold walk from the deposition site.

Chrissy immediately made for the kitchen to check out the food. Minutes later she reappeared to inform Rhona that it would be curry tonight, the full works apparently, and it would be ready in half an hour.

The cottage was all on one level. A small sitting room, tiny kitchen, a bathroom with a shower and two bedrooms. The back window of the sitting room gave them a view of a long sandy beach which was a two-minute walk away. It was traditionally built like the cottage on Skye, with three-foot-thick walls, and Rhona suspected its last renovation had been at least fifty years before.

According to Derek, the owner lived on a farm in the west of Sanday and the cottage had been the original family croft house, used now for the family visits of those who no longer lived on the island. Pictures on the walls suggested the history of the place. There was even one of the nearby schoolhouse when it had served as the local school. In black-and-white, it was a class photo taken outside. Two rows of children, more boys than girls, a mix of ages and a woman teacher. No one was smiling.

Maybe they weren't allowed to smile back then.

There were other framed scenes of the croft house before renovation, indicating that the bathroom had been an addition as had the porch and single bedroom. Further photographs looked as though they'd been taken during wartime, with groups of construction workers, Home Guard members and smiling RAF personnel. The final image was of a beached First World War German destroyer with the inscription *B98 Lopness Bay*. A large framed map of Sanday indicated where they were in the far north-eastern corner, just across a narrow causeway from Start Point with its famous black-and-white-striped lighthouse.

Rhona checked her mobile to discover there was no signal, then called through to Chrissy that she was planning a shower. Chrissy indicated she would hop in after her and revealed that there was Orkney ale, plus a bottle of Highland Park.

It seemed Derek had done them proud.

An hour later, hunger satisfied, the real ale tasted, Rhona said she was planning a walk along the beach. Erling had told her that she could pick up a signal towards the light-house.

'I'll head for the schoolhouse,' Chrissy said. 'Check for a signal there. I want to call Mum and check on wee Michael.'

Chrissy's baby son was her pride and joy, although the relationship with his father, Nigerian medical student Sam Haruna, wasn't going so well.

'And make sure Officer Tulloch's not fallen asleep on the job?' Rhona suggested.

'Well, we wouldn't want to lose any more bones, would we?'

Bundled up against the cold, Rhona took her torch and headed out the back way.

The sky was clear of cloud, a crisp moon in evidence with an accompaniment of stars. To the north-east she could see the rotating beam of the lighthouse, like a bright eye in the velvety darkness. She headed along a path towards the sound of the sea.

Between the moon and the lighthouse, she found her eyes growing accustomed to the dark, so she switched off her torch. As she crested the final dune, moonlight found a long strip of white sand. At the water's edge the sea was an inky black.

Rhona sat down, knees drawn up, and surveyed the scene. Her home island of Skye had some of the best views ever, but she decided what made Orkney special was the feeling of being on the edge of the world.

The sound of a series of messages pinging in as her mobile found a signal put an end to that train of thought. Rhona checked through them, opening a brief text from Sean saying all was well in Paris and one from Erling saying he'd be back tomorrow.

As Rhona slipped the mobile into her pocket, it rang, the drill sharp in the silence. She glanced at the screen to find McNab's name.

'How goes it, Dr MacLeod?'

'Okay. We'll reach the body by tomorrow if the weather holds.'

'And if it doesn't?'

'We stick around until the job's finished. How was the PM?'

She listened as McNab gave her the details, Dr Sissons's theory of dehydration ringing true; the story of an intruder who didn't steal anything, less so.

'I checked through Jock's effects again before they went to the lab,' McNab said. 'There was something tucked in the back of the wallet. An old newspaper cutting about a World War Two radar station, Whale Head at Lopness—' He stopped as Rhona interrupted him.

'That's here,' she said in surprise, 'on Sanday.'

'I know. I googled it. His neighbour said Jock talked about gathering seaweed as a boy and that he came from up north somewhere. I wondered if he came from Orkney.'

Rhona asked if he wanted her to run the name past DI Flett. 'Or maybe the Ranger here, who seems to know everything and everyone about the place. If Jock had a connection with the radar station that might be a starting point.'

McNab muttered his thanks.

'You okay?' Rhona said, sensing something wasn't quite right.

'I'm fine, Dr MacLeod, and no, I'm not back on the booze.'

Rhona recalled McNab's bright blue eyes, the trimmed auburn stubble and his general demeanour at their meeting the day before, and decided he was likely telling the truth. He wasn't back on the booze, yet something was bothering him. She knew McNab well enough to know that. She briefly contemplated asking after Freya, but something warned her not to.

They said their goodbyes and Rhona rang off, keen to be back in the warmth of the cottage. Walking back she now noted a scattering of lights signifying the other inhabitants of the far north-eastern corner of this far northern isle. Looking seawards, there had been nothing but an empty horizon. Looking landwards, Rhona didn't feel quite so alone.

12

Rhona slept well, waking only on the alarm call. She'd banked up the stove before bed, as instructed by Derek, and woke to a warm house. Chrissy appeared as Rhona filled the kettle and informed her that they would have a cooked breakfast before work. Rhona didn't argue.

'I'll make sandwiches for later. Or we could come back here for lunch?' Chrissy suggested.

'We'll work through today. Erling says the weather will worsen later,' Rhona said. 'I want the bones bagged by then.'

'So we're staying another night?'

'That depends on the weather, and the availability of the police chopper.'

As Chrissy served up, she gave Rhona a rundown of her conversation with Officer Tulloch.

'He says the whole island knows about the bones *and* the flowers in the attic.'

'What flowers in the attic?'

'Mike found magic flowers in the attic of the schoolhouse. They're flowers that have been made from the hem of a dead child's smock. The magic flower represents the soul of the child.' Chrissy gave Rhona a knowing look. 'I told you there was a Wicker Man feel about all of this.'

Rhona was trying to make sense of how these flowers

79

Chrissy was talking about had anything to do with the body they were excavating.

Seeing her puzzled expression, Chrissy carried on. 'Mike took one of the flowers to the heritage centre and the guy there, who's DI Flett's relative, by the way, warned him to put it back where he found it. He didn't and that's when the digger unearthed the body.' Chrissy examined Rhona's dubious expression before adding, 'I'm just reporting what's being said. I'm not agreeing with it.'

'What did PC Tulloch make of the story?'

'Ivan says some folk aren't happy about the excavation. They say the dead should be left in peace.'

'But if it was a murder victim?'

Chrissy shrugged. 'They think it's just an old grave. There's loads of them on the island. After one storm, they discovered a Viking burial in a sand dune, complete with the skeletons of three people.'

Rhona rose. 'I think they're probably right, but there's a procedure that has to be followed, and that procedure got you your jolly up here and an opportunity to meet PC Tulloch.'

The tarp looked undisturbed although a small puddle of water had accumulated, indicating there had been rain overnight. There was no sign of PC Tulloch, and Mike Jones came out to tell them that the officer had gone home to catch up on some sleep.

'I just listened to the forecast. High winds and squalls of heavy rain are coming our way, predicted to reach Orkney by mid to late afternoon.'

Rhona was already in the process of kitting up. The light

wasn't ideal but they would have to make a start if they were working against the clock. Mike beat a hasty retreat as she and Chrissy prepared to release and pull back the tarp. It seemed what lay beneath still gave him the jitters.

Rhona was pleased to find there had been no water seepage into the grave and it looked just as it had done when she'd left the night before. Today's procedures would follow the same as yesterday's. Following the grid, cutting small sections or spits and bagging the soil until the skeleton was fully exposed. Rhona felt a flicker of excitement at the prospect.

The further down they'd dug, the sandier the soil had become. It had taken more than two hours of careful bagging and recording to expose the remains fully. The skeleton lay on one side, the upper torso on a higher level than the feet, the remains of one shoe dislodged, the other with the sole still encasing the bones of the foot. The clothing had disintegrated, but where copper had inhibited bacterial degradation such as around buttons and eyelets, fragments were visible. A small metal brooch lay among the ribs.

As Chrissy captured this on camera, Rhona made the call to Kirkwall.

Erling answered immediately.

'It's female,' she told him. 'And definitely not ancient.'

There was a moment of studied silence before Erling answered.

'Can you give me any indication of how long she's been there?'

'The remains are fully skeletonized, but there are some

personal effects which might help decide the timeline. And by the scraps of material that have survived, I'd say the clothes and shoes were of natural fabrics.'

'And that means?'

'We may be looking at fifty years or more.'

'So a cold case?'

'A suspicious cold case,' Rhona said, knowing Erling would be aware that meant the involvement of an MI team.

'So what happens now?'

'I'll process what I can before the bad weather hits and do what's necessary to preserve the rest until we can get back to it.'

Rhona found Mike standing at the open door as she rang off, the look on his face suggesting he'd been party to her side of the conversation at least.

'It's serious?' he said.

'It's suspicious enough to warrant bringing in an MIT,' Rhona said.

'What's that?' he said worriedly.

'A major investigation team.'

Mike stepped back a little. 'More police?'

'More specialized officers.'

'But I thought it was an old grave?'

'It is,' she assured him. 'But not so old that we're not interested.'

The personal items she extracted first. The silver brooch was a small pair of wings, with a crown above and the initials RAF below. There was no engraving on the back to indicate either giver or receiver.

As she'd told Erling, most of the clothing had gone. Plastic was long living, but natural materials like cotton and wool decayed just as flesh did, apart from areas protected by copper. From the scraps that remained, she thought a woollen buttoned cardigan had been worn over a cotton dress.

The soles of the shoes, though not complete, had survived reasonably well. At close quarters, Rhona could see a film of what looked like crushed shells coating the underside. Different particle sizes of sand bound themselves together under pressure, like concrete. That was why getting rid of sand from your shoes was so difficult. This covering wasn't sand, but shell fragments, the colours and patterns of which were still visible, indicating that the female in this grave had walked over a shell beach before her death.

Under an increasingly threatening sky, Rhona began to recover the bones. There was no hard and fast rule as to how long it took for bone to decay, but it would be pretty slow in sand, so she was hopeful they might retrieve most of the skeleton. It was important not to rush the proceedings, despite the sense of urgency the weather was placing on them.

Excavating the areas around the hands and feet first, she bagged the bones of each one before tackling the left limbs, then the right. Vertebrae she bagged together, confident by now that the bones weren't fragile. As each bone was retrieved, Chrissy coloured it in on a bone chart.

Eventually Chrissy said, 'Okay, that's it, except for the missing skull,' which, had it still been there, would have been placed in its own box, any mandibles paper-wrapped and stored separately. But they didn't have the skull and its absence seemed even more pertinent now.

With a skull we had more chance of putting a face to the victim.

Rhona glanced upwards at the scurrying clouds. They'd been lucky until now, both the rain and the wind had held off, but for how much longer?

'Have we time to take out the lower layer?'

Even as Chrissy asked this question, Rhona felt the first drop of rain on her face. As though on cue, the wind flicked at the cover on the camera. Rhona was keen to complete the excavation, but that didn't look likely now. In fact, they had probably been lucky to get this far.

A stronger gust of wind shook the tripod, deciding her. They couldn't carry on with the excavation if they weren't able to record it. They would have to admit defeat, for the moment.

Climbing out of the grave, Rhona shouted to Chrissy to pull over the tarp as the first of the squalls hit. In anticipation of the deteriorating weather, everything they'd excavated had already been taken to safety in the shed. It just remained for them to secure the tarp and get the camera under cover.

Ten minutes later, very wet and not a little blown about, they took refuge in Mike's kitchen.

'There's a severe weather warning out,' he told them. 'All flights and ferries are cancelled.'

'Did they say how long it would last?' Rhona said, accepting the welcome mug of hot coffee Mike offered her.

'No.'

'What about the party?' Chrissy said.

'Party?' Mike looked taken aback.

'Live music at the hotel,' Chrissy said. 'Ivan said the weather won't make any difference.'

'I don't normally go to things at the hotel—' he began, before being interrupted.

'How long have you been living here?' Chrissy demanded.

'Eight months.'

'No wonder you don't know anyone.'

'Chrissy,' Rhona remonstrated, shooting Mike an apologetic glance.

Mike suddenly smiled, transforming his face. 'You're right. I haven't made a big enough effort.'

'Everyone will want to talk to you,' Chrissy told him. 'With a body buried in your back garden and magic flowers in the attic.'

'How d'you know about the flowers?' Mike came back, the smile disappearing as swiftly as it had appeared.

'Everyone knows, according to Ivan.'

It seemed Chrissy had struck a nerve. Mike rose in what appeared to be a gesture of dismissal. 'If you don't mind, I have to get back to work.'

Rhona swiftly thanked him for the coffee and indicated they would head back to the cottage.

'I take it your shed will withstand the storm?' she said. 'Otherwise I should move everything to the cottage, although I'm not sure where we would store it.'

'No need. The shed's as robust as this place. I'll lock the door too,' Mike assured her.

Rhona's plan had been to get the evidence off the island and down to the lab as swiftly as possible. But that wasn't going to happen. Not yet anyway.

13

The chopper dropped suddenly as though yanked earthwards by an invisible chain. McNab's stomach fell with it, hitting the floor between his feet. Then just as suddenly it rose again, filling his stomach with what felt like the frantic beating of a giant seagull's wings.

'Fucking hell!'

'You okay back there, Detective Sergeant?' Doug Cameron, the pilot, grinned round at him. 'A little livelier than a squad car, is it not?'

'You did that on purpose, you bastard.'

'Didn't want you falling asleep just as we're coming in to land.'

McNab forced himself to look out of the window. Already semi-dark, the beams of the chopper picked out where they were headed.

'That's the airport?' he said in disbelief. 'That field?'

'You should have landed here when it really was a field. Once we're down, I need you out and heading for that shed. We want to make it out of here before the storm hits.'

McNab checked his seat belt, as though that would make any difference to staying alive, and gripped the edge of the seat, no longer caring what Cameron and his co-pilot thought of him.

*

The mad impulse that had brought him here now seemed like something he would have done after downing a bottle of whisky. It appeared caffeine might be proving just as dangerous on the mad impulse front.

He'd been with the boss when the call from Orkney had come in with news of the body. McNab had listened to the one-sided conversation, heard Rhona's name mentioned and, picking up the gist of what had happened, interrupted and offered to go there on the spot as part of the major investigation team. When the call had ended, he'd talked up his chances by throwing in the story of Jock Drever and his Sanday connection.

By the look the boss threw him, he knew that had been a mistake.

'This isn't about the Drever case. It's about a suspicious death.'

'Yes, boss.'

'I thought you had a strong aversion to the wilds of Scotland, Sergeant?'

'I managed to overcome it on the Stonewarrior case, sir.' The moment the words were out, McNab had regretted them. He had basically gone AWOL during that time, chasing the suspect through the western Highlands on his own, which had understandably led to his subsequent demotion.

The boss had regarded him with a baleful eye.

This could go either way.

'Are you ready to go *now*, Sergeant?'

'Yes, sir,' McNab had said, wondering just how soon *now* actually was.

'Then get down to the chopper station. Apparently there's a brief window for them to get in and out again before the weather closes in.'

As he'd exited, he heard a *good luck* follow him.

McNab muttered a mixture of blasphemy and silent prayer as the ground swiftly approached. His annoyance at Cameron dissolved into admiration as a gust of wind hit the chopper and the pilot swiftly brought their descent back under control.

Then the door was open and he and his bag were ejected. Even as he dipped his head and began his run towards the shed, he heard the chopper rise behind him. When Cameron had indicated they would be in and out again before McNab had reached shelter, he'd been right.

McNab turned to watch the black and yellow bluebottle rise and head south-west, saying a silent thanks for his safe landing. The rain was falling in sheets, driving into his face as well as his back. Hitching his bag over his shoulder, he made his way towards the vehicle lights next to a small building, assuming it had come to pick him up.

As he approached, a figure stepped out of the jeep.

'DS McNab?' A hand was extended. 'Derek Muir. Resident Ranger. DI Flett asked me to meet you. He sends his apologies. He's stuck on the mainland.' He gestured to McNab to get into the jeep.

'I didn't think they'd manage to land you,' he said, engaging the gear and releasing the handbrake. 'Couldn't have been a fun journey.'

'It wasn't,' McNab said.

'Well, it's going to get worse,' the Ranger said. 'The weather that is, not the journey. I'd rather be down here than up there.'

He swung out of the gate and onto a tarred road, the wind hitting the side of the car.

'Where are we headed?' McNab said.

'Dr MacLeod and her assistant have taken the old Harkness cottage for the duration. It's within walking distance of the deposition site.'

'How's it going up there?'

'They had to give up when the weather came in, but I believe they've retrieved all the bones, except the skull of course.'

'There's no skull?' McNab said in surprise.

'There *was* a skull which the digger unearthed. It went missing the first night. We think local kids may have taken it.'

'I didn't think grave robbers would be a feature of Orkney,' McNab said.

'There are a great many graves and bones scattered over the islands. Most of them ancient of course. We used to unearth them when I was a kid. So I was probably a grave robber too. We'll find the skull.'

The darkness outside was impenetrable, with an occasional glimpse of lighted habitation blinking at the passing jeep. In the headlights, the narrow road was a dark ribbon with a thin edging of white sand on either side.

'The cottage is stocked up,' Derek said. 'So there should be enough food for three, but I can always get more from the shop, if you need it.'

'Chrissy's appetite hasn't been diminished by grave digging?'

'Not according to Dr MacLeod.'

McNab recalled his earlier conversation with Rhona and decided this was a perfect opportunity to bring up the subject of Jock Drever. 'Dr MacLeod said as the Ranger you know all there is to know about Sanday.'

Derek cast him a swift glance. 'I wouldn't say all.'

'What about former residents?'

'How former?'

'During wartime, when Lopness was a radar station,' McNab said.

'The island was overrun by army and navy personnel and contractors then. So I doubt if I could help. If it had been a local . . .'

'The name was Drever, James Drever,' McNab tried.

A moment's silence followed, then the Ranger said, 'A common family name hereabouts. Is that all you have?'

'He may have been a Bevin Boy during the war.'

'Then he'd be a good age now.'

'He died recently in Glasgow,' McNab said. 'We're trying to trace his family.'

Derek looked thoughtful. 'Leave it with me. I'll see what I can find out.'

As they turned a ninety-degree bend in the narrow road, McNab caught a sudden glimpse of something jutting out of the waves just offshore.

'What's that?'

'The famous First World War German destroyer that broke free from a tow and went aground here,' the Ranger said. 'I take it you don't know much about Sanday?'

'Probably as much as you know about Glasgow,' McNab joked.

'Oh, I know Glasgow all right. My family moved there when I was nine.'

'You don't sound like it,' McNab said, surprised.

'I could if you wanted me to.' Derek demonstrated this by going into a diatribe that could have graced any East End pub.

'You were brought up in the East End?'

'Let's say I spent a few of my formative years there before my mother brought me back.'

McNab found he was enjoying himself, even if he had stepped off the edge of the world.

'That's the schoolhouse.' The Ranger indicated a long stone building with tall windows as he pulled into a rougher track. 'You're along here.'

The rain had halted for the moment, although the wind still howled like a banshee. McNab felt its force on the side of the jeep. They crested, not a hill, merely an undulation in the ground, and turned right.

A sign immediately informed them not to go any further due to erosion, before the road became a sandy track with a raised grassed centre. Had they been in a car, the undercarriage would have had difficulty making it past this point. Then McNab saw the cottage. Two windows like bright eyes, a small porch with a front door, the roof comprising large flagstones.

'Home sweet home,' the Ranger said.

14

Samuel Flett had been born in the house he lived in now. A war baby, he'd made his appearance in the box bed next to the fire, the only child born to Ella and Geordie Flett. Sanday winters had almost done for him on a number of occasions. Perhaps 15 January 1952 had provided the most spectacular of these.

Then, it hadn't been illness that had almost finished him off but a hurricane. Of unprecedented violence, it had hit the Orkneys, recording a wind velocity of 130 miles per hour at Costa Head on the mainland before the anemometer had stopped working. Experts believed that at the height of the storm the wind speed had been even higher.

The warning had come the previous evening when a strange aurora had spread across the sky. Sam had watched this sky dance from his favourite spot on the beach. His already vivid imagination had conjured up invading space-men, the lights of their landing craft providing the show.

By midnight the barometer had stood at 28.7 inches and was falling steadily, much to his father's concern. The hurricane had broken at 4.30 a.m. with a squall that had shaken even this solidly build stone cottage.

The wooden henhouses that covered the island at that time had no chance at all and neither did the hens, although

Sam had sought to save his favourite one, nearly losing his life in the process.

Telephone wires were snapped as if with wire cutters, their whipping frenzied dance as dangerous as the flight of the shattered wood of outhouses and roof slates that could have sliced off a man's head.

Into this melee the boy had attempted to run. The henhouse still stood with his favourite hen inside, but at the moment of his heroic rescue attempt, the hurricane had smashed the shed to pieces, throwing them at the rescuer.

Sam had no memory of what happened after that before waking up in the box bed hours later with his mother's worried face bending over him. By rights he should have had a beating for disobedience, but his father felt the wind had already done that for him.

There had been other hurricanes after that. One the following year accompanied by a high tide had seen the sea from Otterswick flow across fields onto Cata Sand, but the physical damage hadn't been as great.

Tonight, he concluded, would be rough, but not on the scale of either of those two years.

Sam rose from the fireside and went to put on the kettle.

His disquiet, he knew, wasn't because of the storm – of which he'd seen and heard many – but because of the discovery at the schoolhouse. As he brewed the tea, taking time to make it in the teapot which had been in the family for as long as he could remember, he allowed himself to contemplate what Derek had told him.

He'd known Derek Muir since the boy had returned from Glasgow with his mother nearly fifty years before. Back then, Derek had struggled to readjust to island life, having spent his childhood in the East End of Glasgow. His rough accent and attitude hadn't made him many friends. He'd thought himself tough and superior and had played this out by starting playground fights. Eventually, his poor mother had sought Sam's help. As a young teacher himself, with only a couple of years' experience, Sam had nevertheless found a way to reach the tough kid Derek had been back then. Sam wasn't even sure why what he'd said or done had worked, but Derek Muir was every inch a Sanday man now and knew more about the island and its inhabitants past and present than anyone, except perhaps himself.

Yet even Derek had no explanation for the discovery of the remains in what had been the grounds of the old primary school. He had come to see Sam at the museum as soon as the story of the unearthing by Hugh Clouston's digger had become common knowledge.

Sam poured his mug of tea and added milk and sugar – *too much sugar* – the words that entered his head were of course those of his late wife, Jean, who was always trying to keep him healthy. Her hard work on that score had succeeded in keeping him alive into his seventieth year. Unfortunately, Jean hadn't looked after herself as well as she had her husband and had departed this life two years before. Something he'd not yet got used to, and never would.

He stirred the mug and carried it back to his seat by the fire. Placing it on the hearth, he put another couple of pieces of peat on the blaze.

It wasn't fashionable to burn peat any more. There were easier ways of warming your house nowadays. In his youth, Sanday, without its own peat banks, had had to rely on the neighbouring northern island of Rousay for fuel. In modern times, it would have been simpler to heat by electricity, powered by the island's three giant windmills, or burn those little nuggets of smokeless fuel that everyone bought for their fire. But Sam liked the scent of peat in the house and the comfort of its glow in the fireplace. And Jean had preferred it too.

As he supped his tea, he contemplated the conversation he'd just had on the phone with Erling. The boy, as he still thought of him, although Erling was in his thirties now, had questioned Sam about the flowers in the attic. Sam had been as blunt with Erling as he had with the newcomer Mike Jones. The flowers, he'd told him, shouldn't be disturbed. They were, after all, the representations of the souls of children who had died. Removing them would be like exhuming a body from sacred ground and putting it on display to the public.

Sam didn't consider himself superstitious, but he did believe that the dead were as much a part of Sanday as the living, and their lives and deaths should be respected. And, he thought again, if you are going to make your home in an old building you should pay heed to what had already happened between those walls.

Mike Jones, as far as he was aware, had – like him – been a teacher and the place he'd chosen to make his home had housed hundreds of children in its time as a Sanday school. The very stones had rung with their voices, their fears, hopes and dreams.

Maybe they still did?

Some of those pupils had died young, their siblings too. That was why the flowers had been fashioned and left there, so that they might watch over those who came after – even Mike Jones.

Sam hadn't said that to the man. His first reaction, he had to admit, had been disquiet. A disquiet which he hadn't been able to fully explain, but definitely involved the certainty that nothing good would come of the flowers being disturbed. That's why he'd urged Mike to put the flower back and not to touch the others.

You can leave the past behind, but it will never leave you.

And then had come news of the unearthing.

A coincidence of course. And yet?

Sam wished that Jean was still there with him. She might have set his mind at rest.

He glanced at the empty chair opposite.

'You know what I'm worried about, don't you?' he said quietly.

He rose and went to the window. There were no lights now, not the way there had been back then. Yet the concrete-clad buildings still stood, resolute against whatever the wind might throw at them. According to his mother, the area around them had been alive with people. Incomers who had changed the island and its way of life forever.

Sam had been born in 1944 at the height of the war. During that time, the island had doubled in population, four hundred servicemen stationed there over the term of the hostilities. Before that, three hundred labourers, skilled workmen and technicians had arrived in 1940 to start work on the wireless station – a vital link in the radar and wireless system designed to warn troops stationed around Scapa Flow when enemy aircraft were approaching.

As a baby he'd known nothing of this, but as a boy he'd explored the empty concrete-clad buildings, and heard plenty of stories about those years. Before the war many Sanday folk had rarely strayed beyond the limits of their own parish with its local shops, school, kirk and chapel. During those years, everything had changed in that respect. Mechanical transport was suddenly in abundance and islanders outside the North End were transported to events at camp. There had, unsurprisingly, been quite a few marriages between islanders and service personnel, and plenty of liaisons, both admitted to and secretive. Babies had been born, like him, in the final days of the conflict, many more in the aftermath.

Then the airmen and soldiers had left, taking some of the island women with them.

The war years were past, but perhaps not the fallout from them.

His initial thought had been that the grave Hugh had uncovered would prove to be yet another manifestation of Orkney's distant past, like the numerous brochs and standing stones that littered the islands. Sand was a great preserver of bones as he knew from his work at the museum.

Then Erling had revealed that the bones weren't so old after all.

Sam addressed the empty seat on the other side of the fire. 'The scientist, a woman who's in charge of excavating the grave, told Erling that she's lain there fifty years or more.' He paused to let that sink in. 'A lassie, Jean, buried in the old playground. How could that be?'

Sam tried to imagine her reaction to the startling news, but wasn't able to. That was the problem. As their time apart lengthened, her voice, once so easily recalled, had grown fainter.

His mood, disturbed by news of the magic flower and darkened by Erling's call, had now reached rock bottom. The reason of course being that he thought he might know the answer to his own question.

*

The child shouldn't be out on a night like this.

The face at the window had seemed at first like a pattern made by raindrops. His eyesight being what it now was, both distant images and those up close had assumed the quality of an old film. He needed new glasses, but chose to make do, because he didn't like life to be too magnified. Then he could see the dust that had accumulated, the smeared marks he hadn't cleaned.

He rose to open the door.

Her face and hair were wet. She wore a waterproof jacket but had chosen not to raise the hood. When he scolded her for that she just smiled. She removed the jacket, shook it and hung it on a hook next to the door, then took the seat opposite him.

'Have you eaten?' she said, in a verging-on-scolding tone.

'I have.'

'Have you eaten enough?'

He told her what he'd had, enlarging the portions somewhat.

She nodded as though satisfied. 'Tea?'

The mug by the fire was lifted, rinsed, and then he watched her go through the motions he had undertaken a short while before.

His tea delivered, she sat down again.

He had a question to ask her but wasn't sure when and how to accomplish it. She normally did the talking. Telling him stories about school and walks on the beach. Tonight she sat silently staring into the fire. He wondered if the sound and fury of the wind attacking the roof was worrying her, then remembered she'd come calling despite the storm.

'You shouldn't have come out in this,' he said.

'I had things to do.' She looked at him with her bright blue eyes.

He thought again how lucky he was to still be able to talk with the young. When he'd retired from the classroom, that's what he knew he would miss the most – the everyday chat of the children.

But that hadn't happened, because of the young girl before him.

He hadn't taught her. Sam had retired well before she'd come to the school. They had met in a different way. She'd turned up at the heritage centre of her own free will. Declared she'd come with her mother to live on Sanday and wanted to know all about the island.

The intensity of her desire to discover the place he felt so strongly about had made them firm friends. That and the fact that she and her mother had become tenants of the neighbouring farmhouse. Coming from near Carlisle, they were more used to the mountains of the Lake District than the flat fertile fields of Sanday. But it seemed that two generations before, her family had been Orcadian, as evidenced by her mother's choice of name for her daughter, Inga.

'What things?' Sam said, returning to the conversation.

'I've been looking for the skull,' she told him.

15

McNab hadn't slept a wink and, glancing at his mobile, realized there wasn't much time left to do so. The settee was at least six inches shorter than required, but that hadn't been the main impediment to sleep. He was used to dreich weather, Glasgow endured plenty of that. But in the city he was enclosed by other flats and surrounded by tall buildings. Despite the three-foot-thick walls on this one-storey cottage, he'd never felt so exposed to the elements.

As he'd lain there, he'd imagined the scene outside. Wind stripping everything from the surface of the earth – buildings, creatures, humans. At any moment he'd expected the roof to be torn off, exposing the people inside in all their frailty. He'd thought of that German destroyer beached not that far away, the sea further demolishing that which it couldn't blow to smithereens.

Why would anyone choose to live in such a place?

According to the brief lecture he'd been subjected to last night by Chrissy, it appeared that people had chosen to live in Orkney before anywhere else on the British Isles. When he'd questioned that assertion, she'd told him Neolithic remains proved her point.

Rhona hadn't intervened in the heated discussion, preferring to write up her notes at the kitchen table on her laptop. On his surprise arrival, he'd been greeted with a hug from

Chrissy and a questioning look from Rhona. McNab had quickly explained how he'd arrived on the last helicopter, courtesy of the boss.

'Because it's a serious crime.'

Rhona had thrown him a look at that point which had dented his bravado somewhat.

'It could have waited until the weather improved.'

'What's a bit of bad weather?' he'd said, deliberately forgetting how his stomach had performed on board the chopper.

It was at that point a gust of wind had hit the building with such force that he'd risen to his feet, then realizing what a prick he looked had headed for the fridge and the beer to cover his sudden attack of the vapours.

As he'd opened the fridge door, his eye had caught sight of a bottle of unopened Highland Park nearby on the worktop. What he would have given at that moment to pour himself a glass. The fact that he had made it through the night on the settee only yards from the whisky was a cause for celebration, even if he'd had no sleep, he decided.

McNab rose with a groan for his cramped limbs and went in search of the bathroom. There were no sounds from either of the women's rooms. He found himself impressed by the thought that they might well have slept through the storm, unlike himself.

The howl of the wind had abated somewhat, but rain still lashed at the small windows and he could see the white-topped waves crashing onto the beach. As he stood, in awe of the edge-of-the-world scene, a very large cat made its way past the window, pausing briefly to examine him on the way. It was, he'd learned last night, one of ten wild felines who called the outhouses home and were fed by the farmer's wife.

That's all I need. Ten fucking cats.

He stripped off and turned on the shower, catching sight of the bullet scar on his back via a wall mirror. Being out of normal view, he usually managed to ignore the life-threatening injury he'd acquired when Chrissy had been pregnant with baby Michael – until he'd met and bedded Freya, that was. She, he'd come to realize, was obsessed by it. She liked to trace it when they made love. Often spoke of it. Interrogating him on what had happened when he'd died in the street in Rhona's arms, then been brought back to life in the ambulance.

McNab held no beliefs in the afterlife and, if he was honest with himself, he had no desire to examine either his feelings about his death or what had happened in the interim between breathing his last and his reappearance.

But Freya was a Wiccan who believed in resurrection, if not of the body, then of the spirit. McNab also suspected she'd been trying to resurrect the spirits of her murdered fellow Wiccans, Leila and Shannon. He'd woken up in the middle of the night to find her in her temple, chanting. Listening through the door, he'd caught their names, discerning words in her spell that caused him disquiet.

Then she'd brought Leila's cat to live in the flat with her.

McNab turned the shower abruptly to cold. In his mind's eye he saw the angry red of the scar pale as he forced his own anger to fade.

His feelings towards Freya he'd interpreted as love. He had risked his own life to save hers. Yet here he was, getting angry because of a bloody cat.

He forced himself to stay under the cold water longer than need be, then stepped out and rubbed himself dry.

Which is why I asked to come here. The man who's more alarmed by wide open spaces than he is of a knife fight, or a bullet for that matter.

McNab glanced at his face in the mirror, surprised at the honesty of his thoughts.

Well, he was here now and there was a job to do. Including finding a bed more comfortable than that couch, preferably somewhere that didn't have cats.

The scent of frying met him on entry to the sitting room. Through the open door to the small kitchen he could see Chrissy at work. Rhona was nowhere to be seen.

'She's gone to check on the grave,' Chrissy informed him. 'Although it's not calm enough yet to start work again. What do you want in your fry-up?'

'Everything,' McNab told her.

Rhona walked the short distance along the sandy track, the sea beating the white shore on one side, empty fields on the other. The squalls of rain and wind had subsided from last night, but according to Derek they were entering the eye of the storm and there was more to come.

Which meant she would spend today viewing the images she'd taken of the excavation so that McNab could see what they were dealing with. When McNab had surprised them with his appearance last night, Rhona realized he was the result of her conversation with Erling. She hadn't expected a response quite so quickly, which suggested McNab had definitely put himself forward. But for what reason?

Since the formation of Police Scotland, specialist units were drafted in to help the local force deal with homicides, many of whom had never encountered a murder on their doorstep before. In those cases, the first few days of an investigation, if carried out properly, usually produced a result. The community officers would work with the local population, backed up by the expertise of seasoned officers.

The discovery of the body at the schoolhouse didn't fall into that category, although McNab was on the MIT list. Last night he'd spoken of Jock Drever's death and the likelihood that he had come from Sanday, which made Rhona suspect McNab was here as much because of Jock Drever as the skeleton she'd unearthed.

The playground was covered in sand whipped up by the wind. Even now she could feel it on her face like pinpricks and taste it on her lips. The tarp, she was glad to note, had stayed secure. A quick peek below determined that the lower layer of sandy soil remained undisturbed.

Rhona, pleased, headed for the shed. Solidly built from the flat stones Orkney was famous for, its roof was, like the cottage, constructed with larger flagstones.

No wind, she thought, however fierce, could dislodge this building.

She tried the door, then suddenly remembered that Mike had said he would lock it – and was surprised when it opened under her hand. She had stacked the equipment, the bags of recovered soil and, of course, the bones carefully at the rear of the shed. In the dim light she was relieved to find that all looked as it had done last night. The shed had proved as robust as Mike had promised.

Hearing footsteps, she turned to find Mike, looking a little startled and wielding what appeared to be a length of driftwood.

'Sorry, I saw the door lying open. I didn't realize it was you,' he said, lowering his weapon. 'How did you get into the shed?'

'It wasn't locked.'

'It was,' Mike said in a determined fashion. 'That's why I came with this.' He gestured to the driftwood cudgel, then looked around wildly as though expecting an intruder to suddenly appear from the shadows. 'I definitely locked the door.' He flashed a key at her.

Rhona wondered if he had, in fact, forgotten his promise and, spotting her arrival, wanted to cover his forgetfulness.

'Maybe the elusive children came back?' Rhona tried to make light of the situation.

It didn't work.

'Why do you say that?' He darted her a suspicious look. 'You think I'm making them up?'

'No, I—' Rhona halted as Mike strode past her.

'Have you checked your evidence is okay?'

'I was just about to.'

Mike located a light switch and flicked it on, then headed for the rear of the shed, Rhona at his heels.

From her viewpoint at the door, the carefully stored evidence had looked secure, but not from where she stood now. Rhona stared down at the torn evidence bags and scattered soil, a rush of emotions sweeping over her, guilt being the main one. If only she'd transported everything back to the cottage. But how would that have been possible?

'An animal got in?' she tried.

'There's no entry other than the door. And,' Mike said, catching her thought, 'no cat or any other animal could have done this. This is wilful destruction.'

As Rhona studied it, she was inclined to agree.

'I'll call Erling,' she said, internally reminding herself that McNab would have to be told too.

At the policeman's name, Mike blanched. 'Please make sure he knows I had nothing to do with this.'

Rhona, shaken and puzzled by what she had just witnessed, took herself outside.

In all her time in forensics, she had never had the evidence she'd collected tampered with. True, she'd had a severed foot found in the waters off Skye removed from the lab fridge, but that had been by order of Her Majesty's Government, a situation she'd had no control over, however much she'd complained.

Here, it had begun to look like someone was trying to thwart this investigation.

But for what reason?

She assumed young people could be as mischievous on Sanday as anywhere else. Derek had assured them the skull would turn up, and she'd bought his explanation that it might be children who'd removed it. Tampering with and destroying evidence collected in the course of an investigation was a very serious matter.

When Rhona called DI Flett from the schoolhouse landline to report the latest developments, Erling listened in his usual calm manner, before asking, 'Is Constable Tulloch with you?'

Rhona had forgotten Ivan.

'I haven't seen him this morning.'

'I understand DS McNab managed to land last night?'

'He did.'

'Have him and Tulloch work together. Tulloch's no detective, but the locals will answer his questions. Hopefully I'll get out there by tomorrow, although it's not looking promising.' He paused. 'As for the remaining evidence, I would suggest the safest place to store it would be at the heritage centre, next to the community shop. I'll ask Derek to help you transfer it down there.' He paused. 'I'm sorry this has happened.'

'In normal circumstances, the evidence would have been off the island and at my lab by now,' Rhona told him.

Chrissy and McNab appeared as she rang off.

'What's up?' Chrissy said swiftly, seeing her expression.

'Come and see.'

'The wee bastards,' McNab said.

'You don't know it was kids,' Rhona said.

'Kids or cats,' McNab thundered.

'You just have a downer on cats,' Chrissy said, dropping to her knees beside the mess. 'And we all know why.' She studied the reason for his outrage. After a few minutes, she gave her expert opinion. 'It's not as bad as it looks. We've lost five maybe six bags. I think the rest's intact and I have it all logged. What about the recording?'

'I took the camera back with me,' Rhona glanced about, 'and left the stand over there.'

'Well, it's not there now,' Chrissy said. 'So even if the weather improves we can't continue the excavation.' She looked to Rhona. 'Someone's screwing with us.'

At that point Mike Jones appeared at the door, causing the trio to fall silent.

'That was PC Tulloch on the phone. He'll be here shortly.'

16

McNab observed the four children before him, who ranged between eight and twelve years old. The girl, who seemed most inclined to speak, was the eldest and definitely an incomer by her accent. The biggest boy regarded her with annoyance, as though he thought he should be the spokesperson. It was like any gang, with a sprinkling of the clever, the not so bright, the foolhardy and the timid. He had pegged the younger boy with the shock of blond hair to be foolhardy. The talkative girl with the dark hair, the brightest. The younger girl was just plain terrified.

They had been given an empty office at the school to chat to the group, all of whom lived within a short walking distance of the excavation site. PC Tulloch was apparently known to all of them – a local boy turned cop. A female teacher was there too, in place of the parents. This wasn't a formal interview, just a chat about the excavation, and in McNab's opinion, Tulloch was doing pretty well.

He'd addressed the kids in the local dialect, switching to English when he realized the older girl was struggling to understand. He knew all their names, where they lived and what their parents did. He made them laugh. Then he'd asked them about the skull.

At that they'd fallen silent and looked to the girl.

McNab had a sudden memory of a book he'd read in

school, or been forced to read, about a group of children born in strange circumstances in an English village. The book had been made into a film, called *Children of the Damned*. McNab had preferred the book's title, *The Midwich Cuckoos*. In the story the children had all been born on the same day, at the same hour, in the same place. And they'd all thought the same thing at the same time, which was, in McNab's opinion, what was happening now.

Three faces turned to the girl at exactly the same moment and waited for her to speak.

Her bright blue eyes sought his, rather than Tulloch's, as though she was aware who was really in charge.

'We didn't take the skull,' she told him. 'We could help you try and find it.'

Of course, the skull wasn't the only item missing now. McNab acknowledged the girl's earnest offer and nodded at Tulloch to continue.

None of the group had given any indication that the girl was telling porky pies. McNab had looked for all the fairly recognizable signs, and spotted none. No one shuffled or avoided eye contact, licked their lips or scratched their nose or looked out of the window.

McNab found himself believing that they hadn't taken the skull.

Tulloch now spoke about the storm and how wild it had been, encouraging them to tell their own tales of the previous night. Had anyone seen the flashes of lightning? Heard the wind? Been out in the rain?

They each in turn said they'd been confined indoors, or had slept through it.

Except the girl.

'I visited a friend,' she said. 'Mr Flett.'

'You went out in the storm?' Tulloch asked.

'His house is minutes away. I wanted to make sure he was all right.'

She's telling the truth, McNab thought, *but maybe not all of it.*

'Sam Flett was a teacher here. He's retired now and runs the heritage centre,' Tulloch told him in an aside. 'He's related to DI Flett.'

The girl interrupted their exchange. 'Sam was nearly killed in the 1952 hurricane. It reached over 130 miles an hour. He was trying to rescue his favourite hen before the henhouse blew away.'

She said this in such an earnest fashion, McNab had to smother a smile, then the thought occurred that she'd just successfully averted the line of questioning.

'What did you and Mr Flett talk about?' McNab said.

He had nonplussed her. She drew her eyes away from him and refocused on Tulloch.

'I checked whether he'd had his tea. He doesn't eat enough since his wife died. He misses her a lot.'

'And you like to keep him company?' McNab tried to draw her back to him.

'I'm new here so he tells me stories about Sanday. Like when the troops were here during the war,' she added. 'He knows everything about the place. That's why he runs the heritage centre.'

A bell rang and the teacher stood up. It seemed their time together was at an end.

McNab thanked them all, his Glasgow accent jarring in his ears after PC Tulloch's musical cadences.

When the door closed behind the platoon, Tulloch said, 'Well, what do you think, sir?'

'You're the local. What do you think?'

'They didn't take the skull, and they're trying to find it.'

McNab agreed. 'My feeling exactly. Inga has them on the job.'

'Do we stop them, sir?'

'And how exactly would we do that?' McNab shook his head. 'The girl is bright and inquisitive. She might find out something we can't.'

'But will she tell us?'

'If not us, then maybe DI Flett.' McNab made for the door. 'Where to next?'

'The hotel, to see if we can organize a bed for you tonight?' suggested PC Tulloch.

McNab was very much in favour of that.

'Rain and gales. Or gales and rain. That's Sanday weather for you,' PC Tulloch said cheerfully as he pulled into a passing place to give way to an approaching car.

Staring out at what he regarded as a bleak landscape, McNab wondered how anyone who lived here could be so cheerful.

'Are there no trees at all?' McNab wasn't a big fan of trees, but even he missed them a bit.

'There used to be woods at Otterswick. They found the remains of ancient trees buried beneath the sands. They're marked on an old Admiralty chart from 1858. And there's an old poem that mentions them.

> *'The Ba' Green o'Runnabrek*
> *The Horse Buils o'Riv*
> *If it wasnae for the woods o'Otterswick*
> *What wey wid wae liv?'*

111

McNab hadn't a clue what Tulloch had said and didn't ask for an explanation, as a large red-brick building loomed up on the passenger side a few metres from the road.

'What's that?'

'The old mortuary from the Second World War. It's the only building that wasn't concrete clad against bombardment – I suppose because the people inside were dead already.'

As PC Tulloch smiled at his own joke, McNab wondered just how many hours of good humour he would be able to stomach.

He'd been promised a town, which to McNab meant more than a scattering of buildings by a small harbour, even if one of them was a hotel. Catching his perturbed expression, PC Tulloch offered an explanation.

'It was busier, when the ferry docked here. Now the roll-on roll-off comes in at Loth on the southern tip of the island.'

He drew up next to a red telephone box that had seen better days and didn't look as though it functioned at all.

'The hotel has wireless and a decent mobile signal,' Tulloch offered by way of compensation.

'But are they open and do they have a room?'

'I called ahead. They're willing to put you up as you're on police business. The pub opens in the evenings. In fact, there's live music there tomorrow night.'

McNab wasn't sure how to respond to that, so didn't.

They were met at the door by a young man who apparently worked behind the bar. As he led McNab up to view his room, he revealed that he and Ivan had gone to school together. McNab tried to look on that as a positive, even though he was feeling more the outsider with every moment. Surely he would get good service having been brought here by a friend?

McNab surveyed the room and, in particular, the bed, with surprised pleasure. Tonight he would get a sleep. The only disadvantage seemed to be that the window overlooked the sea, which appeared to be at war with itself. At that moment a squall hit the window with, he suspected, a mix of salt spray and rain.

According to PC Tulloch, the font of all knowledge, the wind had subsided a little this morning because they were in the eye of the storm. It would, he'd assured McNab, in his usual jovial manner, get back up to speed tonight.

McNab stood for a moment, enjoying the quiet in the room, deciding that, high winds or not, nothing would keep him awake tonight. Leaving his bag, he locked the door with a good old-fashioned key, and headed back downstairs, where he found PC Tulloch and his mate in the bar, with its main windows also facing the sea.

Tulloch pointed at a large sign on the wall which explained how to get onto the Wi-Fi connection.

'It's best to sit near the window,' he explained. 'And Torvaig says do we want some lunch?'

Twenty minutes later, McNab was feeling a whole lot better after consuming a substantial plate of fish and chips. The meal would have reached perfection if accompanied by a pint of beer, but being on duty, he'd refrained.

'If there's no police officer permanently on the island, how do you enforce the drink-driving laws?'

'The locals enforce them themselves,' PC Tulloch said. 'In an emergency someone calls Kirkwall and the police launch comes out.'

'What about a fight?'

'We pull them apart and take them home.'

'Guns?'

'Plenty of them for shooting geese.'

'But not people?'

'No.'

'Knives?' McNab was enjoying himself.

'For gutting fish and skinning rabbits.'

'So you don't need the police at all?'

PC Tulloch's face darkened. 'There was a murder here in 2010. A man battered another man to death and buried the body in shallow sand at Sty Wick. Nobody here believed the story that the victim had left the island. They called the police.'

'So we can expect as much help with this one?'

'There's not many folk left who were here in wartime.'

'Yet somebody removed the skull and tried to destroy the evidence.'

'It looks like that, sir.' Tulloch was obviously troubled by the thought.

'And it's our job is to find out who, Constable. And why.'

17

It would take two trips in the Land Rover to transport the soil and bones to the heritage centre. On the arrival of the first load, Sam Flett offered Rhona space in a room used for newspaper cuttings and recorded material of the war years.

'I guessed you wouldn't want it stored in the back shed.'

Rhona thanked him. 'The centre's locked up at night?'

He nodded. 'And I'm here most days, even out of the tourist season. I can give you a key, so you can come and go as necessary.'

'Hopefully it won't be here for long.'

When Derek departed to fetch the next load, Sam offered to make them a pot of tea.

'I have some biscuits too.'

They were seated now, teapot between them, at a table in the centre of the room. On the surrounding shelves were blue folders of cuttings and written recollections of the residents of Sanday during both the First and the Second World Wars.

'I was born in forty-four, but I heard plenty later from my mother. Then there were the buildings they left behind, that are still standing. I used to play in them as a kid. All except the old mortuary.' He looked straight at her. 'I hear from Erling that it was a lassie you found and she may have been from back then?'

'That's still to be confirmed, but yes, it looks likely.'

'D'you think she was a local lass?'

'I don't know,' Rhona said honestly. 'Are you aware of anyone going missing during that time?'

'No.' He indicated the shelves of folders. 'Maybe in some of the local stories of the war years you might find a mention of someone who went missing.'

'So a long shot?' Rhona said.

'Sanday was a different place during the war. Before then, we knew everyone on this island, parish by parish. It wasn't possible to "go missing". To leave the island you had to go by ferry from Kettletoft to Kirkwall. Most folk even knew why you were going. A trip to the dentist took two days. We knew one another's business. City folk don't like that idea, but that's how it was. And,' he added, 'still is, to a certain extent.'

'So the answer might be here?' Rhona indicated the shelves.

'And in talking to those Sanday folk left alive from those times.'

'How many are there?'

'Not many. If you're talking of folk to the north of the island, Don Cutts is probably the one you want to talk to. He's in a wheelchair now, but still has all his wits about him. There's plenty other auld folk on the island, but most of them are incomers, who've moved here in the last twenty years or so.' He paused. 'Were there any personal items with the body that might help?'

'There was a brooch,' Rhona said.

His eyes lit up. 'Can I see it?'

Rhona extracted the clear evidence bag from the collection and brought it over.

Sam studied it through the plastic. 'This is a sweetheart brooch, very popular during war time. RAF personnel gave them to their girlfriends or wives. We've a selection in a glass case out in the main area.'

'So it's not likely to identify the wearer?' Rhona had suspected as much.

He shook his head. 'Without an inscription, no. If we knew what she looked like, that might jog a memory.' He observed Rhona thoughtfully. 'But without the skull, I take it that's not possible?'

There was no point in denying it. 'Height, build and age, even shoe size – but her face, no.'

'You think that's why the skull was removed?' Sam said worriedly.

'According to DS McNab, the neighbourhood children didn't take it. He spoke to them today at the school.'

'Then who did?'

If someone such as Sam couldn't answer that question, then Rhona doubted she could.

'DS McNab and PC Tulloch are talking to anyone who might have information regarding the body and the skull at somewhere called Heilsa Fjold. I gather it's next to the school.'

'The Sanday Development Trust run the place. It's the new community and youth centre. They'll get plenty folk turning up. Probably more from curiosity than actual knowledge.'

Rhona's mobile rang. When she answered it was Erling.

'The weather is set to worsen again tonight, then ease enough over the following twenty-four hours for you and the excavation material to be transported out.'

'I can't go yet,' Rhona said. 'I still have the soil under the body to collect.'

'You'll send the evidence anyway?'

Rhona agreed. 'Chrissy can go with it. I'll manage the rest of the excavation on my own, provided I can replace the camera tripod.'

'I'll get a replacement to you as soon as possible.'

'By boat or plane?'

'When I come with the police launch, if not before.'

When Rhona rang off she said, 'That was Erling.'

'I guessed as much,' Sam said with a smile. 'I'll leave you to it then. I have some paperwork to be getting on with.'

As Sam rose to go, Rhona suddenly remembered.

'Have you heard of a man from here called James Drever? He'd be ninety by now.'

Sam shot her an incredulous look and put down his mug.

'Jamie Drever's alive?'

Rhona didn't see the point in not telling the truth, but first she wanted to establish that they were talking about the same man.

'Your James Drever,' she said. 'Has he any relatives here on Sanday?'

Sam shook his head. 'He left during the war and never came back. My mother used to talk about him, and wonder if he'd survived the war.'

'If I had a photograph of him in his twenties, would you or someone else be able to identify him?'

'My mother would have, but she's long dead. Why do you ask?'

Rhona decided to be blunt.

'We found the recently deceased body of an elderly man called James Drever in a Glasgow flat. We're trying to trace any relatives he had.' She told Sam about the newspaper cutting of Lopness in his wallet and the fact that he'd told his neighbour he'd gathered seaweed as a child, which led them to think that Orkney might have been his home at one point. 'He was tall and slim and sandy-haired. He got married in Newcastle to a woman called Grace Cummings in 1948.' She looked at Sam. 'Does that sound like your James Drever?'

'I have no idea, but if you have a photograph from back then, I could see what I can find out.'

'I'll arrange with DS McNab to let you see a copy.'

Sam had been unnerved by his conversation with the forensic woman. Having the excavated material here in the heritage centre wasn't pleasant, but it wasn't the bones and the soil that had upset him.

It was what had happened to him at the mention of the name Drever. Drever was a common Orkney surname, found on most of the islands in the archipelago. Why had he immediately thought that the man she spoke about was *that* Jamie Drever? And why had that brought such a sense of dread?

He'd found himself trembling in the aftermath of her question, and had been keen to get away from both the woman and the room of evidence. Ever since they'd dug up the bones he'd had the ill feeling that the past was coming back to haunt them.

A past long buried, like the flowers in the loft of the old schoolhouse.

He shut and locked the door of his tiny office as foreboding overpowered him. He'd experienced such sensations before, particularly in his youth. They'd waned during adolescence and while Jean was alive had faded away almost entirely. She'd called them his dark fogs, which she'd dispelled with love and laughter.

Sitting there in the gloom, he could taste the horror of the fog as it descended. It was always the same feeling. He knew something bad was about to happen yet he didn't know what, nor had he any means to prevent it. Feminine fancies, his father had disparagingly called them, firmly dismissing them. His mother had been more forgiving, but hadn't encouraged him to speak of them. Instead she gave him jobs to do, one after the other, so that he had no time to think at all. Eventually he'd given up mentioning them.

The blackness usually lasted a couple of days, then abated. At first he linked them to deaths on the island or accidents that happened to their neighbours, feeling sure as a child that he had been foretold of the event. The importance this gave him eventually proved too frightening, and he'd worked as hard as his mother to ignore them.

Marriage and teaching had helped. As he'd grown older, the intensity of the feelings had dissipated. Except when Jean had lost the two bairns during pregnancy. He'd felt, no, known it would happen, although he'd never shared his fears with her on the matter, in case she thought he was the one to jinx the pregnancies.

At the darkest moments of his premonitions, he thought that maybe he had.

He thought of his mother, married to an older widower with a son not much younger than herself. Still young, still pretty. She'd enjoyed the coming of the radar station, welcomed the change to the grinding routine of running a farm. She'd loved going to the dances and the cinema. Then a baby had come along to spoil her fun, or so she used to joke, as she'd reminisced about those days when the outside world had come to Sanday.

And Jamie Drever had been a part of that world. A big part.

I owe it to her to find out if the man in Glasgow was Jamie.

If it was, then perhaps he can be brought home and buried here, near her.

The thought comforted Sam a little, but not enough to counter his dark premonition.

18

Heilsa Fjold – what language was that?

The name rolled off PC Tulloch's tongue with ease. McNab, on the other hand, had decided he wouldn't attempt it, but opted for 'community centre' instead.

Still, the place had been a good choice for the interview sessions. Light and airy, coffee and home baking on constant supply. (McNab had been seriously missing his espresso fixes.) A good internet connection and a constant stream of folk interested in talking to them, or more obviously, keen on finding out what all the fuss was about. After all, uncovering old bones on Sanday was almost as frequent an occurrence as high winds and rain.

McNab had assembled his materials to help stimulate memory. A map of the exact location of the burial. Photographs of the brooch and what was left of the clothing. A description of what the victim may have looked like, in dimensions at least.

Most folk already knew that the skull had gone missing and had their own opinions on why, mischief-making by kids being the most prevalent. Teenagers from the school showed a great interest in the forensics involved and were obviously fans of *CSI* or other forensic TV programmes. At that point having Rhona there would have been an advantage.

During the first two hours, he and PC Tulloch spoke to

about thirty folk. Though the majority wouldn't have been born when Sanday had been invaded by servicemen, they seemed to know quite a lot about the island during that time, a tribute he thought to the heritage centre, the school or the work of Derek Muir.

PC Tulloch was, McNab decided, ideal for this job. He put folk at ease, made them feel they were contributing, but most of all, generated the sense that it was a community endeavour to solve this crime.

Just as with large profile cases on the mainland – when someone went missing the local community was organized to search for them – here on Sanday the community was being marshalled to help discover the identity of the woman found buried in a school playground.

'More coffee, Detective Sergeant?'

McNab looked up to find the young woman who'd been keeping them supplied with refreshments all morning. Tall, blonde, pretty, she'd introduced herself earlier, but her name, Hege, sounded a bit like the name of the centre and he'd therefore not registered it properly. Her voice had a slight accent which he thought initially was the same as PC Tulloch's, but now wasn't so sure.

'A double espresso this time?' She smiled at his reaction to her offer. 'The machine makes them too.'

'How did you know?' McNab said.

'I heard you mention it to Ivan.'

'Ivan?'

She flushed a little. 'Sorry, PC Tulloch.'

McNab hadn't given a moment's thought to Tulloch's first name and now here it was. Ivan had vacated his seat and gone to the Gents, although having exited there, now seemed to be in animated conversation with an elderly man who'd just entered the building via the wheelchair ramp.

'That's very kind of you.' McNab gave her what he hoped was a winning smile. 'I was getting withdrawal symptoms.'

'Too much caffeine—' she began.

'Is bad for you,' McNab finished for her.

'But it also stimulates the brain,' she offered. 'How are things going?'

'I've learned a lot about Sanday's invasion during the war.'

'It's an interesting story, but not a true invasion, not like what happened to Norway.'

'Your country?' he tried.

She nodded.

'I thought the accent sounded different from PC Tulloch's,' McNab admitted. 'Are you just visiting or have you moved here?'

'I'm here for a year.'

McNab didn't ask her why, as PC Tulloch approached with the elderly gentleman in a wheelchair.

'This is Mr Cutts, sir. His family used to work on Lopness farm when it was bought over by the government to build the radar station.'

The old man's expression suggested a grievance about that which hadn't yet waned.

'They let the crop die in the fields that year. We weren't allowed to harvest anything,' he said.

Up to now, most of the folk offering stories of that time had been positive about the impact of the camp on the island. McNab had a feeling this interview might prove to be a little different.

Fifteen minutes later, he'd learned that prior to the influx of servicemen, Sanday had been a God-fearing island, Lopness folk had gone to the kirk, relationships led to marriage and bairns weren't born out of wedlock.

'The war changed all that,' the old man said. 'They held dances at the camp and sent buses to pick up the local women. There was a cinema showing American movies.' He regarded McNab with a rheumy eye. 'As a young man, I have to say I loved it.'

McNab wondered where all this was leading. He didn't have long to wait.

'There was a girl worked on the camp. I don't know what she did there. Her name was Beth Haddow and she was from somewhere in England. We met at one of the dances, but she wasn't interested in me. There was someone else for her, although she was kind enough to a sixteen-year-old ploughboy.'

By his expression he was reliving those times.

'I asked her to dance with me that night. She did, but she was watching for someone else. I don't know who. I went outside to the toilet and when I came back she'd disappeared.' He paused. 'I never saw her again. I tried asking about her but they were a secretive lot up there. You could come to the parties and watch the movies, but you weren't allowed to ask questions.'

McNab showed him a photograph of the brooch.

'She was wearing this when she died.'

Mr Cutts picked up the picture and studied it. 'Sweetheart brooches were very popular back then. I don't remember her wearing one.'

'What was she wearing when you last saw her?'

He smiled. 'I was just a lad. I never paid any attention to

what women wore, just dreamed of what was underneath the clothes.'

McNab was warming to Don Cutts as a teenager, and as an octogenarian.

'Describe Beth for me.'

'Small, maybe just over five feet tall. Slim with dark hair, cut short. Pretty with very blue, intense eyes. Light on her feet, like a bird.'

'Could she have left the camp, gone back south?'

'She could have, but I don't think she did.'

'Why?'

'She was never on the ferry to Kirkwall. They didn't go as often as they do now and I knew most of the men that ran it. She didn't leave from Kettletoft.'

'Maybe the army transferred her out?'

'She wasn't in the forces. She was a civilian. When I kept coming back asking about her, they got shirty with me. They were hiding something.'

'Why would they do that?'

'There were a lot of secrets between the local folk and camp personnel. Mostly of a personal nature. After all, it was wartime. And bear in mind there were more of them than there were of us.'

'Have you a photograph of Beth anywhere?' McNab asked.

'No,' he said sadly. 'Just a memory of her.'

We have no chance with this, McNab thought as Mr Cutts wheeled himself away. *It's too long ago and whoever killed her would likely be dead anyway.*

PC Tulloch presented himself again. 'How did that go?'

'Go ask that nice Norwegian lady to make me another espresso.'

*

McNab settled himself in a seat by the window and checked his mobile. The signal was intermittent everywhere but for a few bright spots, such as here at the hotel and at the community centre.

He noted that Freya had been trying to call him and had left a message.

In normal circumstances he would have been keen to hear the message, but somehow this place and the circumstances didn't feel normal. Being cut off gave you a different perspective on life, as though you were cocooned.

He was on a job, yet it didn't feel like it. No requirement to explain to his superiors how things were going. No working against the clock. No feeling if you called it wrong, someone might die, as it had been in the previous two cases.

And the prospect of a home-cooked meal shortly to accompany his pint, and a good night's sleep to look forward to.

Maybe the edge of the world wasn't so bad after all.

Especially now that PC Tulloch had left for home.

'The centre opens at ten,' he'd informed McNab on departure.

'I thought we'd spoken to all the oldies who were around during wartime?'

'There are relatives who may have heard stories from back then and want to help,' PC Tulloch had said.

The islanders certainly seemed keen to help. Most of the information they'd imparted in the interviews had no bearing on the investigation, except in the case of Don Cutts. There was also a slight feeling on occasion that someone's name was being brought to police attention over an unrelated matter. Those he had passed on to PC Tulloch. After all, he wasn't here to police the island as such, that was the responsibility of Kirkwall.

Then there were those who tried to take the investigation into the realms of fantasy land, such as the woman earlier today who'd suggested that witchcraft had played a part in the death.

Thinking about witchcraft brought McNab's eye back to the mobile screen, and Freya's number.

He stared at it for a moment, then muttered, 'Here goes,' and pressed call back.

It rang out three times, then went to the messaging service. McNab, a little relieved, apologized, explained that the service was rubbish here and he would try again later. Satisfied that he'd done his duty, he turned his attention to his pint.

19

He'd answered the knock fully expecting it to be either the forensic team or one of the policemen. He didn't mind the two women, but found the newly arrived detective sergeant intimidating. Mike was pretty sure the one they called McNab could read every thought he had, and frankly, that terrified him.

He'd come to Sanday to escape the nightmare and it seemed that another had been waiting here for him.

When he saw who stood at the door, his stomach flipped, then rose into his throat, and he had to make a swift dive for the kitchen sink.

'Are you okay?' The voice that followed him was sweet and concerned, and the sound of it made him retch again.

Mike gripped the edge of the sink, not daring to turn round.

Was she real after all, and not a figment of his imagination?

He ran the cold water and splashed his face, trying to get a grip on reality. At that moment the back door slammed in the wind, shutting her in there with him.

He turned, stricken, and there she was in the flesh, the face he'd drawn when he found the flower in the attic. Her bright blue eyes, the dark hair cut shoulder length. The nose, the mouth.

How was that possible?

Mike glanced from the face before him to the back view of the easel that still held the drawing. It was uncanny, the resemblance. He remembered how swiftly her face had come to him. He must have seen her before and simply forgotten or only registered it in his subconscious. Perhaps at the shop in Lady Village or passing by in a car on the road.

'Who are you?' he said.

The creases on her brow eased and she gave him a bright smile.

'My name's Inga and I live near Mr Flett from the heritage centre,' she said earnestly, in an accent he registered as Cumbrian. 'Are you feeling all right now?'

He wanted to tell her to leave, that she shouldn't be here alone with him.

Instead, he said, 'Have we met before?'

Her brow furrowed again. 'I don't think so.'

'Have you and your friends been playing nearby?'

'We go to the beach sometimes,' she offered.

'Do you sing songs, playground rhymes?' he tried.

'Mr Flett's been teaching me some old Sanday songs,' she said, obviously puzzled by his line of questioning.

Mike had been striving not to look towards the easel again, but couldn't stop himself.

Her eyes followed his. 'You're an artist?' she said excitedly. 'Can I see what you're painting?'

'No.'

She'd been poised to move towards the canvas, its contents hidden by the angle at which it stood. His response had surprised her. She shrank back, unsure now of her ground.

'I don't show things until they're finished,' he said, to soften the blow.

Don't be nice to her. You must make her go. Now.

He heard the internal warning, but didn't heed it.

'Why are you here?'

She brightened then, pleased finally to be asked.

'I'm helping the police with their enquiries,' she said in a semi-important tone.

The phrase she used struck terror in his heart, and he was suddenly back there in that police interview room, reliving the horror.

'How are you doing that?' he said.

'By searching for the skull.' She observed his reaction to this. 'I know they think we took it, but I explained in school today to PC Tulloch and Detective McNab that we didn't and we would help them look for it.'

'Who's we?' he said, his alarm rising even further.

'My friends who live close by.' She reeled off names, none of them registering with Mike as he panicked at the thought of not one, but four kids hanging about the place.

I can't have them near me.

'I came to ask if it was all right if we searched the grounds around the schoolhouse.'

'The police have already done that.'

'But they haven't searched all of the beach or out at the lighthouse.'

Suspicion bloomed. 'Did you take the skull and bury it in the sand, so you could find it again?' he demanded.

The blue eyes clouded over and she looked mightily offended.

'I wouldn't do that.'

Mike decided he'd had enough. He strode to the door and opened it. Immediately the rain entered on a gust of wind.

'I think you should go home.'

She hesitated and he sensed that she wanted to make

things right between them. He was struck again by the captivating combination of innocence and determination on the girl's face.

That's what got you into trouble before.

'Your parents won't like you bothering your neighbours,' he said, desperate that she shouldn't mention her visit to anyone.

By her expression, she was accepting defeat, although he sensed she wasn't the type to give up that easily.

As she exited, Mike said, 'I don't want you or your friends hanging around here. It's a crime scene after all.'

He watched the small slight figure trudge off through the rain, then shut the door and immediately went to the easel. Studying the portrait only confirmed his initial reaction. The girl he'd drawn looked exactly like his young visitor.

How was that possible?

Even if he had seen her at the community shop, or just passing by in a car, how could he have remembered her in such detail?

I can't keep this picture. Not now.

What if the policeman from Glasgow should see it?

He's suspicious already. The way he looks at me.

'Policemen are suspicious of everyone. It goes with the job,' he said out loud to calm himself.

He knew he should remove the picture from the easel and either destroy it or bury it out of sight somewhere. And what of the painting of the flower that had inspired it? His eyes were drawn to the kitchen table where the original flower still sat in its evidence bag.

If I put the flower back in the loft like Sam Flett told me to . . .

Maybe if he did that, life would return to normal.

Mike fetched a bedsheet and draped it over the easel.

I should move it from this room at least. What if the detective takes a look? He's seen the girl at the school.

Mike lifted the easel and transported it through to his bedroom, still dressed in its shroud.

It's safe in here.

Even as he thought that, he wondered if anywhere was safe for the drawing, or for him.

20

Rhona found a list of seven recorded marriages between servicemen and Sanday girls. One was between an RAF sergeant James Lee stationed at Whale Head, Lopness, and Jessie Tulloch Marwick of Cross Parish.

That romance at least seemed to warrant an RAF sweetheart brooch.

The folders, she discovered, made fascinating reading, with tales of the Home Guard and a visit from some Norwegians heading westward, who were given 'a great welcome'. It seemed their pilot, Lief Lyssand, had gone on to join the RAF and had been based on mainland Orkney.

Sadder stories were in there too. A body from a plane downed north of Sanday washed up on the shore and buried in Lady churchyard. A man from Leith killed by a bomb while working in the camp mortuary. Sam had said that as a boy he'd played in all the camp buildings except the mortuary. She wondered if that had been the reason.

When Derek had delivered the remainder of the evidence, he'd offered to run her back to the cottage, but Rhona wanted to spend more time in the centre, trying to get a picture of what life had been like in Lopness at the time, she believed, when the victim probably met her fate.

The contrast of life then from now seemed even greater having read the recollections. During the war years this small top corner of Sanday had changed dramatically, from a sparsely populated area where everyone knew everyone else, to a densely packed hive of a thousand service personnel, brought together for the purpose of war. And in war, normal rules didn't apply, because you might not be here tomorrow.

There might have been only seven recorded marriages, but there would have been, she surmised, many more liaisons. Some of them hidden. One of them perhaps resulting in death.

McNab's call brought her out of her reverie.

'We have a possible missing person from 1944,' he told her. 'A woman in her early twenties who worked at the camp. Not local. Just over five feet tall, dark hair, blue eyes. Name of Beth Haddow. The old guy, Don Cutts, who reported it, was a teenager working on Lopness farm at the time. He had the hots for Beth, but she preferred someone else, he doesn't know who. It seemed Beth disappeared, but no one at the camp would answer his questions.'

'Was she service personnel?'

'He says not. And he was pretty adamant he believed she never left the island, although he has no way of proving it.'

'Could she have simply been avoiding him, and that's why the camp people gave him the brush-off?' Rhona asked.

'Maybe, but the dances and cinema showings went on as normal and she didn't appear again at any of them.'

'Has he any photographs of her?'

'No, but he says he remembers exactly what she looked like.'

With a skull a facial reconstruction would have been possible and confirmation of whether the body was that of Beth Haddow made easier. McNab knew that as well as she did.

'I think someone on this island knows who that body is,' McNab said. 'And doesn't want us to find out.'

Rhona was beginning to think the same way. She told McNab what Erling had said about the weather and the transportation of the evidence.

There was a short but pregnant silence, followed by, 'You're not going with it?'

'And leave you here alone in the wilds?' Rhona said.

'Exactly.'

'You were the one that wanted a jolly,' she reminded him.

'A jolly requires good company.'

Rhona finally put him out of his misery. 'Chrissy's going. I'll stay and finish the excavation.'

'Then you can save me from Ivan the Terrible's constant good humour.'

'Ivan who?'

'PC Tulloch, the cheeriest bloke on the planet.'

'Unlike you,' she countered.

'A good night's sleep will improve my mood.' McNab explained about his room at the hotel.

'Excellent. There's live music there tomorrow night.'

He groaned. 'It's not a ceilidh, is it? Or worse, karaoke?'

'Not sure,' Rhona said, to worry him further.

'Can I come back to the cottage once Chrissy goes?'

That, Rhona thought, would be a bad idea. She said so. 'I'll be going soon too.'

She could tell the idea of being abandoned on Sanday to investigate a murder from seventy years back wasn't what McNab regarded as fun. To cheer him up she told him there could be news on Jock Drever.

'Sam Flett thinks he might know who he is.'

McNab audibly brightened when she explained about her conversation with Sam.

'Can you get a copy of the wedding photograph to him?' she asked.

'Will do.'

Rhona glanced at the window as she rang off, registering how dark it was outside despite it being only mid-afternoon. Rain still beat at the glass and, as Erling had predicted, the wind had risen again. It looked as though the eye of the storm had passed and they were in for another night of gales. According to Sam, late October was a wet time on Sanday. It was certainly proving to be.

Rhona put the blue folders back on the shelf and turned her attention to a pamphlet about shells found on Sanday. The beaches around the deposition site were, as far as she was aware, fine white sand, yet the sole of the shoe found in the grave had been crusted with clearly distinguishable shell fragments.

The answer to this puzzle eventually presented itself in a booklet entitled *Sanday Voices*. One of the men stationed at the RAF camp had noticed that on the Sanday side of Start Island, where the lighthouse stood, there was a substantial deposit of shell sand composed mainly of mussel shells – a veritable goldmine at a time when England was importing shell sand for grit in its poultry feed from Holland, and even from as far away as the USA.

It seemed Sanday folk had taken advantage of this and built a lucrative, albeit backbreaking industry, reaching its peak in the late forties.

So there was a shell-sand beach close to the RAF camp.

Distinguishing between types of sand was tricky unless the grains were of different sizes. Shell sand was easier as it was often possible to identify species, or at least *genera*, of marine molluscs from fragments, as long as they weren't too small.

Of course, which molluscs were present seventy years ago and which were present now might have changed, but if Start beach was the only shell beach on Sanday, then that's the beach the victim had walked on prior to her death. A beach which was close to the former RAF camp.

On the journey back to the cottage, she questioned Derek about the shell sand without stating exactly why.

'The company that exported it built a rough concrete causeway to transport the shells via a lorry, but high tides and rough weather kept breaking it up. You could take a look yourself, when the wind drops.'

'And it's going to?'

'Without a doubt. Check the tide clock on the kitchen wall of the cottage. Assume a couple of hours to get out to the island, take a look round, and come back again. Aim for the centre of that time zone to be low tide.' He checked his rear mirror, then drew into a passing place to let the local minibus with its complement of passengers pass.

'The eastern side of the causeway is treacherous underfoot, rocky and slippery with seaweed. The western side is sandy and can be waded easily at low tide, but the water rises there more quickly. I prefer a barefoot crossing on the sand myself. Don't leave it too late to come back,' he warned. 'The island is bigger than it looks from here. It was home to a fully functioning farm back then. The buildings are still there, plus a row of cottages for workers.'

They were approaching the schoolhouse now. Rhona asked to be let out there and she would walk the final leg.

'I'd like to check the excavation site,' she said.

'Don't get blown away,' were Derek's parting words.

Rhona quickly sought the leeward side of the building. As she turned the corner, she noted the outside light come on as the door opened and a small figure emerged. It was a little girl, dressed in a waterproof jacket and wellington boots. Then the back door banged shut.

In moments, the figure had disappeared into the rain and wind.

Rhona approached the grave and checked the cover to find it secure; then, curious about Mike's visitor, she knocked at the kitchen door. He didn't answer at first, so she tried again. Eventually his tall figure appeared on the other side of the glass and, seeing her there, opened up.

'Is there something wrong?' he said, looking worried.

'No, I was just checking the cover was secure.' Rhona expected him to invite her in. When he didn't, she said, 'May I come in for a moment?'

As though he'd just remembered his manners, he apologized and ushered her inside.

'Your assistant's checked a few times today already,' he said.

'I'm glad Chrissy's on the job.'

They stood there awkwardly, with Rhona realizing he desperately wanted her to leave. Mike Jones had never been at ease with the presence of an investigative team on his property, but it seemed the incident in the shed had served to make matters worse.

'The evidence is safe now?' he enquired.

'We hope so.'

'Did you locate your tripod?'

'No, but DS Flett's bringing a replacement tomorrow.'

His face fell. 'I thought you'd finished the excavation.'

'The soil below the body has still to be collected.'

'Why?'

'It may contain evidence,' she explained.

They stood a further few moments before she decided to come right to the point. 'I see you've made contact with one of the local children.'

His face went white, red, then white again. 'What?' he said stupidly.

'The girl who was visiting when I arrived.'

She realized he would have denied the child's existence, but the certainty of her announcement gave him nowhere to go.

'She was only here minutes,' he rushed on. 'She asked for permission to search for the skull around the house. I told her you'd done that already.'

'DS McNab spoke to some of the local children at school today. They're keen to help.' She smiled, hoping to ease his obvious discomfort. 'Maybe those are the kids you've been hearing around the place.'

He didn't respond to this, his mouth now set in a stubborn line. Rhona decided to take the hint.

'DS Flett says the weather will improve by tomorrow night, so I should finish up the next day, all being well.'

'And then you'll go?' He looked relieved.

'My work will be over, but not DS McNab's.'

He looked frightened by that. McNab had that effect on people, the innocent and the guilty alike. Rhona bade Mike goodnight and was shown the door.

As she battled her way along the path to the cottage, she continued to wonder about Mike Jones. Everyone had secrets, things about them they didn't want others to know. Herself included. Having the police on your doorstep was an unnerving business. Sometimes those responsible for a crime sought to put themselves in the spotlight, craving the attention, while acting the innocent.

Mike Jones was the opposite of that. Every moment the investigation team was there was apparently torture. And his reaction to the children was odd. If he'd been a teacher, why did he seem so afraid of kids?

21

When he'd moved back into the family croft house, Sam had changed virtually nothing. The house sat in a time warp and he liked it that way, particularly now he was alone. When Jean died, he'd given up the house they'd shared, and come back here. Why he wasn't sure, except that it felt right to be where his life had begun.

And his and Jean's house had become the home of a young couple, who now had two children to play in the garden and on the beach beyond, where Erling had played as a youngster during the long summer holidays twenty years before.

Because he'd never thrown out any of his mother's belongings, except her clothes, Sam was certain he would eventually locate what he sought.

It took him some time to unearth the photograph, but find it he eventually did. The box contained an assortment of black-and-white photos, mostly of people he had no recollection of.

His mother had enjoyed taking the box out of a winter's night and rifling through its contents, telling him the names of those pictured and events that had been captured. It had seemed to a younger Sam that the whole world was in that box. A world of stories of Sanday, Westray and Kirkwall, and even on occasion further afield, especially the pictures featuring people from the camp, some in their uniforms.

A young Sam had been impressed by those uniforms, even though, by the time he was old enough to admire them, the camp had been disbanded and the excitement it had brought departed with it.

He'd often thought as he played soldier or pilot among the empty buildings that he too would like to join the forces and wear a smart uniform and see the world. He had certainly left the island for a time. Secondary school in Kirkwall during the week, then off to university, then back to teach another set of young Sanday residents.

That, he decided, had been adventure enough for him. So he had never got to wear a uniform, although he'd worn a teacher's gown for a while before it stopped being a requirement, like the tawse had stopped being used to administer punishment in the classroom.

Sam drew his fleeting memories together and focussed on the photograph.

His father and stepbrother Eric stood at the back. His mother sat on a chair in front of them with no sign of Sam, the late baby – yet.

Sam checked the back of the photograph and found his father's neat spidery writing with a date, 17 June 1944. His half-brother, Eric, had been a strapping seventeen-year-old in the photograph. And beside him on the far left was another figure, someone near Eric in age, but tall and thin, where Eric was broad-shouldered and sturdy.

'Jamie Drever,' he said.

Snatches of conversation came back to him. Not from when he was young, but when his mother had been fading. Her body frail, yet her eyes still burning with life. She'd always been like that, glowing with life. His father, older by nearly twenty years, had been the taciturn one. Sam had often seen his father steal a glance at his Ella, as he called her, as though he couldn't believe his good fortune to have married her.

There were plenty of times they'd argued, mostly about his mother's 'fanciful ideas' as his father called them. Fanciful ideas about new curtains or her attempts to cultivate a small flower garden which had to have a wall of flat stones built round it to give shelter to the few things that would grow there.

Red hot pokers and red poppies with dark blue stamens. And prickly wild rose bushes, much loved by the blackbirds that sheltered in them, singing their hearts out. To an Orkney farmer, fertile land was for growing crops and grazing beef cattle. What flowers grew naturally were to be found in the machair, the grassy plains that lined the shore.

Despite this, his father and Jamie, who'd worked on the croft with them, had built the wall for her garden.

She would sit in it, tucked in a sheltered corner, catching the sun on her face, watching the birds flit in and out of the bushes. As he'd grown older Sam had realized that Eric had the same disposition as his father. Taciturn, hard-working. Sam, everyone said, took after his mother. Sensitive, bookish. He was predicted to go to university and become something other than a farmer, which turned out to be true.

Sam had no lingering memory of Jamie or his big brother Eric. It was in his mother's latter days that she'd spoken of him, and often. Then Sam had come to know the affection she'd had for the tall lanky lad, who'd spent so much time at their house.

Looking at the photograph reminded Sam of other memories, ones that weren't as pleasant. As the dementia had taken hold, his mother had grown confused, vividly reliving times when she'd been unhappy, worried or upset. And during those times, Eric's name had kept occurring.

She'd gone back too, in her mind, to when the camp had dominated this part of the island. When she'd stopped going to the dances because of her pregnancy, but when his half-brother had spent a great deal of time going there, much to the annoyance of their father.

There had been a girl involved. That much Sam had deciphered. A girl from the camp. Trying to recall the confused ramblings of a woman who spent more time in the past than the present, Sam had gathered that his father had disapproved, and that there might have been some rivalry between Eric and Jamie for the girl's affections, which had resulted in a fight, after which Jamie was banished from the house.

Sam had no idea if his recollections were true, or whether he was reinterpreting his mother's ramblings in the wake of what had happened recently. But one thing he was sure of. Eric had been a man who enjoyed a fight, and who liked to get what he wanted.

As Sam shut the tin, a glint of something metal below the photographs caught his eye. Tipping the contents onto the fireside rug, he discovered it was a sweetheart brooch similar to the one Dr MacLeod had shown him, with the RAF insignia.

Who had that belonged to?

His mother had never mentioned it, nor shown it to him, even when she'd been reminiscing about the war.

Everyone who knows what happened is dead.

What was the point in raking up the past like the body in the schoolyard, and the flowers in the attic? None but the dead were left to tell the tale.

Sam put the brooch back and shut the lid.

He would show the photograph to the policeman. Compare it with the one he had. If the man they'd found in Glasgow was Jamie Drever, he would arrange to have him brought home to Sanday. That was the best he could do.

22

If the wind howled all night long, McNab didn't hear it, and when he opened his eyes, he found a different Sunday, quiet and apparently calm.

Rising, he found himself whistling as he headed for the shower, which surprised him. Emerging ten minutes later, he caught the scent of bacon being cooked below, and his mouth started to water in anticipation. At that moment he experienced a brief but almost fond thought of PC Tulloch, who'd found him such good digs.

Heading downstairs, he followed Torvaig's instructions from last night and made for the kitchen, where he found his breakfast ready at the agreed time.

'Have a seat, Sergeant,' Tor gestured to the big kitchen table. 'I take it you'll have a bit of everything on offer?'

McNab indicated that he would, and with pleasure.

'I can't do you an espresso, but I can make the coffee strong?'

'News travels fast around here.'

'Strangers are like a book. Folk are keen to turn the pages. Find out their story.'

'And that doesn't take long?'

'It depends on the stranger.'

Tor placed a heaped plate in front of McNab and a pot of strong coffee.

'Enjoy. Oh, I almost forgot, this came for you.' He handed McNab an envelope with 'For the policeman' written on the front.

McNab turned it over, to find it sealed.

'How did this arrive?'

'I found it on the front mat when I came into work,' Tor told him.

McNab tore the envelope open to find a single sheet of paper inside, with the words 'Ask Mike Jones why he's here' written on it.

McNab put it back in the envelope.

'A lead?' Tor looked interested.

'Maybe,' McNab said, and proceeded to attack his plate of food.

After breakfast, he decided to wait outside for the arrival of PC Tulloch. After all, as Tor had intimated, this might be the only day he would experience Sanday without a gale-force wind blowing.

The previous evening, while McNab had enjoyed his pint, Tor had told him how, back in the day, the pub windows were directly over the water. 'Unfortunately drunk folk had a habit of falling out of them, so the new owners moved the bar back a bit and built the wall. If they fall out now, it's only a few feet.'

The tide was out and the stretch of shore below the sea wall was thick with rocks and seaweed, or tangle as Tor called it.

'It used to make folk a packet of money. Tons of it gathered and sent to the mainland. It contains a natural gel like gelatine.'

Tor had kept him entertained with such stories in between serving two darts players, a couple who were more interested in checking their mobiles than drinking, and the Norwegian girl, who'd popped in to ask when he wanted the music to begin the following night.

Her appearance had been a welcome surprise, but unfortunately short-lived, and although she'd acknowledged McNab's presence, she hadn't indicated a need to hang about and talk to him. His disappointment at this had resulted in a stab of guilty conscience and he'd attempted to call Freya. When it had gone to voicemail, he'd covered his relief with a jokey message about being cut off in the wilds, and said he would try again tomorrow.

If I call now, there's a chance I'll catch Freya before she heads for the university library.

Before he could make up his mind on this, his mobile rang. McNab glanced at the screen to find an unknown caller.

'Sergeant McNab, Sam Flett here. I've found an old photograph of Jamie Drever.'

McNab thanked him, and they arranged to meet at the heritage centre, after the interviews at the community centre.

'I'll be there most of the day. PC Tulloch has a list of folk wanting to speak to us.'

'You're the big attraction around here at the moment,' Sam told him.

McNab brightened momentarily at the thought of a morning being served espresso and home-made Battenberg cake by the young lady from Norway, then PC Tulloch drew alongside him, wearing a beaming smile.

Erling reached out to discover Rory's side of the bed empty and already cold.

149

The wind's dropped so he's headed back to Flotta.
And I'm bound for Sanday.

He swung his legs out of bed and stood up, his head suddenly reminding him how much red wine they'd drunk the previous evening. Erling smiled, deciding the residual pain was worth it. He headed for the shower, noting that Rory's toilet bag had already been removed, which meant he'd been out of here early.

Turning on the shower to full power, he reflected on the night before with some pleasure. In particular when Rory had told him what he believed was the explanation for the mysterious phone call that had so worried him.

It turned out that Rory had a sister. Well, a half-sister to be precise, and that's who'd called him. Based in New York, they rarely saw one another.

'I thought a trip to the Big Apple might be our first holiday together,' Rory had then suggested.

Erling had been pleased by both the explanation for the call and the offer. Of course, he hadn't exhibited relief, or admitted that he'd been aware of the sister's call in the first place. Although at one point in the proceedings, he'd intercepted a look from Rory that made him wonder if he had in fact been spotted in the porch that night.

That's the policeman in me.

His mood on the way to Kirkwall was improved even further by the transformation in the weather. Scapa Flow and the hills of Hoy were in full view, with hardly a breath of wind to ruffle the waters. The forecast had promised a calm break of at least forty-eight hours, hopefully sufficient to let Dr MacLeod finish her excavation, and have all the evidence transported south.

The mystery of the body buried beneath the playground

would take longer to solve, if solve it they could, with most of the witnesses of the time already dead.

And probably the perpetrator also in his grave.

According to PC Tulloch, Sanday folk were turning out to help with their enquiries, and they had been given at least one possible name for the victim, which Erling was following up on. Had they located the skull, a photofit would have probably avoided an unnecessary search.

Just like the more recent destruction of some of the evidence, the removal of the skull now looked like a wilful attempt to disrupt police enquiries, but to what end he had no idea.

The police were no more popular on Sanday than anywhere else. Regarded as a necessary evil to the majority of the population on the mainland of Scotland, it was the same on Orkney.

Sanday, unused to a police presence, didn't think it needed one and there would be a few folk keen to see them leave. But tampering with evidence wouldn't help that happen. On the other hand, implicating someone in the tampering might settle an old score, and like anywhere else, there were always scores to settle.

And thus the call that had arrived from DS McNab just as he'd left the house, alerting Erling to a finger being pointed at Mike Jones and asking for his background to be checked. Something he planned to set in motion, but as discreetly as possible.

23

'You're sure about this?'

'Quite sure,' Rhona said.

'I could stay, help you finish more quickly.'

'It's important you get back to the lab and start processing the material. I'll be back in a couple of days.'

'If the weather holds.'

'It will, according to Derek,' Rhona said. 'I'll work on the grave today, visit the island for a sample of the shell sand tomorrow. Then I'll be home,' she promised.

A pair of arms was waving at them from the helicopter, indicating it was time to depart.

'Right, that's me off, then.'

Rhona watched as Chrissy ran towards the chopper, its blades already turning. She was pulled inside and, with a brief wave, the helicopter rose and headed off in a south-easterly direction.

Rhona waited as Derek's jeep approached and pulled up alongside.

'Where to now, Dr MacLeod?'

'Back to the excavation.'

The contrast to her earlier work was marked. Then she had been checking the advancing sky and constantly thinking about the rising strength of the wind. Today, erecting a forensic tent was a distinct possibility. One which Rhona decided to take.

She found herself pleased to be in the blue confines once more, free from observation. Not that Mike Jones had bothered them much, being unnerved by the presence of a grave in his back garden, but the solitude of the tent was something she enjoyed.

As she'd intimated to Mike, the soil from beneath the remains was as important as the soil above. In different circumstances and weather, they would have sifted the material as it was extracted, to discover anything buried in it. Worm action distributed items throughout soil, which meant that because something was near the surface didn't mean that it had started off there.

Rhona worked steadily, using the camera as before, a replacement stand having been delivered via the helicopter this morning. Up to now, her most interesting find was a handful of broken shells. This time they weren't attached to anything, suggesting that they might have been in a pocket of an item of clothing, long since disintegrated, or perhaps dropped into the grave at the time of the burial.

The morning passed into early afternoon undisturbed. She took a break then, writing up her notes, the sun still free in a cloudless sky, dancing light on the tent roof. Despite their early rise, Chrissy had made up sandwiches and filled a thermos for her.

Rhona emerged now from the tent, determined to seek out a sheltered spot to enjoy her lunch with a view to the island and the distant lighthouse. She could hear hammering and guessed that Mike was working on the section of the building still under renovation.

He hadn't approached her all morning, in fact she

suspected he was intent on avoiding her completely. However, there had been a note on the back door inviting her to use the toilet whenever necessary. Rhona decided to take up his offer before she set off for lunch.

She hadn't been alone in the schoolhouse before, and now took a moment to admire what Mike had done to the place. The rural primary school she'd attended on Skye had resembled this one – the main classroom with its open rafters, and tall windows to make the most of the natural light. As a little girl, she'd often looked out of windows like these towards a deserted beach that she longed to play on.

Making her way to the bathroom, Rhona noticed what she thought might be an intervening door and decided to go and warn Mike she was in his house.

As the door swung open, she realized her mistake. Rhona hesitated, a little embarrassed at being in Mike's bedroom, yet not immediately withdrawing. Invading someone's private space wasn't something she usually did, but she was curious about Mike Jones, particularly since the previous evening, when he'd been loath to admit the existence of his child visitor.

Now she was perhaps looking at the reason why.

The drawing stood on an easel, a sheet pulled up to expose a girl's face, wide-eyed and innocent. Dark hair cut just below the chin, eyes intensely blue. There was an old-fashioned feeling about the sketch, as though it was of a pupil of the schoolroom next door.

Rhona edged forward, drawn by the image, then realized another smaller canvas sat next to it, hidden by the sheet. She eased the cloth back.

The second was a painting of a flower head, apparently made of a strip of muslin, intricately woven.

A magic flower.

The hammering had stopped and footsteps now approached. Rhona ducked out of the bedroom and made for the back door, just as Mike appeared. They faced one another for a moment, before Rhona said, 'I saw the note about the toilet. Thank you.'

'No problem.'

His eyes darted from her to the bedroom door and back again.

'I'm just off to have lunch on the beach,' Rhona said to cover the moment. 'How's the renovation going?'

'Okay.'

She opened the back door, keen now to make her exit.

'I won't be long. I plan to make the most of the light.'

She didn't wait for a response. Once outside, she retrieved her sandwiches and flask and immediately set off to find a place with a decent view of the island.

Eventually she chose a sheltered spot and began her lunch, while contemplating what had just happened at the schoolhouse. She hadn't seen Mike's young visitor properly, but it now occurred to her that the girl may in fact have been his model for the drawing. If that were the case, could it explain his reticence in mentioning her visit?

Two sandwiches and a cup of coffee later, Rhona was none the wiser. She could of course ask Mike, but that would expose the fact that she'd been in his bedroom, not something she wanted to admit.

She abandoned her seat on the sand dune and walked a little further, training her binoculars on the causeway. Derek had indicated that it was easier to cross on the western flank where it was sandy underfoot, and true enough the seaweed-covered rocks that jutted out of the water to her right looked tricky to negotiate.

The shell beach apparently lay on the eastern side of Start Island, although it wasn't visible from here. Provided all went well today, she would wade across at low tide tomorrow. She'd said as much to Derek on their way back from the airfield.

'Just make sure you pay attention to the time,' had been his response.

Glancing at her watch, Rhona estimated she had an hour before the light was too poor to continue. Enough time, she hoped, to finish. She'd excavated more than two-thirds of the grave floor when she unearthed the object.

Twenty-five centimetres in length, with a cork handle, the blade was rounded, with a row of seven small holes lining the blunt side, finishing with a larger hole at the top. It was definitely a knife, a specialized model. But for what?

She fetched her forensic case. The discoloration on the blade could simply be rust, but a presumptive test would indicate whether that was the case or not. Rhona folded a piece of absorbent paper in half, then half again to make a point, and scraped it across the stain.

As she did so, a fly entered the tent, made for the knife and immediately settled on the blade, suggesting her belief that it was dried blood was correct, even before she tested.

A brief examination of the bones as she'd bagged them hadn't found any surface damage. The hyoid bone had been intact, which suggested that the victim hadn't been strangled. The knife, buried with the victim, might well have been the murder weapon.

Rhona switched on the arc light and settled down to write up her notes. The satisfaction at completing the excavation was tinged with sadness at what had been unearthed here. Discovering a Neolithic or Viking grave would have proved fascinating and illuminating. The death, even if violent, would have been far enough removed in time not to affect the community.

This grave was something different.

'It looks like a pilot's knife,' Derek said, holding up the bag to the light. 'Carried in the boots of aircrew to cut their parachute lines.' He peered more closely through the plastic. 'It should have an RAF Stores serial number on it somewhere.'

'So we might be able to trace who it belonged to?' Rhona said.

'Maybe, but it's a remote possibility. The knives were also issued with the larger multi-man survival dinghies. The rounded end was to prevent puncturing the dinghy. The handle was buoyant and –' he pointed at the larger hole – 'a lanyard attached here made sure it wouldn't be lost overboard.' Derek looked at her. 'I take it this was in the grave?'

She nodded.

'I suggest you check what I've said with Sam. He might even have a photograph to compare it to. I expect there were a few of these at the Lopness camp.'

Rhona had suspected as much.

'You think that was the murder weapon?' Derek said.

'It's a possibility.'

'So what happens now?' he asked.

'I head back to the forensic lab and process all the material.'

'And DS McNab?'

'That's up to him, and of course DI Flett.'

24

The police launch had brought him over at midday, dropping him at Loth terminal. From there he'd caught the community bus to Heilsa Fjold, rather than have PC Tulloch come and collect him. The bus was a good way to catch up with what was happening on the island and, in this instance, what folk thought of the discovery up at Lopness.

The driver, a relative of Hugh Clouston, was bang up to date with developments. He knew that Dr MacLeod's assistant, 'the lassie with the pink hair', had gone off in the police helicopter this morning, 'along with a lot of stuff, delivered there by the Ranger'.

'And Dr MacLeod got her replacement tripod,' he assured Erling.

Erling said he was very pleased to hear that.

'So do you think it was that Beth Haddow, the lassie that old Don Cutts was speaking about?'

At that point, Erling realized either the driver was ahead of him in the game or the story was growing legs. When he didn't respond, Dave Clouston tapped the side of his nose knowingly. 'I know you cannae divulge details of the investigation, Inspector.'

Erling didn't think there was anything else left to divulge.

When he reached Heilsa Fjold, he found DS McNab holding court in the room directly behind the open area, which was busy with folk either checking emails and accessing the internet or waiting to be interviewed.

His own arrival caused a stir of interest. Erling spoke to those he knew, and asked after families and life in general. Through the glass partition he could see that DS McNab was deep in conversation with a woman in her thirties, whom he didn't recognize.

PC Tulloch arrived at this point and, spotting his superior officer, looked horrified and examined his watch. 'Sir, I—'

'I came over on the launch instead of waiting for the afternoon ferry. The bus brought me here.'

Relief flooded his constable's face.

Erling drew him to one side. 'How are things going?'

'They all ask to speak to the Glasgow detective.' He looked dismayed by this.

'Who's in with the sergeant now?'

'Inga Sinclair's mother, sir. One of the children we thought might have taken the skull.'

In the following silence, McNab observed the woman who sat before him. His gut feeling was she was telling him the truth about her daughter and what she was up to. Then again, who the hell really knew what their children got up to or what they were thinking? He was pretty certain his own mother never had. If he was honest, that was one of the reasons he didn't fancy settling down and having a family. He would be on their backs all the time, interrogating them, worried about them, not like a father, but like a policeman.

People lied. Big lies, small lies, evil lies, innocent porky pies. Looking the other way when answering could be a lie, because the truth was often written in the eyes. Then there were shy folk who just couldn't meet your gaze, yet were telling the absolute truth. In the end you just had to trust your instinct.

'Maybe she'll grow up to be a detective,' McNab said.

The mother's face flushed, and she dipped her head to avoid his gaze. 'There's something I haven't mentioned. It's not relevant to this case, but . . .'

McNab waited.

'We left Carlisle to get away . . . from Inga's father.' She hesitated. 'This was where my mother's family came from. I thought we'd be safe here.'

The eyes that met his were fearful.

'Have you any reason to think you're not safe?'

She shook her head. 'It's just . . . if the children didn't take the skull or damage the evidence, then who did, and why?'

'If I asked you that question, Miss Sinclair, what would your answer be?'

'My name's Claire,' she told him.

'Well, Claire. What do you think?'

She'd obviously thought about it, but was unsure whether to give her opinion.

'Someone who wants to hide the identity of the body you found. Or . . .' She hesitated.

'Or what?'

She shifted in her seat. 'Maybe someone who wants to cause trouble for Mr Jones.'

'Why would they want to do that?'

'Most people here welcome incomers, but not everyone does.'

'Did you have someone particular in mind?'

She shook her head. 'No.'

McNab made a decision and, pulling out the letter, pushed it across the desk at her.

The seconds it took to register the contents heightened the flush on her face.

'That's terrible,' she said. 'Why would someone do that?'

'Have you any idea who that someone might be?'

'No.'

'If you do have an idea, will you come back and tell me?'

'I will.'

As she rose to go, McNab caught sight of DI Flett through the intervening glass.

That man is my way off this island.

McNab swallowed his espresso. His hopes of being served by the Norwegian girl had been dashed. It seemed the task of keeping them fed and watered had passed to the elderly Mrs Skea, whose rich Sanday accent had proved problematic to someone more versed in Glasgow patois. They'd eventually succeeded in establishing understanding by pointing and nodding. Mrs Skea's age suggested that she might be a good interviewee on the subject of wartime Sanday, so McNab had willingly passed her on to PC Tulloch. A few seconds listening to their unintelligible conversation had convinced McNab that Orcadians were probably closer to Norwegian than they were to him.

Now seated in a small private room with DI Flett, plus an espresso refill, McNab was intent on finding an escape route from this 'jolly'. It seemed DI Flett had picked up on his intention.

'You want to leave us, Detective Sergeant?'

'Once we've completed the interviews and established whether Jamie Drever is our man in Glasgow.'

DI Flett eased himself back in the chair. 'I've been talking to DI Wilson about that.'

'You have?' McNab had been using the 'no signal' excuse and had thus barely had a conversation with the boss since his arrival.

'He said your Jock Drever died in suspicious circumstances?'

There was only one answer to that and McNab gave it. 'Yes.'

'He'd been tied up, perhaps interrogated?'

'I don't know about interrogated,' McNab said.

'He hadn't been gagged?'

'Not to our knowledge.'

'Then he wasn't secured to keep him quiet or, you've established, to rob him.'

McNab had no idea where this was going, but the fact that he hadn't thought along these lines irritated the hell out of him.

'There are few people left alive who might shine a light on what happened in Lopness when the woman was murdered,' DI Flett said. 'What if James Drever was one of them?'

The journey to Lady Village and the heritage centre was the first occasion McNab had had a proper view of the Sanday landscape, and it only served to convince him that, much as he disliked trees, they were less threatening than all this open space.

PC Tulloch having been abandoned at the community centre, DI Flett had taken the wheel.

'Not much road congestion here, Sergeant?'

McNab smiled politely in acknowledgement of the fact

they hadn't met a car since exiting the car park at the community centre.

'I take it country life isn't for you?'

'You could say that.'

'Yet you volunteered to come, according to DI Wilson.'

'Things were quiet at home.'

'Quieter than this?'

As they entered an area where the mobile signal picked up, McNab heard a series of pings as the outside world intruded. Not to appear uninterested, he checked the screen, skimming past all but one, from Rhona, which he opened.

'Dr MacLeod's headed for the heritage centre.' Even he could hear the pleasure in his voice.

DI Flett gave him a swift look. 'Then we can have a strategy meeting.'

25

The two photographs lay side by side on the table. A young Jamie Drever standing with Sam's family, then the man known as Jock Drever as a newly married man. The likeness between the two was unmistakable.

McNab watched as a riot of emotions crossed Sam Flett's face. He had seen such turmoil before, but it was usually on the faces of those people who'd been forced to identify a body in the police mortuary.

'How did he die?' Sam said finally.

McNab glanced at DI Flett before answering.

'Dehydration.'

'He was ill?'

'He was restrained in a chair next to a fire.'

Sam looked horrified. 'Restrained? You mean tied up? Was it a robbery?'

'We wondered about that, but in fact nothing was taken, not even the money in his wallet.' McNab changed tack a little. 'His neighbour said Jock used to talk about someone called Ella?'

The two Fletts looked at one another.

'That would make sense, Sergeant,' Sam said. 'Ella was my mother's name.'

McNab cut off what he had been about to say next. In

Mrs Connelly's opinion, the Ella that Jock had talked of had been more than just a friend.

'Your mother looks very young in the photograph,' he said instead.

'She was twenty when she married my father.'

'So not much older than Jamie?'

'And my half-brother, Eric,' Sam said.

McNab took a moment before getting to the real point of the conversation.

'There aren't that many people left alive who would have been here when the girl was killed. Jamie Drever would have been one of them.'

McNab watched as his words sank into Sam's thoughts. The result was, in his opinion, utter panic. Sam stood up suddenly and gripped the table.

'You're saying Jamie's death has something to do with that body in the schoolyard?' He swayed then as though about to keel over. DI Flett was there immediately, urging him to sit down.

'The sergeant's only echoing my thoughts, Sam. We have nothing to suggest that's the case, and Jamie Drever probably died before the body was discovered.'

McNab watched as the old man crumpled back into the seat.

'I want to bring Jamie home. Give him a decent burial in Lady churchyard near my mother and father.'

'We'll do that,' Erling promised.

When Sam went to make them some tea, McNab headed for the toilet. He would have much preferred to have questioned Sam Flett on his own. To his mind having DI Flett there had been a mistake. Of course, Sam wasn't a suspect in either case, having been a baby at the time of the first killing and having been on Sanday when Jock Drever died.

Assuming he was here.

In normal circumstances he would have requested a check on whether Sam had left the island around the time of Jock's death. After all, there were only a couple of ways he could have travelled. But he hesitated to do so, because DI Flett was his superior officer and a relative of Sam's.

McNab ran the cold water and splashed his face, since there was no hope of a dose of caffeine until he got back to the community centre or the hotel. As he dried his hands, he heard Rhona's voice and felt his spirits rise.

Now that they'd established who Jock Drever was, he would suggest to the boss that he head back with Rhona and let DI Flett and PC Tulloch take over here. Buoyed up by his decision, he headed out to the so-called strategy meeting.

Sam entered the small office, shut the door and turned the key. Not to keep anyone out, but to encourage himself to stay in. His overwhelming desire to listen at the door of the research room being the reason.

He hadn't liked being questioned by the Glasgow detective about his mother and he was fully aware what was being implied when his mother's age had been mentioned. By Erling's expression, he too had picked up on it.

If it's true it was years ago and they're both dead anyway.

Just another island secret.

'Of which there are many,' he told himself.

There was no mirror in the room, so Sam sat down at the desk and examined his reflection in the computer screen.

Now that Erling had seen a photograph of Jamie Drever, would he guess what Sam himself suspected? The gaunt face looked back at him. A face that resembled neither his pretty mother nor his father. His half-brother had, on the other hand, resembled Geordie, in temperament as well as looks. Dark, handsome and brooding with a strong and resilient work ethic, but a fiery temper. A temper that exploded on occasion.

As a young child he hadn't been aware of it, but in Ella's latter years her stories of the past had been frequent and vivid, in contrast to her grip on the present. And both Eric and Jamie had featured in many of them.

I think in her own way she was trying to tell me.

Sam switched on the screen and his image was replaced by the desktop.

Dr MacLeod had shown him a pilot's knife she'd found in the grave. With the aid of her magnifying glass she'd picked out a reference number, 27C/2125 and wanted to know if he could trace it. Concentrating on that task would take his mind off the other secret he had no wish to reveal.

McNab was on edge. Rhona suspected it was due to a lack of caffeine, rather than too much, and the tea that Sam had served them, however strong, wouldn't supply the required fix. He was also angling for a return to Glasgow and DI Flett seemed happy to let him go.

Jock Drever had been identified as a Sanday man, and could be returned here for burial once his body was released, and the excavation had been completed. The continuing investigation into what was a definite cold case could go on without him.

The jolly, it seemed, was over.

Having established this, McNab produced a letter which he passed round. Erling seemed familiar with its contents; Rhona wasn't.

'What's this about?' she said.

'Someone has it in for Mike Jones.'

'I got that,' Rhona said. 'Do we know why?'

'I suspect it's just an anti-incomer thing. Or he's annoyed someone with the renovation work. We're running a check on him just in case. There's nothing back as yet,' Erling told her.

A fleeting thought crossed Rhona's mind. One she wasn't happy about having.

'What is it?' McNab said, noting her expression.

'I saw a girl coming out of the schoolhouse this morning, and when I asked about her, I'm sure Mike was about to deny she'd been there.'

'What did this girl look like?' McNab said.

Rhona described her.

'That's Inga Sinclair. I interviewed her mother this morning. Inga and her gang are searching for the skull. That's probably why she was there.'

'Possibly, although he's been drawing her, along with the flower he found in the loft.' Rhona explained how she'd happened on the painting. 'He definitely didn't like me knowing she'd been there,' she added.

'I got the impression he didn't like the idea of kids hanging around the place,' McNab said.

Erling looked uneasy. 'We have no reason to suspect Mike Jones of anything untoward. He's cooperated with us fully up till now,' he reminded them.

Sam stepped away as movement within suggested the meeting was coming to an end. Despite his best intentions he'd been drawn to the door when he heard Inga's name. Then he'd heard them mention the magic flower.

I warned him to put that back where he found it, and he promised he would.

The terrible sense of doom was back. Sam felt it wash over him like a powerful wave, fear in its wake. Fear for the child.

You're being stupid. Inga has no connection with the past. It's the secrets of the past that we have to worry about.

26

A dense mist had descended while they were in the heritage centre. Even the car, parked yards away, had been swallowed by it. Unlike a city fog, Rhona tasted salt rather than exhaust fumes on her lips. In the field across the road, the white shapes of sheep grazed like ghostly apparitions.

When Erling spoke, his voice sounded muffled. 'Who wants dropped off first?'

Rhona looked to McNab. 'You're the closest.'

'Why don't you eat at the hotel tonight?'

Erling came in then. 'It's your last night, and there's live music on. You can watch Sanday folk enjoying themselves.'

'Are you headed back to Kirkwall?' Rhona said.

'I plan to catch the last ferry.' The signpost for the school loomed out of the midst. 'I'll pick up PC Tulloch, drop you two off at Kettletoft, then he can take me to the ferry.'

They lapsed into silence after that. Darkness had descended both outside the vehicle and in. Rhona was seated in the back behind McNab and recognized by the set of his shoulders how deep in thought he was. They hadn't had a proper conversation since he'd arrived and eating at the hotel would remedy that.

If that was all that happened.

They'd been skirting round one another since the witch-craft case. She'd been delighted when he and Freya Devine had become an item. He had seemed so happy at first.

But not any more.

She and McNab went back a long way. They had history, none of which Rhona regretted, but she had no desire to rekindle the past.

I have with Sean, more than once.

That thought sent her to check her mobile, but there was no signal. A visit to the hotel, McNab had assured her, would remedy that. One of the things she'd enjoyed about her stay on Sanday was being offline. The constant interruptions, the need to check, had dissipated. The outer world seemed both far away and unimportant.

The journey between the community centre and the hotel complete, PC Tulloch dropped them out front, promising to be back later.

'You fancy a drink?' McNab said.

When she raised an eyebrow, he laughed. 'I'm on the beer, not the whisky, Dr MacLeod.'

Rhona followed McNab inside where he led her, not to the bar, but into a kitchen where a young man greeted them. McNab introduced him as Tor and expressed an opinion that he was a very good cook.

'Is there enough for Dr MacLeod?'

'There's plenty. An Orkney roast with all the trimmings?'

'Sounds perfect,' Rhona said.

'If you want to go to the bar and help yourself to a drink, I'll bring the food through,' Tor offered.

The bar was empty. Rhona headed for a table at the window. Peering out, she could see a narrow passageway bordered by a waist-high flagstone wall. To the right, the harbour wall tailed off in the mist, just one boat's mast visible.

McNab arrived back with a pint and a large glass of white wine.

'You're not fond of red, as I recall?' he said as he set the wine down in front of her.

'Sean's working on my palate,' she told him, then laughed at McNab's expression. 'Don't say anything,' she warned him.

'As if.'

'How are things with Freya?' Rhona strove to change the subject.

'I'm pretty sure she prefers the cat to me.' McNab took a slug of his pint.

The meal arrived then, carried aloft by Tor. When he placed the heaped plates on the table, Rhona gave a gasp.

'I could have served what we call our small portions, but DS McNab said he preferred the *normal*-size plate,' Tor explained.

They settled down to eat, foregoing further conversation. As they did so, the place began to fill up. Seated at the window, looking into the room, Rhona took a keen interest in who was coming in. A mix of ages, more males than females, with a distinct mixture of accents. Had she to guess what the make-up of the population on Sanday was, she'd have plumped for equal numbers of locals and incomers, the incomers for the most part coming from south of the border.

There were lots of curious glances coming her way too. Having been marooned in the north of the island, her only contact had been the immediate team and Mike Jones. Now she was viewed here with the Glasgow detective, her part in the investigation would be apparent.

The band had arrived and were setting up at the other end of the room – a couple of mike stands and a set of speakers. One of the singers was a young woman.

'No karaoke machine,' she told McNab.

'Thank God for that,' he said with obvious relief. Glancing round, he indicated the young woman. 'That's Hege from the community centre.'

Rhona shot McNab a look.

'What?' he said in exaggerated innocence.

Ten minutes later, despite the size of the portion she'd been served, Rhona had cleared her plate.

'That was a Chrissy-sized meal,' she said.

'Have you heard from her?'

'She was planning to deposit everything at the lab, then head home, to see her wee one.'

Rhona congratulated Tor on the food as he removed the plates, then checked her mobile. As McNab had suggested, there was a reasonable signal near the window, probably even better outside on the walkway.

A flurry of messages downloaded. She skimmed through them, conscious that most would have to wait until tomorrow when she would be back in Glasgow. Chrissy's message she opened to confirm what she'd already told McNab.

'Aren't you going to check yours?' she said as McNab indicated that he was off to replenish their glasses.

'It can wait,' he said. 'I'm home tomorrow anyway.'

Rhona settled back as the music started up – a mix of traditional and country and western seemed to be on offer, which suited her fine. It was certainly a change from The Jazz Club, which was their usual haunt after work in Glasgow.

Sensing someone's gaze, Rhona looked up to find a man at the bar studying her intently. It was a face she hadn't seen before, although there was something about it that seemed familiar. He was dark-haired, with a short beard.

Dressed in oilskins, she took him to be a fisherman. His eyes in the tanned face were a marked blue.

For a moment she thought he intended coming over, then McNab reappeared with the drinks.

'What's up?' he said, swivelling round to see where her gaze had been. 'I think you've got an admirer,' he ventured. 'I could sit elsewhere. I don't want to cramp your style.'

Rhona ignored the innuendo. 'Have you interviewed him?'

'Never seen him before.'

'He seems familiar.'

'You just like guys with black hair and blue eyes. Wonder if he plays the saxophone?' McNab said.

Rhona smiled, knowing he was referring to the man's likeness to Sean.

'I get the impression he's not the only one watching us,' she said.

'Yeah, it's like a scene from *The Wicker Man*.'

'You've been listening to Chrissy,' she accused him.

At that moment the door opened and Mike Jones walked in. It took moments for the atmosphere in the bar to change. McNab cottoned on to it immediately as the crowd parted to let Mike reach the bar.

'Maybe you weren't the only one who received a letter about Mr Jones,' Rhona said.

A series of eyes were now observing McNab as though expecting him to say or do something. What, Rhona had no idea.

'What the fuck!' McNab said under his breath.

Mike Jones was attempting to order a drink, but Tor appeared too busy to serve him.

'They're blanking him,' Rhona said.

While Mike hesitated, unsure quite what to do, Rhona rose and headed for the bar.

'Hi, Mike, can I buy you a drink?'

His relief at her sudden appearance was obvious.

'A pint of lager shandy, thank you.'

'Tor, can you pour this man a drink and put it on DS McNab's tab, please?'

Tor was at a loss for a moment, then did the decent thing and poured the pint. Beside him, the dark-haired man looked stonily on.

'You have a problem?' Rhona said.

He met her challenging look. 'I do.'

'And that is?'

'I don't like paedos being served in my pub.'

The interchange had reached those around them, who'd fallen ominously silent.

The colour drained from Mike's face as McNab, sensing a fight, appeared alongside Rhona.

'Take a seat, Mike. You too, Rhona.'

Rhona did as asked, more for Mike's sake than to let McNab fight her battles.

From the table by the window she watched the two men square up. McNab's comfort zone was an East End pub, where he would take on anyone. Here was a different matter. There were rules wherever you went, and they were always different.

Just then the door opened and Ivan walked in. Rhona could have sworn she heard a collective sigh of relief from the assembled company. He immediately read the situation and headed for the contretemps, where he gave the dark-haired man a friendly slap on the back and called McNab 'sir', while mentioning DI Flett in the process.

The tension in the room visibly lessened. Tor waved at the band to start playing again. Only then did Rhona realize that they'd fallen silent. Beside her, Mike reached for his drink with a shaking hand.

'In Scotland, we call that a stushie,' Rhona said, trying to make light of the situation.

It didn't work. Mike took a long draught of his pint.

'He called me a paedo.' He looked sick at the thought.

Rhona wasn't sure what to say.

'It's a common term of insult these days,' she tried.

She thought for a moment he was about to cry.

'PC Tulloch sent him packing,' she said. Her news didn't bring any colour back into the man's cheeks.

McNab appeared to take a seat beside them, adrenaline beating the pulse in his neck.

This is the most fun he's had since he got here.

'Who was that?' she asked Ivan, who'd taken the seat beside her.

'He's working on one of the fishing boats, but he's not from Sanday.'

McNab turned to Mike Jones. 'He called you a paedo. Why do you think he did that?'

'It was a mistake. I made a mistake, that's all.' Mike stared straight ahead, as though trying to convince himself of that.

Once Ivan, Rhona and the paedo had left, McNab ordered a double whisky, drank it down in one and took himself outside. For the first time in months he felt in need of a cigarette. Even as he thought of one, he could taste it in his mouth and feel the heat in his lungs and the nicotine hitting his bloodstream.

He also felt slightly nauseated at the story they'd just been told.

The excuses of the sad bastard.

The fog was just as thick, with no wind in evidence, as he headed round the back. The waist-high wall was built like all the others he'd seen as he'd travelled the island – flagstones, carefully laid one on top of the other. At the far end, an old plough stood atop the wall, rusted red. The tide was in, slurping and sucking at the main sea wall below, seaweed trailing the water like a tentacled monster.

What was the point in standing out here when he had no cigarettes? He should go back inside and straight upstairs. And yet . . .

The whisky had hit his bloodstream, making him crave more. If he didn't go straight to bed after this, his long spell of abstinence was in serious danger of coming to an end.

His secret desire, which only now did McNab admit to, had been to coax Rhona MacLeod back into his bed tonight – a forlorn hope.

I'm a sad bastard too.

He was used to Glasgow fogs, although since the city had been smoke free, they didn't taste the same, or so he'd been told. Car fumes now, rather than coal dust. Whatever its make-up, a Glasgow fog didn't freak him the way that this mist did.

He suddenly recalled an old horror movie he'd watched about a little Oregon seaside town. Isolated in an old lighthouse, doing a late-night radio show, the presenter had watched a fog roll in below, bringing evil with it.

I'd rather have the wind.

He could still taste the whisky on his tongue. A Highland Park, Magnus Pirie's favourite. He might order another and take it up with him. Once back on his home turf, the craving would ease, he assured himself. He'd get back into his routine. The press-ups, the cold showers, the sex.

If Freya will have me.

The story he'd just heard from Mike Jones presented itself once again, despite his best efforts to forget it. Still, the guy had come clean before they'd found him on the sex offenders' register. According to him, it hadn't been kiddie fiddling, *just* an affair with one of his fifteen-year-old pupils. Fifteen, sixteen, who could tell the difference? McNab swore under his breath. Who was he to judge after Iona?

She wasn't fifteen.

But she might have been. He'd never checked. Just celebrated his promotion to DI with a pretty nineteen-year-old who'd thrown herself at him, after Dr MacLeod had turned him down.

Thinking back to then, he could of course blame the booze. Another reason why he should lay off the whisky.

An image of Inga Sinclair suddenly presented itself, the earnest wee face telling him how she and her gang would find the skull, and he found himself deeply troubled by the thought of the girl visiting the schoolhouse. Even more so by the idea that Mike Jones had been sketching her. When challenged on that, he'd vehemently denied it. Apparently he'd just drawn a girl's face that turned out to look like Inga.

Aye, fucking right!

The bile rose in his throat again.

McNab turned from the wall, his mind now made up. He would have that second double, then head for bed. Tomorrow he would be off this fucking island, and back where he belonged.

The mist had thickened, the neighbouring harbour no longer visible. McNab reached out, feeling his way along the wall, the concrete underfoot slippy with water droplets and sea slime.

Somewhere out there a fog horn sounded, like a long blast of pain.

McNab halted, the skin on his neck suddenly prickling.

Whoever came on him from behind must have been waiting there all along, biding his time. McNab felt the sudden impact of a fist on the back of his head. Stunned, he staggered against the wall, reaching out for a handhold to prevent himself falling to his knees.

Before he could collect his wits, a second blow landed square between his shoulders.

McNab swung round, thrashing blindly into the mist at his ghost attacker. His fists met nothing and no one.

He heard the muffled sound of retreating footsteps and a shouted, 'Fuck off back to Glasgow, filth!' Then silence.

McNab leaned over the wall, his head swimming, the nausea taking over.

Below, the sea swallowed his watery vomit and came back for more.

Get back inside.

Out here in this mist he was a sitting duck, should his assailant – or assailants – take another shot at him.

He pulled himself upright and moved towards the door, but not quickly enough.

Never turn your back.

The full weight of a heavy male body slammed into him, propelling him against the wall. There were no fists this time. McNab's stomach hit the sharp edge of the top layer of stones, winding him. He bent over the wall, gasping, trying to draw air into his lungs, the sea spray flying up to meet him.

McNab now knew what was planned, but could do little to prevent it. Almost immediately, his feet were swept from under him. Up and over. That was the plan. The Glasgow cop who forgot that the mean streets existed everywhere. Who forgot to watch his back. The swiftness of the action saw him balance there a moment, then he was over and scrabbling madly for a handhold to prevent his descent.

No chance.

Seconds later he hit the water.

The tentacles of seaweed reached out for him, binding his flailing arms. He shouted as he briefly surfaced, but his voice was drowned as the fog horn repeated its mournful warning call.

27

PC Tulloch dropped her at the road end. Walking through the mist to the cottage didn't bother Rhona, the sandy track being clearly visible under her feet, the porch light she'd learned to leave on, her guide.

Mike's pickup was already parked outside the schoolhouse, a light shining in the big room.

Rhona contemplated knocking and asking to speak to him. After the incident in the pub, he'd confessed to an indiscretion with a pupil who was underage, which had resulted in his dismissal from his job and his flight north to Sanday. Rhona had accepted that part of the story. It was the reason he'd given for the existence of the drawing that she'd found difficult to believe. According to Mike, he'd imagined a face and sketched it. He'd never seen Inga before she'd knocked on his back door.

Yet what he'd created was a portrait of the child.

As she hesitated, the light in the schoolhouse went out, deciding for her.

I'm going home tomorrow, she reminded herself. *After I collect a sample of shell sand. My job here is over.*

The thought both pleased her and made her a little sad. There was something to be said about living remotely. Life did seem simpler, and more real.

But bad things happen everywhere.

The almost brawl in the pub had confirmed that. The guy at the bar hadn't been the only one who'd wished Mike Jones ill tonight. Was that because they were aware of his past before the police had even checked him out, or was it something else?

People came here to hide from the world. People like Mike Jones. But there was nowhere to hide in a community this size. Nowhere at all.

She headed along the track. There was still no wind and the fine droplets of mist were a soft curtain against her face. She couldn't see the sea, but she could hear it, beating the shore.

Reaching the front door, she went for the key, strategically placed under a stone.

Taking off her boots in the porch, she welcomed the draught of warm air that met her when she opened the inner door. The place was just as she'd left it and yet . . .

Rhona sniffed the air, the way she did when first stepping onto a crime scene. The scent of diesel was faint but definitely there. As though someone with oily hands had been in the room.

Her first thought was that Derek had visited while she was out. But he knew she was getting a lift back from the community centre with the rest of the team. He'd even joked about having a night off from police work.

A thought occurred, sending her out and round the back of the cottage with her torch. Maybe her visitor hadn't come by road. Maybe they'd come by boat.

The grass directly behind the cottage was kept short and there was a washing line strung between a stone-built turret and the house. There were numerous similar flagstone edifices along this northern section of the coast. Derek had told her he believed they were used by fishermen to mark their location, or by the wives to hoist signals to bring them ashore.

After the cut grass were the dunes, low and rolling, the grass spikey and much longer than the back lawn. It only took a few minutes for her to accept that, in the mist, it was impossible to see what she sought. If someone had come ashore here, then they would have trampled the grass, and the mark of the bow of the boat where they dragged it ashore would be visible in the sand.

Rhona cursed now at the mist and the darkness. It would have to wait until morning.

She retreated inside and made a point of locking the door.

She was used to living alone and in truth she preferred it that way. Her relationship with Sean, on and off, functioned better when he wasn't a permanent feature in the flat.

But tonight she would have preferred company, and wished Chrissy was still here. She would have welcomed her take on all of this. What had happened, both in the bar and here at the cottage? Her forensic assistant had a knack of seeing things for what they truly were, and for saying so outright.

Rhona prepared for bed, realizing that the silence was all encompassing and that she missed the sound of the wind. As she shut the curtains, she caught a light on again in the schoolhouse and suspected Mike had doused it on hearing her arrive, hoping she wouldn't do what she'd intended and knock on his door.

As she pulled the curtain to, she saw something through the mist. A ghostly light she realized was the lighthouse. Somewhere a fog horn sounded a muffled warning. This area of Sanday had seen countless shipwrecks before a light-house had finally been built on Start Point. According to Derek, Sanday folk hadn't pillaged the cargo and endangered the survivors such as in the tales of Cornish wrecks. The tradition of the island had been to save the men and their cargoes, for which they were well rewarded by the companies whose ships had gone aground.

Rhona slipped under the duvet.

If the fog didn't lift, the likelihood would be that she'd leave tomorrow by the teatime ferry to Kirkwall. There was little point in asking the helicopter to chance a landing in this soup when she could make her way by sea. Once in Kirkwall she could await a normal service flight south.

She thought about McNab and hoped that he'd forsaken the bar and gone to bed. It was obvious all was not well between him and Freya, thus his desire to come on what he thought would be a jolly. She smiled at her memory of his expression on seeing the empty landscape. Having been brought up on Skye, places like this didn't faze her. Chrissy was impervious to whatever environment you put her in. McNab, on the other hand, was an urban warrior, ill at ease outside the city limits.

Her phone buzzed, startling her. There was a signal inside the cottage, precocious and entirely dependent on the time of day and the weather. It seemed the fog was better than the wind.

She glanced at the screen and answered.

'Hi.'

There was a pause as though the caller hadn't expected a response.

'How are things in the north?'

'How are things in Paris?'

'I'm home,' Sean said. 'Missing you.'

'I'll be back tomorrow,' she said, hearing the sad note in his voice. 'Have you been drinking?'

'Have you?' he countered.

'Some white wine in the local hotel.'

'Never red.'

'The food was great. As good as yours,' she countered.

'I'll cook for you tomorrow?' A question, not a statement.

'I'd like that,' Rhona said.

'The meal might require red wine to compliment it?'

'Okay,' Rhona conceded.

'Until tomorrow, then?'

'Until tomorrow.'

She rang off wishing Sean was here beside her.

The banging on the door had become one with her dream, of spectres rising from the sea, covered by the mist in their approach to the island.

Rhona sat up, wondering what time it was. At this time of year, Sanday was dark well into the morning, and she wondered if she'd slept in. Glancing at her watch, she found it was only an hour after she'd gone to bed.

Rising, she shouted, 'I'm coming.'

She had no idea what she expected to find when she opened the door, but it hadn't been a dripping McNab being held up by Derek Muir.

'What—' Rhona didn't get a chance to finish the sentence.

Derek propelled McNab into the room and deposited him on the couch.

'I'll strip him. Bring blankets. A duvet, anything to get him warm.'

Ten minutes later, McNab was encased in the duvet from Chrissy's bed, a hot-water bottle tucked inside.

'What happened?' Rhona finally said.

'He went over the wall behind the bar.'

'How did that happen?'

'We won't know until he can tell us. Tor saw him go outside and eventually went looking for him. God knows how he spotted him among the seaweed at the foot of the sea wall. They brought him up and called me. I thought it better to bring him here. If someone with access to the hotel has got it in for him . . .' He tailed off.

McNab was shivering. At regular intervals, a raft of shudders swept through him.

'We should get him into bed.'

'Chrissy's room,' Rhona said.

'Is it warm in there?'

'I've kept the stove stoked, the radiators are hot.'

Together they hitched McNab up, who was acting like a drunk man.

'How much did he have to drink?'

'I don't think it's alcohol. I think he's approaching hypothermia.'

Fifteen minutes later, they had McNab tucked into bed. It was obvious from his colour that the warmth was penetrating. 'I'll keep an eye on him, if you want to head home,' Rhona offered.

'I'm happy to take the couch, if you want to get some sleep,' Derek offered.

'You've done enough already,' Rhona said.

'I feel responsible.'

'How can you be responsible?'

'This is my island. We did this to him.'

'That's like saying that everything bad that happens in Glasgow is my fault,' Rhona countered.

'There are six hundred people here; you have, what, a million?'

'Not any more,' Rhona said. 'In the heydays. You go home. I'll look after his lordship.'

As she let him out, Rhona said, 'Have you any idea who might have done this to McNab?'

'Plenty of ideas, but no proof,' Derek told her.

Dawn didn't break at this time of year on Sanday, it eased its way in, and after the time most people needed to rise. It was still pitch black outside when Rhona showered and went into the kitchen. On her way she checked on McNab. He was sleeping peacefully, his bristled face a much improved colour from the stagnant look of his arrival the previous night.

Gazing on him, Rhona had a moment of madness, remembering the odd occasion they had come together sexually, and she'd wakened to find McNab beside her, looking like that. It was usually followed by his eyes opening and some pointed remark which she immediately had to rebut. Rhona wondered if that was what it had been like with Freya. The jokes covering his real feelings, only getting so close and no further.

A bit like myself.

Her plan for today, McNab not included, had been to collect shell sand and investigate the remains of the radar station, including the old mortuary. She hadn't changed her mind.

McNab was renowned for pissing folk off and getting into trouble for it. Rhona had no idea what had happened after she'd left the bar, but if he'd hit the whisky? There were stories of drunks tipping over the back wall into the sea. In Glasgow he could stagger home. Here, on Sanday, he may well have crossed a wall, rather than a busy street, and ended up in the water.

She began a fry-up, trying to be like Chrissy, not sure she was succeeding.

I did it in Skye, I can do it here.

She fried bacon and slice sausage and potato scones and kept them warm in the oven. As she started on the eggs, McNab appeared.

He sniffed the air. 'Tell me you have baked beans.'

'You're alive,' she said.

He cocked an eyebrow at her. 'And hungry.'

Rhona shovelled the fry-up onto his plate and added an egg. 'No beans,' she said.

'If Chrissy had still been here.'

'Well, she isn't,' Rhona said and served herself.

It was apparent that McNab was not about to enlighten her on last night before he filled his stomach. They ate in companionable silence. Rhona had already set up the coffee machine, putting in a few extra spoonfuls to give McNab his required caffeine fix. He accepted the cup of thick black coffee with a grateful smile.

'So,' she said, when he'd drunk it and had a refill, 'what happened exactly?'

'I went outside and someone jumped me in the mist, and tipped me over the wall into the water.'

'Any idea who?'

'None.'

The stubborn set to his mouth suggested that even if he had, he wasn't planning on telling her.

'Well, if someone has a grudge, it's just as well you're heading home today.'

'Oh no I'm not,' McNab said.

'But I thought . . .'

'Not without finding the bastard who tried to kill me.'

'Is that not Ivan's job?' she tried.

'Some bastard punched me,' he rubbed the back of his head, 'then tried to drown me. Big mistake. And not one for smiling PC Tulloch to remedy.'

'DI Flett may not agree.'

'He's back in Kirkwall, I'm here.' He changed the subject. 'What about your plans?'

'I have some forensic work to finish, then I'm heading back to Glasgow.'

McNab glanced at the window. 'You only get off this island if there's no mist and no wind.'

'That's by plane. If it's misty the ferry still goes,' she challenged him.

'Godforsaken place.'

'I like it.'

'But you were brought up in Skye, which explains everything.'

Rhona left him there, plotting his revenge, and went to check the tide clock. It seemed low tide was at ten this morning. She got dressed in her outer gear and walking boots and headed out. The mist hadn't completely dispersed, but it had definitely thinned, probably aided by a faint breeze that stirred the grass.

Rhona had said nothing to McNab about her suspicions that someone had been in the cottage in her absence. He was already fizzing about the attack on him, plus Mike Jones's confession, which he'd muttered on about during his third cup of coffee. He had serious concerns about Inga Sinclair visiting the schoolhouse and had made that pretty plain.

Rhona wondered if the attack on McNab had had something to do with him sticking up for Mike in the pub. By rights it should have been her who'd taken the fallout. After all, she'd insisted on buying him a drink, even though she'd put it on McNab's tab.

Reaching the flagstone tower, she stopped, determined now to check if anyone had trekked through the longer grass from the shore. Eventually she found a flattened track to the east of the tower which led down to the beach. Whoever had walked up from there had crossed a patch of seaweed, dried and crusted on top, but gooey and green beneath. Nearer the water were the marks of a boat's keel in the sand.

So she *had* had a visitor. The question was who?

She was well aware folk called in unannounced all the time on Sanday, as they did on Skye. If the door was left unlocked, you might find your visitor inside awaiting your return.

But my door was locked, although it wouldn't be hard to find the key.

She made up her mind to broach the subject with Derek. It was he who knew the owner of the cottage and had organized their stay there. He would probably know if she were likely to get an unannounced visitor who came by boat.

Rhona checked her watch, conscious of the time. In Derek's estimate she should allow a couple of hours for her trip to Start Island, paying attention to the tidal clock. She had no wish to get stranded there in the mist or the dark.

Had the day been clearer she would have liked to check out the entire island including the lighthouse, but the main reason for her visit had to come first.

Derek had been right. The distance was deceptive, even more so with the lingering mist. The track ran to the north of the spit of land that stretched towards the causeway, keeping close to and a little above the shore. In parts, the double track had been so eroded by the sea that it had become single, with no chance of even a Land Rover negotiating the narrow passage between the field wall on the right-hand side and jagged rocks on the left.

Strange droppings underfoot caused her to stop for a closer look. Definitely not from sheep, they were black and fairly sizable. At a guess she would have said a big cat, but since the path was littered with the droppings, that would require a veritable pack of them, which of course was nonsense. Eventually she decided they'd most likely been deposited there by geese.

According to a leaflet she'd picked up at the heritage centre, the burgeoning wild geese population was a growing problem for farmers on Sanday – large flocks of the birds landing to strip the fields bare, ruining the crops. By the abundance of droppings, she could appreciate the problem.

At the end of the track the sand dwindled into shingle covered with rotting seaweed, both crusted and fresh. Rhona took a seat on a larger stone and removed her walking boots and socks, tying the laces to sling about her shoulders. She'd already decided to tackle the sandy crossing. Although the water was deeper there, it looked far less treacherous than the seaweed-strewn rocks amid the broken concrete of the former causeway.

I should have put on my wetsuit and swum across.

She'd brought the wetsuit with her in the hope that she might manage a little wild swimming from Sanday's famous white beaches. That hadn't been possible up to now, and since she was headed back later today, unlikely.

Maybe I'll come back to Sanday under different circumstances.

Reaching the water's edge, she braced herself and stepped in. It was certainly cold but not as freezing as some Highland rivers she'd swum in, particularly when they were running with melted snow. Beneath the clear water, the white sand was rippled in glorious patterns, with fronds of bright green seaweed spread out like fans.

The water at its deepest was past her knees. She realized the northern side of the causeway would fill rapidly as the tide came in, and wading like this would become swiftly impossible. Having made her way safely across, she donned her socks and boots and set out along the southern shore, ignoring the desire to follow the track to the lighthouse. Out here, the mist roamed the surface in tendrils, like long grey wisps of hair.

Eventually the shell beach crunched beneath her feet.

She'd completed the collection of her shell samples, and now with time to spare, Rhona didn't see why she shouldn't take a look a little further afield. The mist had fragmented and the distinctive black and white stripes of the lighthouse were clearly visible at least at the upper level.

She initially contemplated heading for the old farm buildings, which weren't that far from the causeway, then decided instead to venture as far as the earth mound that sat a third of the way along the southern side.

According to the map, Start Island's entire shoreline

consisted of large slabs of flat rock, apart from the shell beach, which was probably why so many ships had foundered here. The main track that led to the lighthouse ran along the north coast. On the south side there was no obvious trail and she would just have to pick her way alongside the field walls that marked the division between farm and shore.

Birds swooped and called about her as she walked. Rhona wasn't a bird watcher, but it was clear to see and hear that, even in autumn, Sanday was a place to come if you were a twitcher. She intermittently checked her watch, aware that once the tide began to turn, she had an hour or so to cross the causeway before things got tricky. Added to that, she'd planned to take a look at the old wartime mortuary before she headed for the ferry.

If I run out of time, I can always delay my departure until tomorrow.

Chrissy hadn't been in contact yet, but that didn't concern Rhona. Chrissy's first task would be to properly log everything taken south, and besides, there was no signal out here on her mobile to take a call.

Across the stretch of Lopness Bay, she could now make out the distant shapes of the concrete-clad buildings of the radar station, although the two giant masts and the wooden huts that had housed a thousand personnel had long gone.

As she turned back to face the land, the burial mound emerged from the mist, or at least the summit of it did. Apparently Mount Maesry, or Mount Misery as it had come to be known, was a chambered cairn like Maeshowe on the Orkney mainland, or Quoyness, further south on Sanday. According to Sam it had been used for potato storage by the lighthouse men back in the twenties until the entrance had collapsed. It seemed a sacrilegious use of something so beautifully constructed to house the dead.

As she walked across the field, the sky darkened and the first heavy drops of rain met her face. Rhona upped her pace, hoping to find some shelter among the ancient stones.

28

Sam had barely slept. The fear he'd had for the child had continued to grow overnight, fed by the snippet of conversation he'd overheard through the door. He'd only met Mike Jones once, when he'd brought the magic flower into the heritage centre. The man had been staying close to home, not mixing much. Most Sanday folk were happy with that, content to give him time to get used to the place.

The island had many incomers now. It hadn't been like that during his childhood, when most of the population had been born and raised here, or in the case of his mother, had come from Westray or the neighbouring North Ronaldsay. He didn't mind people coming to live on Sanday. Without new blood, the island would have died long ago. They sometimes had false ideas about what island life was like, and found reality very different. Many couldn't deal with the weather, or the isolation, and soon gave up.

Derek had been of the opinion that Mike Jones wouldn't last the winter. Sam thought back to the tall, gangly figure. The man's inability to meet his eye. His reaction when Sam explained what the flower stood for.

But is he a danger to the child?

That he couldn't answer.

Rising before dawn, he prepared breakfast, taking solace in routine tasks. The continued absence of the wind was beginning to bother him. The house seemed too quiet, and the mist that enveloped the landscape a thick smothering blanket.

Being Saturday, he knew the child wouldn't be at school, so he could expect a visit from her, usually accompanied by a request that she come to the museum with him. Her mother seemed happy with such an arrangement, pleased that Inga was interested in the history of the island her family had come from. Sam liked the child's company, especially at this time of year, when there were few visitors to the centre.

Thinking of Inga and the school sparked another thought.

While he awaited the child's arrival, Sam went back to looking through his mother's things. Ella had been the keeper of the Flett family history. It was she who'd held the family bible, with all the births, deaths and marriages written inside the back cover. Being from Westray, she hadn't gone to the school here, but his father had.

Maybe she kept information about the school and his father's time there.

The thirteen flowers in the attic of the schoolhouse had bothered Sam enough to make him search the archives for any reference to multiple child deaths from pestilence or famine. Sanday had had its fair share of both, but having thirteen flowers laid together didn't mean that those they represented had died at the same time. Derek apparently had said as much to Erling and Mike Jones. The flowers might have been originally kept in local crofts, then moved to the schoolhouse when it was built.

Sam hadn't paid much attention to Ella's bits and pieces after her death, feeling he was invading her privacy. Only the legal documents necessary to bury her and manage her estate had been sought. The tins and boxes that contained her memories, he'd felt were hers, and he hadn't wanted to intrude.

Going through the contents now, he realized she must have saved every drawing he'd done for her as a child. He pulled out another of these. Not a war plane this time, or a space ship, but a sketch of the old red-brick mortuary. A shudder went through Sam.

I hated that place. I still do.

It wasn't only drawings she'd kept. A bundle of his letters from university were there. A couple of postcards from when he'd gone travelling in Europe.

Then it struck him.

There were no childlike drawings done by Eric in Ella's collection, which was hardly surprising since he'd been a teenager when Ella had married his father, but where were the letters from him after he'd left Sanday?

Sam hadn't been born when Eric had left the island, so had no personal memories of his half-brother to call on. Later, his mother had told him that Eric had left to work down south somewhere, like Jamie, and they'd lost touch.

His father had never mentioned Eric or Jamie, and had frowned if Ella talked about them. Over time, the young Sam had come to understand that something bad had happened between Eric and his father. Something that must never be talked about.

An old faded school photograph was the final item in the box.

It had no date on it, but it must have been taken before the parish schools had amalgamated and the pupils moved to the central school. He wasn't even sure that the building the children stood outside was the local schoolhouse. There were a few such photographs available on the heritage website, but this wasn't one of them.

Sam searched the line of boys for someone who might possibly be his father. The boys, of different sizes and age, all looked very similar with their blank or startled faces, shocks of ill-cut hair, short trousers, thick socks and tackety boots. There was no one to his eye who looked like Geordie Flett, but then again, he'd only ever seen his father as a grown man.

Sam ran his eyes over the girls . . . and saw her. Dark hair cut straight just below her ears, a bright-eyed expression. That familiar smile so full of joy and excitement.

With a surge of pleasure Sam realized that he might be looking at an earlier version of Inga, a great-grandparent perhaps, or a long dead great-aunt? He thought how pleased the child would be when he showed her the picture. She would of course want to know who the girl was. Perhaps her mother might be able to pinpoint who in their family history it might be, and whether it had been taken at the local school.

If she didn't know, he could display the photograph at the museum and ask if anyone could identify the children. If that didn't work he would send a copy to the library in Kirkwall for their archives and see if anyone from further afield might throw light on where and when it had been taken, and the names of the pupils in it.

Pleased with his discovery, Sam tidied the box away and noted the time.

The child is usually here by now.

He went to the door and looked out but couldn't see her house through the mist.

I'll go there. Show Inga and her mum the picture from the newspaper. See if she wants to come to the museum with me.

Sam banked up the fire and headed out.

29

'The creepy bastard. I knew he wasn't telling us the whole story.'

'He spoke to you about it, Sergeant?'

'Last night in the hotel bar after someone called him a paedo,' McNab said.

There was a moment's silence as DI Flett absorbed this.

'The kid Inga Sinclair's been at his house,' McNab said. 'Rhona saw a drawing he'd done of her.'

Concern travelled the distance between them.

'The girl involved was just short of her sixteenth birthday,' DI Flett said. 'She wasn't twelve.'

'Who the fuck cares? She's dead, isn't she?'

'He didn't kill her.'

'But she died.'

'Apparently the girl was troubled by bullying at school.'

'And Mr Jones her Art teacher took pity on her. Thought if he painted her portrait and had sex with her it would help.'

DI Flett had had enough of his tone and told him so, which only served to remind McNab that he was no longer a DI himself.

'Sorry, sir,' he said with just enough forced humility to make matters worse.

'When are you heading back to Glasgow, Sergeant?'

At that moment he realized that DI Flett had no idea

what had happened to him. McNab almost licked his lips in anticipation.

'I don't think I can leave now, sir.'

A pause.

'Why?'

'Because last night someone tried to kill me.'

Being interrogated by a superior officer over the phone was, he decided, much more fun than face to face. DI Wilson would, of course, have demolished him by now, either way. DI Erling Flett, McNab thought, was too nice, or he wasn't sure of his ground.

'I believe,' McNab ended by saying, 'that the attempt to silence me has something to do with the remains we found.' He wasn't certain that was true, but it was a sure-fire way of keeping him here.

There was a considered moment before DI Flett said, 'Speak to the girl's mother about her visit to the schoolhouse. We don't know how much about the Jones case is common knowledge on Sanday, so keep it low key.'

McNab rang off then, thinking if he'd learned anything since he'd landed on this island, it was that news travelled fast.

He poured another cup of coffee before phoning PC Tulloch to ask where the hell he was.

'I tried to call you, sir, but your phone was engaged.' The constable sounded fraught. 'Something's happened, sir.'

'What?' McNab said.

'Inga Sinclair's gone missing.'

The child had left home around nine thirty, telling her mother she was going to Sam Flett's and would be at the heritage centre with him most of the day. Sam had arrived at the Sinclair house at eleven wondering where Inga was. The track between the two houses had been searched as had the neighbouring beach. There had been no sign of Inga. The little gang of children had been contacted. All agreed that there had been no arrangement between them to meet. Inga usually went to the museum with Mr Flett on Saturdays.

Inga's mother was distraught. Sam Flett even worse. When McNab had questioned why, the old man said he'd feared something bad would happen to the girl ever since the flowers in the attic had been disturbed. At that point McNab thought the pensioner had lost it, and stopped listening.

Rhona was nowhere to be found either. Calls to her mobile went unanswered. Her last remark to McNab had been that she had some forensic work to do before catching the late-afternoon ferry to Kirkwall. What work she'd referred to and where, McNab had no idea. The Ranger, Derek Muir, appeared to be off the radar too, so chances were he was accompanying Rhona.

McNab ordered PC Tulloch to organize as many locals as he could muster for a search party in the few remaining hours of daylight they had left. He then indicated that he was heading to the schoolhouse.

'Sir, maybe it would be better—'

McNab's expression froze the words in Tulloch's mouth.

'Call DI Flett. Tell him what's happening,' McNab ordered. 'You use the vehicle to rally the troops. I'll walk.'

It was a short but winding road from the Sinclair house to the old school. McNab reckoned he could walk it in ten minutes if he left the road and went cross-country, although he didn't fancy meeting any of the local livestock, less keen on them than drunks on a Friday night in Sauchiehall Street.

Glasgow livestock I can manage.

The mist seemed reluctant to disperse, despite a movement of air that couldn't yet be called a breeze. It was hard to believe he was in the same place where a gale had been lifting the roof only the other night.

The first three fields proved empty; the fourth had a herd of cattle that decided to check out the human emerging from the mist. McNab made for the wall at this point and climbed over onto the road.

The schoolhouse lay ahead, a couple of lights on, although it was only midday.

McNab realized that he disliked this room, almost as much as he disliked the man who stood facing him.

A rattled Mike Jones had professed to knowing nothing about Inga's disappearance, insisting that he'd woken early and immediately gone to work on his extension.

'So she didn't come knocking at your door this morning?' McNab said.

'No.' Mike Jones flung his head from side to side to emphasize the fact.

'According to police records, the last girl whose portrait you painted hung herself. Something you forgot to mention last night.'

Jones looked like a man who'd just taken a punch and was reeling from it. He reached for the table to steady himself, shaking his head as though he didn't want to think about it.

'And now you're drawing Inga,' McNab said in an accusing tone.

'I didn't draw Inga.' Jones was desperate now, his face devoid of all colour except for under his eyes, which were a dark shadowed grey.

McNab wasn't listening. He was already on his way to the bedroom with Mike Jones stumbling behind him, a look of horror on his face.

'You can't invade my home,' he tried. 'I haven't done anything wrong.'

McNab threw open the door, hoping what Rhona had professed to find was still there. He approached the easel and threw back the sheet.

He heard Jones gasp behind him. McNab almost gasped himself, because the likeness was so extraordinary.

'How the fuck could you do *that* if you'd never seen Inga before?'

Jones was attempting to pull himself together. McNab could almost hear him saying the mantra, *Stay calm. They can't prove anything.*

'I drew the face I imagined when I looked at that magic flower.' He indicated the small painting that stood alongside. 'When I opened the back door and she was standing there, I was sick in the sink. I couldn't believe she existed.'

'Who are you trying to kid?' McNab said in disbelief. 'You persuaded a girl of twelve to have her portrait done. Is that all you persuaded her to do?'

Mike Jones was crying now, small, almost silent sobs. He sank down on the bed.

'I didn't do anything wrong.'

'Are we talking about the fifteen-year-old or the twelve-year-old?'

'Neither of them.' Jones stood up, making an attempt to gather himself together. 'I'd like you to leave now.'

'After I check the house for Inga,' McNab said.

'She isn't here.'

'Then you won't mind me looking.'

In truth, there weren't many rooms to search. The reno-vated section was open plan apart from the bedroom. The area yet to be converted was empty of anything except a ladder and some tools.

McNab glanced upwards.

'I'd like to take a look in the loft.'

Jones's face, which had assumed some colour, lost it again.

'I don't think . . .'

McNab dragged the stepladder over, and climbing up, eased open the hatch. He spotted a bulb fitted to a beam and, feeling around for a light switch, flicked it on. The loft looked empty, but he wanted to be sure.

Pulling himself up and onto the narrow wooden walkway that ran between the beams, half stooping, he eased his way along, checking each gap in turn. There was nothing stored here, or if there had been, Jones had cleared it.

A layer of what looked like ash lay between the rafters, he assumed as an attempt at insulation. Spotting one of the infamous flowers he'd heard so much about, McNab crouched for a closer look. Lying partly buried in the ash and of a similar grey colour, it wasn't obvious at first.

As McNab reached for it, Jones's voice came to him from the open hatch.

'Please don't touch it,' he pleaded to no avail.

McNab cupped it in his palm and examined the intricately woven shape. The material felt stiff to the touch, brittle almost, but despite its obvious age and condition, it did resemble the petals of a flower. He laid it back down, then went in search of the rest.

There were twelve of them as he'd been told, and a gap where one had been, signified by a small empty grave in the ash.

McNab moved back towards the hatch and dropped down onto the ladder. As he emerged, he found Jones's troubled face staring up at him.

'You didn't remove any of them?'

McNab ignored the question and signalled that it was time to leave.

'We'll be organizing a search party for Inga. You could join in.'

Mike Jones looked terrified at the thought.

'Then again, maybe it's not a good idea now that your cover's blown.'

Exiting by the back door, McNab noted that the tarp had gone and the grave now stood open to the elements. Rhona had obviously been here, but where the hell was she now?

The car came towards him as he made his way back along the tarred road. The face that looked out seemed to have aged ten years. PC Tulloch was no longer the cheery-faced bloke he'd met at the onset. McNab had grown pissed off at Tulloch's eternal good humour. Now he wanted it back. Pronto.

He climbed into the passenger seat and awaited news of the child's death.

'I've rounded up about thirty folk,' Tulloch said.

She's alive.

'Do you know how to organize a search?'

'I've done it on the mainland before, but it wasn't a child we were looking for.'

Relief sweeping over him, McNab was about to joke about a missing sheep, but managed to stop his tongue.

'We need more officers.'

'The police launch is on its way from Kirkwall,' Tulloch said.

However many they managed to squeeze on the launch, it wouldn't be enough. McNab said as much.

'Locals know the terrain,' Tulloch said. 'Even in poor light.'

McNab suddenly realized the mist had gone and he could see the field on one side of the car, the beach on the other. He glanced upwards to discover a leaden sky.

'It's going to rain,' Tulloch said.

'Rain and gales. Gales and rain. Sanday weather.'

Even as McNab spoke the first heavy drops hit the windscreen, propelled by a northerly gust.

McNab had been involved in searches before. Folk strung out across the landscape in all weathers, men, women, old and young, determined to help. Nine times out of ten, by the time the search took place, the missing person was already dead. If it was a child, that was almost a certainty.

30

She was running as the deluge hit. The early mist had dissipated. Now the sky had become a cauldron of grey and black seething clouds fighting one another in their efforts to drop their load on Sanday. A wind from the north had come to their aid, biting through her jacket. She'd abandoned attempts at keeping her hood up, and her hair was soaked already.

Rhona stumbled as the ground rose swiftly through a tumble of loose slates. Screaming gulls, riding the wind, swooped down on her, as though forbidding her passage. Scrambling up the slope, she finally dropped into the hole that fronted the mound.

Pressing herself against the stones, she waited and watched as the thundering clouds fought their way across the causeway to the main island. A shaft of watery light broke through to illuminate the rain sheet where it now descended on the area surrounding the cottage and schoolhouse.

As the rain eased, Rhona emerged from under her rock for a better look.

On the outside, she estimated the mound to be around twenty-two metres wide and four metres high. Inside, according to her research, there was a circular chamber eight metres wide by one and a half metres high – the space lighthouse keepers had once used as a potato store. The entrance tunnel had collapsed in part, a jumble of smaller stones blocking it, although the larger slabs that framed it were still upright.

As Rhona crouched to peer between the rubble, she noted that someone else had been there not long ago. The grass was trampled and the clear marks of boots bigger than her own were visible. Directing her forensic torch through, hoping to catch a glimpse of the tunnel beyond, she saw to her surprise that there was an open area beyond the blockage. Excited by the thought that someone had broken through recently, Rhona began to work at the pile of rubble. Fifteen minutes later, she had a space big enough to peer in.

Her torch beam found its way through the passage to illuminate what looked like an entrance to the inner chamber. It too appeared partially blocked. Rhona checked her watch. She would have to go soon, and yet if she moved a few more stones, she might squeeze through and view the inner chamber.

Ten minutes later she was on her knees, between the upright slabs, approaching the tunnel's end. In here there wasn't a whisper of sound. It was as though the howling wind and the crashing waves no longer existed.

The silence of the grave.

She wondered how many people had been entombed here. The care that the Neolithic people had taken in the construction of this burial place indicated how important their ancestors had been to them. The huge stones had been so well put together that they still stood resolute against the wind and weather after thousands of years. A remarkable feat of engineering and determination for a people whose average lifespan had been only a quarter of a century, according to a study of their bones.

She'd reached the end of the tunnel. Here, a large flat flagstone had been manoeuvred into place, partially blocking the entrance to the main chamber. Positioning herself, she directed her torch through the gap. As the beam ran over the side wall, she could make out a series of rectangular chambers where the dead had been laid. Above was a beautifully constructed corbelled ceiling.

The nagging thought that she'd already spent too long here made her begin her retreat.

As she eased her way back, the torch slipped from her hand and rolled under the flagstone. Reaching for it, she realized the beam had caught something in its circle of light.

What she saw startled her, although in theory it shouldn't have, because this was a grave.

But a grave long since cleared of bones.

Rhona hurriedly pulled off her boots, keeping on her socks in the hope that they would give her traction on the slippery rocks. The sandy crossing was no longer viable, the depth and speed of the water pouring in on that side the impediment. The rocky path was less submerged, but finding a firm footfall was going to be a problem.

She moved out into the water, which felt a great deal colder than on her way here.

How could she have got it so wrong?

According to the tidal clock in the cottage, she should still have half an hour to get across the causeway, but it certainly didn't look that way. *I shouldn't have delayed at the mound.*

As she waded deeper, the shock of the cold hit her thighs. Only a couple of yards in, it was obvious that by midway the water would likely be chest high.

If I can keep my feet, I might make it.

Rhona felt for another step, bracing herself as the power

of the incoming tide threatened to take her with it. Her water-logged clothing was making things more difficult. She eyed the distance yet to travel, knowing that she was barely halfway.

She could keep going and take her chances, retreat and wait for the tide to turn in eight hours' time or abandon her outdoor clothing and attempt to swim. None of the proposed options were attractive. Marooned on the island for eight hours in wet clothing would be as life-threatening as trying to complete the crossing. As for wading back and undressing . . .

A white-topped wave swept towards her as the sea strove to take over the channel between Start Point and the bigger island. This time it met her chest. She gasped as its icy cold grip caused her heart to momentarily stop.

I must be more than halfway by now.

The wave passed but it had unbalanced her. She felt herself floundering and strove to locate something flat and solid on which to plant her feet, and all the time the current tugged at her legs, keen to show who was in charge. Her toe slammed against what she knew to be broken concrete, which meant she was in the region of the old causeway, built to transfer the shell sand by lorry.

Which means I'm on the right path.

She felt something sharp stab her sole and realized that concrete had torn her sock and, she suspected, cut her foot. Deciding she couldn't get much wetter, she plunged forward, half walking, half swimming, her boots abandoned to float off with the tide, intent now only on getting to the opposite bank and crawling up onto dry land.

The final lap saw the heavens open once again. What little of the top of her clothing had been dry, was within minutes as wet as the rest of her. Rhona didn't care. Her feet were on dry land at last, or at least on crusted seaweed.

She didn't stop to assess her injury. She just walked on as swiftly as possible, knowing if she stopped even to get her breath, the shivering would increase tenfold.

She was on the coastal track now, a field wall on her left, a plunge to the rocks below on her right. She walked for ten, then ran for ten, like a soldier in training, her eye on the distant prize – the smoke curling up from the cottage chimney.

By the time she reached the front door, the shudders had set in and she could barely retrieve the key from under the stone. Getting it into the lock was even more difficult, any instruction she gave to her hands being ignored.

Eventually the door opened and she fell inside. Once in the hall, she stripped, dropping the clothing in a wet bundle on the floor. Stumbling through to the bathroom, she put the plug in to capture the water, then turned on the shower as hot as was bearable and stepped into the bath.

The water swirled at her feet, reddened by her blood.

She wasn't sure how long she stood there, steam filling the room, condensing on the mirror to run in streams down the glass. When the chittering cold had eased, she stepped out and dried herself, using the towel roughly, persuading blood to rise to the skin surface.

Dressed again, she set the kettle to boil, then fetched the Highland Park and poured herself a large measure. It went down like fire and she poured another, the craving for warmth as strong inside as out.

As she'd undressed at the front door, she'd extracted her mobile and placed it on a table. She fetched it, hoping against the odds that it had survived the crossing. Taking it to the seat near the stove, she now took time to view what she had discovered in the Neolithic mound on Start Island.

31

'No CCTV, no police station, no Wi-Fi, no mobile signal most of the time. How the fuck do you catch criminals?'

'We don't have many to speak of,' Tulloch had said.

The answer had only served to infuriate McNab further. 'Give me the mean streets of Glasgow any day,' he'd muttered under his breath.

He'd set up shop at the heritage centre, which had a reasonable Wi-Fi connection. Sam hadn't accompanied him. The old man, shaken by events, had nevertheless insisted on joining the search party. For the moment, they were checking all farm outbuildings and derelict properties, of which there were many in the vicinity of the girl's home. The various beaches and their neighbouring dunes were also on the list.

Sam Flett seemed particularly concerned about the water, as though he expected to find that Inga had drowned, but he could offer no rational explanation for that fear.

The last known sighting of the girl had been by her mother, as she'd left the house to go to Sam Flett's. The walk there, along a single-track road, or a shorter way through the site of the former camp, should have taken less than ten minutes.

Apparently, no one had seen her after that, although the mist that morning had been blanket thick.

Had McNab been able to muster a helicopter, a sweep over the farmland would have been useful. With no trees to block the view and few buildings, it would have been easy to spot a body, alive or otherwise.

But they didn't have a helicopter. And it would soon be dark.

Glancing out of the window, he was struck again by how quickly the night descended here. The girl had told him she, or her gang, were searching for the skull. According to the other members of the gang, Inga had taken over. She thought she knew where the skull was. Where, they had no idea. How she knew had brought an equally blank response.

The kids were as puzzled as everyone else.

Or someone is lying.

McNab took out a flask of coffee, laced with Highland Park. He'd made it in the cottage before he left, anticipating something – probably his inability to cope.

His mobile pinged, delivering a text message from an unknown number.

McNab opened and read it.

Magnus stood on the police launch watching the approaching island, remembering the last time he'd visited Sanday. Then, home from university for the holidays, he'd been recruited for the Stenness football team, who were short of a goalkeeper, and frankly would have accepted anyone who'd offered. It had been midsummer's day. The team had met up in a Kirkwall pub and boarded a ferry, hired for the occasion. The trip had taken a couple of hours.

It had been a fine night to cruise up through the islands, though Magnus hadn't seen much of them as he'd spent the journey, like the others, in the bar. Everyone had tumbled off the boat at Kettletoft and headed for the football field near the school. They'd played the game in broad daylight at midnight. Stenness had lost, down to Magnus's inability to save goals. Then they'd adjourned to the Kettletoft Hotel to consume food and further alcohol, after which they'd boarded the ferry home and spent the return journey back in the bar. Someone had profited from the excursion, but it hadn't been the players, who'd depleted their bank accounts and attacked their livers with the fury of a Scottish battle.

Yet I remember the excursion with great pleasure.

Just as he remembered Sam Flett.

Magnus had accompanied Erling as a young teenager on one of his summer outings to Sanday to stay with his 'adopted' uncle and aunt. Magnus's memory of that time was as powerful in image as it was in smell. Sanday had made an impression on him. Sam Flett and his wife, Jean, even more so.

It was during those weeks together that he'd sensed an awakening in Erling. It had, in the end, come down to scent. Erling, he suspected, had a crush on him. But it was more than just an adolescent crush. Magnus could smell his desire, even if Erling couldn't, or wouldn't, acknowledge it.

That summer together on Sanday had been, for Magnus, magical. It had also been a break from the past. An acknow-ledgement that no matter how much he loved Orkney, every island in the archipelago, his future, at least in part, would lead him elsewhere.

They'd swum off the nearby beaches and cooked fish on an open fire in the dunes. Sam and Jean had left them to their own devices, sensing this was the end of childhood for them both, and that tomorrow would be a different day.

And it turned out to be true.

They'd remained friends, though they'd gone their own

way in the world. But Magnus had never forgotten the role Sam Flett played in that.

It had been Sam's most recent email which had prompted this visit. When it arrived, Magnus had been considering a long weekend at home in Orkney. Sam's message had made up his mind on that front. The storms of the previous week having abated, he'd reached Kirkwall from Glasgow just as the fog descended, so had no hope of a quick hopper trip to Sanday.

Until now, he hadn't talked to Erling about his recent correspondence with Sam, preferring to talk to Sam face to face about it first.

Sam had been 'seeing' things. Darkness and evil that involved a local child. Apparently the unearthing of a collection of muslin flowers in the loft of the old schoolhouse had triggered his angst. The discovery of a body buried in the old playground had served to make things worse.

'I can talk to you. You won't think I'm going mad,' he'd told Magnus.

Magnus had recruited Sam's help a while back, with a paper he'd been writing on the second sight, asking for local stories and legends that might indicate its presence in Sanday. Sam had been very helpful, sending material from the museum archives and eventually admitting to his own experiences.

And now the child he was worried about had gone missing.

Magnus's call to Erling this morning, indicating his intention to catch the ferry to Sanday to see Sam, had resulted in his presence on the police launch. It was as swift a passage as Magnus could have hoped for, but he sincerely wished that it hadn't been necessary.

He had hoped to talk Sam through his fears, help him establish psychological reasons for them. Learn a bit more about the muslin flowers that had so disturbed him.

Magnus hadn't thought that any such discussion would involve the disappearance of a child.

From his own experience with criminal profiling, he was aware that the window of opportunity for finding a child was small. By the time the troops were assembled, half that time had gone.

Erling was in the cabin with his small group of men. They would be relying on locals to do the majority of the work. They were there to offer support and to investigate behind the scenes. He'd given Magnus a brief résumé of what had happened up to now. When Rhona's name had come up, Erling had said, 'I thought you may have known she was on Sanday?'

'I've been in Germany,' Magnus had told him. 'A lecture tour.'

'Her assistant's gone back to Glasgow with the remains. Dr MacLeod was intent on following later today.'

The two men had exchanged a look that indicated Rhona wouldn't be going anywhere if the child wasn't found alive.

'And DS McNab?' Magnus had asked.

'He had a run-in with a local and got pitched over the wall at the Kettletoft Hotel. Torvaig fished him out, soaked, but otherwise unharmed.'

'A bit like the old days?' Magnus had smiled, remembering the drunken escapades of their youth.

'DS McNab didn't find anything amusing about it,' Erling had told him. 'He saw it more as attempted murder.'

Now that did worry Magnus.

'He maintained it was linked to the cold case.' By Erling's expression, he hadn't dismissed such a thought.

'What's happened to Sanday since I was last there?' had been Magnus's reply.

32

Putting the mobile in a sealed evidence bag had been a good idea. A little moisture had entered in her struggle to negotiate the causeway, but not enough to do damage. The photographs she'd taken at Mount Maesry were good. Or at least the ones taken outside were, including the footprints she'd recorded on the ground leading to the tunnel. Those she'd taken of the central chamber, not as clear.

'But it's definitely a skull,' Rhona told the screen.

Tossing off the duvet, interest taking over from a desire to get warm again, she fetched her laptop and downloaded the images.

The resultant pictures were better but were they good enough? She would send them through to Chrissy and see what the IT lab made of them. The best solution would be to go back there, clear the tunnel, get inside and take a proper look.

The more she thought about it the more the idea of the missing skull being secreted there made a kind of sense. The mound was a place to incarcerate the dead, with a great deal more respect than had been afforded to the victim in the playground.

But who would have done it?

Many people felt deeply uncomfortable about exhumation. All cultures had their own way of dealing with the dead. Each Orkney island had its own idiosyncrasies, its own history and pattern of beliefs, although they shared a common Scandinavian heritage. Magnus had said that there was also an Inuit influence, because of the intermarriage between Orcadians working for the Hudson Bay Company and the inhabitants of the vast north of Canada.

Magnus's hero, the Arctic explorer John Rae, had spent a great deal of time with the Inuits, learning how to survive in their world, and apparently they believed that a person's soul was contained in their blood. A tricky scenario for forensics to deal with in that part of the world.

Religion didn't appear to play a dominant role on Sanday, not the way it did on the western islands of Scotland. But someone hadn't liked the idea of the bones being exhumed and taken off the island. Or maybe they just didn't like the idea that the skull might help identify the victim. Either way, the skull she'd seen in the mound would have to be retrieved to check whether it was the missing one.

Revived now, and keen to make contact with the outside world, Rhona went in search of a possible signal. She'd heard nothing from Derek all day, but then she'd indicated she didn't require transport until the late ferry. A ferry she wouldn't be catching now.

When Derek's mobile rang out unanswered, she tried McNab.

'Where the fuck have you been? I've been trying to reach you for hours,' he said.

'I got stranded on Start Island,' she began, but he wasn't really interested in hearing her story.

'Inga Sinclair's been missing since nine thirty this morning. We have a search party out looking for her. Sam Flett's losing his nut over it. As is her mum.'

Rhona went cold, colder than she'd felt when she'd exited the water at the causeway.

'When was she last seen?'

'Nine thirty, setting out for Sam Flett's. I've searched the paedo's place. It's clean and he swears he never saw her.' There was a short pause. 'There's something else.'

Rhona waited.

'I got another poison-pen letter, by text this time.'

'And?'

'Seems the DI's relative may be keeping something from us.'

There were no records kept of who had been on the ferry as a foot passenger, not unless they'd paid for the crossing by card. Of course in a small community, somebody usually knew your business, including when you were headed to Kirkwall. There was no evidence to suggest that Sam Flett had taken a trip to the town, or further afield, in the last couple of weeks.

Yet to McNab, in terrier mode, that thought persisted.

Elsewhere, Sam Flett would be a suspect. He was the only one who seemed to know anything about Jock Drever, and he was, in McNab's opinion, holding something back on that front.

As for the kid. She'd last been seen by her mother heading to Sam's house. He maintained that she'd never reached his place and that had been accepted without question. Why? In any other child disappearance case, his house would have been the first one to be searched. But, hey, he was related to DI Flett, a pillar of the local community, and therefore completely trustworthy.

In my experience, you're guilty until proved innocent.

On the announcement of Inga's disappearance, the local car hire firm had offered their four vehicles for police use, so they were no longer restricted to Derek's Land Rover and the car PC Tulloch had brought over.

The police launch would be arriving soon with DI Flett and two or three of his merry men from Kirkwall, so they would need the extra transport. Professor Magnus Pirie was on his way too. McNab checked his feelings on that front. If he was honest, he could do without Pirie full stop. Yet, he had to admit, they had come to an understanding of sorts during the last case they'd worked on together.

And here they were together again. Why? Because Pirie was an Orcadian buddy of DI Flett's or because he had some mystical knowledge of Sanday and so-called magic flowers, or even worse, men who preferred their sexual partners young enough to be their daughters?

Memories of his own dalliance with Iona followed that thought, so he swiftly moved to the mystery text.

Ask Sam Flett about the girl. That's what it had said.

What girl? The one lying dead this seventy years in a grave next to the schoolhouse? Or the girl with the short dark hair and big eyes who'd told McNab she would find the skull for him?

I should have told her not to look. Maybe she did discover who took it. Maybe that's why she's missing. McNab didn't want to go down that route, but couldn't prevent himself.

He heard a car draw up. It could be good news or bad news. Or it could just be the cavalry.

'There's no chance she could be on Start Island?' McNab said. 'And we've been looking in the wrong place?'

The three men now turned in unison to Rhona.

They'd convened in the research room of the heritage centre, DI Flett and Magnus coming from Loth and Derek bringing Rhona from the cottage. Asking Derek to wait in Sam's office, Erling had ushered them in here.

The search had ended for the night, with no sightings of Inga since she'd said goodbye to her mother that morning. The girl, it seemed, had simply disappeared.

Rhona had outlined what had happened to her, and that she'd seen a skull in the Maesry Mound. Hence McNab's question.

'I suppose it's possible Inga might have gone there,' Rhona said. 'But if she did track the skull to the mound, there was no evidence of a child's footprints around the entrance, only an adult's.'

'How long before we can get back across?' McNab demanded.

'Not until the next low tide, unless we go by boat,' Erling said. 'And we can't search the island in the dark anyway.'

'Maybe she got cut off like Rhona?' McNab said.

'I suspect every local knows about the tide and the causeway,' Erling said. 'And the kids will have been warned. That was the case when I used to visit. Sam and Jean were very particular about it.' He looked to Magnus, who nodded in agreement.

'Derek told me to check the tidal clock in the cottage,' Rhona said. 'I thought I'd read the clock correctly but—'

'There's something else,' McNab interrupted her.

Rhona registered McNab's expression and realized what he was about to reveal.

'I received an anonymous text about Sam Flett.'

'What about Sam?' Magnus said.

'It said, "Ask Sam Flett about the girl."'

When this announcement was greeted by a puzzled silence, he went on, 'My first response was that it referred to the remains in the playground. Then I thought of Inga.'

'And you have no idea who might have sent it?' Magnus said.

'No. I can get the Tech department on to it—'

Erling interrupted him. 'Has Sam's place been checked?'

'I searched the schoolhouse . . .'

'Has Sam Flett's house been searched, Sergeant?' Erling repeated.

'I'm not sure it has,' McNab finally admitted.

Rhona had never seen Erling angry before. The anger was controlled but it was unmistakable.

'When did Sam turn up at the girl's house?'

'Ninety minutes or so after Inga left.'

Erling bristled still further. Rhona sensed that had she and Magnus not been there, McNab would have received a dressing-down.

Sensing an impasse, Magnus intervened.

'I'm heading to Sam's. What if McNab goes with me and conducts a search?'

There had been plenty of time for Sam, should he be guilty of anything, to remove evidence of it. That was something they all knew. Then again the likelihood of Sam Flett harming Inga didn't seem a possibility to Rhona. She said so.

'Sam's email to me was troubled,' Magnus said. 'He appeared concerned for the girl's safety. He also mentioned something about the disturbance of muslin flowers in the schoolhouse loft.'

McNab stood up, ending that discussion. 'Let's go.'

33

The house was in darkness apart from an outside light which came on at the car's approach. Rhona saw no sign of Sam's jeep. It was dark by now, with no evidence of moon or stars. Rain and wind had accompanied them there, not constant, but registering as intermittent squalls. Rhona didn't like to think of the child anywhere outside on a night like this.

McNab, the driver, had remained silent throughout the journey as Rhona had got Magnus up to speed on what had brought them here, and what had happened since. Even to Rhona's own ears, it sounded strange.

McNab drew up alongside the walled garden to the front of the house and killed the engine. All was quiet.

'Doesn't look as though he's in,' McNab said.

'He was expecting me,' Magnus told him.

'That was before the kid went missing.'

'Maybe he's with Inga's mother?' Rhona suggested.

'Let's take a look around,' McNab said, getting out of the car.

Magnus looked ready to remonstrate, but Rhona touched his arm. 'The door's probably open,' she suggested. 'And as you said, he's expecting you.'

McNab was already in the porch. Seconds later the hall light came on.

'Sam won't mind,' Rhona told Magnus. 'I'm sure he'll be glad we checked if he hasn't done so already.'

They stood in the small living room that looked very like the interior of the old croft in the grounds of the heritage centre. The fire had been banked up and was smouldering away in Sam's absence. The open fire wasn't the only thing in the room that belonged to the past.

Nothing's changed in here for decades, Rhona thought. An Orkney chair either side of the fireplace, the box bed, the small items of brass, polished and shining.

'It was his parents' home,' Magnus said. 'He sold his own house and moved here when his mother died. Jean had died a couple of years before and he was on his own.'

The room was as tidy as it was old-fashioned. If Inga had been here, there was no evidence of it. Nothing untoward, everything in its place. On the table, a book about Orkney during the war sat next to an old floral-patterned tin, possibly pre-war.

McNab had already deserted them, heading to the downstairs bedroom and bathroom.

'There's an upstairs too,' Magnus said. 'I visited with Erling once. He sometimes stayed here with Sam's mother.'

The wooden staircase was steep and narrow, with a platform at the top and a door on either side. Through the right-hand one they found a spare bedroom. Tidy and apparently unoccupied, although the bed was made up. Through the other door was a study. An open laptop sat on a desk below the skylight. One wall was shelved. Running her eyes over the spines, Rhona noted that most of the books related to Orkney and its various islands through the ages.

'His main interest,' Magnus said.

When they went back downstairs McNab was in the living room, looking about as though willing something suspicious to appear.

'Anything?' he said.

Rhona shook her head.

'We'd better check the outhouses.'

Most of the buildings that clustered to the back of the croft house were semi-derelict. In the time it had been a working farm, they would have all been in use. Now, one seemed to be kept for the use of stray cats, which hissed threateningly at McNab as he shone his torch about.

'What is it about you and cats?' Rhona said in sympathy.

'Your cat likes me.'

'Tom's the only one.'

They ploughed their way through all the sheds but in truth it was hardly a proper search in the dark. Old bits of rusty machinery could have hidden more than just a few stray felines.

Rhona shouted Inga's name throughout, just in case.

'Do you have a mobile contact for Sam?' McNab said when they'd reconvened in the living room.

'No. He got in touch by email.'

'Can I see the interchange?'

They trooped back upstairs. McNab stood back to allow Magnus to take a seat before the laptop. It was obvious that Magnus was uncomfortable about this. Checking through someone's laptop was like searching through their belongings without a warrant, but by McNab's expression, he wasn't going to take no for an answer. Rhona guessed that Erling's reprimand had left its mark.

Magnus seemed to have come to the same conclusion, because he attempted to do as bid.

The laptop, like the front door, wasn't secured. There was no password set for access and the desktop layout was pretty obvious. Magnus had no difficulty in finding Sam's emails and a search on his own name soon brought up their exchange. The first emails were on the subject of the second sight, followed by Sam's tale of 'the souls of dead children being disturbed' and his subsequent fear for the child.

There was silence as McNab read them through, disbelief registering on his face.

'I thought the old guy was losing it. Now I'm sure.'

Magnus looked as though he might remonstrate. Rhona, thinking an argument wasn't what they needed at this moment, intervened.

'I think we should check for Sam at Inga's house.'

McNab struggled to bite off whatever further retort he had planned, and nodded. 'Okay, let's go.'

As the car drew away, Rhona glanced back. The old croft, with its roof constructed of flagstones coloured orange in places by the growth of lichen, might have been an image of not only seventy years ago, when the surrounding land had been occupied by soldiers and airmen, but even further back when children were mourned by representing their souls with muslin flowers.

In contrast to Sam's, the Sinclair house was a blaze of light. Three vehicles stood out front, one a jeep. It appeared as though the neighbours were rallying to Inga's mother's aid.

'Maybe all three of us would be too much,' Rhona said. 'What about just Magnus going in? After all, Sam's expecting him. If the jeep's his, Magnus can bring him out and we could go home with him and have a chat?'

McNab grudgingly agreed, watching Magnus's departure with an expression of exasperation.

'Stop it,' Rhona said.

'Stop what?' He now assumed an expression of injured innocence.

She decided not to continue with the conversation but watched the door instead. Some five long minutes later, Magnus emerged, alone.

'The old boy isn't here,' McNab said, his voice tinged with frustration.

Magnus got back in the car. 'They're all in there. The parents of the other kids Inga played with. They're hopping mad and there's a lot of talk about Jones. No one's seen Sam since the search began. They thought he'd gone home.'

'How's Inga's mother?' Rhona said, knowing it was a stupid question.

'Blaming herself because she didn't stop the girl looking for the skull. Apparently Inga's been obsessed by it.'

'I didn't discourage her either,' McNab said quietly as he started up the car.

'Can you drop me back at Sam's?' Magnus said. 'I'll wait there for him.'

'Search resumes at first light.'

'I'll get in touch the moment Sam gets back,' Magnus promised.

'If he comes back,' McNab said, after they'd dropped Magnus and were making their way along the sandy track towards the cottage.

'Why do you say that?' Rhona challenged him.

McNab shrugged. 'If he has harmed the girl . . .'

'You can't believe Sam Flett would hurt Inga intentionally.' Rhona didn't buy that idea.

'Bad things happen. Intentionally or otherwise,' McNab said.

*

When they pulled up Rhona attempted to wish McNab good night. 'I'll see you in the morning.'

'Any chance I could take the couch again?'

'You said the hotel was a big improvement on my couch. And the food was better.'

'DI Flett's staying there tonight.' He pulled a face.

'Won't he want to talk to you?'

McNab's face clouded over. 'He shouldn't be here anyway. He can't be the investigating officer and have a relative as a suspect.'

'I'm sure he's aware of that.'

There was a stand-off for a moment before Rhona took pity on him.

'You can have Chrissy's room, just for tonight.'

Once in the cottage, McNab immediately made for the kitchen, opened the fridge door and peered inside. Seconds later he emerged with a couple of beers and some eggs.

'There's not much left,' he complained.

'I hoped to be back in Glasgow tonight.'

'No doubt with Mr Maguire preparing a feast for you,' McNab said sarcastically.

He rummaged in the bread bin, then extracted a large tin of baked beans from the overhead cupboard.

'You said there were no beans,' he accused her.

'I must have missed them.'

His expression suggested he didn't believe her. 'What would you say to French toast and beans? With Orkney ale to wash it down?'

'I'd say yes,' Rhona replied.

Rhona replenished the stove, glad to see the fire was still alive. She accepted the bottle of beer offered by McNab, and a glass to drink it from. McNab took a swig straight from the bottle and set about whisking eggs.

'You've become quite domesticated,' Rhona said.

He threw her an affronted look. 'I've always been able to cook. You just never stayed around long enough to find that out.'

Which was true. An occasional, *very* occasional, one-night stand had been more their style.

'The Irishman, on the other hand, got to demonstrate *all* his skills,' he added.

Rhona threw him a warning look.

'So,' he said, above the sizzle of the frying toast. 'What's your take on all of this? Do you believe Jones set forth a curse when he took that flower from the loft?'

'You have to believe in curses for them to work on you.'

McNab glanced over, his face serious. 'Freya doesn't think so.'

So he's brought up the subject of Freya at last, Rhona thought.

'She believes it's the power of those who create the curse that decides its fate.'

'The flowers represent children. Why would removing one from the attic result in the harming of a child?' Rhona said. 'Shouldn't it be designed to harm the person who removed it?'

'Well, Jones thought he'd found a good hideout here and the flower and the discovery of the body proved him wrong.'

'Who says the two are connected?' Rhona challenged him.

McNab carried the plates to the table.

'There's something about all of this we're not getting. What's happened to Chrissy and the forensics?'

'She's barely had time to log everything, let alone start sifting and testing.'

McNab started to eat as did Rhona, suddenly hungry. They said nothing more until they'd cleared their plates.

'That was delicious,' Rhona said.

'I have talents other than as a detective.'

Rhona ignored his promotional tone and continued talking about the forensics. 'I went to Start Island to collect shell sand. The victim I believe was there prior to her death. There was shell sand embedded on the soles of the shoes.'

McNab looked thoughtful. 'I wish we knew who she was.'

'If the skull I saw inside the mound is the missing one, then we can create a picture of her.'

'We have the far past, the distant past and the present all colliding here.'

'They're colliding in time, but that doesn't mean they're connected,' Rhona said.

'Always the scientist.'

'Always the detective.'

Rhona rose, sensing the atmosphere was getting too cosy.

'I'll see you in the morning.'

As she left, she realized the bottle of Highland Park still stood out on the counter.

What the hell. She wasn't McNab's lover, or his mother. If he drank it, that was his lookout.

McNab chose the seat nearest the stove. Heat beat from the metal. Through the glass came a rosy glow. Domesticity. He allowed himself a moment to enjoy the idea of Rhona next door in bed, lying waiting for him to join her, however ludicrous that notion might be.

34

Mike Jones watched the car headlights pass by on the way to the cottage. He continued to sit by the window in the dark, until he was certain whoever had been in that car wasn't walking back to call on him.

Ever since the visit from the Glasgow detective, he'd been contemplating flight.

He could catch the early morning ferry. Be in Kirkwall an hour or so later. Then take the *Hamnavoe* to Scrabster and start the long drive south. Here on Sanday, he was isolated and exposed. Once the news of his 'misdemeanour' was out, no one would want him here anyway, and after the scene in the pub, it was clear that his past was no longer in the past.

He heard again the word 'paedo' and cringed. He wasn't a paedo. You could get married at sixteen in Scotland without your parents' consent.

But you weren't in Scotland and she wasn't sixteen. Not when you painted her. Not when you had sex with her.

He tried the 'age is arbitrary' argument, especially when the difference was a couple of months. Then his conscience took over and reminded him that Alice had hanged herself, possibly because of him.

All the months of denial buried in the hard physical work of renovating the schoolhouse evaporated and he was back wallowing in guilt and self-recrimination.

Has it all come back to haunt me because of the flower?

Even as he thought that, he was listening. Tuning in to hear the children's voices, one girl's in particular. He was frightened of hearing her again, but at the same time willing a recurrence. As though what she might say would provide a clue to Inga's disappearance. Thinking her name immediately conjured up an image of the girl standing at his door, her face friendly and eager.

Just like Alice.

He stood up, contemplating bed, although sleep was no longer a friend.

The wind had returned and was playing the eaves. He realized that he'd missed its presence and that without it he'd felt lonely. In the city the noise of the traffic had kept him company. Here, it was the elements – the wind and the sound of the sea.

That thought made him don his jacket, deciding that being out in those elements might lead to better sleep.

The clouds had cleared and a fullish moon hung in a midnight sky. The wind was brisk, catching him in the face as he turned north-east, intent on walking in the direction of the island and the lighthouse's comforting beam.

Although he carried a torch, he decided he had no need of it, as the moon's rays glistened on the white sand of the path. As he walked, he knew with a sudden pang that he would be sad to leave this place.

There are other islands, he thought, *other places to settle . . . until someone finds out about my past.*

Maybe he could just sit it out here instead. He didn't mingle much anyway. As long as the local shop would sell him food, and he had fuel for the fire, he would survive. Alone if need be. But what if they decided to drive him out?

No one wanted a paedophile living next to them. And now, with Inga missing, things could only get worse. *Maybe they'll come and burn me out?* He recalled the anger on the man's face in the pub and realized that might be a possibility.

Glancing back at the schoolhouse, he imagined it in flames, with him inside.

Shaking his head to dispense with both the image and the thought, he turned his back to the bay, looking across to the field that had once housed a thousand service personnel. The white concrete-clad buildings seemed to glow in the moonlight, in contrast to the distant dark mound of the mortuary. He'd wandered among the buildings on numerous occasions, trying to imagine what it had been like back then, when this corner of Sanday had been filled with people.

All of them incomers, like me.

He shivered suddenly, as if the wind had risen and brought colder northern air to meet him. Then he heard it. Had it been spring, he might have taken it for the bleat of a lamb or a calf. But it wasn't spring. He thought of the many wild cats that made their homes in the unused outhouses or derelict farm buildings.

No. It sounded like a child's voice.

Mike imagined for a moment that it might be Inga, trapped on Start Island and calling for help.

'Inga!'

His voice rang out, edged by fear.

He repeated the call, taking time in between for the reply that never came.

Uncertain now what he'd heard, he walked towards the causeway, slithering over the wet rocks.

The water was low. Should he try and cross? Could she be on the other side?

He wondered whether the tide was going out or coming in. *I never did get a handle on the way the tide's times change.* As he stood, uncertain, a gull suddenly flapped upwards, like a white shrieking phantom. Startled, he stumbled into a rock pool, feeling the seaweed covering give way beneath him and icy water enter his boot. He righted himself, shivering with both surprise and cold.

Was that the cry he'd mistaken for a child?

The seabird was descending again, keen, it seemed, to return to its previous roosting place. As it dropped, he realized where it was bound.

A dark hump lay among the broken concrete of the old causeway about midway across the Sound.

His first assumption, that it was a seal, he quickly dispensed with. The seals he'd met had watched him inquisitively from the water as he'd walked the beach. Or they'd observed him passing by on the path, as they basked on the rocks below. None of the sightings had been at night. None of them had looked like the bundle curled in a rock pool full of seaweed.

Mike's first instinct was to turn and walk away. Leave the gull to whatever it sought.

But something stopped him. Some memory of his humanity before things all went so wrong. He pulled the torch from his pocket and switched it on, directing the beam at the questionable object.

When that didn't help, he marshalled himself and moved forward, squelching and slithering through the seaweed, coming to a halt a couple of yards away. His heart pounding, his breathing short and painful in his tightened chest, he tried playing the beam over the object again.

Could it be the girl?

A wave of fear swamped him.

He'd been told that bodies were occasionally washed ashore here. Often from fishing accidents miles away, eventually carried here, months, even years after they'd drowned.

You don't even know if it's human.

He took his courage in his hands and moved closer.

The warmth from the stove and the whisky had combined to send him to sleep. Instead of moving through to Chrissy's bedroom, he'd curled up on the couch instead, forgetting the fact that he would be crippled by morning.

McNab came to with a start. The room was still warm and his legs were cramped, but that wasn't what had woken him. He sat up, groggy. Glancing down at the empty tumbler, he tried to recall what he'd had to drink, but could register nothing more than the one dram, and of course the Orkney ale with the meal. Added to that, his mouth tasted okay. No aftermath from too much booze furred his tongue. No sign of dehydration. A quick glance to the bottle found it at the same level.

All this happened in a matter of seconds before the pounding, which must have been what woke him, resumed.

'All right, all right!' he shouted back and, standing, made his way to the front door.

Mike Jones looked like a man possessed. McNab's first thought was that the paedo had lost it. Followed by the thought that a lynch party was behind him.

'Come. Quick. There's a body.'

His words hit McNab like a bullet. He felt his heart stop.

'Inga?' he forced out.

'I don't know.'

At that point McNab heard Rhona's voice calling, asking what was wrong.

'Where?' he said to Jones.

'In the middle of the causeway.'

Rhona appeared beside him in hastily donned trousers and a sweater. Her hair was tousled and her cheek creased by sleep. McNab, even in that moment, thought how lovely she looked.

'Any signs of life?' she said as she pulled on a jacket and stuck her feet into wellington boots that were obviously too big for her.

'I couldn't . . . I didn't get close enough to check.'

'Show me,' Rhona said. She pushed past McNab. 'Get a hold of DI Flett then follow us down. You'll get a signal at the rear of the cottage.'

It had only been hours since she'd stumbled back along this path, sodden and near to hypothermia. Drowning while crossing the causeway had been a definite possibility. A slip underwater. A failure to regain your footing. The current against you. Your clothes waterlogged, pulling you down.

Half walking, half running, hampered by the oversized boots, she made her way back along the track, a reluctant Jones at her heels. Already she was trying to decide how she would handle this. The expression 'dead weight' was even truer for wet bodies. It could take four to six people to lift them. But maybe Jones was wrong and whoever it was wasn't dead.

She'd reached the end of the path, with Jones panting a little behind her. She looked to him for guidance and he pointed to the right-hand side.

'Over there.'

Rhona jumped down onto the beach. She retraced her steps from earlier, over dry sand, sinking into crusted seaweed, until she was below the high-water mark. Waterlogged sand gave way to slippery rocks. She turned, checking she was still heading the right way, and shone her torch in the direction of Jones's outstretched arm.

Then she spotted what he was pointing at. About halfway across.

Rhona splashed into the water.

He'd dressed for the weather when he'd joined the search party for Inga. But not well enough to protect him from a sea of water. Rhona crouched beside the body that had once been Sam Flett. His skin had a spongy look, the cheeks and eyes nibbled as though they'd been the starter, the main course waiting beneath the waterproof clothing.

Rhona did a quick calculation. Tides were semi-diurnal, twice a day with a period of roughly twelve hours and twenty-five minutes between. So the time between high and low tide was just over six hours. She'd read the tide clock wrong before, but going from when she'd made her return crossing, she estimated the next low tide had been around midnight, which meant it was likely to be on its way back in.

The body would have to be moved from here as soon as possible. But where? Protocol said secure the body, and keep it clean and safe. It certainly couldn't stay here on a tidal causeway. The cottage was too warm, but an outhouse might work until they could transport it off the island.

As Rhona made her way back, McNab came running along the track.

'Is it Inga?'

'It's Sam Flett,' she said.

Relief flooded McNab's face, to be replaced by puzzlement. 'How?'

Rhona didn't attempt to answer his question. 'I need you to bring me a new tarp from my gear and a roll of brown parcel tape. We have to secure the body and bring it ashore before the tide turns.'

McNab, who knew all about drowned bodies, glanced back at Jones. 'Three of us won't be enough to lift him.'

'Is Erling coming?'

'Yes, and both his men.'

'Then we'll manage.'

'Where are you planning to put him?'

'The shed at the schoolhouse,' she said. Seeing McNab's expression, she added, 'It's too warm in the cottage and the outhouses there are full of cats.'

'I take it you'll tell Jones the good news while I fetch the gear?'

It was the second time in two days she'd felt sorry for Mike Jones. She was making a habit of it.

'Just until the helicopter arrives,' she promised. 'And I'll stay with the body.'

Her assurance appeared to ease his fear a little. 'I thought it might be Inga,' he admitted. 'That's why I couldn't go close enough to see. I should have checked.'

'You were right to come and get us.'

'Did he get caught in the tide?'

'I don't know,' she said honestly. 'I'll go back to the body. Could you wait here? We might need your help lifting it.'

That prospect didn't appeal, but he nodded anyway and

238

headed back up the beach, to take a seat on the grass and await McNab's return.

Sam Flett would have known these waters, this causeway, like the back of his hand. Surely he wouldn't have allowed himself to get caught by the tide? Rhona directed her torch beam at Sam's head, looking for any obvious wounds.

Maybe he lost his footing and banged his head on the rocks. People might drown in a few inches of water if they were unconscious. As far as she could see, there were no open wounds, no bloody gash, but that didn't mean he hadn't suffered a blunt-force trauma.

Other things might have made him fall down and drown. A heart attack or a stroke. Sam was an elderly man. Fit, as far as she'd been aware, but past his three score years and ten.

She felt a surge of sadness. Sam had been nice to her. Helpful. So concerned about Inga. That in itself could have put his heart under strain.

But why was Sam near the causeway in the first place?

Had he suspected that Inga had crossed to the island and gone looking for her? That was one possible explanation.

Another one occurred which she didn't welcome.

That Sam had something to do with the missing skull. That he had been the one to take it and hide it in the mound. It was obvious he wasn't happy about the grave being disturbed or the flowers for that matter. Or maybe he hadn't wanted the skull to be reconstructed.

Maybe Sam suspected he knew who the victim was.

Rhona shivered as the breeze found its way under her jacket. Not fully clothed, she would have to put on another couple of layers if she was intent on sitting up the rest of the night with Sam's body.

McNab was coming towards her carrying the tarp.

Ideally she should wrap and secure the body here then carry it ashore, but Rhona had been watching the level of the water in the rock pool and suspected it was rising.

McNab was observing her, awaiting instructions.

'How long before Erling gets here?' she said.

'He was picking up the community ambulance and hopefully the doctor. He said twenty minutes or so, but a vehicle that size won't get along this far, half the path's crumbled into the sea.'

Rhona made her decision.

On her right was a stretch of sand with fewer rocks.

'Lay the tarp out there,' she instructed. 'We'll roll the body onto it.'

35

Protocol said she should touch nothing without a witness or forensic help. At this moment she wished with a vengeance that she hadn't sent Chrissy home.

McNab had done as bid while Rhona attempted to clear the seaweed that had tangled the body.

The water was rising. She was sure of that now.

'We'll need Mike's help,' she said.

McNab baulked at that.

'In normal circumstances—' he began.

'These aren't normal circumstances.' Rhona called to the figure still waiting on the shore.

Jones came sloshing through the water towards them.

'Okay,' Rhona said. 'Here's what we do.'

Twenty minutes later, they had dragged the body via the tarp to a spot above the waterline.

'What now?'

'Is there any chance they'll bring a body bag?'

'I didn't think to say.' McNab looked put out by the omission.

Rhona hoped the doctor or Erling would have thought of that.

'I'll parcel it up for the moment,' she said.

'What about the clothing?'

'We leave it on.'

She had plenty of evidence bags with her gear, enough to use one for each item of clothing, but here wasn't the place to undress him.

Rhona set about making up her human parcel, instructing McNab when necessary, securing it all with tape. By the time Erling arrived, the body would be cocooned, with no chance for him to look on Sam's dead face.

He doesn't even know who it is yet.

'Maybe you should call Erling. Warn him about the body.' Reading McNab's expression, she added, 'Or would you rather I did that?'

'No, I'll do it.'

Rhona registered his determination but didn't comment on it.

'There's a signal here. You should let Magnus know too. Stay with the body. I want to check out the rock pool we found him in.'

Mike Jones moved away as though he didn't want to be within earshot when McNab made his calls.

Leaving McNab to it, Rhona re-entered the water. In normal circumstances the locus would have been thoroughly lit and searched. In this case she would be rooting around in the dark, and the next tide would wash this scene of crime clean (if it was the scene of a crime).

Rhona came to a stop, pretty sure she was at the right place, marked by a larger upright rock that had probably halted Sam's passage across the causeway.

The sand patch they'd used was waterlogged now. The disturbed seaweed was back and floating in the rock pool. Rhona knelt down on a flagstone slab and began to search the water in which the body had lain. She'd thought she'd caught a glimpse of something earlier among the tendrils of seaweed, but had been too preoccupied with getting the body to safety to investigate.

Now she rooted around with one hand while the other held the torch. Her reluctance to give up eventually paid off.

'Got you.' Rhona extracted the small object and held it in front of the torch beam.

It was a brooch, or more exactly a sweetheart brooch, not dissimilar to the one in the grave. She turned it over and examined the back. On this one there were initials.

EF BH

As Rhona bagged the brooch, she heard voices from the darkness.

It took five men to carry the corpse to the ambulance, which waited at the turn into the cottage. It had been decided to transfer Sam's body directly to the doctor's surgery to await the helicopter dispatched by MIT West which would arrive sometime tomorrow, both weather and schedule permitting.

Sam was now double-wrapped. Dr Cameron, who hailed from Manchester, had supplied the body bag. A man in his fifties, he'd deserted the city some five years back to be the resident jack-of-all-medical-trades on Sanday, and had planned to spend his spare time birdwatching.

'I haven't had quite as much spare time as I thought,' he'd told her as they'd made their way back along the dark single-track road.

'I'd like to strip and forensically examine the body,' Rhona said. 'Is that possible?'

'I have somewhere I do minor surgery, but you could

wait until you get it to the mortuary in Kirkwall, or better still Inverness or Aberdeen.'

'I'd like to take a look while it's still here.'

Their conversation for the remainder of journey was about Sam Flett. The doctor knew Sam well, having spent time at the heritage museum researching the island he'd come to live on.

'Sam knew everyone. He was a good bloke.'

After a pause, he brought up the subject of Inga. 'I take it there's no word on the girl?'

Rhona's silence gave him the answer.

'I haven't spoken to the detective yet because it involves patient confidentiality.' He thought for a moment before continuing. 'But I believe Inga's mother told DS McNab why she and the girl moved here.'

Rhona had heard nothing of this from McNab, so she waited for more.

'There was a problem of domestic violence. I treated Claire Sinclair shortly after she arrived on Sanday. There were some cuts to her arms that had healed, bruising, old cigarette burns.'

Rhona intervened. 'What about Inga?'

'She was fine. Her mother assured me of that and I believed her. Often in such circumstances the women take the beatings to protect the children.'

Rhona had a sudden thought.

'Her partner doesn't know where she is?'

'She's certain he doesn't.'

'Why is she so sure?'

'Apparently she never revealed that her family came from these parts. She said he would never contemplate that she would leave the Carlisle area, let alone come to Scotland.'

The ambulance had drawn to a halt.

The back door was thrown open and McNab peered in. 'We're here, Dr MacLeod.'

The treatment room served her purpose very well. Brightly lit, clean, with a range of equipment to supplement what she always brought with her on jobs.

The body having been carried in, Rhona suggested that she bring Erling back in once she and the doctor had unwrapped the body, so that he might see his 'adopted' uncle.

'There's a machine in the waiting room,' the doctor had said. 'It produces not bad coffee.'

McNab's expression had brightened at this, then realizing he would be sharing the space with his superior officer, didn't look quite so keen.

'Come on, I'll buy you a coffee, Sergeant,' DI Flett had said.

Left to their own devices, Rhona offered the doctor a forensic suit to don.

'I'm not sure what's required here,' he said.

'I just need a witness. This isn't a post-mortem. I need to check out his clothing then pack it, each item separately. I'll examine his body, take samples and make notes about what I find.'

He nodded without comment, although she was pretty sure this wasn't a common occurrence for Dr Cameron in his general practice. He would be called to certify death on occasion, but as far as she could gather, anyone *in extremis* was normally whisked to the nearest hospital, that being Balfour Hospital, Kirkwall. If not there, then Aberdeen.

As she unzipped the body bag, the tang of the sea filled the room. The cocoon she'd created to preserve Sam was still intact. Rhona carefully cut the tape and unwrapped the tarp.

She pondered at this moment whether it might be better for Erling to see Sam fully dressed, rather than stripped naked and covered with a sheet. Under the waterproofs Sam was wearing a thick sweater and trousers. All of which were sodden. But at least he looked normal. Okay, his face showed signs of being in the water but . . .

The puddles on the floor decided her.

McNab was definitely not in his comfort zone, despite the two double espressos he'd drunk since arrival at the doctor's surgery. DI Flett had asked him to describe in detail what had happened both in their visit to Sam's cottage and to the Sinclair house, then the circumstances that had led them to recovering his body from the causeway.

McNab had given him every last detail, down to the expression on Jones's face when he'd opened the door to him.

'When did you search the schoolhouse?'

McNab gave him an estimate, because he couldn't remember exactly.

'Did you check the outhouses?'

McNab stumbled over that, knowing he had, but not as thoroughly as he might have.

DI Flett was looking at him in a manner he didn't like, because it reminded him too much of the man he regarded as his real boss, DI Wilson.

'You think what happens here doesn't warrant a proper investigation, Sergeant?'

McNab didn't have an answer to that, at least not one he wanted to give.

'Well?'

As he opened his mouth to speak he knew that what he was about to say was a mistake, but he found himself saying it anyway. 'I think, sir, that it's difficult to investigate a small community if you are familiar with its residents.'

He'd shot his bolt and his opinion, which was that DI Flett shouldn't be here and probably PC Tulloch too.

'But *you* are in no way familiar with the residents of Sanday, Sergeant, and it's you we're talking about here.'

Things deteriorated after that, until the point when DI Flett suggested McNab accompany the body south on the helicopter. 'As you originally intended.'

As McNab was about to argue to the contrary, the door to the treatment room opened and Rhona emerged to tell DI Flett that he could come in and see Sam now.

Erling had looked on death before a number of times. It never got any easier. The first time had been as a student. A friend had got high and drunk and leapt over a wall for bravado, not realizing there was a huge drop on the other side. A young life, full of intelligence and hope, had been annihilated in an instant. The shock and horror of that brief moment had stayed with him and would, he felt, remain forever.

He'd attended fatal road accidents, which thankfully weren't frequent on Orkney, collected fishermen's bodies from the waters surrounding the islands and dealt with the results of a serious fire on Flotta, which haunted him still, especially when he thought of Rory.

But I haven't had to face this.

Sam Flett had been more than just an 'adopted' uncle. He had been a friend. He and his wife, Jean, had dealt with his younger self with a skill Erling could only now appreciate. His own parents had been more distant. Loving, but he had found it too difficult to speak to them about the growing realization of what he might be. He had always thought of it as 'might' as though there was some way things might turn, like the tide, and he would wake up to find he was normal.

And I wanted so much to be normal.

He had felt no such contradiction while with Jean and Sam. In fact, he had never worried for a moment about who or what he was when on Sanday with them. Maybe that was why he'd exuded the pheromones that Magnus had smelt and remarked upon.

Erling observed the face that was no longer Sam Flett. The fish had claimed it. Sam had become a part of the food chain of the ocean. That aspect of his death Sam wouldn't have minded.

'What happened, Sam?'

Erling listened intently, as though he might hear a response.

'He thinks I've screwed up,' McNab told Rhona. 'He wants me to leave.'

Rhona remained silent and drank her coffee.

'When I said someone tried to drown *me* outside the hotel, he suggested it might have been horseplay. He's the one not investigating properly, because he's too close to this place and the people involved.'

He waited again for her to comment, but she didn't,

despite her concerns. McNab didn't scare easily. If he believed someone had tried to kill him, then from her experience, his claim had to be taken seriously. On the other hand, Sanday folk were used to policing themselves. If an incoming officer of the law had been seen to fall short of what was required, i.e. take steps against the infiltration of a known paedophile, then they might see that as a punishable offence. And he had been rescued pretty quickly, which suggested Torvaig had been given a heads-up on the fact that McNab was in the water.

'What if the same person attacked Sam Flett?' he said.

Having stripped and processed Sam's body, the evidence of a blunt-force trauma to his head had become apparent. Something she still had to tell Erling.

'I don't think you should leave,' she said. 'You're part of the team sent in here. But perhaps you might try to work better with local officers.'

'You sound like the rule book for MIT.'

'I meant to.'

'You'll back me up?' he urged.

'Sam Flett's death changes everything,' she told him.

Erling turned on her re-entry to the treatment room. 'Can you tell how Sam died?'

'It'll take a post-mortem to determine that for certain.' She gave the stock answer.

'But you have an idea?'

'There's evidence of a blunt-force trauma to the back of the skull.'

'He fell on the causeway and hit his head?'

'Maybe.'

Erling went quiet, appreciating he was putting her on the spot. Dr MacLeod wasn't a forensic pathologist and wasn't conducting a post-mortem. She was there to strip forensic evidence from the body.

'I found this,' she said. 'In the rock pool where his body lay.' She held up a bag.

Through the plastic he saw a metal object. Studying it, he realized what it might be.

'A sweetheart badge?' he said, trying to imagine why Sam would have such an object on his person.

'There's a pair of initials,' she said.

'What are they?' As he posed the question, Erling realized he was worried what her answer might be.

36

Magnus had been dozing in one of the Orkney chairs when the mobile rang. Startled into sudden wakefulness, he was puzzled as to where he was for a moment, surrounded as he was by an image of the past.

His shock at the news of Sam's death had been followed by a deep disquiet, and the realization that though Sam had been afraid for the girl, it may have been his own death he'd been forewarned of. Magnus's investigation of the second sight had unearthed many similar stories, but he hadn't wanted Sam to feature in one of them.

He'd immediately asked McNab if he might help in any way.

McNab had answered no, then amended that somewhat. 'Can you take another look around Sam's place?'

'What am I looking for?'

There was a pause, then McNab said, 'I never thought he was being completely straight about the business of the cold case. And Rhona found a sweetheart brooch with the body, a replica of the one in the grave, only this time it had the initials EF and BH on it.'

'Do we know how Sam died?'

'He was in the middle of the causeway, so drowning comes high on the list of possibilities.'

'Sam Flett knew Start Island. He would never have got caught out by the tide.'

'We all make mistakes.'

With that McNab had rung off, after which Magnus had fixed himself some strong coffee and started his search.

He had begun with the laptop. That in itself had taken some time. Magnus had looked at, he thought, every file on there. No doubt the police IT department would do a more thorough job, but it appeared that Sam hadn't been in correspondence with anyone apart from himself regarding the current case on the island.

And our correspondence focussed primarily on Sam's fear for Inga.

He checked the sent folder to find nothing more recent than their last exchange. Then he noted that one email lay in the draft folder. Clicking it open, he found it had been written to him.

I've found, I believe, the girl for whom the magic flower was made. And I think she may have been an ancestor of Inga, because she looks so like her. I'm going to take the newspaper cutting with me to Inga's mother and ask if she can identify the girl.

Weariness had set in for Rhona. That and despair. The longer they remained here, the worse the situation seemed to become. Her excavation of the wartime grave, or maybe the discovery of the flowers in the attic, had apparently started an avalanche which continued to roll down the hill, creating havoc and death in its wake.

Such thoughts ran contrary to Rhona's scientist brain, yet they presented themselves nonetheless.

No time had as yet been set when the helicopter would arrive to take Sam's body away. Rhona didn't have to be around when that happened. Everything was ready, including the forensic report and the clothes and samples she'd taken from the body. It would be up to the pathologist to decide if he agreed with her findings on the nature of Sam's death.

McNab had driven them back, as silent as she had been. Rhona had immediately gone through to bed, assuming he would do the same. Sleep hadn't come easily, but eventually she must have drifted off, because daylight filtering in through the salt-encrusted window eventually roused her.

There's little wind, was her first thought, *which means the helicopter can land*.

Her second consideration was the child and the continuing search for her. Start Island had to be part of that search. Along with the Maesry Mound, and the possibility of finding the skull.

Rising and showering, she entered the kitchen to discover McNab up and already cooking. What he'd found in the fridge, she had no idea.

'Someone left eggs at the door,' he told her. 'I hope it wasn't that bastard Jones.'

'Maybe it was Derek Muir,' she said, then suddenly remembered they hadn't informed Derek about the death of his old friend.

'He'll have heard already,' McNab responded to her concern. 'Nothing's a secret on this island. Except the things they definitely don't want you to know about,' he added with a shake of his head.

He handed her a plate of scrambled eggs. This time Rhona didn't mention his cooking skills, but ate them gratefully, along with a mug of strong coffee.

After breakfast they both went round the back of the cottage to try for a signal. The sound of messages arriving in quick succession was partially drowned out by bird calls. Rhona glanced through the list to find Magnus's name as the most recent.

'Magnus wants us to go over to Sam's. He thinks he may have found something,' she told McNab.

McNab was staring at his mobile screen.

'What is it?' Rhona said.

'I asked Ollie in the Tech department to run a check on my mobile history. See if he could discover where that text message about Sam came from.'

'And?' Rhona said.

'It was sent from Sanday, from a mobile belonging to Hege Aaker.' He looked put out by this.

'You know her?' Rhona said.

'She's Norwegian. Working here for a year. She served me coffee and cake at the community centre. And she was in the band that night at the pub.'

'Why didn't she speak to you if she knew something?'

McNab shrugged. 'I've given up trying to figure out how folk in this place work.'

'She's not a local,' Rhona reminded him.

'Well, she's into secrets like the rest of them.'

If there had been a summons from Erling, McNab never mentioned it.

Magnus looks as though he's had about as much sleep as we have, Rhona thought as he led them into the small living room. The laptop from the study now stood on the table. A tin box lay open beside it, with a selection of old photographs and what looked like children's drawings and postcards spread out alongside. An email was open on the screen.

'I went through all our emails again and anything I thought might have a connection to Sanday during the war, or the cold case.' Magnus looked to McNab. 'Your guys no doubt would do a more thorough job.'

'What did you find?' McNab said.

Magnus indicated they should read the open email.

McNab's face clouded over as he did so. 'What has this got to do with anything?'

'Last night, Inga's mother never mentioned this picture, although in the email he said he was planning to show it to her.'

'So?'

'I just thought that odd,' Magnus said, sounding almost apologetic. 'Also, you mentioned the brooch? The tin box held a lot of memorabilia, his mother's I believe. I wondered if he might have got the brooch from there.'

McNab still wasn't impressed.

Magnus kept trying. 'Then the initials. Sam's half-brother was called Eric. He would have been a teenager during the war. His initials were EF. The young woman who Mr Cutts named as going missing was called Beth Haddow. EF and BH?'

At last he'd generated a spark of interest.

'Sam's brother was in the RAF?' McNab said.

Rhona intervened. 'Sam said the brooches were fairly common currency, even if you weren't a serviceman.'

'There's one more thing.' Magnus looked a little put out by what he was about to say, while McNab waited impatiently.

'You saw the photograph of Jamie Drever as a young man

with the family?' He extracted it from the pile and laid it on the keyboard. 'That's Eric and his father, Geordie. They look very much alike, don't you think?' He pointed at the third man. 'That's Jamie.'

McNab peered at the picture.

Rhona knew what Magnus was hinting at almost immediately, having studied Sam Flett recently and at close quarters. She looked to McNab.

'What?' he said.

'We can compare the DNA samples from both bodies,' she told Magnus, while waiting for the penny to drop with McNab.

It finally did. 'You think Sam Flett was Jock Drever's son?'

'I think there's a strong possibility he was,' Magnus said. 'Once Sam saw this photo, I believe he may have come to the same conclusion. He mentioned in our correspondence that his mother had developed dementia prior to her death and talked a lot about the past. Apparently Eric never wrote to her after he left Sanday and, according to Sam, his mother kept returning in her mind to one summer in particular, which seemed to have given her both great joy and a terrible sadness. It was the summer she discovered she was expecting Sam. The summer Eric left home. And Jamie Drever went south. Possibly the summer the young woman died.'

The woman standing before him was barely recognizable from their previous meeting at the community centre. Inga's mother appeared to have aged ten years since he'd last spoken to her. Of all the tasks he had to face as a detective, dealing with the parent of a missing child was, McNab felt, the worst. As he apologized for the intrusion, she interrupted him.

'It's about Sam Flett, isn't it?'

When McNab nodded, she said, 'I heard you found his body on the causeway last night. Poor Sam, he was kind to Inga and she was very fond of him.'

Her belief in Sam's innocence of anything untoward in her daughter's disappearance was obvious. McNab wasn't so certain. Experience had shown that those known to the girl were the most likely suspects, particularly when the child liked and trusted them.

'How did he die?' Inga's mother was saying. 'Did he drown?'

McNab used the standard get-out clause. 'We won't know until the post-mortem.'

'I thought he was too old to be out searching, but he insisted.' She halted as tears took over. 'He was our first friend on Sanday.'

McNab chose that moment to ease her round to the subject of the photograph Sam had planned to show her.

'It was a newspaper cutting,' she said. 'I have it here.'

She fetched a plastic folder from a nearby shelf and handed it to him.

Through the plastic, the cutting looked old and fragile. A group of rather startled children stared at the camera. The clothing suggested the thirties or forties, but McNab was no authority on dress through the ages. Two rows, one of boys, the other girls. The girl in the middle had dark hair cut in a bob. She was the only one with an excited smile on her face.

'She looks very like your daughter,' McNab said.

'She does, doesn't she? When Sam arrived with it looking for Inga, I didn't pay any attention. I was too worried by the fact that she hadn't reached his house, although she'd left more than an hour before.'

Asking her who she thought it might be seemed inappropriate at that moment, so McNab changed tack.

'What route did Inga normally take to Sam's house?'

'I told Ivan Tulloch that already,' she said.

'Tell me.'

'She crossed the fields in between.'

'Always?'

'Usually, unless there were cows. You shouldn't walk through a herd of cows.'

'Were there cows there yesterday morning?'

'I'm not sure.'

'If she didn't cross the field?'

She thought for a moment. 'She sometimes went along the beach rather than use the road.'

'How much traffic is there?'

'Very little. Just local, except in the summer when we get visitors coming to see the lighthouse.'

'So you haven't seen any strange cars about?'

She shook her head.

'What about boats in the bay?'

'People do fish out there, but . . .' She ground to a halt.

'You've had no mystery phone calls? No feeling you were being watched?'

'No.' She appeared puzzled by his questions.

'Did Inga mention Start Island at any point?'

Her mother thought for a moment. 'They did a project in school about the lighthouse. Derek Muir, the Ranger, took them over to see it. They climbed to the top. She liked that.' Her eyes misted over.

'But she didn't mention going there to look for the missing skull?'

She shook her head.

McNab now came back to the photograph.

'Have you any idea who the girl in the photograph is?'

She seemed to be expecting the question. 'I think it's probably my grandfather's sister, Ola Sinclair.'

'And the school?'

'The local one.' Her face clouded. 'Where Mike Jones lives now.' She shot McNab a look. 'Is it true what they're saying about him?'

'What are they saying?'

'That he's a paedophile, hiding out on Sanday. How he had sex with a fifteen-year-old pupil, and she killed herself.'

'When you first spoke to me, you were willing to give him the benefit of the doubt.'

She didn't look so sure of that now.

37

They dragged Derek's small boat up the shell beach, just beyond the high-water mark. The journey over had been uncomfortable for Rhona. Derek had attempted to ask her about the discovery of Sam's body and she'd had to indicate she couldn't answer his questions, regardless of the fact that he was obviously upset.

At that he'd announced, 'They said that he got caught in the tide. I don't buy that. Sam knew the movement of the tides and the crossing. He wouldn't have made a mistake like that.'

Rhona tended to agree, but could hardly say so.

As the boat met the shore, Derek jumped out first, followed by Magnus, and the two men pulled the bow high enough for Rhona to step onto the shell sand with her forensic bag.

The weather seemed to be in their favour today. Scudding clouds indicated the presence of a brisk breeze, but the sky was bright and the rain had apparently deserted them for the moment. Having secured the boat, Derek suggested he walk ahead to the lighthouse. He was due to make a routine check there anyway. The lamp was powered by solar panels, but during the winter that had to be supplemented on occasion by diesel, and the tank needed checking.

'I'll go up top. I can see the whole island from there, provided the weather stays like this.'

With a good pair of binoculars and Derek's knowledge of every inch of the terrain, if there was a body in view, he would spot it. No one voiced that, but all three thought it, although there was also the lochan that bordered the northern shore to consider, its expanse of water a haven for reeds and birds.

They agreed that Rhona and Magnus would search the derelict farm steading, and then head for Maesry Mound, meeting Derek there. They all checked their mobiles, to find Derek was the only one to have a signal of sorts.

Before he set off, Rhona reminded him that if he did discover anything suspicious, he should immediately come and get her.

'Don't touch anything,' she repeated.

Derek set off along the track that followed the north shore, while Rhona and Magnus climbed a low stone dyke to make their way across a field to the farm.

She'd viewed the farm during her earlier walk along the southern shore. From there she hadn't appreciated the number and variety of the buildings clustered together, their backs turned to the sea. It was more of a small settlement, with a row of tiny cottages, a main house and numerous outbuildings.

They agreed to split forces for the search. Magnus would take the outbuildings, while Rhona checked the main house and cottages. As she entered what must have been a small garden to the front of the main house, Rhona paused to listen to the relative silence. The layout of the buildings was such that they all faced inward, allowing the residents shelter from the winds that came from the surrounding sea.

Here too, as in the fields, lay evidence of the wild geese

that plagued the farmers, the same black droppings littering the grass of the forgotten garden.

Rhona focussed on the main house, the only building which had an upper floor. Gazing through the hole where a window had been, she saw the remains of an ancient rusty kitchen range, the only symbol left inside of its previous occupants.

The lower half of the wooden front door was rotted and broken. Through the gap, scattered piles of broken lobster creels and old fishing floats were visible. When she tried to open the remainder of the door, it refused to budge, so she went back to the window and climbed through.

As she shouted Inga's name, her voice, no longer whipped off by the wind, met the interior stone walls and played back to her. But no answering call came, however often she tried.

Eventually she established that there was nothing in the lower rooms but rubble, old fishing ropes, scraps of nets and the decomposing remains of a number of birds and small animals. At a guess, a wild cat or two were using the space to store and eat their meals. They appeared to be the building's only visitors. Making for the narrow staircase leading upwards, and noting their poor state, Rhona tested each step before using it.

The layout in the attic was much the same as at Sam's place, although there were no walls or doors to separate the two low-ceilinged rooms. Bird droppings, broken slates and dust were the only things up there.

Rhona retreated downstairs, and exited the way she'd come in.

The row of tiny cottages proved just as empty. Relieved to discover no evidence of Inga, Rhona was also frustrated that their journey to the island had brought no clues as to what had happened to the girl. She couldn't escape the thought that Sam's visit had had something to do with Inga's search for the skull.

As she emerged from the final building, Magnus jumped the wall between them.

'There's no sign of anything or anyone having been here,' he said.

'I agree. Let's head for the mound.'

They set out across the intervening field. Scanning the horizon for Derek, Rhona couldn't spot him anywhere.

'Chances are he's in the lighthouse,' Magnus said.

Approaching the mound from the north, there was no sign of the entrance. Magnus followed her round, marvelling at the shape and size of the Neolithic hill.

'It's like a smaller version of Maeshowe,' he said.

'Wait until you see inside,' Rhona promised, excited now at the prospect of checking for the presence of the skull.

On reaching the access tunnel, Rhona looked for the footprints she'd photographed earlier, only to find they were no longer visible. In fact, it looked as though the soil had been raked, the object used, she suspected, a piece of drift-wood lying nearby.

'Someone's swept the ground clean,' Magnus said.

'It certainly looks like it.'

Rhona re-photographed the area, then entered the tunnel to find the large slab that had blocked the opening had been moved to one side. There would be no problem seeing into the central chamber now. There would be no difficulty entering it either.

Which could only mean one thing. There was no longer anything there for them to find.

*

The jeep stood in the middle of the bay like a stranded whale. A vast, shallow bowl with a narrow inlet, Cata Sand had a thin film of water at high tide. At low tide, as now, it was transformed into a vast expanse of golden sand populated by the worm-like spirals of razor clams or spoots as they were known locally.

The farmer who'd reported seeing the jeep had initially assumed that someone was taking a shortcut across the bay to the ruins of Tresness Farm on the neighbouring peninsula, a common enough occurrence. Or that a joyrider was taking advantage of the wide expanse of firm sand while the tide was out.

Neither had been the case.

Having finally realized it might be Sam Flett's vehicle, he'd called the community centre looking for the 'Glasgow detective'.

McNab didn't like crossing the large area of wet sand, but wasn't prepared to display his discomfort in front of PC Tulloch. As well as being nervous of wide open spaces, he also wasn't a fan of beaches. He mistrusted the sand's intentions, believing its real goal was to suck him down, like quicksand. Neither was he keen on tramping across what looked like an army of worms. Even as he did so, spoots of water erupted on all sides, marking his progress.

If Tulloch picked up on his discomfort, he neither mentioned nor showed it, although he did explain why they were being fired at.

'The razor clam feels the movement on the surface and digs down deeper to avoid you. That causes the fountain of water.'

McNab made no comment.

They'd left their own vehicle next to a small squat concrete building, which Tulloch had referred to bizarrely as the brickie hut, telling him it had once served as a lookout shelter. McNab would have preferred to drive rather than walk across the sand, but Tulloch had advised against it. 'The chassis's too low on the car. We could get stuck.'

As they neared the small jeep, McNab felt his pulse quicken. The man who'd called in said he hadn't approached the vehicle, just checked it out with his binoculars. He didn't think there was anyone inside, but couldn't be sure.

McNab upped his pace, the surface of the sand no longer an issue.

The film of water was a little deeper here, indicating that the jeep stood in the lowest part of the bowl, halfway across. McNab sloshed through it.

The driver's window was down, the seat wet with the rain that had fallen overnight. The passenger side was empty too, the window on that side wound up. On the floor round the pedals was a sprinkling of what looked like shell fragments.

McNab moved to the back door and opened it with gloved hands.

The narrow back seat lay empty, but not the floor.

He hesitated, registering the find, feeling the blood rushing to his head, his throat tightening. And all the time, the word *No* was repeating in his brain, like a mantra.

McNab reached down for the child's anorak that covered the motionless bundle, and drew it back.

38

'There was a pair of wellington boots under the anorak.'

Rhona had imagined the scene, seen the bundle on the jeep floor and tasted McNab's fear as he'd pulled back the coat.

'But it wasn't Inga's body,' she'd said firmly. 'And the boots will give us some indication of where she's been.'

Rhona had expected the soles of the wellingtons to have deposits of shell sand on them, similar to that retrieved from the jeep's pedals. Instead she'd extracted soil which, by its scent alone, contained a high proportion of manure. The floor of the back seat had yielded more of the same mix. It seemed the girl had likely been on farmland prior to the jeep picking her up, whereas the driver of the jeep had last been walking on shell sand. The tyres of the jeep may yet give them more evidence, but driving it onto Cata Sand had resulted in both the sand and seawater removing the surface deposits. Perhaps that was the reason it had been abandoned there, in the hope that it might be washed clean.

The evidence she'd already extracted had conjured up a variety of scenarios, which she and McNab had discussed at some length. The most common being that Inga had been intercepted as she'd taken a shortcut across the fields on her way to Sam's place.

The question was, by whom?

McNab had voiced his opinion at this point that Sam was the chief suspect.

'He could have met the girl, something could have happened between them, then he went to her home looking for her,' he'd said. 'We both know it's often the one who declares a child missing who made it happen in the first place.'

Rhona hadn't argued, because McNab was right. It looked as though the girl had been in Sam's vehicle. The anorak and wellington boots were definitely Inga's. She recognized them herself from her encounter with Inga at the schoolhouse. There could of course be a different explanation for their presence in the vehicle. They may have been planted there to make it look like Sam had abducted the girl.

And now Sam Flett was dead and couldn't defend himself, which to Rhona, at least, seemed a little too convenient.

'Maybe he couldn't live with what he'd done?' McNab had responded to this.

'There was evidence of blunt-force trauma to the back of the head,' she reminded him.

'He could have hit his head *after* he drowned,' McNab said.

And there they were, back round again to the post-mortem results.

'The most important thing is to locate Inga. And the soil deposit may be our way of doing that.'

They'd retrieved the jeep and it now stood behind the heritage centre. In normal circumstances, a SOCO team well versed in forensically examining vehicles would have taken over. She'd discussed with Erling transporting the jeep to Kirkwall for examination and they'd decided it would be swifter for her to process it here, and have the evidence lifted off the island and down to Chrissy as quickly as possible.

Rhona would have given anything to be back in her lab, or any lab, but if she left the island, there would be no one on hand to process what they might find next.

And everyone involved, including Erling, thought it was likely to be a child's body.

McNab was glad to be alone for the short journey from the museum to the community centre. He had to concede that PC Tulloch had conducted himself well up to now, but his presence in the car would have been a distraction. He needed time on his own to think.

In most of the cases he'd worked on, there had been a sudden moment of insight, when experience, intuition or a mixture of both drew aside the intricate layers and showed you what lay beneath.

Not here. Not in this place.

Whatever he'd learned on the job in Glasgow, plainly didn't work on Sanday. He'd played it all wrong. Been too accommodating. Far too polite, even when he suspected folk were lying. And who was afraid of being interviewed in a community centre? If he'd been able to conduct the interviews in a police station. Put the fear of death in them. He would have got the truth then.

Maybe even prevented some of this from happening.

McNab drew into a passing place as a car approached, and was rewarded with a wave of a hand.

Fuck, he was even driving like them.

He put his foot hard on the accelerator, kicking up sand

as he rejoined the road. Things would be different from now on, he vowed.

Hege Aaker denied the accusation. Again.

'It came from your phone.'

'That doesn't mean I sent it.' She met McNab square in the eye.

'Who has access to your mobile?'

'When I'm here, anyone and everyone.'

'How's that?'

'I leave it by the coffee machine while I'm working.'

They both glanced at the said machine where at least five people were gathered.

'See,' she said, 'anyone might have used it.'

'What about your access code? Who knows that?'

'I don't use one. It irritates me to have to keep putting it in every time I want to use the phone.'

'The text arrived on Saturday,' McNab said.

'I did come in that morning.' She looked thoughtful.

'Who else was here?'

'I'd need to check the diary. The place is used for different meetings, family gatherings. Plus we get individuals coming to check emails and to use the internet.'

'Get the diary,' he told her.

It seemed there had been a meeting of the directors of the Sanday Development Trust. The group who worked on Sanday archaeological sites had also been there. And a Golden Wedding tea party.

'Is there a list of names available?'

'For the first two groups probably, but I'm not sure about the tea party.'

'Anyone apart from that?'

'There were a few folk popping in and out. There always are.'

'I take it my number is on your mobile?'

'You asked everyone to take it down, remember?' she reminded him. 'In case we thought of anything else to tell you.' In that moment her face clouded over. 'Everyone liked Sam Flett. Who would want to harm him, or Inga?'

McNab wanted to say, *That's what I fucking need to know.* In different circumstances, he would have said exactly that. But he wasn't in Glasgow. He was on Sanday. Hege had given an explanation for the text from her mobile. Looking at those around him in the centre now, plus the diary, he recognized it was probably true. Plus, he didn't think she was lying, and he didn't believe she'd try to point the finger at Sam.

But then maybe he was going soft?

The next interviewee was Don Cutts. McNab had offered to visit him at home, but the old man had declined. 'I don't get out much. This is exciting for me.'

He wheeled himself in, like an actor coming on stage. His expression suggested he had something to say and was looking forward to it. When McNab asked if he wanted coffee or tea, he dismissed this with a wave of his hand.

'Mr Cutts—' McNab began.

Before he could get any further, the old man interrupted him. 'I heard about the sweetheart brooch you found with Sam.'

McNab wanted to ask, *How could you know about that?*

Before he was able to, Mr Cutts came back in. 'I had to think back. I couldn't be sure.'

'About what?'

'Eric Flett. Beth Haddow was seeing Eric Flett, Sam's half-brother. And, maybe, the guy that was staying at the Flett's house at the time.'

'Jamie Drever? Tall, skinny, with ginger hair?'

The old man nodded, a glint in his eye. 'Aye, Jamie. But there was another one. A veritable triangle of them. It's a long time ago. But the memory of that time seems stronger every day. The other guy was older. Eric and Jamie had no chance really. Like me.' He shook his head, recalling, it seemed, the adolescent trauma of it all.

'Who?' McNab urged him.

'Tall, dark-haired, local, although he worked away a lot on the fishing. He liked a drink, I remember that much, and he had a way with the women. I wanted to learn what it was. But I don't think I ever did.'

'Who was he?' McNab tried again.

He shook his head. 'I'm damned if I know. And he'll be dead now anyway.' A mix of pain and sadness swept his face. 'There were only a few local surnames back then. No incomers, you see, except for the military personnel. Get Sam Flett to tell you the family names in the north of the island.' He looked pleased by his solution, then his face crumpled. 'But Sam's gone now too.'

'Did Sam talk to you about this?'

His rheumy eyes focussed on McNab. 'His mother had dementia. Sam said she was spilling the family secrets.'

'And they were?'

'What are they always?' he said.

39

The chopper would be returning from Sanday bearing Sam's body and the evidence that Dr MacLeod had collected on the island. But it wouldn't land here in Kirkwall.

The thought of Sam heading south to be dissected in a Glasgow post-mortem disturbed Erling more than he'd thought possible. He could have insisted it go to Inverness, but for what purpose? So that it might stay above the Highland line? His 'adopted' uncle had never regarded himself as a Highlander, nor even Scottish. Sam Flett had been a Sanday man, an Orcadian, through and through. So what did it matter where they cut him open, if it wasn't here on the island?

He was aware too that Sam had to feature as a suspect in the child's disappearance, particularly now that his jeep with her jacket and boots had been found. But why would he harm the child?

The fact that it had become a distinct possibility meant he could no longer be directly involved, and the ongoing investigation would have to be managed by DS McNab with local support. His thoughts on McNab he'd kept mostly to himself, not even divulging them to Magnus. He'd heard tales of the detective, particularly during the Stonewarrior case, in which Orkney had featured, but had never met the man in person until now.

McNab, if he was honest, had really got under his skin. He didn't like the detective's dismissive attitude to Sanday, its way of life and its people, but he was used to townies thinking themselves superior, whatever their profession.

Irritation wasn't the only emotion he felt. There was another. Envy.

Envy because McNab didn't care about his position, his future, even his own well-being. He didn't care what people thought or said about him. In that he was like Rory. In fact, there was a lot about the two men's characters that was similar. Apart from the fact that McNab was so demonstrably straight. He seemed at times to play the gung-ho tough guy just to make that more obvious.

Is that why he pisses me off?

Even as he asked himself that, he knew the real reason for his dislike of the Glasgow detective. McNab was rooting about in his family, opening up the past. A past that Erling had his own preferred version of. A version he didn't want to see destroyed.

Their latest phone call, in which McNab had brought him up to date regarding their search of Sam's cottage, and the discovery of the jeep and its contents, had left Erling with a profound feeling of unease. Sam's declared affection for Inga had been transformed in his mind into an obsession. Added to which, his preoccupation with the second sight, his belief in the significance of the flowers in the schoolhouse attic and his declared fear for Inga's safety, all pointed to the likelihood that Sam had been losing his mind.

Had Sam been fearful that he might harm the girl himself? Was that what he'd been trying to prevent?

Sam's possible involvement in Inga's disappearance hadn't been the only bombshell McNab had dropped. Old Don

Cutt's recollections of a triumvirate of possible lovers for the missing Beth Haddow had included both Eric Flett and Jamie Drever. Old Mr Cutts could of course be telling lies, revisiting adolescent grievances or just stirring the pot. Although if Dr MacLeod had seen the missing skull in Maesry Mound, then someone currently on Sanday was trying to prevent them discovering the identity of the remains at the schoolhouse.

No one wants to discover a murderer in the family. Including me.

Rhona had set up the Skype call in the research room, where Sam Flett had installed her when she'd first arrived on the island. Back then the mystery had centred on a cold case. Not any more.

Chrissy peered into the screen as though she was looking through a window at her. Rhona felt a surge of affection and relief at seeing Chrissy again and realized just how much she'd missed her forensic assistant's straightforward evaluation of everything.

'So, you're still there?' Chrissy said.

'I'm still here,' Rhona agreed.

'But no more Sam Flett.' Chrissy looked over Rhona's shoulder as if searching for the museum curator. 'What the fuck's going on up there in Sanday land?'

'We found his body on the causeway.'

'A man who knew all about the tides died on a causeway? I don't buy it.'

'His body's on its way to Glasgow. Will you attend the post-mortem?'

'You bet I will.'

'There's other stuff.' Rhona proceeded to talk about the samples she'd sent from Inga's boots, plus the shell sand.

'I need you here at the lab,' Chrissy said. 'But I know why you're not coming back.'

'I don't think she's dead,' Rhona found herself saying.

There was a moment's silence as Chrissy absorbed this.

'For a scientist, that's a pretty big statement.' She waited for Rhona to respond.

Eventually she did, trying to put into words what had occurred to her as a possibility.

'Sam Flett was freaked by the muslin flowers found in the attic,' she stated. 'He found an old school photograph that featured a girl that looked like Inga. His fear for Inga wasn't rational but it was very real, and growing. What would he do?'

There was a long pause as Chrissy thought about this. 'If it was me, I would hide her, until I worked out what the threat was.'

'I wondered about that too.'

'What about her coat and boots in his jeep?' Chrissy said.

'It's too convenient. As was the jeep's placing on the sands. Whoever did that, I don't think it was Sam, although I'll need the post-mortem to confirm the timing.'

They talked then of the missing skull.

'Someone's screwing with you and you know now it's not kids.'

Rhona agreed. 'If that someone knows or thinks they know who killed that woman seventy odd years ago, they don't want it broadcast.'

'Which suggests it's someone living there,' Chrissy said. 'Otherwise why would they care what their ancestors had done?'

'Maybe the killer isn't dead,' Rhona countered.

'Someone that old can't sneak about, removing a skull and hiding it on Start Island in a cave.'

'Not a cave, a Neolithic tomb,' Rhona corrected her.

'If the killer was from Sanday, isn't it likely they would have come from a family local to the area around the radar station?'

Chrissy was right. Back then, family names had been local to parishes. Fletts, Drevers, Sinclairs, Weirs.

'Sam Flett was the authority on all of that,' Rhona reminded her. 'And he's dead.'

They talked then of what the grave had produced.

'There's a lot of soil to sift,' Chrissy said. She didn't add, 'On my own,' but Rhona caught the silent words anyway.

'And the pilot's knife?'

'The staining on the blade was blood, and I retrieved a DNA sample from the handle. I'm trying to trace the serial number via the MOD, in the remote chance it may provide us with the name of the person it was issued to.' She paused. 'I sent your photo of the skull to IT as requested. They managed to get a much better image, which I forwarded to the Human Identification Centre in Dundee.'

A 2D-reconstruction was possible from a photograph, although a 3D-scan of the actual skull was by far the better option. Normally the facial reconstruction examiner would take the photograph or at least give instructions on how to. Rhona had been the recommended minimum of six feet away, which avoided any lens distortion, and the camera in the mobile was high quality, but the conditions hadn't been ideal. She could only hope that it was enough.

'Any luck tracing Beth Haddow?'

'Nothing so far. How's his nibs?'

'He hates it here, but you know McNab – once he's fastened on something, he won't give up.'

There was a snort of agreement.

'I've sent you the evidence I collected from the jeep, including soil from Inga's boots,' Rhona went on. 'I'm hoping we can use soil analysis to pinpoint where she was when she last wore the boots.'

According to the soil map, the north-east corner of Sanday was predominantly calcareous sand, which was alkaline with low organics. Lopness, on the other hand, where the old radar station had been, was acidic with a high organic surface.

'Okay. I'll have that checked out. Any idea when you'll be back?'

'Give it another twenty-four hours. If we haven't located the girl by then, I'll come anyway.'

Rhona rang off. Talking things through with Chrissy had helped, particularly when they'd agreed on the remote possibility of Sam hiding the girl. Now she had to run the idea past McNab, and she didn't think it would go down quite so well with him.

'She has a point,' Magnus said. 'Sam was frightened for Inga, but couldn't explain why. That's why he wanted me here.'

McNab shook his head. 'You're asking me to believe that he hid Inga, then went to her mother and frightened her half to death by declaring her daughter missing, which set off a hunt for the girl?'

'It didn't necessarily happen like that,' Rhona broke in.

'Well, how did it happen, Dr MacLeod?'

Rhona ignored the bullish look.

'Sam Flett didn't drive that jeep onto Cata Sand,' she said. 'He was likely dead when that happened.'

'So who did?'

'Someone who wanted to implicate Sam in Inga's disappearance.'

'Like you, you mean?'

God, he could be annoying when challenged.

'Let's for the sake of argument assume that Inga might be in hiding, for whatever reason.'

'I'd have to have evidence to believe that,' McNab warned. 'And don't tell me stories about magic flowers.'

Rhona then revealed the thought that had been simmering at the back of her mind. 'You said her mother came here to escape from an abusive partner.' She hesitated. 'Is there the remotest chance he found out where Inga and her mother were?'

40

It was her. He was sure of it.

But am I sure of anything?

The rain had come on as he'd walked along the headland. He had his torch, but as usual wasn't using it. He found over time his eyes had become accustomed to the shadowy darkness that descended by mid-afternoon this time of year. Above him, rainclouds scudded across the sky, with a faint moon making an occasional appearance. It had been in one of those moments that he'd seen her.

She'd appeared, he thought, from behind the old mortuary building. At first he'd assumed the shadowy movements to be one of the herd of cattle, already knowing that it wasn't true. The slight figure was accompanied by another taller one, a male.

He lost them for a moment as they passed like shadows behind a concrete building, then he spotted the two figures yards now from the beach. Reaching the edge of the grass, the male jumped down, then turned to lift her after him. He thought he heard her laugh, then the sound of the sea swallowed everything.

He didn't know how long he stood there, his heart crashing, unable to make his feet move, but eventually he'd walked towards the spot.

The edge of the dunes hung above the sand here by three

feet, the underside eaten away with the tide. He shone his torch down, looking for what, he had no idea. It seemed to his fevered imagination that he saw a bowl hollowed out in the sand as though someone had lain there. He ran his eyes seaward. The tide was out, the wet sand glistening under his beam.

Were those footsteps?

In that moment he thought he heard the faint throb of an engine and caught the distant shadow of a boat out in the bay.

If he was certain of the sighting, then why not contact the police? Say he'd spotted someone who might be Inga Sinclair near the beach with a man, although it had been dark and when he checked again, she was no longer there.

Because doing that would thrust me into the spotlight again.

Firstly the discovery of the flowers in the loft, then the unearthing of the body in the playground, after which the girl in his portrait had turned up on his doorstep. He thought it couldn't get any worse than that, and then it had. He'd taken a walk to clear his head, and found Sam Flett's dead body.

How can I go to that detective and tell him I think I've seen Inga?

The small voice, the one he didn't like listening to, was back. At times invidious and recriminatory, it could turn suddenly into wheedling and flattery. First he was bad, then good, when others were bad. It was all his fault, then everyone's fault but his own.

His own version of Jekyll and Hyde.

During the enquiry into Alice's death, he'd been accused

of all manner of horrors. The distaste of his friends, colleagues and the general public had been so powerful it had removed all sense of himself. He could no longer think of a single moment he'd spent with Alice – as she'd sat for her portrait, as they'd talked and laughed together – without pain and self-loathing. As for the few times they'd been intimate. Those he'd refused to recall, only to find them being replayed in his dreams and to wake horrified at himself.

But to deny Alice's existence had seemed the biggest crime of all.

That was when she'd not only come to him in dreams, but physically walked back into his life.

I see the ghost of Alice everywhere.

Was that what was happening now? Had the stress caused by the discovery of the remains in the playground, and the subsequent outing of his guilty past, given rise to him 'seeing things' again? But it wasn't the ghost of Alice he was encountering, he reminded himself. It was the girl in the portrait. Inga Sinclair.

He was back in the bedroom, flicking on the light switch. Drawn to the portrait, which by its very existence made him a possible suspect in Inga's disappearance. Every time he gazed upon it, it appeared to have gained in both detail and power, as though it was coming alive before his eyes.

It's the best thing I've ever done.

As he studied it, he noted that the wind had returned, and felt safer because of it. The sound travelling the eaves and skirting under the grey slates of the roof could be blamed for the voices of the past.

He didn't hear the back door open, although the touch of cold air on the back of his neck should have warned him. There were no footsteps, or perhaps he was too engrossed by the portrait to notice. When he did register there might be someone in the house with him, his first thought was that the detective had returned to grill him again.

He disengaged from the portrait and went to check.

Derek Muir had never been a friend. The truth was Mike had no friends on the island. But the Ranger had always been civil to him, at least. The man's blank stare, which he normally used when dealing with Mike, had disappeared, to be replaced by a look so hostile that Mike halted mid path.

'Where is she? Where's Inga?' he demanded.

'I have no idea.'

'They say you painted her. Is that true?'

'I drew a picture of a girl that looked like Inga, but that was before I even met her . . .' His voice petered out then, aware how improbable his story sounded.

Derek Muir obviously didn't believe it either.

'How did you know Sam Flett was on the causeway?'

'I didn't. I found him by chance.'

Muir's eyes were dark and full of venom. Mike wondered if the man had always hated him, for coming to Sanday, for working on the schoolhouse, for being an outsider, or had the hatred arisen because he now knew of his past?

'You're not wanted here. Your kind are not wanted here,' he emphasized.

My kind?

Mike found a small spark of courage and fanned it. 'I'm not the only one with secrets. I'm not the only one with a past.'

His words had a bigger impact than he'd intended, because Muir suddenly launched himself towards him. Mike stepped back, startled.

'What do you mean?' Muir said, directly into his face.

Mike didn't know what he meant, other than everyone had secrets whether they lived in cities or on small remote islands.

Having encountered the kitchen table, Mike could retreat no further. He thought Muir was about to hit him and flinched in preparation, but the blow never came.

'Leave,' Derek spat at him. 'Leave Sanday as soon as possible.'

The little flame of courage flickered again. 'Or what?' Mike said, astounded at the challenge in his voice.

'Or we'll make you.'

It was what he'd feared as he'd looked back at the school-house after he'd discovered Sam Flett's body and imagined a mob at his door. Maybe he hadn't been wrong about that after all.

'I'm not going anywhere,' Mike heard himself say.

Muir looked deflated by the reply, as though the fight had suddenly gone out of him.

'Then don't say I didn't warn you.'

When Muir left, Mike turned the key in the lock, then went to do the same with the front door.

He'd never felt totally at home here, but he'd never felt frightened before. Not the way he had in his home town. Local newspapers there had carried his face on numerous occasions and brought the hounds to his door. Here, it had only been the prospect of a hard winter that had concerned him. But not any more.

I was lying when I said I wouldn't leave. I'll leave tomorrow. Come back when things settle down. Kirkwall might be sufficiently far enough away, or maybe Thurso on the mainland. He could rent somewhere over the winter. Let the police know where he was, so that it didn't look as though he was running away.

Derek Muir was right. He couldn't stay here. Not until they found the girl. And what if they didn't find her? Or what if they found her body?

Things would only get worse.

At this thought, he started packing, throwing clothes into a rucksack. It was happening all over again. He was cursed for what he'd done to Alice.

41

The hotel looked deserted, but when McNab tried the front door he found it open. Inside, the lights were already on. God, Glasgow could be bleak in winter, but losing daylight this early he couldn't live with.

McNab made his way through to the kitchen in search of Torvaig. When he found no one there, he checked the bar to find it deserted too. He contemplated helping himself to a drink, but when he found himself looking at the whisky bottle rather than the beer, he went upstairs to his room instead.

This time he did need a key, having locked the door when he left the day before.

Stepping in, he had the immediate sense that someone had been in there. He wasn't a bloodhound like Magnus Pirie, so it wasn't smell that did it. He stood in the one spot and, taking his time, swept the room. Once, twice, three times.

It hadn't been tidied, nor had the bed been made. Torvaig had made it clear that his stay in the hotel wouldn't involve the usual room service. He would be fed and watered only, and expected to come and go as he pleased.

The room was untidy with scattered sand visible on the carpet, but was this particular untidiness his own?

Beyond the window, the sea was a thick grey moving mass, meeting an equally slate-coloured horizon. McNab shuddered, remembering how the water had swallowed him up and the seaweed had clutched at him.

Apparently, he hadn't been in the water long, although it had seemed an age to him.

Torvaig said he'd heard his cry as he went over the wall and had come looking for him. McNab suspected it hadn't happened quite like that, although any attempt to extract a possible name or names of his attackers from Torvaig had proved useless.

McNab had told DI Flett he suspected the assault had had something to do with the cold case. He'd done that in order to stay on the island. The truth was he suspected the attack had more to do with standing up for Mike Jones in the bar.

Which brought a face to mind. One he hadn't as yet interviewed. Nor did he even know his name. When he'd asked Torvaig, he'd said he thought the man was part of the crew on one of the boats that occasionally came into the nearby harbour. That was all he knew about him.

It irritated McNab that he hadn't followed up on the guy, but when he'd checked the harbour the following morning, the boat had gone.

Then more pressing matters had taken his attention.

They were no further forward in finding the girl. If she lay dead on this flat island, surely her body would have been found by now? No woodland or scrub to hide her in. No inaccessible areas. And most of the able-bodied population had joined in the search.

Of course, if the sea had taken her, as predicted by Sam Flett, it might never give her up, or it might deposit her on some far-off shore, or at least what was left of her. Was that a worse outcome than finding her dead on Sanday?

Forgetting his unease about a possible visitor when he'd entered the room, he crossed to the window. The signal here was reasonable, his room being directly above the bar on the seaward side. Immediately a series of recent emails and messages came dropping down. Among them, three missed calls from DI Wilson, all made that morning. The boss was keen to talk to him and unwilling it seemed to leave a message to say why.

The CCTV footage was reasonably clear. The man it featured had been seen in the vicinity of Jock Drever's flat around the dates in question. It seemed Chrissy had been the one to suggest who it might be.

'Do we know if Muir was off the island at that time?' DI Wilson asked.

'We don't,' McNab said.

'I suggest you don't alert him, but that you speak to Dr MacLeod and organize a routine DNA swab of all those connected to Sam Flett and Inga Sinclair. We'll check the airline services from here. I'll get DI Flett to do the same for the ferry.'

'Then he'll find out,' McNab said. 'The only secrets here are the ones they want to keep.'

'We'll ask for a list of vehicles crossing around that time. We won't say who we're looking for.'

The boss has no idea how it works up here.

'Can I talk to you, sir?'

A pause.

'Go ahead, Sergeant.'

McNab proceeded to run his mouth off, big time. Would he have been so honest if he'd been standing in front of the boss? He didn't think so. His first admission was that Rhona had dealt much better with the isolation and the outsider feeling than he had. Maybe because she'd been brought up on an island like this. He felt like an alien, with bad breath and a rank smell. The 'Glasgow Detective' was a label used more as an accusation than a description. Okay, he was hated in Glasgow too, but it didn't bother him there, because it didn't usually arise from the people he was trying to help. Sanday inhabitants were for the most part law-abiding and had been policing their island themselves for a long time. Hence no police station. McNab had the distinct feeling that they thought he'd somehow brought trouble with him, or at least made it worse by his presence.

'And they could be right, sir.'

'You believe had you done things differently, Sam Flett might still be alive? And the child might not be missing?'

That about summed it up.

The boss took his studied silence as an admission.

'I'll be in touch with the post-mortem findings on Sam Flett,' he said. 'You set up the DNA screening with Dr MacLeod. As for the search, go over old ground again, including outbuildings previously searched. If her abductor is local, they'll know where you are all of the time. They could be playing cat and mouse with her body.'

'Maybe she's still alive, sir,' he ventured.

The silence this time was on the boss's side.

'Keep in touch, Sergeant.'

McNab rang off then and went downstairs. The bar was still deserted, but this time he did pour himself a drink and chose a whisky.

*

'You're certain?'

'Not certain,' Chrissy hesitated. 'It was out of context, and he was dressed differently.'

Rhona was very aware that clothing and location could play a big part in witness identification. She also knew that eye-witness testimony was notoriously unreliable. In the past it had put numerous innocent people behind bars. Nowadays, the psychology behind how and why witnesses 'recognized' someone from a scene of crime was established, but not yet fully understood.

'But you think there's a possibility it was Derek Muir?'

'I do.' Chrissy paused. 'Also, Bill's been trying to speak to McNab about the DNA screening programme. Is he answering his mobile at all?'

'Intermittently,' Rhona said. 'I'll find him and sort out a schedule.'

'Looks like your twenty-four-hour window might not be enough,' Chrissy said.

There was no answer to that, so Rhona didn't offer one.

42

The search would eventually have to be scaled down. The people of Sanday had work to go to, farms to run, families to look after. If a large-scale search hadn't found Inga by now, it was unlikely to. Perhaps her remains would eventually be discovered years from today, like the numerous other graves that littered Sanday, from Neolithic times through to the Vikings and the possible Beth Haddow. Rhona didn't want to think of that being the outcome, but the more time passed, the likelier it became.

Thick velvety darkness enveloped the car as she made her way back to the cottage, her headlights picking out shadowy buildings, the concrete remnants of the last time the island had been at war. Back then, when government forces had invaded Sanday, the people had accepted their presence, even when it had forced locals off their land and allowed their crops to wither in the fields.

The latest invasion of police personnel hadn't been so welcome.

For many islanders the interest the police had shown in the decades-old grave at the schoolhouse had been deemed disruptive and unnecessary. Sam Flett had definitely been one of them. The theft of the skull and the interference with the soil evidence could have been prompted by such disquiet.

On the other hand, both actions could have been done to try and protect the identity of the victim.

And now a possible sighting of Derek Muir near Jamie Drever's flat in the run-up to the discovery of his dehydrated body. Scotland was a small place, and plenty of folk from Orkney travelled to Glasgow for a variety of reasons. But . . .

Rhona didn't hold entirely with the 'there's no such a thing as coincidence' theory on crime. Life had a habit of ignoring carefully formulated theories on what did or should happen.

By ferrying them about and providing local information, Derek Muir had been close to the investigation. According to her most recent discussion with McNab, he'd run Jock Drever's name past the Ranger the day he'd arrived. So Derek had been forewarned and forearmed about their interest in the man. What he couldn't do was wipe out his trip to Glasgow, if indeed it had ever happened.

Assuming it had, and he had gone to visit Jock Drever, why would he tie up the old man and interrogate him? Had it had something to do with the unearthing of the remains at the schoolhouse? Was that even possible time wise?

For a scientist, it seemed her imagination was taking over. *Imagine the imaginable.*

As she turned a bend in the road, her headlights picked out the strange red-brick building, the only war edifice not to be concrete clad, although it did have a series of concrete supports, perhaps to protect against the shockwaves of any nearby bomb impact. Standing at right angles to the road, the mortuary, like all the other buildings, had been searched and nothing found. One thing had struck her at the time, and a memory of it swept back now.

Unlike the other buildings, the floor of the mortuary had

been raised by at least two feet of manure and sandy soil. How so much of this mix had got inside, she had no idea, except perhaps it being used as a shelter by cattle who'd managed to get in through the doorway. The smell had been pungent, the quantity of muck rising almost as high as the two windows that sat one on either side.

At that point she recalled Inga's boots and the remnants of something similar on them. When surveying the building, she'd given no thought to soil sampling, but talking to Chrissy about it had strengthened the need.

Rhona pulled into the side of the road, and switched off the engine.

The walk across the darkened field to the mortuary wouldn't take long. With her forensic torch to guide her path, her only concern was that livestock using the building as shelter might take umbrage at her visit.

Once out of the vehicle, she realized the night was thick with sound. A short-eared owl, registering her presence, barked in alarm, its flight illuminated by the beam of her flashlight. A group of cows mooed loudly at her passing, but thankfully shifted away rather than towards her. Then her light caught the red-brick wall as it loomed, an ominous shadow before her.

Beyond lay the dark mounds and white hollows of the dunes. After that the moving waters of Lopness Bay. She felt as though she was walking into the past. Seventy-odd years ago a young woman had wandered through here on her way to a shell-sand beach, never to return. Yesterday a little girl had perhaps walked this way in her wellington boots and anorak and not come back either.

The owl's worried alarm call had followed her here and was now joined by the warning beat of the sea. Under her feet, the grass ended and the churned-up sand, manure and mud began.

Rhona hesitated, but only briefly, then made her way towards the seaward end of the building, and the dark open portal of the old mortuary.

43

Inga's mother was alone this time, and when she opened the door to him, he could read her terrified thoughts and sought immediately to reassure her, although the words he used weren't really comforting.

'We haven't found Inga yet.'

Her face, initially showing signs of panic, now dissolved into despair. McNab wasn't sure which expression was worse.

'May I come in?'

She nodded and he followed her into the sitting room, where she sat down next to the fire, staring at it rather than him.

'You'll stop the search soon,' she said.

'We'll scale it down, but we won't stop.'

Huddled into herself, she barely acknowledged his reply.

'Can I ask you a few questions?'

'I don't know any more than I've told you.'

'It's about your life before you came here.'

Her eyes flicked up at him. 'I told you about that.'

'Do you have a photograph of your former partner?'

'Why?' She regarded him suspiciously.

'If you have one, may I see it?'

She seemed to give up on the answer or denial she'd planned and rose.

Leaving the room, she returned a few minutes later and

handed him a passport-size photograph. 'That's Joe. I threw out the rest,' she said. 'I don't know why that one survived. Maybe to give me a focus for my hate.'

McNab studied the face in the photograph. Dark-haired like his daughter, and handsome in a bullish way. He was clean-shaven in this, but McNab sketched in the three-day stubble.

'His height?'

'About the same as you, but broader.'

'What did he do as a job?'

'Shipyards for a while, manual work, some time on a fishing boat.'

'If he was to come here looking for you, what would happen?'

Now the fear was as bright and hot as the fire that burned behind her.

'There's no way he would know to come to Sanday. I've been very careful about that.'

'Would Inga be able to contact him?' McNab tried.

She shook her head. 'Inga wouldn't do that. She knew . . .'

'About the beatings?' McNab finished for her.

Her face crumpled. 'I don't know. I tried not to make a noise, but sometimes . . .'

'Did Joe ever threaten or hurt Inga?'

She shook her head.

'But you thought he might?'

'I was afraid . . . if she tried to intervene. That's why I left.'

McNab looked again at the photograph. 'How recent is this?'

'It was taken about ten years ago.'

There was no easy way to tell her, so he came right out with it. 'I may have seen this man. Here on Sanday.'

'What?' She sprang to her feet in shock.

'He came off a fishing boat docked in Kettletoft harbour.'

She covered her mouth with a shaking hand.

'He warned me not to take her away from him. He warned me.' She looked at McNab with pleading eyes. 'Please. You have to get her back.'

'Can I use your landline? The signal here . . .'

'Of course. It's in the hall. Will I make us some tea?'

McNab nodded, not because he wanted tea, but because she needed something to do.

DI Flett listened intently as he spun his latest tale, then talked about the police launch and the coastguard. McNab felt immediately out of his comfort zone when dealing with the sea rather than inner-city streets.

'We'll make contact with any fishing boats in the vicinity. See if we can track him down.' There was a moment of silence before DI Flett said, 'Well done, Detective Sergeant.'

More used to reprimands than being congratulated, McNab had no idea how to respond, so hung up instead.

Inga's mother was waiting anxiously in the living room.

'What are you going to do?' she said, handing McNab a mug of tea.

'You said he never hurt Inga,' McNab reminded her. 'If I'm right and the man I saw was your former partner and he has snatched Inga, there's no reason to suppose he would hurt her now. His intention may have been to hurt you by taking her.'

That made a sort of sense to her.

'Until we check this out, I'd rather you didn't mention it to anyone. If he is here, it might alert him.'

'Okay,' she said, although she didn't look convinced.

'I've called PC Tulloch. He's on his way and will stay with you overnight.'

She looked relieved.

'I'll make up a bed for him on the couch.'

Her mention of the couch reminded McNab of his own sleeping arrangements. He'd fully intended going back to the hotel, but in view of the latest developments, he decided he should call in on Rhona on the way back and let her know what had happened.

The schoolhouse was in darkness when he passed. McNab had little time for the paedo, but if they did find the girl with her father, it would let Mike Jones off the hook, for this one at least.

Feeling the undercarriage hit the raised grassy centre of the track, he slowed down. Having got himself on the right side of DI Flett, he didn't want to ruin it by wrecking a police vehicle. That thought made him recall being brought here by Derek Muir the night he'd arrived on Sanday. How he'd run Jock Drever's name past the Ranger.

McNab tried to recall the man's reaction. There had been, he thought, no disquiet at his enquiry. Most of the uneasiness had been on his own side, as he'd looked out on the emptiness of Sanday and realized what he'd come to.

If it was Muir that Chrissy had spotted on CCTV, he could have been in that part of Glasgow for any number of reasons. With nothing at all to do with Jock Drever.

And yet.

Derek Muir had exhibited little emotion about any of the subsequent events that had happened on Sanday. McNab had read this as the natural reticence of an Orkney islander. Sam Flett, on the other hand, had been much more emotional in his dealings with the police, on both the cold case and Inga's disappearance.

I even thought the old guy had lost his wits. Particularly over those muslin flowers.

McNab revisited that night in the pub when he'd almost met a watery grave. It had been Derek Muir who'd brought him here to Rhona. He owed the man that at least.

Drawing up in front of the cottage, he noted that only the porch light was on. He'd expected Rhona to be home by now. Either she wasn't or else she'd decided to have an early night.

He sat for a minute with the engine running, hoping if the latter were true, the sound of his arrival might rouse her. When that patently wasn't the case, he made a decision and got out.

His knock brought no response, so he checked below the stone to find the key was no longer there. Either she *was* inside or she'd taken the key with her. As a last resort, McNab headed round to the rear of the building in search of the elusive mobile signal.

The schoolhouse had been in darkness as she'd approached, yet Mike Jones's pickup stood outside. Rhona imagined him switching off the lights every time she spotted a car on the distant road, whether they were destined to turn his way or not at the crossroads.

And she couldn't blame him for that.

He'd come to Sanday thinking to start a new life and instead had walked into a nightmare, not this time of his own making. His past, which clearly haunted him by his blurted confession in the pub, had become even more untenable here, where there was nowhere to hide.

Then a thought occurred.

If Mike Jones was so obsessed with watching the road for possible visitors, was there a chance he'd spotted Sam's jeep going past on its way to Cata Sand?

Rhona drew up behind Jones's car and doused the engine.

The wind had picked up, whipping at her body as she stood awaiting a response to her knock on the front door. When one didn't materialize, she checked and found it locked. Aware he rarely used it as an entrance, leading as it did through the part of the building still being renovated, she decided to head round the back.

The outside light sprang on as she turned the corner of the building, illuminating the mound of broken tar and earth from the excavation. Her pinned tarp was gone, of course. As she'd removed it, she'd advised Mike to put plyboard over the gaping hole until the digger came back to fill it in. He'd said he would, but by the looks of things, the hole hadn't been refilled yet.

Or Hugh Clouston, having discovered Mike's secret, had refused to come back and do the job.

Which, she thought, was a possibility. Whether proved innocent or not of any wrongdoing with Inga Sinclair, Mike Jones – his past misdemeanours now common knowledge – was unlikely to remain on Sanday.

From her own island experience, she knew that the background of incomers to remote parts of Scotland was rarely more colourful than those who'd been born and bred there.

But people, whether town or country dwellers, shared a particular aversion to the thought that their children were in danger from a paedophile, and once branded as such . . .

The outside light, on a timer, went out. Rhona moved, hoping the sensor would spring it on again. When it didn't immediately do so, she switched on her torch. There were no lights on in this section of the building and no smoke coming from the chimney, which was in itself unusual.

Rhona approached the back door and was surprised to find it standing partly open. Perturbed now, she pushed the door wide and called out.

'Mike, are you there? It's Rhona MacLeod.'

Her call entered the building and was swallowed by the shadows.

In all her visits to the schoolhouse, she'd never encountered such a feeling of emptiness. Now on high alert, she stepped inside, to find the air in the big room chilly, confirming that the stove had burned too low or gone out.

That wouldn't happen. Not if he was here.

As Rhona called out a second time, she caught a scent she immediately recognized. The older the blood, the sweeter it smelt. This smell wasn't old. Some people couldn't smell blood at all; others might smell a bottle cap's worth of blood in a large room. Sensitivity depended on the person. Magnus, with his hyperosmia, might have found a myriad ways to describe blood deposits, both human and animal. Rhona, on the other hand, knew only that this blood had been spilt recently.

Swinging her beam around the room, she sought its source. When she couldn't find it, she located the nearest light switch and, covering her hand with her sleeve, turned it on.

The room burst into light, blinding her for a moment.

Now frantic to find the source of the smell, she surveyed the dishevelled room, aware that in all likelihood this was a crime scene, and if she entered without kitting up, she would be contaminating the locus.

Yet Mike Jones might still be alive, if I can locate his body.

Minutes later she'd established that the scent of blood that had drawn her inside had come from a struggle, and not directly from a body itself. In fact, the scattered trail led from the centre of the room back to the door she'd entered by.

Wherever Mike Jones was bleeding, it wasn't in here.

Rhona retreated, checking the step to find more blood splatters on the concrete and the lower part of the door. Her exit, picked up by the sensor, fired up the outside light and it sprang on again, its circle terminating just short of the mound of earth and broken tar.

Directing her beam at the immediate area around the back step, she established two sets of prints in the disturbed soil, the larger she assumed to be Mike's. The footprints moved on, Mike's leading, the other following. Keeping to one side of these, she followed their path, which led beyond what looked like a scuffle, towards the excavation site.

Her heart upping its pace, Rhona followed, already knowing where Mike's flight had led.

Her beam eventually found him, face down in the open grave he had so feared. It looked as though he'd fallen into it by accident. His legs, too long to fit, were spread awkwardly up the side nearest the door.

Like a raggedy doll, she thought.

In the light of her torch, blood had streamed from the area of his ear, explaining the trail that had led her there.

Rhona crouched and reached down, seeking a pulse, yet knowing that in a neck that lay at such an angle, she was unlikely to find one.

44

He poured the strong coffee into a flask, ignoring the desire to add a tot of whisky, and headed back to the tent. The wind had been kind to them, allowing Rhona to process the scene under shelter, but there was no guarantee it would stay that way for much longer. The darkness had eventually been broken by moonlight, but daylight was still some way off.

Whatever had happened to Mike Jones had begun in the bedroom. That had been evident from the state of the place.

As Rhona had processed the body, McNab had worked the schoolhouse. Waiting for forensic help from wherever they might send it had seemed like a non-starter. He'd managed enough crime scenes to know what was required, but still found himself checking with Rhona to be certain he'd thought of everything.

As he walked back along the track to the sound of the sea and the eerie cry of an owl, he found himself desperate to be back among sandstone walls, noisy polluting traffic and the sound of Glasgow voices.

The longer we stay, the worse it gets.

Their arrival had been the catalyst for all that had followed. Their poking about in the past had unleashed a darkness that had set neighbour upon neighbour and destroyed the tranquillity of the island.

Fuck it! People do bad things everywhere.

McNab composed himself and, throwing the flap open, entered the tent, brandishing the flask.

'Coffee?'

The eyes Rhona turned on him were tired, but there was a resolve there he recognized. Often that same resolve had played against his wishes, both personal and professional.

She carefully laid her notes aside and accepted the cup he poured for her.

'I told Sean I would be back yesterday, or maybe the day before. I've lost track,' she admitted.

'You should call him,' McNab said.

She met his eye. 'Have you called Freya?'

He shook his head, then voiced something he'd been avoiding. 'It's not going to work. With Freya,' he added.

'Can I ask why?'

He could have said, *because I'd rather be with you*, but didn't. 'Because she's clever and young and she makes me feel old and sad.'

She looked distressed by his attempt at an upbeat admission. 'That's not good.'

'No,' he acknowledged, 'it isn't.' Deciding he didn't like where the conversation was headed, he quickly changed the subject. 'How did the paedo die?'

'His neck's broken. Probably when he went into the grave.'

'And the head injury?'

'It's bloody round the ear, but superficially it doesn't appear severe enough to kill him.'

'Was he murdered?'

'There are fingermarks on his back which suggest he was probably pushed into the grave.'

'Would you be able to match the marks to hands?'

304

'Possibly.' Her voice faltered, as though the well of determination had just run dry.

'Go and get some sleep,' he ordered. 'It's my turn to stay with the body.'

'The ambulance is coming?'

'At daybreak. And the police helicopter.'

'Okay,' she nodded. 'Will you stay with him until they come?'

He noted she didn't say 'it' but 'him'. That, he realized, summed up Rhona MacLeod.

'I will,' he promised.

'Then I'll grab some sleep.'

She left then, and it was McNab's turn to commune with the dead.

The ambulance arrived as dawn streaked the sky. This time the doctor didn't accompany it. Mike Jones's body was to be directly transferred to the helicopter waiting at the airfield, then taken south.

Watching the helicopter rise in a flurry of noise and wind, McNab wondered if he could have done more to prevent the latest death. He'd accused Jones of terrible things. Some true, some unproven. Yet still they were back in a world where a child was missing and two of the suspects in her disappearance were already dead.

45

Something was happening on Cata Sand. Something that involved pickup trucks and piles of wood. DI Flett instructed McNab to pull up next to the brickie hut.

'Bonfire night,' he told them. 'It's a tradition on Sanday to have the fire on the sands.'

McNab opened his mouth, no doubt to emit some sarcastic remark, then thought better of it. Something had happened between McNab and Erling. Something positive. And it was plain to Rhona that McNab was trying to maintain the mood.

Having deposited a load of wood, a jeep recognizable as the Ranger's was heading their way from the beach. Rhona now understood Erling's reason for stopping. None of them had seen Derek Muir since Chrissy's revelation and the discovery of Mike Jones's body. Erling, she suspected, having recognized the vehicle, was about to address that.

As the jeep climbed from the beach, Erling got out of the car and walked towards it.

From where they were sitting, the interchange between the two men appeared cordial. Once or twice the Ranger glanced at their car, but whatever Erling was saying didn't appear to worry him unduly.

Moments later Erling was back, but they had to wait until they were on the main road before he revealed what had been said.

'I told him we're planning a mass DNA sampling and asked him to help spread the word.'

'How did he react?' Rhona asked.

'As always. Interested and helpful.'

McNab came in. 'What about Mike Jones?'

'He was obviously upset about that. Said he'd called in on Jones yesterday.'

'Why?' McNab demanded.

'He was worried by the pub incident and wanted to check that Jones was okay.'

That sounds like Derek, Rhona thought. 'Did he say at what time?'

'Around five.'

'Did he have wind of someone heading Jones's way?' McNab asked.

'No.'

McNab made a sound that suggested disbelief. 'How close is Muir's place to the schoolhouse?'

'He lives on the headland at Lopness. The house is only really visible from the bay.'

Before McNab could respond, a pickup stacked high with wood came bombing towards them. Erling told McNab to draw into the next passing place and let it have the road, which didn't please McNab one bit, but gained him a raised salute in thanks from the driver.

'It's better if we keep the locals on side,' Erling said in response to McNab's disgruntled expression.

McNab caught Rhona's eye via the mirror. 'I intend interviewing Muir about the Glasgow connection later today.'

Rhona immediately intervened. 'Is that wise? I thought we planned to run the DNA check first?'

Erling came in next, surprising her by his response. 'I

agree with Sergeant McNab. Let's see what Derek Muir has to say about his visit to Glasgow.'

McNab's head shot round. 'You know he was definitely there?'

'I heard back from Kirkwall airport this morning. They confirmed that Derek Muir flew to Glasgow three days before you discovered the body of Jamie Drever, and returned the day before the body was discovered,' Erling said.

Rhona heard McNab's expletive, which wasn't remarked upon by his superior officer.

'You're okay with me interviewing him, sir?'

'You're MIT. I'm just the local contact, Detective Sergeant.'

Silence fell as they travelled the remaining few kilometres to the community centre. McNab's jawline was set, his eyes fixed on the road. Thankfully they didn't meet another car. Rhona couldn't imagine McNab giving way a second time, even on the orders of a superior officer.

Rhona had taken up residence in one of the back rooms normally used for meetings. The additional manpower Erling had brought with him on the dawn helicopter meant her help wasn't required to take either prints or mouth swabs, which left her free to do other things.

She'd told Chrissy she would head back today regardless of whether they'd found Inga or not. That, of course, was before they'd discovered Mike Jones's body, but having pro-cessed that particular crime scene, she was free to leave the island and return to Glasgow and her lab.

Except that she didn't feel she could. Not yet anyway. Which is what she told Chrissy.

'When I heard about Mike Jones, I guessed as much.'

'Any word on Sam Flett's post-mortem?' Rhona said.

'There's a report winging its way to you, but in a nutshell, he drowned.'

'The head injury?'

'The pathologist found rock and seaweed fragments in the wound.'

'But the blow didn't kill him?'

'No. The water did. With no evidence to the contrary, the conclusion was he lost his footing, banged his head and drowned.' Chrissy was quiet for a moment. 'I do have some good news, however. I assume you're currently online?'

'I am.'

'Then take a look at what they've fashioned from the photograph you sent of the skull.'

Rhona waited impatiently as the email attachment downloaded.

'Is it there?' Chrissy said.

'It is.' Rhona clicked it open.

She found it difficult to conjure up the image of a human face from the bare bones of a skull. Thankfully it hadn't been a problem for the digital artist who, with imagination and skill, had created this.

'What do you think?' Chrissy's voice expressed her own excitement.

'It's very good,' Rhona said.

'Will someone recognize it?'

'Someone already has.'

Magnus looked from the old photograph to the reconstructed face on the screen and back again.

'The likeness is strong,' he finally admitted.

'But?' she prodded.

'But if we desire something enough, we can often convince ourselves that it's true.'

'I don't *want* it to be her,' Rhona countered.

'Maybe not, but it might offer some explanation for Sam's fear for Inga.'

'It doesn't help us find the child.'

'No,' Magnus said, his expression one of deep thought.

'But if Inga's great-aunt did go missing during the war, surely her mother would have known about it from her grandfather?'

'Do you know everything about the generations that came before you?' he countered.

Rhona was aware that she was adopted and that her birth mother had been the woman she'd called Aunt Lily, her adopted mother's sister. She even knew that her biological father had been called Robert Curtis. But further back than that, no. She had no idea.

'In those times,' Magnus reminded her, 'folk didn't discuss family business with their children. Or with anyone else for that matter.'

'So there's no one left alive now on Sanday to confirm the identity of the victim.'

'There's Don Cutts,' he reminded her. 'You were planning to show him the reconstruction, if only to confirm it isn't the Beth Haddow he spoke of.'

Rhona nodded. They would ask the old man to come in. Show him the reconstructed image.

There was another way to confirm if the body in the grave was a member of the Sinclair family, and that was to test their DNA. The same was true of the relationship between Sam and Jamie Drever. Although it hardly seemed important now that Sam was dead.

'I wondered if Sam suspected and looked for Jamie Drever. I thought he might have been the one to interrogate Jock,' she admitted.

'But he never left the island?'

'Apparently not.'

'And Derek Muir did.'

Rhona nodded.

'So what, if anything, was the connection between Derek Muir and Jamie Drever?'

'I have an aunt in Glasgow. I visit her twice a year.'

The Ranger looked relaxed and not remotely put out by McNab's opening question.

'Where does your aunt live?'

Derek Muir gave an address McNab recognized as being in the East End, not far from Jock Drever's place.

'You can check with her if you like, although her memory's not so good these days. She has Alzheimer's.'

'Did you speak to anyone else on your travels?' McNab said.

'I don't know anyone else in Glasgow, so no.'

'Not even Jamie Drever?'

That brought him up short. The Ranger observed McNab, a puzzled expression on his face. 'Jamie Drever? Is that the man you spoke about when you arrived? Wasn't he called Jock?'

'We're all Jocks in the army.'

'You have experience of army life, Sergeant? I didn't realize.'

McNab ignored what he regarded as an obvious deflection.

'You were seen in the vicinity of Jock's flat, just before he died.'

The Ranger looked puzzled. 'If he lives near my aunt, then I suppose that's possible.'

'Why did your family leave Sanday?'

The sudden shift in topic seemed to catch Muir off guard and for a moment he didn't appear so sure of his ground. Then he came back. 'My father got a job in Peterhead. Why?'

'Doing what?'

'Same as before. On a fishing boat.'

'But you spent your childhood in Glasgow?'

He looked nonplussed at that, then shrugged. 'It was a long time ago, Sergeant. My parents parted company, that's all I know.'

'Where's your father now?'

A shadow crossed his face. 'He's dead.'

'You're sure of that?'

'I have the death certificate to prove it.'

McNab sat back in his chair. 'So now that Jock's gone, there's no one left to tell the tale.'

'What tale?' The Ranger fashioned a look of bewilderment.

'Why the girl buried in the schoolhouse grounds died.'

There was a knock at the door. McNab checked his watch, then called, 'Come in.'

Don Cutts, it seemed, was a stickler for timing. The door opened and the wheelchair entered.

The two Sanday men exchanged surprised looks.

'Ranger?'

Muir collected himself and smiled at the old man. 'Don. How are you?'

'Good.'

'I take it you're helping the police with their enquiries?' Muir said, with a twinkle in his eye that annoyed McNab.

'I just gave my DNA sample,' Cutts said, full of self-importance. He looked from Muir to McNab. 'So, Detective Sergeant. I believe you have something you want me to take a look at?'

'I have.' McNab turned the laptop round so they could both view the screen. 'This is an image of the young woman in the schoolhouse grave.'

Whatever either man was expecting, it wasn't this.

'How did you do that without the skull?' the old man said, impressed.

McNab smiled. 'Don't you just love forensic science.'

Muir said nothing, but his eyes were immediately drawn to the screen. McNab watched as both faces assimilated the image. It wasn't a photograph, but it was real enough. Don Cutts muttered something under his breath. A phrase McNab couldn't interpret. Muir's expression never changed and he remained silent.

The old man eventually spoke. 'That's not Beth Haddow, although it does look a peedie bit like her.' He continued to peer more at the screen.

'Have you any idea who it might be?'

McNab watched as a thought took root and grew. Eventually the old man turned to him, and now McNab could see how distressed he had become.

'It might be Ola Sinclair.' He shook his head in dismay. 'God, is that what happened to the lass? We heard she'd gone to work on the mainland.'

'Tell me what you remember about her.'

It took a few moments for Cutts to muster himself.

'The women like Beth Haddow, who came with the forces,

were,' he hesitated, 'more available, so to speak, than island women. Ola kept herself to herself, although I did see her at the camp dances occasionally.'

'Can you remember who may have been interested in Ola back then?'

'Just about everyone, I'd say. She was a bonny lass.' A thought crossed his face. One that obviously disturbed him. 'I did see her once or twice with Eric Flett, but I didn't think it was serious. I thought Eric was keen on Beth Haddow, but it's so long ago, Sergeant. I'm not sure if what I remember is even true.' He shook his head.

'What about the other man you mentioned. The older one?'

McNab watched as Don Cutts probed his memories of seventy years ago.

'The truth is, that guy hung about all the women. And for the most part, they liked it. I told you I wanted to know what it was about him that made them so keen.'

'Describe him for me.'

'But I did that already,' the old man said, puzzled.

'Do it again.'

As Don repeated his description, McNab watched the Ranger. Muir's face remained impassive, but the emotion in his eyes couldn't be blanked.

It was strange how a dam was breached, the wall of lies swept away, the truth cascading out like a flood. In the job, McNab had seen it happen many times, with good and with bad people. With a truly evil person, it might never happen. A natural-born killer, from McNab's experience, nursed a belief in their divine right to do whatever was necessary for their own self-gratification, or survival.

Derek Muir, in his opinion, was not such a person.

After the revelation of the image and his story, Don Cutts had departed, none the wiser as to why the Ranger had been present during the discussion. So much a part of island life, McNab realized that Muir's presence was natural and acceptable anywhere, at any time.

McNab waited until the door shut behind Cutts, before asking, 'Was the man Mr Cutts described your father?'

Derek Muir said nothing, his expression as closed as before. McNab wondered if that particular look had been fashioned in childhood, as a means of protection. Sam Flett had drawn a picture of Derek Muir as a troubled youngster, hardened by city life. He'd brought that toughness back with him, making his return to the island difficult. But Muir had succeeded in making himself an islander again. He'd been accepted back into the community. Built a reputation. Become a valued member of the community, of the stature of Sam Flett.

Then the body was unearthed . . .

'When did you know?' McNab said quietly.

Derek Muir's eyes finally met his and McNab viewed the agony behind the stony countenance.

'That my father was a murderer?' His voice shook with emotion.

'You know that for certain?'

Muir shook his head. 'No, but I suspect it, as do you, and no doubt once she examines all the forensic evidence, your Dr MacLeod will prove it.'

His face, although still impassive, had turned a sickly grey colour.

'We're not responsible for the sins of our fathers,' McNab found himself saying.

Muir gave him a small but pitying smile. 'You think so, Detective Sergeant? And what if your father was exposed as a murderer? How would that sit with your job as a detective? How would it sit with you as his son?'

McNab didn't answer the question, knowing full well that it would fuck up his job. As it would fuck with him too.

They sat in silence for a moment, although McNab sensed that now the dam had burst, Muir was keen to reveal everything.

'How did you find Jock Drever?' he said.

'My aunt told me, in one of her moments of clarity, that she'd seen him near her place. I already knew my father had been a violent man, and that my mother had found out something he'd done that had frightened her enough to make her leave Sanday. I didn't want to dig around here for the answer, so I went looking for Jock to ask him.'

'What happened?'

Muir had been waiting for that question and immediately answered. 'He refused to discuss anything about Sanday back then. I suspected he was keeping something from me, so I . . . persisted.' He looked stricken by the admission. 'I know now he was keeping quiet to protect Ella, and of course Sam, but I was desperate to find out the truth . . .' There he halted.

'You tied him up?'

He nodded. 'But I didn't hit him. Nothing like that. Eventually, he asked about Ella and his son. I told him Ella was dead but that Sam was alive and well . . .' He hesitated.

McNab, recognizing there was more to come, kept silent.

'Then the body was unearthed.' Muir glanced at McNab.

'I knew right away that the fearful ramblings of my aunt were true.' His voice broke. 'Was it my fault Jamie Drever died?'

'You untied him?' McNab said.

'Yes. And gave him water. He asked me to turn on the fire. He said he was cold. What happened after that?'

'He died in the chair. Dehydration probably.'

A terrible silence followed.

Muir turned stricken eyes on him. 'Then I'm a killer. Just like my father.'

McNab asked one final question.

'Why are you so sure your father killed Ola Sinclair?'

'Once my father decided he wanted something, he would never be denied it.'

46

McNab understood the sentiment. He didn't relish being denied either. And he never gave up. Did that make him bad? Or capable of murder?

If a job's worth doing, it's worth doing well.

Those had been his mother's constant words to him. Though McNab wasn't certain he'd always followed her instructions the way she'd intended. Determined, against the odds, to complete a job? Yes, he'd done that. It was the way he'd done it that could be called into question.

I've been on my best behaviour up here on Sanday Island. I've attempted to be civil to the locals. I haven't come on to Rhona, even when the opportunity presented itself.

But he'd definitely screwed up his relationship with Freya. What if they'd had a child together? How would he have felt if she'd taken the child away from him?

But Joe Millar was violent to his partner. I would never do that. Never say never.

McNab's intimate thoughts, not expressed on his face, he hoped, were now interrupted by a question from his island superior, DI Flett.

'Where's Muir now?'

'He's writing a statement, sir. PC Tulloch's with him.'

By DI Flett's expression, he hadn't been fooled by McNab's deferential tone.

'He's been swabbed?'

'Yes, sir, and his fingerprints taken.'

'Did you question him any further about the girl and Mike Jones?'

McNab decided attack was his best defence, so went for it. 'I chose not to interrupt the confession, sir. Also we need someone, who isn't connected to Muir, to sit in on any further interviews.'

DI Flett raised an eyebrow. 'Which, Sergeant, rules out just about every officer currently on Sanday, including myself.'

'Yes, sir.'

'What about Dr MacLeod? Or Professor Pirie?' DI Flett offered.

McNab wanted to say a definite no to Pirie, using the fact that he'd been a visitor to the island as a teenager, and undoubtedly would have met the Ranger then, but something stopped him.

'Let's use them both,' he said.

'We'll ask any further questions required here, Sergeant, before transferring Muir to Kirkwall.'

Muir would be charged with regard to the theft of the skull and the destruction of the forensic evidence. In relation to the death of Jock Drever, things weren't so clear. McNab found himself concerned by the imminent removal of the Ranger. And not for altruistic reasons.

'Why not keep him here, sir, until we work out what happened to the girl? He's the one with the most extensive knowledge of the island, and its inhabitants.' He didn't add, *after Sam Flett*, but it was implied.

'I agree.'

DI Flett was observing him in such a positive manner that McNab almost squirmed.

'I'd like to get a coffee, sir, before joining the others.'

'Go ahead, Sergeant.'

McNab made for the coffee machine, as keen to get away from DI Flett as he was to satisfy his caffeine craving. He found Hege on duty at the coffee table and they exchanged nods.

'A double?'

'Make it a treble,' McNab ordered.

As he accepted the cup, she said, 'Will you be at the hotel tonight?'

McNab shot her a glance. 'Why?'

'I'd like to talk to you about something.'

Immediately suspicious, McNab wanted to ask what, but was thwarted by DI Flett signalling him to hurry up.

'I should be there by six,' he said. 'I'll meet you in the bar.'

'Muir admitted to taking the skull from the deposition site and hiding it in the mound,' McNab told the assembled group.

'And afterwards?' Rhona asked.

'He noticed you checking out the place. Waited until you left, then removed it, this time to the lighthouse,' McNab said.

'I have photographs of the footprints from the mound entrance, which should match those of Derek Muir if his story's true. We can also compare the DNA of the victim to the Sinclair family and possibly confirm if it was Muir's father who wielded the pilot knife.'

'You doubt it?' McNab interrupted.

'I prefer to prove it,' Rhona said. 'Or are we taking Don Cutts's word on everything that happened back then?'

'Muir believes his father did it,' McNab countered.

'That doesn't mean it's true.' Rhona looked to Erling. 'Is there anyone else alive on Sanday that might corroborate Don's story of Derek's father and Ola Sinclair?'

'I'll find out,' Erling said.

Rhona nodded her thanks. Putting thoughts on the cold case to one side, she drew their attention to the soil map of Sanday that was now displayed on the big screen.

'A friend and colleague, an expert in forensic soil analysis, has done a rush job on Inga's boots to see if we can pinpoint where she was on the island when she last wore them.

'The deposits indicate that Inga was in an area of the map which is coloured pink. As you can see, there are only two sections on the north of the island where she could have encountered such material. The major one lies here,' she indicated the northern edge of Lopness Bay. 'That's where the remnants of the RAF camp are, through which Inga would have walked to Sam Flett's house. The other segment lies along the southern shore of Start Island not far from the shell beach.' She waited until they'd assimilated the significance of the information, before continuing.

'The same classification of soil was found in the grooves of Sam's waterlogged boots, yet the pedals of his jeep were encrusted with shell sand, suggesting Sam wasn't the person who drove the jeep onto Cata Sand.'

'Did you retrieve any other trace evidence from the vehicle?' Erling said.

'I lifted fingerprints from the steering wheel and the door handle, and from the child's wellington boots.'

'But how does all this help us find Inga?' McNab said, a note of frustration evident in his voice.

'We know that Sam was in the habit of leaving his jeep at the gate near the road end, and walking from there to the croft house,' Rhona said. 'When we visited Inga's mother the night the child went missing, the jeep wasn't there, neither was it outside his croft or at the road end.'

Rhona waited, as a small light began to dawn on the faces around her.

'The bastard used the jeep to abduct her,' McNab said. 'The kid thought it was Sam waiting for her to go to the museum.' He halted. 'But wouldn't Sam have noticed his jeep was missing, when he went to Inga's house that morning?'

'Why would he bother to check? No one steals your car on Sanday,' Rhona reminded him. 'And immediately afterwards he joined the search.'

They all turned to Magnus at this point.

'The idea's a plausible one,' he agreed. 'According to her mother, Inga liked and trusted Sam Flett. Therefore she had good reason to approach his jeep, especially since it was Saturday, a day she would normally accompany him to the heritage centre. But if it was a stranger behind the wheel . . .'

McNab interrupted him. 'What if it wasn't a stranger?'

All eyes turned to the photograph which now appeared on the screen.

'Dr MacLeod and PC Tulloch will confirm that this is the man who threatened Mike Jones the night I was attacked at the hotel. He has since been identified by Inga's mother as Joseph Millar, Inga's father, who has a history of domestic violence.

'The fishing boat Joseph Millar was on left Sanday on

Saturday morning. DI Flett has made contact with the captain of the *Lucinda* and he confirms that Millar didn't report back and as a result they left Kettletoft without him. Inga's mother believes her former partner could have taken Inga, in revenge for her leaving him.'

'Is he likely to harm the girl?' Rhona said.

'According to the mother, he hasn't,' McNab said. 'Up till now.'

'Is it likely then that Millar was involved in the attack on Mike Jones?' Erling said.

'Forensic evidence collected in the schoolhouse went south this morning with the body,' Rhona confirmed. 'It'll also be checked against what we found in the jeep.'

McNab was the one to break the silence that followed. 'If Millar did use the jeep to snatch his daughter, then abandoned it on Cata Sand, where did he go from there? And what did he use for transport?'

Rhona now voiced what she'd been thinking all along.

'What if he had a boat somewhere within walking distance of Cata Sand?'

A brief silence followed, before Magnus said, 'Dr MacLeod could be right. The majority of small crafts are already laid up for the winter. The chances are an owner wouldn't miss one right away, particularly if it was taken from a holiday home.'

'So we start looking for the boat,' McNab said.

47

When they'd dispersed for the night, McNab had indicated he was heading back to the hotel to eat. Rhona had turned down his invitation to accompany him.

'I'll pick something up at the community shop.'

'You sure?'

At that moment she'd almost acquiesced. After all, they'd have plenty to discuss over whatever delicious meal Torvaig prepared for them, but McNab's expression, half inviting, half pleading, had decided her.

'I'll see you in the morning,' she'd said.

Now, entering Lady Village, Rhona drew up outside the community shop. Its neighbour, the heritage centre, lay in darkness, the door shut and no doubt locked, although she still had the key Sam Flett had given her. Thinking of the old man now, she felt saddened and perturbed by his death, because she too had crossed the causeway. She knew how simple it would be to lose your footing and fall, hitting your head on the rocks. She also recognized how easy it could have been for someone to make that fall happen, and for there to be no evidence to show that had been the case.

And if Joe Millar had used Sam's jeep to abduct Inga . . .

Locking the car from an urban habit, Rhona crossed to the heritage centre.

Since McNab had revealed the possible identity of the

body in the schoolhouse playground, and the man who might be responsible for her death, she'd been going over and over it in her head, trying to work out the geography of what had happened that night, all those years ago. Sam would have been the person to discuss the layout of the RAF camp with, but of course Sam was no longer there for her to ask.

But the material he collected is.

The key turned easily and, stepping inside, she threw on the light switch. Standing there in the sudden brightness, she realized she'd hardly spent five minutes in the museum without Sam's benign presence. That thought, plus the solemn emptiness of the place, only served to emphasize the sense of loss.

Gathering her thoughts, she looked around at the familiar display of Sanday through the war, knowing that what she really needed was a map of the general layout of the former camp, with its proximity to the causeway, the shell beach, the schoolhouse and the Sinclair place.

Such a thing had to be in the research room.

Opening the door, she was reminded of her first visit, recalling how captivated she'd been by the material she'd discovered there, most of it seemingly nothing to do with the excavation.

How wrong she'd been.

Locating an Ordnance Survey map of the area, she spread it out on the table and, retrieving various sketches from the folder, placed them alongside. She then fetched the booklet prepared by people who remembered Sanday at that time, and who'd worked in or visited the camp. Their descriptions of life would help her identify the buildings, and how they'd been used. Plus, she had her own selection of photographs of those left standing.

Bringing up the soil map on her laptop, Rhona settled down to study the collage she'd created.

The single road ran north, hugging Lopness Bay, eventually forming a loop round the North Loch with a single rough track veering off towards Ayre Sound and Start Island. The only other paths led to isolated houses, many now derelict.

But not back then.

The land requisitioned for the erection of the radar masts and the RAF camp had been lost to locals, but not their homes. And one of those houses had been occupied by Derek Muir's family, even though his father had been away at sea most of the time.

Studying the map, aware now of the proximity of possible pathways, Rhona could see how a meeting between Ola Sinclair and her attacker might have taken place. Judging by the remains of her clothing, she'd been on a night out, possibly attending a dance at the camp. After which, she'd never reached home. So why had her family not raised the alarm?

Maybe she thought she was leaving the island, and left a note to that effect?

Was that where Don Cutts's story of her going off to the mainland had come from?

They might establish her identity and even the likely identity of her attacker, but they would never know the whole story of what had happened that night, nor why Eric Flett had disappeared straight after.

The chances are we'll never know.

Jamie Drever's parallel departure, she suspected, had more to do with his relationship with Ella than any contact he'd had with Ola. Perhaps Geordie had discovered their relationship and that had been the outcome.

How terrible to discover his young wife had betrayed him.

And yet it seemed that Sam Flett, however he'd been conceived, had enjoyed a happy childhood. His father hadn't punished the child, or his wife, for Sam's conception. It appeared the sombre figure in the family photograph had truly loved Ella, because he'd brought up her child as though it had been his own.

The thought of that child brought Rhona back to Inga.

Rhona hadn't admitted this out loud, or even to herself, but the odds were definitely against the girl being alive. Her fleeting hope that somehow Sam had hidden Inga because of his irrational fear for her seemed hollow now.

Also, the suspicion that Mike Jones had been involved in Inga's disappearance hadn't been dispensed with by his death. The nature of the attack on Jones could mean that someone believed him guilty of a misdemeanour with the child. If that were true, Jones couldn't reveal it now. Whoever had attacked him and pushed him to his death had only made matters worse.

We are all too close to this case, and the people involved.

At that moment her mobile rang. Rhona glanced at the screen expecting McNab, only to discover Sean's name. Despite McNab's suggestion that she call Sean in the wake of processing the body of Mike Jones, she hadn't done so.

As she hesitated, the call switched to voicemail. Rhona contemplated listening to the message, but couldn't bring herself to. She didn't want to think about anything outside of now and the problems she faced here. Pushing the mobile away, she refocused her attention on the map.

Ola Sinclair's path the night she was killed was plain now. *But what of her great-niece's route?*

The soil evidence suggested Inga had made her way through the former camp en route to Sam's place. There was no forensic evidence to show she'd gone by way of the beach or crossed a different soil formation.

Rhona still held true to her belief that the girl had been picked up in Sam's jeep. That seemed the most likely explanation for her sudden and immediate disappearance. The alternative being that, though her boots and coat were taken from the camp area, the girl was not.

They had combed the area extensively, so that didn't seem possible, and yet . . .

With that thought came a memory of a photograph she'd seen in the research room, in one of the pamphlets featuring Sanday at war. There had apparently been only one death and that had been when a bomb, falling on the camp, had killed someone working in the mortuary.

Aware that the camp might be a target for enemy bombers, a false radar station had been set up on the northern shore to draw enemy aircraft away, along with air-raid shelters at Lopness for the real camp.

She eventually located the picture. Small and embedded in a page of text, it featured an indentation in an otherwise flat field, fronted by what looked like a long narrow opening. Below were the words, 'A former air-raid shelter'.

Rhona checked to see when the pamphlet had been printed, but couldn't find a date. She hadn't recalled any mention of the presence of underground shelters, but then again, Sam, the most obvious person to know about such things, had disappeared shortly after the search for Inga had begun.

She returned to the map and, using a first-hand account of the camp layout, plotted the position of the air-raid shelter on it.

It was then it struck her.

If it still existed, the bunker in the picture lay midway between Sam Flett's place and the old Muir farmhouse, where the Ranger now lived.

48

The hotel bar was busy, although McNab got the impression none of those in the room had any wish to stand next to him.

They blame me that Inga hasn't been found. And if you bring in a detective from Glasgow, who's supposed to know how to deal with such a thing, then you're entitled to blame (and despise) the said detective when they fail.

The realization of this made him want to punch something, or alternatively take the edge off his failure, the way he knew worked. McNab's eyes moved to the whisky bottles, of which there were many.

I could sample them all and still not understand what happened after Inga Sinclair left her house on that fateful morning.

In a city, her every move would have been recorded. He would have used that, thinking it was his wonderful intuition that had solved the case. When it had been CCTV.

Here, without it, I'm crap.

A nearby wall poster advertising the bonfire and fireworks on Cata Sand only added to his general feeling of angst. Regardless of where he was, McNab hated bonfires and fireworks in equal measure, although he could think of a few folk in Glasgow he would cheerfully offer up as a guy to the flames.

Torvaig, coming to ask for his order, caught him eyeing

up the poster. 'You planning on coming to the party, Sergeant?'

When McNab shot him a horrified look in response, Torvaig shrugged his shoulders. 'And here I was about to offer you the loan of a pair of wellies.'

'It's a weird place to have a bonfire,' McNab said.

'The local firemen organize it on the sands because it's safer than on land. It'll be a big blaze, with lots of free food and drink.'

'Thanks, but no thanks.'

'Suit yourself. Have you eaten?'

McNab shook his head.

'I'll get you something.'

McNab watched Torvaig go through to the kitchen, at the same time sensing that their exchange had been both watched and listened to. When he swivelled round to face his audience, his defiant look was met by some, while the rest resumed their own conversations and ignored his challenge.

McNab pointedly lifted his pint and headed for his usual table at the window.

Looking out into the darkness, he thought back to the night Inga's father had squared up to him over buying Jones a drink. Had he known then that his daughter was on the island? McNab didn't think so. He suspected he'd heard the story about Jones, and was looking for someone to pick on.

So how had he found out about Inga? Had it been a chance remark in the pub? A discussion of the body that had been unearthed in the schoolhouse yard? The fact that they'd thought one of the local kids had taken the skull? A mention of Inga's name?

It didn't matter how he'd discovered that the mother and

daughter were on the island. But once he had, McNab had no doubt he would have decided to do something about it. McNab recalled Inga's mother's terrified expression when he'd told her he'd seen her former partner.

McNab had a list of folk he hated and paedos and wife-beaters came pretty well at the top. Ironic that, in this case, one should be pitted against the other.

And now one of them was dead. *And maybe not the right one.*

The mother had told him that her partner had never hurt Inga. When McNab had met the child, he'd thought her bright and well-adjusted. He had experience of children that had been abused by their parents and Inga's behaviour and openness hadn't suggested a frightened child to him. Of course, that could all be down to her mother. Or the father had made sure that the child had never witnessed the violence.

Families, he decided, were strange beasts. Personal relationships even more so.

Which is why I avoid them.

At that moment his mobile, discovering a signal, sprang into life. McNab, thinking it would be work related, answered it without checking the identity of the caller.

'Michael?' Freya's voice sounded tentative, with just enough hope to cause him concern.

'Freya. How are you?' Even to his own ears, his response sounded lame.

She was hesitant in her answer. McNab had been with Freya long enough to be aware that she always tried to be honest.

I'm about to be dumped.

He tried to get in first. 'I'm sorry I haven't been in touch.

There's no signal and it's been flat-out work.' He added, 'I told you it would be like this,' for good measure.

Like it was her fault!

'I understand.' A bleak silence followed, filled by McNab's troubled, frantic thoughts.

Then she said, 'I've decided to go home to Newcastle.'

'Why?' He hadn't expected this.

'I think I'll work better on my thesis there.'

McNab heard the unspoken words, *without remembering the fire and Leila's death.*

He realized then that being with him had probably made that more difficult, which was why Freya hadn't wanted him to stay at her place. And all the while, he'd thought he'd been the one to make that decision.

'Maybe it's for the best,' he said.

For the best? Fuck's sake.

'Look after yourself, Michael.'

She ended the call before he could respond.

McNab sat for a moment, surprised by the strength of his feelings, the biggest of which, he realized, was relief. Then he considered calling Rhona.

Why? To tell her I'm free and available? Like she would care.

As Hege entered the bar, all heads turned. Well, all male heads, anyway, reminding McNab just how attractive she was. She made for the bar without glancing in his direction.

McNab, nonplussed, wondered if she'd spotted him, or alternatively didn't want to show she had. He headed for the counter with his empty glass and, noting her presence, offered to buy her a drink.

Her surprise at his sudden appearance obvious, or pretended, she said hesitantly, 'That's very kind, Detective Sergeant McNab. A whisky and water, please.'

'Any one in particular?' he asked.

'Highland Park.'

McNab immediately added one for himself to the order.

Aware now that all eyes in the room were on them, McNab suggested she might join him at the window seat. Hege provided a perfect study of a woman who has no wish to accept such a proposal, but was doing so under embarrassed duress.

Reaching said table, McNab set the drinks down and slipped into his seat, facing the room, allowing Hege the advantage of her face not being visible to the remainder of the room.

'*Slàinte*,' he offered.

She touched her glass to his and said something indecipherable, which he assumed to be Norwegian. McNab sampled his whisky and decided that it tasted like nectar.

'So, what did you want to talk to me about?'

She waited a moment, then lowering her voice, said, 'I'd rather not talk about it here. Maybe we could keep it until later, perhaps in your room?'

McNab thought he must be hearing things, so strove for clarity.

'You want to come up to my room?'

She gave a sideways glance. 'Not yet. Later.'

McNab sampled more of his drink. 'So what do we do now, while we're here?'

'Have a drink and talk about normal things.'

Normal things. McNab had forgotten what they were.

Hege turned out to be good company, made even better by the whisky they both consumed. She told him about

Norway, and the little fishing village she came from. How she'd travelled over most of Scotland, but was fond of the northern isles, in particular Sanday.

'The people are very welcoming.'

'You think so?' McNab said.

'It's different for you. As a policeman,' she added.

'How?' he challenged.

She considered her response. 'In small communities there are many secrets. Here, as in Norway. Unlike in cities, like Glasgow, everyone knows everyone else's business, but we keep our own counsel, particularly with outsiders.'

McNab realized she didn't know Glasgow, where you were asked your business at every bus stop.

'You're not an outsider, then?'

She allowed silence to invade for a moment, before answering.

'I thought I was, until all this happened.' She smiled, as though they were discussing something much more light-hearted. McNab wondered if it was for the benefit of the room, or for him in particular.

'I have to go.' She rose, her expression indicating that this was awkward, yet necessary.

McNab played along, and in a moment she was gone and speaking to those in the room as she departed, her voice so relieved that they knew her sojourn with the 'Glasgow detective' had been under duress and nothing more.

49

Hunger beset her as she locked the door of the heritage centre. Having boasted that she'd planned to cook for herself, she'd singularly failed to buy any ingredients and the community shop now lay in darkness. She could of course, even at this late hour, take up McNab's offer and head for the hotel.

That thought lasted seconds, because there was an alternative.

Magnus answered her call almost immediately. When Rhona explained her dilemma, he told her to come straight over to the croft house. 'Erling gave me the go-ahead to make use of everything in the fridge, and the cupboards for that matter.'

'Is Erling with you?'

'He took the police launch to Kirkwall. Someone he wanted to see.'

Relieved, Rhona said she'd be there shortly.

Packing the box containing the accumulated material from earlier, Rhona set off northwards. The night was clear, the moon on the wane but still bright enough to lay a filter over the flat landscape. To someone conditioned to the claustrophobic nature of a city, with its tall, tightly packed buildings and swarms of people, such a landscape could generate a feeling of exposure and fear.

Rhona had watched McNab's reaction to the emptiness of the place, noting his obvious discomfort. She'd appreciated that many of the rules he played by, as a detective, were virtually unusable here. Yet McNab had persisted, and it had paid off. In terms of Jamie Drever and the skull, at least.

But if we have to leave here without finding the child . . .

Exiting Lady Village, she was now on the road that ran along the northern shore of Cata Sand. Even in poor light, the giant bonfire was visible, rising like a Trojan horse from the vast expanse of flat shallow water that surrounded it. Rhona had voiced the thought to PC Tulloch that celebrating Guy Fawkes seemed bizarre on an island that was a world and centuries away from the political intrigue that had begun the tradition.

'I think it's probably more a Viking challenge to the oncoming winter,' he'd told her. 'We, the people of Sanday, plan to be here next spring.'

And they'll do that by knowing who their neighbours are, and watching out for them.

The sea off Lopness had roughened, bringing waves to crash over the sunken destroyer. In the far distance were the scattered lights of the houses that peppered the north-eastern spit of the island. Rhona sought the one that was Sam's croft and spotted it.

Minutes later she was at the gate.

Magnus must have been looking out for her, because his tall figure came along the grassy track behind a bouncing torch beam. Rhona shouted a greeting, then went round to the boot to retrieve her box.

'You didn't bring food with you?' Magnus said with a laugh.

'No,' she assured him. 'Just something I'd like you to take a look at.'

The room was as she remembered it. The two Orkney chairs standing either side of the fireplace. The curtained box bed. The only difference from her last visit was the fire blazing in the grate, where before, Sam's absence had seen it go out.

'Good smells,' she said.

'We aim to please. Take a seat, unless you want to show me the contents of the box first?' he added.

'I'm so hungry I was close to eating the contents on my way over here,' Rhona confessed.

'Then food comes first.'

Twenty minutes later, and much the better for an ample helping of Orkney beef stew, Rhona thanked the cook for saving her life.

'Whatever you were doing in the heritage centre, must have been hungry work.'

'You saw me there?'

'I passed the car on my way home and realized you, unlike me, hadn't stopped for the day. Do you want to show me what you were working on?'

Minutes later they'd cleared the table of dishes, and Rhona had spread out her collage in its place. Magnus listened intently as she described the path she thought had been taken, first by Ola all those years ago, then by her grand-niece.

'You think history was repeating itself?' Magnus said.

'Sam was right to think Inga was in danger. We know that much.'

'Because of the flower,' Magnus said.

'McNab didn't like that,' she told him.

'I can imagine.'

Magnus was observing her with an inquisitive eye.

'I take it you didn't come here to talk about the flowers?'

'No,' Rhona said. 'Were you aware there were underground bomb shelters in the camp?'

'I was, why?'

When she showed him the pamphlet, Magnus stared at the picture, his brow furrowed.

'I thought they'd all been filled in, even by the time I came here as a boy.'

'Then when was this picture taken?'

'I have no idea.'

Rhona pointed at the cross she'd marked on the Ordnance Survey map. 'Studying the material and first-hand accounts, I estimate this is the spot not far from the mortuary. Whether it's this particular bunker, I'm not sure.'

'No one reported an opening like this when the area was searched.'

'Even partially filled in, it would be fairly easy to miss, if you weren't aware of its existence.'

'So you want us to take a look at first light?'

She nodded.

Magnus's expression grew serious. 'What do you expect to find there?'

Rhona had no desire to remind him that her forensic speciality was hidden or buried bodies.

She left Magnus at midnight and was treated to a display of the northern lights on her return trip to the cottage. Stopping the car, Rhona stepped out to watch. The Merry Dancers didn't dance for long and their gowns weren't as brilliantly coloured as she'd seen in video footage, but to view their brief appearance in person definitely lifted her spirits.

Drawing up in front of the dark cottage, she left on the headlights to help her locate the key and open the front door. After this, she took herself round to the rear of the building to search for the elusive signal. A number of emails and messages arrived, including another from Sean, this time with an attachment.

Rhona went inside, to discover that the stove had long since gone out. She plugged in the electric heater left there for such emergencies, and went for a shower before bed. The beat of the water on her head, in the past, had often sparked thought and even insight. She pondered now the timeline they'd drawn for Inga, her possible captor, and for Sam.

Doing that had made her even more convinced that the answer lay at sea, or somewhere on the miles of coast. There were, she suspected, a myriad of places a small boat might pull ashore or be hidden under rock arches or caves. Sanday had many long beaches, but it also had an expanse of rocky shoreline.

She remembered a story Sam had told her of a long cold winter a century ago when Inuit coracles had been sighted off the far north of this parish. The men in them had always made off as soon as they'd realized they were being watched. They apparently never set foot on dry land, but fished, ate and slept on the water in their small, fast but fragile boats.

Joe Millar was a fisherman, and she had no doubt he could survive at sea.

But maybe he's gone already. To a nearby island. Westray, North

*Ronaldsay, even the Orkney mainland, and we're searching here
in vain.*

The earlier elation generated by the dancing lights had
departed, her mood now low.

Sitting up in bed, she finally opened Sean's message.

For you, was all it said. Rhona clicked on the attachment.

It was the song he'd played for her at the beginning of
their relationship. Huddled now beneath the duvet, she
listened to the saxophone's notes of love, and questioned
why they didn't move her as they should.

50

Erling lay awake, staring into the darkness. Sleep hadn't eluded Rory, whose steady breathing beside him only served to accentuate Erling's own wakefulness. He contemplated going to the bedroom next door to try again, or else give up entirely and start the day now, at this early hour.

It wouldn't be the first time he'd done that when pondering a case. His brain seemed to work better at night, when the detritus of the day dissolved into the background, presenting the problems that hadn't been solved more clearly.

He'd taken the decision to return on the police launch, rather than spend the night at Sam's, for no other reason than Rory had said he would be here. Since the child's disappearance, they'd barely spoken on the phone, let alone seen one another. And every relationship needed nurturing.

Maybe this one more than most.

The gnawing feeling he'd had on his return to the cottage when he'd heard Rory on the phone had returned, but this time for a very different reason. Maybe it was the way the past had come back to haunt the residents of Sanday that had sparked his unease.

But it wasn't that which had fed the flames.

It was when I mentioned the Glasgow detective's name.

Now in the kitchen, the coffee machine filled and switched on, Erling recalled the scene at the dinner table in detail.

They'd finished the main course and were tucking into Orkney cheese and biscuits, and making a determined move to finish a second bottle of red wine. Rory had been telling stories of other places he'd worked as a diver. It had sounded like a round-the-world trip. Erling's only sojourn away from Orkney to attend university had seemed embarrassingly timid. When he'd said so, Rory had rebuked him.

'I didn't always choose to go to those places. Often, I had to.'

Erling had waited for him to explain his remark, but he hadn't. Instead he'd changed the subject, asking how things were going on Sanday. Erling had duly answered, but not in any great detail. Just mentioned that they'd had a confession regarding the theft of the skull, and that they also knew what had happened to the elderly Orcadian they'd found in Glasgow. It was at that moment he'd mentioned DS McNab's name.

Rory, who Erling believed had been feigning interest until that point, now really did pay attention.

His head shot up. 'Who's that?'

'The detective they sent up from Glasgow. Why?'

'I didn't realize they'd bring in an outsider.'

'Any murder investigation is allotted an MIT team, particularly if it occurs in a location not used to that level of investigation.'

Rory nodded, but Erling could see that behind the false calm lay unease.

'To be truthful, I didn't take to the guy when I first met him,' Erling admitted, hoping his honesty might prompt Rory to reveal what lay behind the studied neutrality.

Rory helped himself to more wine and another slice of cheese, then said, 'Really. Why?'

'He was arrogant and basically insubordinate.'

It seemed to Erling that a flash of recognition crossed Rory's face before it went blank again.

'But now. . .' Erling continued, his own disquiet deepening.

'What?'

'I still think those things, but I also believe he's good at his job, probably because he does get under the skin.'

Rory was studying his wine intently.

'How much longer is he here for?'

'Until we find the girl, I suspect.'

'Do you think she's still alive?'

'Statistically it's unlikely, but if it was her estranged father who snatched her, then perhaps there's a chance.'

The awkwardness of the moment had passed. With a smile, Rory had refilled Erling's glass and suggested they head for bed.

Pouring himself a mug of coffee now, Erling carried it to the bedroom door. Rory was still asleep. The duvet had slipped down, exposing the muscled chest and tattooed arms. Erling felt a stir of desire and contemplated getting back into bed and wrapping himself round the warm body. If he did, Rory would waken, and they would replay the games of last night.

But his mood of suspicion wouldn't allow it.

He closed the door and went to shower and get ready for the day.

McNab had hung around the bar until just before ten, then gone upstairs. He hadn't watched the TV since his arrival, but did so now, the flurry of channels it offered giving him a glimpse of a world he'd all but forgotten existed.

The ten o'clock news was followed by a shipping forecast that warned of high winds and rain overnight, particularly over the northern isles.

It seemed Sanday was about to get a battering.

Again.

McNab propped himself up on the bed with his final double of the night, relishing the warm fuzzy glow the whisky had bestowed on him, in tandem with fighting the negative feelings that had resulted from his fall from grace.

It was because Freya dumped me.

That would, of course, be the excuse he would feed Rhona should the need arise, despite the fact that it wasn't true.

When Torvaig shouted he was off home, McNab called back his farewells, then headed downstairs to unlock the door that Torvaig had just secured.

He would give it half an hour then go to bed, he decided.

Whatever Hege had planned to communicate couldn't be that urgent or she would have shown up by now. McNab took his disappointment back upstairs with him.

The screen had morphed from the news into some foreign detective story with a female lead that didn't do smiling. McNab pondered why the national broadcaster was so keen on buying in police thrillers from Scandinavia rather than develop more based in this part of Scotland. *After all, it's foreign enough up here.* He wondered if it was because of the weather, but the weather on the screen looked just as bad as Sanday had been promised for tonight.

His thoughts were interrupted by the drill of his mobile, something he'd almost got used to not hearing. Glancing down, he saw Hege's name and answered.

'Has everyone gone?' she said.

'Yes. And the door's open.'

Minutes later, he heard her climb the stairs. McNab immediately stood up, then sat down again. There was only one chair in the room, which he would offer to her. He would therefore have to stand, or else sit on the bed.

For fuck's sake. Get a grip.

He waited for her knock on the door before opening it.

She looked rather startled at his appearance, as though she hadn't expected to find him there.

She's as awkward and embarrassed as me, he thought. *But why*?

As she accepted his invitation to enter, he caught the scent of whisky. Whether from her breath or his own, he wasn't sure.

'Take a seat.' He gestured to the only chair.

'I'm sorry it took me so long,' she apologized, not explaining the reason.

'So,' McNab said, deciding to get to the point. 'Is this police business or is there another reason you wanted to visit me in my room?'

When she blushed, he added, 'Of course, had I a choice in the matter, I'd much prefer it to be the latter.' McNab gave her what he hoped was his signature grin.

His attempts to lighten the moment seemed to work, because she smiled in response and visibly relaxed.

'No female has asked to visit your hotel room before?' she played back at him.

'I wouldn't say that, exactly.'

Silence fell as she contemplated her next response.

Eventually she said, 'I think I know who sent you that text about Sam Flett.'

'Really? Who?'

'The man who picked a fight about Mike Jones being served.'

'He had access to your mobile?'

She flushed. 'Yes.'

McNab waited for her to go on, knowing what would come next before she said it.

'He and I were . . .' She halted there.

'Go on.'

'The boat came into the harbour for repairs two days before the incident at the pub.' The eyes that met his were defiant, but troubled.

McNab rose from his seat on the bed and went to the window. The wind was whipping at the surface of the water, turning it to froth. The mass of seaweed rose and fell among the foam.

He turned. 'And when did you discover that Joe Millar was in fact Inga's father?'

'You know?' she said in surprise.

'When did you find out?' McNab repeated.

'The night of the argument. After you left, someone mentioned the kids who lived near the schoolhouse. How they were easy game for . . .' She hesitated.

'The paedo,' he finished for her, imagining what had been said, and how it might have sealed Mike Jones's fate.

She continued, 'Joe was distraught when he heard Inga's name.'

'So Millar found out on Friday night that his wife and daughter were on Sanday?'

She nodded.

'And his reaction to that?'

'He was angry and upset. He told me later, when we were

alone, that she'd left him for another man, and taken his daughter with her. He'd been searching for them ever since.'

'Did he mention that he used to beat Inga's mother and that she left him before he could do the same to Inga?' McNab said coldly.

Shock and horror filled her face. 'I can't believe Joe would do that . . .'

'Maybe you need a bit more time in the sack with him to find out what Joe Millar *is* capable of.'

As she withered under his words, McNab reminded himself that browbeating a woman was also a form of abuse.

'Inga went missing on Saturday,' he reminded her.

'But everyone thought Joe had left with the boat first thing on Saturday morning,' she countered.

'Yet the text you say he sent me from your mobile arrived on Saturday.'

McNab poured a whisky from the bottle he'd fetched from the bar. She was visibly in shock, her face transparent, her hand trembling as she accepted the glass. She took a mouthful and swallowed. He would have liked to fill his own glass and do the same, but found himself resisting the move. She glanced at him as though to check whether she might finish it.

'Go ahead,' he said.

When she did, he poured her another measure.

She shivered as a gust of wind and rain hit the window. They were in for a wild night, as promised. McNab pulled the duvet from the bed and offered it to her. She took it gratefully, wrapping it round her shoulders.

After a few moments, twin red spots appeared on her cheeks.

When she looked ready, he tried again.

'So, about this text?'

'Just because it arrived on Saturday, doesn't mean it was sent then.' She was fighting back. 'On Sanday, texts get delivered when your mobile locates a signal.'

Which was true.

'You saw Joe on Friday?'

'He stayed over Friday night and got up early to join the boat. My place has no signal. I get my messages when I'm at the centre, or here at the pub.'

'Where's Joe now?' McNab said quietly.

She met his eye. 'I have no idea.'

'He hasn't been in touch?'

She shook her head vehemently. 'Definitely not.'

'And if he finds out you've come to me?'

'I don't know,' she said, worry creeping into her voice.

McNab thought for a moment. 'Where do you live?'

'Just along the shoreline from the hotel.'

'Are there any boats beached nearby?'

She looked puzzled by the question. 'A few, and a couple of boathouses.'

'Could a boat go missing without anyone noticing?'

Catching his mood, she thought hard about that.

'One of the boathouses belongs to a holiday cottage. So I suppose . . .'

'Take me there,' McNab said, reaching for his jacket.

'What? Now?' she said.

But McNab was already at the door.

'It's within walking distance,' she assured him as they bent their heads against the wind.

McNab swore under his breath. Anything further than a couple of yards in this weather, to his mind, did not constitute a walking distance.

Street lights on the left-hand side of the road attempted to illuminate the scene, with little success. He hadn't paid much heed to the route into Kettletoft before now, having always arrived by car, with his sights strictly on the approaching hotel. Now he registered that the long string of houses, bar a few, were on the seaward side of the road, most of them single storey, a few derelict, with some in the process of being renovated. Cars were parked alongside and some open areas between held boats on trailers, or lying on the grass.

Eventually Hege stopped and entered a gate in a wall. Tucked behind was a tiny house with a flagstone patio.

'This is my place,' she said.

'It has a boathouse?' McNab asked.

'Yes, but no boat. It's the holiday house next door I was talking about.'

She took him round the back. Once out of the lee of the building, the wind whipped at them again. On either side of an old stone jetty that jutted out into the surging water stood two boathouses. The one he took to belong to Hege's cottage was dilapidated. The boathouse and house on the other side had obviously both been renovated, and fairly recently.

'A consultant from somewhere in the south of England owns it. He comes up in the summer with his family.'

'He definitely has a boat?'

'Yes.'

Hege walked down the stone jetty. McNab delayed as a wave hit, spilling its wash of water across the green surface.

Noting his trepidation, Hege urged him to follow. 'It's safe,' she called back.

McNab, his memory of his recent ducking still fresh, didn't agree, but he followed her nevertheless.

She jumped down onto the gravelly shore, and having now entered the grounds of the next-door property, climbed back up the rocky shoreline and headed for the boathouse door, where she waited for him.

'I'm used to the terrain,' she said, when he finally joined her. 'I come from a fishing village like this one in Norway.'

McNab ignored her attempts to put him at ease. 'Did Millar know about this boat?'

'He asked about the house next door. Who owned it. Whether he had a boat. I told him.' She looked pained by that.

A sensor on the rear of the house picked up their presence and a light came on, illuminating the boathouse door.

'It's been forced,' McNab said, noting the chipped wood alongside the lock.

He hesitated, albeit briefly, before grabbing the handle and pulling it open.

Inside, all was darkness and shadow, with the sound of the sea surging over the jetty as a backdrop. McNab felt along the inside wall for a switch and eventually found one.

He blinked as a powerful overhead light came on.

The space was large and tidily kept. All the paraphernalia for boat owners stood along the walls. Shelves were laden with tools. There were containers for fuel and water.

A trailer stood centre stage.

The one item that was missing was a boat.

51

Rhona had slept fitfully. The wind, hitting the small seaward window of the bedroom, had crept in around the frame, the spluttering draught chilling the air and fluttering the curtains. She'd given up sometime during the early hours of the morning, and rising, had gone through to the kitchen, to discover the howl of the wind was even stronger here.

She doubted whether the large thick slabs of slate that covered the roof would be shaken by such a wind, but they couldn't prevent the sound of it trying, which reminded her of the high-pitched screech of a banshee. From the sitting-room window, she had a fine view of a tumultuous sea, whipped-up sand and madly dancing grass. The only object that appeared permanent was the striped lighthouse with its steady revolving beam.

By dawn, a level of calm had descended. Now on her third cup of coffee, Rhona ventured outside to take a look. A film of white sand glistened on the flagstones that fronted the door, but otherwise nothing had changed.

She went round to the back of the building and took up her place beside the stone lookout post to await her morning delivery of mail. Having downloaded last night, she found only two new messages. One from Magnus, confirming he would arrive shortly. The other from McNab, sent in the early hours of the morning.

Rhona opened it.

Several attempts later, she still hadn't made contact with him, which suggested McNab was either asleep or no longer at the hotel and in range of its signal.

Hearing a car on the track approaching the cottage, she abandoned her attempts and went to greet Magnus.

'Ready?' he said.

Rhona quickly told him of McNab's message.

'So you were right. He does have a boat.'

'It looks like it.'

'Do you want to find McNab or check for the bomb shelter?'

'Let's head for the camp, as planned.'

They collected a spade and trowel from the shed, scattering the half-dozen cats that had been sheltering there, then set off over the fields. The sea was still high, although the wind had dropped.

As they walked, Magnus told Rhona some of the words in Orkney dialect for the winds that swept the islands. 'You can have a tirl, a gurl, a gussel, a hushle, a skolder, a skuther and a guster,' he finished.

'And the difference between them?' she said.

'The degree of strength. My ancestors regarded the weather as a personal foe with whom they had to cope,' Magnus said. 'My grandfather, and my father, always used the personal term "he" rather than "it" when referring to the weather. You still hear Orkney folk saying, "He's blowan hard," and "He's cleran up."'

Rhona regarded the sky. 'He's cleran up,' she tried.

'Not bad,' Magnus acknowledged, 'for a ferry louper.'

On their left flank, they spotted the large blocks of concrete that had secured the feet of the giant radar masts. Beyond them the rooftop of the Muir house.

'Should we call in on our way back?' Magnus said.

Rhona nodded. Derek Muir hadn't been transferred to Kirkwall, on Erling's orders, but his normal activities had been curtailed. Not so much house arrest as island arrest.

'He would be the one to ask about the boat and its owner,' Rhona said.

They took the route along the shoreline. The overnight buffeting had deposited large clumps of tangle on the sand. Behind these rose mounds of broken slate, difficult to clamber over to reach first the machair then the fenced farmland.

On spotting the brick mortuary, Rhona stopped and, using her map, indicated to Magnus the area she judged to be halfway between the Muir farmhouse and Sam Flett's place.

'So how will we recognize it?'

'The photograph suggests a long low hillock. Imagine something like the Maesry Mound, its surface just above ground, built not of stone, but concrete. The entrance would be a tunnel. I think it was the tunnel entrance that was shown in the picture.'

Producing her binoculars, Rhona slowly swept the flat landscape.

The job had taken her to many open places like this, looking for hidden and buried bodies. Killers could go to extreme lengths to hide their victims, believing that without a body there was no evidence of a crime. In the process, she'd had dogs set on her, been threatened by landowners and once been shot at, albeit with an air rifle. Usually because someone had something to hide.

Here, the only curiosity came from the neighbouring field of cows.

'Anything?' Magnus said, peering ahead.

'No.'

'Could it be behind the mortuary, rather than on the seaward side?' he suggested.

It was worth a try.

They set off towards the building Rhona had last visited in the dark.

'Sam Flett hated this building, but he never said why,' Magnus said.

'No one likes a mortuary, just as no one likes the thought of a grave,' Rhona offered.

'I think something happened to him here as a child.'

'That sounds like a psychologist,' Rhona said.

The last time she'd been here, the field had housed a herd of cattle. This time it was deserted, although the scent they'd left behind was just as pungent.

Rhona glanced at Magnus, wondering if his strong sense of smell was causing a problem. Guessing the reason for her look, he shook his head. 'Now, an abattoir would be difficult, but live cattle, no.'

As they turned the corner of the building, a bird flew out of the mortuary, practically into their faces. Startled, Rhona realized it was the owl that had accompanied her earlier visit. As she turned to watch its flight, she spotted an undulation in the ground.

Magnus, following her glance, registered it too.

Rhona walked in that direction.

The grass here was well churned up by her compatriots of the other night, although last night's rain had been absorbed by the sandy underlying soil.

Approaching, Rhona took her bearings again.

'This could be the spot,' she said.

'So we dig,' Magnus said. 'But where exactly?'

Digging up the ground always disturbed the layers. Filling it in did the same. Those who sought to hide bodies by burying them always forgot that. They forgot too that the grave sank as the body beneath it rotted. Sunken areas in the surface often gave the game away.

But we're not looking for a body, just the entrance to the bomb shelter.

Rhona pointed at just such an indentation. 'Here, but let me go first.'

She didn't use the shovel, but chose the trowel instead, scraping until the metal met a hard surface. The patch of exposed concrete grew under her hand. She could sense Magnus's excitement behind her, but she didn't pause or look round until she'd exposed the top part of what she believed was a tunnel entrance.

'That's what was in the photograph,' she heard Magnus say.

Below the surface the soil became predominantly sand, falling away easily to expose a corrugated sheet serving as a door. Rhona turned away as the smell of decomposition hit her nostrils. Behind her she heard Magnus gasp.

'Help me dig,' she told him.

Ten minutes later, the tunnel entrance was obvious. Rhona sat back on her heels. The strong smell that had first been released had dissipated, although that might have been because of the stiff breeze that had blown up. Despite the wind, a few flies had arrived, deserting the neighbouring cattle for the sweat from their exertions, or the scent of something rotting.

As Magnus dragged the panel free of the entrance, Rhona shone her forensic torch inside. The beam played off a concrete passage, its walls dry.

'So what now?' Magnus said.

'I take a look inside.'

52

It felt like a replay of her entry to Maesry Mound, although this time the walls weren't constructed with ancient flagstones but Second World War concrete. The space between the floor and ceiling had been lessened by an infill of sand, requiring her to crawl rather than crouch. Her body blocking what little light came from behind her, Rhona had to rely on her torch to illuminate her path. The entrance tunnel didn't last long before she found the ground beneath her dipping and the space before her widening.

Rhona slithered inside.

A quick swing of her beam established the height and width of the place. It also illuminated a shelf of what looked like different-sized light bulbs and a collection of shells. On the ground lay a bundle that turned out to be a blue sleeping bag and a pillow, with a soft toy alongside.

A child's hideout?

The smell of decay still in her nostrils, she went looking for its source, eventually finding it between the makeshift bed and the wall. A mound of writhing maggots were busily stripping the remains of flesh from the bones. Rhona got closer for a proper look, already certain it wasn't big enough to be a human corpse, even a child's. The scattered remnants of fur suggested an animal, the size of a fox, though the remains of the coat weren't russet, but a striped grey and black.

The cat's glassy eyes had gone, leaving gaping holes, its small sharp teeth exposed in a mouth now devoid of flesh and tongue.

The remains were undoubtedly those of a large feral cat, one of the many living wild on the island.

Having scanned the entire small space, and certain now there was nothing else alive or dead here apart from the maggots and the flies that had accompanied her entry, Rhona eventually answered Magnus's urgent shout.

'Come in,' she urged him, 'and take a look.'

His big frame eventually eased its way into the shelter. His eyes took in the scene, registering the collection of stored treasures, the bed and the soft toy.

Rhona handed him a school notebook with the name Inga Sinclair written on the front.

'Her diary,' she said.

'So Inga was using this place as a den?'

'According to Sam she was really interested in wartime Sanday. I can imagine this place was a bit of a find for her.'

Magnus was examining the contents of the shelf. 'These look like old bulbs, maybe from the lighthouse?'

'There's a similar collection on the window ledge in the cottage,' Rhona said.

Rhona used her mobile to take a photographic record of the scene, then took a short video.

'How did the search party miss this place?' Magnus said.

'Inga made a pretty good job of burying the entrance. She obviously didn't want anyone to discover her den.' Rhona gestured to the jotter. 'Let's go outside and take a look at this.'

Trying to study the diary in a whipping wind proved difficult, so they decided to make their way back to the cottage. A few yards from the building, they made a dash for it as a squall hit, with hailstones rather than rain this time.

Once inside, Rhona put on the coffee maker again. Then they sat down at the table with the jotter.

Each entry had been dated, and assuming she began the diary when she'd discovered her den, then Inga had been using the bomb shelter since the summer. The beginning of the school holidays in fact. Inga hadn't written an entry for every day, but apparently only when she'd visited the shelter.

1st July

It's coorse wither for summer, but I'm cosy enough in my den. I've brought some of the old bulbs Mr Muir gave me for the shelf and my favourite shells from the beach on Start Island. Mum doesn't know about this place. It's just for me. ☺

Rhona skimmed through the other entries which talked about birds she'd seen while lying hidden in the entrance tunnel. She'd recorded too what she thought was the Orkney name for each bird and a little drawing. Eventually they neared the present day.

They've found a body buried in the old playground! The man who lives there called the police and two forensic women in white suits came to dig it up, but someone had stolen the skull!!!!

There followed an entry on her determination to find the missing skull.

Lachlan, Nele and Robert have vowed to help, but they're not true detectives. Lachlan and Robert would rather play computer games or football and Nele's too frightened, so I'll have to investigate myself. The Glasgow Detective said he would be glad of my help.

The discovery of the flowers in the schoolhouse loft had definitely fired her imagination.

I have this feeling that one of the flowers belongs to my family from long long ago.

Then she'd recorded her visit to Mike Jones.

He looked at me as though I was a ghost, then was sick in the sink. I saw one of the magic flowers on the kitchen table and he had a picture on an easel, but he wouldn't let me look at it.

'So Mike Jones's story of their encounter was true,' Rhona said.

The final entry was dated Friday.

I'm going to the museum with Mr Flett tomorrow. We're going to try and discover who the thirteen flowers were made for. They represent the souls of dead children! ☹

P.S. Mr Flett told me not to cross the causeway.

Magnus met Rhona's gaze.

'Sam was afraid for her and that fear centred on water,' he said.

'I'm going to try McNab again. If I can't reach him I'll try Erling. Then we'll head for Kettletoft.'

The squall had moved south-west, darkening the sky over Eday. Here the sun was out, its shafts of light like stairways to heaven. In Scotland, she thought, you could experience every season in one day. Here on Sanday, you could face all the seasons within ten minutes.

Sheltering behind the lookout, she tried McNab's number again. It didn't even ring out but informed her there was no connection. She was luckier with Erling.

'I'm docking at Loth as we speak,' he told her. 'I'll head for Kettletoft to see this boathouse, then McNab and I will go to the community centre, where we can keep in contact with the coastguard.'

Rhona quickly told him of finding Inga's den.

He listened in silence. 'You were looking for her body?'

'At one point, I thought I'd found it.'

On the road to Kettletoft, Magnus in the driving seat, Rhona ran her thoughts out loud.

'Assuming he has her on board this boat. Where would he go?'

'If he launched it on Friday night, it would have been before dawn. The girl was taken on Saturday morning by jeep.' He considered this. 'He got rid of the jeep on Cata Sand, so chances are he'd anchored by then in the Bay of Newark, north of Cata, or Sty Wick, to the south.'

'Sty Wick,' Rhona said, trying to recall where she'd heard the name. Then it came to her, with a shudder. The last victim murdered on Sanday had been found buried in the dunes of Sty Wick.

But that won't be the case for Inga.

'Then where?' she said.

'If he wanted to hide, then somewhere not easily accessible from the land or the sea.' Magnus paused. 'I don't know the coast of Sanday well enough to guess where.'

'Wouldn't he just sail to another island, or Orkney mainland, or even Caithness?'

'It's possible, but he'd be noted on one of the smaller islands. The girl's disappearance is big news. And –' he paused – 'it all depends on his reason for snatching her.'

Rhona waited for Magnus to explain further.

'Did he really want the girl with him or did he just want to punish her mother?' he said.

'Maybe he had no plan other than to snatch her,' Rhona said.

'That's possible,' Magnus conceded. 'Domestic violence is all about control of the partner. Torment and torture feature strongly. Of course,' a shadow crossed his face, 'the ultimate torture for the mother would be . . .'

'If he were to kill the child,' she finished for him.

They settled into an uneasy silence, each party to their own thoughts. Rhona's transitory relief at discovering that the old bomb shelter hadn't contained Inga's body had long departed. The flat fields rolled by the window. Magnus drew in at a passing place to let a local car pass and was given the customary wave. The surrounding scene of island life suggested peace and tranquillity, made more beautiful by the watery sunlight that graced their path.

Yet, wherever you are, the surface of life rarely portrays what lies beneath.

The tide was out on Cata Sand and the bonfire had grown larger since their previous visit. A couple of pickups were there now, unloading, with a few figures stacking the wood that had been delivered.

'They'll go ahead with the bonfire?' she asked Magnus.

'It's an island tradition, designed to glue the community together in hard times. It's their act of defiance against the long dark days of winter. The *we will survive* gesture.'

'Despite Sam's death, and everything that's happened?'

'I believe Sam would be the first to wish it so.'

53

McNab had the look of a man who hadn't slept. Wild-eyed and high, on a mix of adrenaline and, she'd hoped, caffeine, although she'd definitely got the whiff of whisky from his breath when he'd come close.

Rhona had seen that look before. Perhaps too frequently. Yet its appearance had often heralded the moment in a case when the breakthrough had happened, or was about to. When McNab's terrier determination had dug up the truth.

All that scouring of the Sanday countryside, the endless interviews, listening to stories that appeared to have no relevance, yet fearful that if you didn't take note of the details, the answer would have passed you by.

McNab's life wasn't that different from hers, she acknowledged. Asking the right questions of a crime scene, and looking for the answers, forensic or otherwise.

He caught her eye and gave her a little personal nod. Rhona felt a rush of . . . what? Annoyance, pleasure, excitement? She broke eye contact before he did, and the wistful look he met that with made her a little sad.

They were back in the meeting room. Erling and Magnus, she and McNab, with PC Tulloch and the other three officers brought in from Kirkwall. Entering the centre, she'd taken note of Derek Muir and Hege Aater sharing a coffee and apparently waiting to be interviewed. Both had looked uneasy, although it was Derek Muir that had most concerned her. The man who'd met her from the helicopter and welcomed her to Sanday was no more, and a stranger sat there in his place.

She roused herself as McNab called them to attention and indicated the photograph of a motorboat which had just appeared on the screen.

'This is the *Antares*. It's owned by a Dr Frank Haynes from Eastbourne, who comes up with his family every summer. It was stolen from the boathouse of his holiday home in Kettletoft sometime on Friday night, possibly in the early hours of the morning, and taken, we believe, by Joe Millar.'

Up on the screen came a list of the boat's specifications. McNab mentioned a few for emphasis. 'Suitable for coastal cruising, a four-berther with all mod cons, including a dinghy and standard navigation equipment. Dr Haynes maintains it's ideal for Sanday, although he wouldn't go out in her at this time of year.'

He continued, 'Some tinned supplies and frozen food has been taken from the storage shed at the Kettletoft shop, which wasn't discovered until today. So we believe he has provisions. There have been no sightings reported as yet of the boat off the neighbouring islands, nor in the intervening stretches of water. We're assuming, therefore, that he's still around Sanday somewhere.'

'After discussions with DI Flett,' he glanced in Erling's direction, 'we decided that Derek Muir was our best bet in identifying suitable locations to hide such a craft.'

McNab nodded at PC Tulloch who, looking decidedly awkward about being the one to do the job, immediately headed out of the room. Minutes later, the Ranger appeared.

He glanced at Erling, discomfort and shame written on

his face. It seemed to Rhona that Erling's return look was non-judgemental. In his quiet but firm Orcadian voice he asked the Ranger to tell them where Joe Millar might have hidden the *Antares*.

The Ranger visibly relaxed at the tone, and requested McNab to bring up the Ordnance Survey map of Sanday. At this magnification, all the locations Rhona was familiar with were there. The cottage, the schoolhouse, the old RAF station, the bays and inlets of Sanday.

'I would suggest that after abandoning Sam's jeep, he went south, tracking round the tip of the island and the ferry terminal. Going north would have meant circling Start Island and the northern coast where we were all searching on land, and the motorboat might have attracted attention.

'I believe he may have been heading for this area.' He pointed to a section of the western seaboard. 'Between the Taing of the Pund and Scuthi Head.'

'Why there?' McNab said.

'It's peppered with caves, hidden inlets and arches.' He pointed at the name Blue Geo just south of Taing of the Pund. 'The Orkney name for a cave or creek is Geo.'

Rhona recognized the area from her soil map. It had been coloured turquoise, indicating thin soil over strongly weathered rock of old red sandstone, hence the numerous abandoned quarries indicated on the Ordnance Survey map.

'He could hide there?' McNab said.

The Ranger nodded. 'The main problem is the weather at this time of year. Most fishing boats wouldn't get close to that part of the coastline in November.'

Rhona saw Ivan nodding vigorously at this.

So he snatched the child and deliberately took her into danger.

'How do we search then? From land or sea?' McNab said.

'Both,' Erling said. 'Broughtown's the closest settlement. It's not a town, just scattered farms. The road doesn't venture near the cliffs, so we approach cross-country. It's a bit like the cliff area of Yesnaby on mainland Orkney, and as spectacular, I understand.'

'Just not in the dark or bad weather,' McNab muttered. 'And since daylight is short, and the weather predicted to be bad, we'd better get going.'

Magnus came in then. 'Can I speak to Hege? She may be able to give us some insight into Millar's frame of mind and the psychology of thought behind his actions.'

McNab opened his mouth to say something, then thought the better of it.

'Go right ahead, Professor.'

The others had gone, taking Derek Muir with them.

Hege had brought them both coffee and now sat opposite, her cup untouched. Magnus had introduced himself, although he was pretty sure she knew exactly who he was.

'DS McNab said that you and Joe Millar formed a friendship during the few days his fishing boat was in the harbour. Are you willing to talk about that with me?'

'I've told DS McNab everything I know,' she said.

'Maybe not everything.' Magnus paused and looked at her steadily. 'It's important for us to understand what drove Millar to take his daughter, and what he intended doing with her if he was successful. If we can understand his motives, we may be able to gauge what he'll do when confronted by the police.'

She looked frightened by that prospect. 'You think he'll hurt Inga?'

'I honestly don't know, but if I could learn a little more about his frame of mind in the hours leading up to the abduction, that might help,' Magnus told her.

She thought about what he'd said, her hands twitching in her lap, her mouth moving as though she was biting her inner cheek.

'Okay,' she said.

'Let's start at the very beginning, when you met Joe.' Magnus purposefully used Millar's first name, trying to emphasize the normality of two people meeting up in a casual way. After all, Hege Aater had done nothing wrong.

'He came into the bar. I was helping Tor that night and we got chatting. He told me he'd come off the *Lucinda*. That she had a little engine trouble and would be in the harbour for two or three days. He had a nice smile and he made me laugh.' She halted.

Magnus let her take her time, and didn't urge her to continue.

Eventually she did. 'He stayed until closing time. Didn't drink much. Just chatted to me at the bar. Even helped me collect the glasses. Tor needed away sharp, so I said I would lock up. Joe offered to walk me home. The wind was up that night. He said he'd stop me from blowing away.' She gave a half-smile in memory before continuing.

'We got soaked between the hotel and my place. It seemed mean not to ask him in until the squall passed.'

Magnus realized she had begun excusing her actions.

'You did nothing wrong,' he said to reassure her.

She nodded, only half believing him.

'We had a nightcap. Whisky. He kissed me. I kissed him back. We went to bed.' She looked directly at Magnus. 'He was gentle and considerate. It was good.'

Magnus nodded at her to continue.

'It was the same next day. We talked about Norway. He knew some words in Norwegian, although his accent was terrible. He went to check on the boat, then we spent the evening together again. He got to chatting to the locals. They seemed to like him. He wasn't pushy. Just interested. Then someone mentioned he'd heard that Mike Jones was on the sex offenders list because of one of his pupils, who'd killed herself. Everyone was shocked about that. Shocked and angry that he'd come to live on Sanday.'

'And Joe?'

'He was the same. Most men are when they think about paedophiles.'

'What happened then?'

'Mike Jones walked in, large as life. The place went quiet. It was horrible. The look on Joe's face. Even Tor didn't want Jones there. He wouldn't have served him. They were intent on freezing him out until Dr MacLeod intervened and ordered a drink for him. DS McNab came over to back her up.' She swallowed and cleared her throat.

'I thought there would be a fight, the way he and Joe looked at one another.' She paused. 'The relief in the place when Ivan arrived. But it didn't end there. After they all left, except the detective, someone mentioned the children who lived up near the schoolhouse. Nele Skea, Lachlan Dunlop, his wee cousin Robert, and Inga Sinclair.'

'What happened then?'

'Joe asked about Inga and her mother.' She stared into the middle distance. 'He didn't say why, but I knew something was wrong.'

'When did he tell you?'

'When we went back to my place. He said he thought

Inga might be his daughter and that her mother had left him for another man, and taken his child. He asked about Inga. I told him what she looked like. That she was bright and clever and spent a lot of time at the museum with Sam Flett.' She paused. 'He asked me a lot about Sam too. Where he lived. What he was like. I thought learning about Mike Jones had spooked him.'

'Did he mention wanting to see Inga?'

'I asked him about that. He said it wasn't a good idea, and now he knew she was okay, he'd sleep easier. I suggested that maybe he could patch it up with her mother. He said no, that wouldn't work, not after what she'd done to him. He seemed sad,' she added.

'So you didn't think he'd try to see Inga?'

'He changed the subject. Started talking about us, making jokes. Mentioned the boat he had at home. Asked if I had access to one here. That's when I mentioned the one next door.' She looked uncomfortable. 'I had no idea he would do what he did.'

Her face grew pale, her eyes suddenly blazing with a memory she didn't welcome.

'What is it?' Magnus said.

'He carries a knife. A bone-handled fisherman's blade with a spike. The type that folds back into the handle. It's very old. He showed it to me when I was talking about my father being a fisherman.' She looked frantic with fear now. 'He won't hurt her, will he?'

54

Heading south from the community centre, they were soon on the long narrow strip that ended eventually at Loth on the southern tip of Sanday.

Passing Bea Loch on their left, two disused quarries were visible on the northern side of the road, testament to the underlying sandstone. At the crossroads near Hobbister, Rhona and McNab parted company with the others, the plan being that they should split into two teams. Erling and his men would head for the campsite at Ayre and begin their search at Taing of the Pund, making their way south.

Rhona, McNab and Ivan would continue on the road as far as Scuthi Head, then work north from there. Erling determined the fate of the Ranger by taking him with his group.

McNab was driving. Ensconced in the back of their vehicle, Ivan gave them a running commentary which, Rhona noted, was setting McNab's teeth on edge.

'That's Backaskaill Bay.' He pointed to a wide golden expanse of beach on their left. 'There are caves and inlets down there too,' he informed them brightly. 'Doun Helzie for one, and more at the tip of the peninsula.'

'Fuck's sake,' McNab muttered loudly.

Rhona turned and gave PC Tulloch a friendly warning

look, which he attempted, against his better nature, to take heed of.

Minutes later, he called on McNab to slow down and take a right at the next farm sign. They turned into a track that headed towards the coast, bouncing their way along until a surface suitable for the vehicle gave out.

'Now we walk, sir.'

The wind was coming directly from the west into their faces. Above them the sky was full of scurrying clouds, all headed east as though fleeing an impending storm.

As Ivan led the way, Rhona walked alongside McNab. They were both dressed for the weather and the terrain, but regardless of how well prepared they were, McNab might as well have been deposited on the moon, he looked, and obviously felt, so completely out of place here.

Reaching the edge, they looked down on the sea, slate grey, in ridges, the watery equivalent of the folded rocks below.

Now McNab did swear, and loud enough for the heavens to hear.

'How the fuck do we find anything down there?'

Ivan beckoned him on. 'If the boat's here, it'll be tucked in a hidden bay, under an arch or a cave.'

'And how do we know where the caves are?'

'You've got me with you, sir.'

The first bay at Balfour's Geo proved empty, apart from some seals on the rocks nearby being showered by the larger waves. Avoiding the wild Scuthi Head itself, Ivan led them north-east, crossing inland, but keeping as close to the shore-line as possible. The bay at Whitefield Geo was empty too, the caves there not suitable for giving refuge to anything larger than a seal or two.

In the meantime, the scurrying cloud had thickened, its colour deepening to ashen grey. Losing the intermittent shafts of light that had played on them up to now had lessened the visibility. Grey rocks, grey sea and grey sky, all now merged together.

They were nearing an area Ivan called the Wheems. Rocky islands dotted the surface of the sea, frothy waves tumbling over them. Rhona looked out, wondering if it was her imagination or was the sea getting rougher? The wind was the same, whipping strands of hair from under the hood of her cagoule, to lodge in her eyes or fasten themselves to the side of her mouth.

McNab hadn't donned his own hood. His hair was soaked, as was his face, water glistening on his bristled chin. Only PC Tulloch's red-cheeked face looked fit for the weather.

Now they were entering the area on the map that Rhona had held out the most hope for.

After the Wheems lay a series of deep sheltered bays. Glancing northwards, she sought some indication of the other half of their party, but in the now-poor visibility, could make out nothing other than flat fields, a few scattered farm buildings and the usual herd of cattle.

Both South and North Feas were empty apart from a small upturned boat, much the worse for wear, on the pebbly shore.

McNab, walking alongside her, was mumbling something. Peppered with curses, it sounded like the specifications of the missing *Antares*.

'What are you muttering?'

'The water tank is twenty litres capacity. The fuel tank holds 135 litres. We don't know what was in them when he left. Even if he's settled in one place, with both of them on board, he'll need to replenish the water at least.'

'So?'

'According to the map, the next section has fresh water run-off and a waterfall.'

It was a good point.

Ivan had come to a halt, his high-visibility jacket defying the weather and the light's endeavour to hide him. Water streamed down his face and dripped from his nose and chin. He seemed impervious to it.

'Okay, we're nearing the spot Derek indicated.' He started to strip off the bright jacket. 'If he is hidden down here, it might be better not to forewarn him of a police presence.'

'You'll get soaked,' Rhona protested.

'I'm soaked already.' Underneath he had a plain black jacket, much like theirs. He dropped the hi-vis jacket on the ground. 'Okay, let's go.'

Even through the swirling wind and rain, the spectacular nature of the coastline was obvious. Below her, centuries of pounding seas had dug deeply into the land to create intricate natural arches, hidden coves and, no doubt, caves, some tidal, others deeper and perhaps dry.

Rhona looked towards the horizon, hoping for a sighting of the police launch or the coastguard, knowing the visibility out there had grown so poor that there was little chance, unless any craft were close to shore.

'Right.' Ivan stood beside what appeared to be a sheer drop. 'We head down here,' he said, then disappeared into the rain.

McNab, obviously perturbed by his sudden disappearance, called out to him to wait, then, urging Rhona to go first, followed her. Used to following the hi-vis jacket, Rhona had to focus hard on Ivan's back as he wove his way down what could loosely be described as a path, except where he suddenly crossed slabs of rock. The rain met them in sheets, blinding Rhona until she had to stop and wipe her eyes.

Halfway down Ivan came to a halt, so suddenly, she almost knocked into him.

'What is it?' McNab's voice came from behind her.

Ivan suddenly dropped to his knees, gesturing at Rhona to do the same. 'There's something down there.' He pointed below.

Rhona followed his hand. Through the sheeting rain, she saw something white against the grey sea and rocks.

'That's got to be him,' McNab hissed from behind.

There was a boat there. Tucked in behind an arch, yards from the shore, rocking madly as a series of waves swept through the arch to break against the shingle.

McNab eased closer. 'Can we get down there without being spotted?'

Ivan was silent at the question, although Rhona could almost hear him ponder his answer.

'We'll edge further round, climb down on the other side and come under the arch.'

'Through the water?' McNab said in disbelief.

'The tide's not full in, so it won't be too deep.'

Rhona got the impression that McNab's estimation of Ivan was rising. Either that or he thought his constable had lost his wits. It seemed to her that both scenarios played out on his rain-drenched face. Finally he nodded an okay.

Keeping low, Ivan moved across, rather than down, leading them past the arch and the hidden beach. As soon as he deemed them out of sight, he straightened up.

'The next bit's tricky,' he said, as though it had been easy walking until now.

As they began the descent into what looked like frothing madness below, Rhona caught the sound, not of the sea, but of swift running water.

'The waterfall,' McNab said.

They came upon it seconds later, dropping down the cliff face in a long white plume to carve its way through the stony beach below, then disgorge itself into the sea.

His water supply.

Now they were slithering down, as any soil that gripped to the rocks became mud under the onslaught of rain. Hood up, ears enclosed, Rhona did not, at first, hear her mobile. The vibration against her body finally alerted her.

She stopped suddenly, causing McNab to collide with her back, nearly knocking her over. She pulled the zip down far enough to get a wet slippery hand inside. Throwing off her hood, she stuck the mobile to her ear.

It was Magnus asking if they'd had any luck. When Rhona told him they'd located the boat, he said, 'Hege says he has a flick knife. A fisherman's special with a second blade shaped like a needle. She's frightened he might use it if cornered.'

The signal died before Rhona could respond or even contemplate trying to contact Erling, and no amount of waving the mobile about in front of her brought the missing dots back.

Ivan had moved on, unaware that he'd lost his followers. As she set a course to catch up, she told McNab what Magnus had said.

'Fucking hell, why didn't she tell me?' he complained.

That wasn't the only thing that had worried Rhona about this sudden revelation. If Hege was suddenly concerned about what might happen when the police located Joe Millar, might she, if she could, try and warn him of their coming?

'Did she have a contact number for Millar?' Rhona said to McNab.

'Just what I was thinking. She swore she didn't, but . . .'

They had reached the beach, although this didn't consist of the usual strip of white sand but a pile of debris that had fallen from the rock face above. Beside them, the waterfall rattled over stones, as noisy as the waves that crashed to shore.

'Now we get really wet,' Ivan promised.

The curved rock that towered above them was greened by lichens and sea anemones clinging on for dear life. The water would, she was sure, have been a midnight blue had the sun been out. As it was, there was nothing inviting about it.

This time she didn't remove her boots, but waded in behind Ivan. Once in the shadow of the arch, they were plunged into an even deeper gloom. All sounds of their movement, the suck and chug of the sea, became exaggerated, resonating against the jagged stone walls. Ivan moved on, wading purposefully forward, apparently ignoring the fact that the water was growing deeper with every step.

Sensing McNab was biting his tongue, keen not to reveal his unease, Rhona put his fear into words. 'It's getting deeper, Ivan.'

He turned, his expression excited but unworried. 'It won't get any deeper than this. Once we turn the next corner, the ground rises towards the beach.'

She had almost got used to seeing only a few yards in front of her. Apart from an occasional drip of water from the roof of the arch, it was no longer raining on them, which was a small consolation for her water-sodden feet. Eventually the gloom lightened and they emerged, within sight of the pitching boat.

Its rear was towards them, but the name *Antares* was clearly visible.

McNab moved past her, keen now to take the lead. If he had a plan, he hadn't shared it with them.

'So,' Rhona said, 'what do we do now?'

All the windows were covered by curtains. Rhona couldn't imagine staying there in the pitching sea in the dark, when dry land was so close at hand. The cliffs alongside were dotted with dark shadows. Some of which would no doubt prove to be caves. Maybe he'd come ashore and taken refuge in one?

She said as much to McNab.

'We check the boat first,' he said. 'Have you got a signal?'

Glancing at the screen, it was obvious there was no chance, tucked down as they were with a wall of rock behind them.

'Coming from the other direction, the others should reach here soon,' Ivan told them. 'Do we wait?'

Rhona could sense by McNab's demeanour that that wasn't in the plan.

'If she's on that boat, we get her off now.' He turned to Ivan. 'The maximum draught for the *Antares* is 0.6 metres. I assume that's when it's loaded?'

Ivan nodded. 'I estimate it's sitting in around a metre at the moment,' he advised.

Rhona used her binoculars, then handed them to McNab. 'I can't see a dinghy. Do you know where it's stored?'

McNab's recollection of that part of the spec seemed to be missing.

'There's no dinghy pulled up on shore that I can see.'

There wasn't, although that didn't mean it hadn't been hidden.

'Okay, here's what we do,' McNab said.

Rhona had insisted he discard his outer garments and boots to get rid of the weight. He quibbled about that, but she'd been adamant.

'The cold will hit you with a vengeance. You'll go numb, then it'll get painful. By that time you want to be out of the water.'

'I know what the North Sea feels like,' he'd insisted. 'I was thrown in it, remember?'

She'd smiled, and that smile made him feel better.

The swim ladder faced him at the rear. From where they were, he could reach it without being seen. McNab managed to discard the cagoule, but struggled with the boots. Eventually he released his feet. By now he was already cold and trying hard to disguise it.

He plunged forward, exiting the safety of the arch. The plan had been to wade and not to swim. It was clear that swim or not, the waves would succeed in soaking him anyway.

The bottom half of his body already chilled and wet, the true shock of the cold only hit him when the water reached its freezing hand between his shoulder blades and took his feet from under him.

Gasping, McNab muttered desperately under his breath, the order to swim.

Gradually, and despite the forward push and backward suck of the waves, the stern of the *Antares* approached.

He looked to shore, seeking Rhona, and saw Ivan helping her to clamber there via the rocks.

So Rhona was safe, at least.

The swim ladder sat to the right of the outboard motor. Reaching out, he found the bottom rung. Grabbing a hold, he floated there, listening. There wasn't a sound from within. His memory of the child included her talking, incessantly. There was nothing being said within his earshot, at least.

He reached for and gripped the ladder, two rungs further up, preparing to pull the heavy weight of his body and sodden clothes from the water. As he did so, the boat pitched in an incoming wave. McNab lost his grip and fell back, submerging.

Caught unawares, he swallowed what tasted like a gallon of salt water, then broke the surface, trying hard not to cough his guts up and alert anyone on board.

His second attempt at the ladder brought him onto the back deck, which swam in a film of seawater.

There was no sound or movement from within, despite the arrival of his weight on the stern. The spec photos of the *Antares* indicated sleeping quarters forward, with a door between it and the main cabin.

McNab checked the shore to find Rhona and PC Tulloch already there. Rhona raised her hand and McNab gave her the thumbs-up.

Seabirds screamed above him as though in warning, and he realized that the rain had stopped.

Water pooling round his feet to add to that which was already there, he reached for the main cabin door and opened it. As he suspected, it was empty. The wheel and pilot's seat on the right, a bunk partially made up into a bed on the left.

He stood for a moment, listening again.

Above all he wanted to call the child's name, but what

if he did and she was in the forward cabin with Millar? Shielded now from the sound of waves, the resulting silence seemed more ominous.

McNab stood, hesitant. Then noticed something smeared on the forward door.

Fucking hell. Was that blood?

McNab grabbed the handle and wrenched it open.

There was something about the sight of a dead child that never left you. The image glued itself to your brain, reran in technicolour when you least expected it. He'd viewed three such corpses and had hoped never to view another.

There was blood on the floor, some spots on the bed, which was made up of six blue cushions laid out on the floor. A pillow, with a blood smear. A sleeping bag with something inside it that gave it shape.

His guts rising into his throat, McNab dipped his head and eased himself into that space. He imagined it smelt of little girl, of tears and terror.

Reaching out, McNab caught the end of the sleeping bag and tried to pull it towards him.

He emerged from the cabin and climbed back onto the side deck. All thoughts of being cold had left him. He looked for Rhona on the shore and found her there. Watching and waiting.

'Michael!' she called, her voice wavering on the wind.

McNab shouted back that the girl wasn't on board.

55

Of the three, this cave was the deepest. Its entrance swam with water, but only at ankle level. Ivan had indicated that the tide was on its way in and that at high tide, the entrance would be wholly underwater.

'If my memory serves me right, the very back stays dry. But don't stay in there too long or you won't get back out.'

The entrance was narrow, one person wide. McNab had sent Ivan back up the cliff to try and make contact with the other half of the search party before the dark descended, while he checked out the other caves. Rhona's insistence that they each carry a dry change of clothing in a backpack had paid off. Stripping, McNab had accepted his with open arms. Now reclothed, his outer garments back on, the only wet items were his boots.

Her despair at the shouted message that the girl wasn't on the *Antares* had been tempered by McNab's arrival on shore with his tale of the bloodstains on the inner cabin. It was clear from his expression that he'd been convinced he was about to find the girl's body.

Which might yet be the case.

Emerging from the narrow entrance, her torch now picked out a heightened inner cavern. The water was less here, just a thin film over sand. Her every movement seemed amplified as though she'd just entered a cathedral in the rock. Lowering her torch, she realized that it wasn't completely dark, and the little light that existed wasn't coming from behind her but in front.

She moved forward, heading towards that dim light, to find the ground rising. Soon she left sand, and her feet found stones again, grey slabs like those outside. The stones were wet but not under water. The passage had narrowed once more, barely wide enough for her to pass through. Ivan or McNab, broad-shouldered and clothed in bulky waterproofs, would have struggled to make it.

Around six feet in length, the passage deposited Rhona onto dry land. Above her, a vertical hole in the rock proved to be the source of the light.

She stood for a moment, listening. Somewhere in the distance was the scream of a seabird, the low boom of water against rock, the rattle of gravel as a wave shifted it. In here, only the sound of her breathing.

She switched on her torch again and ran it around the space.

A scattering of feathers and droppings bore witness to the detritus falling from the bird life on the rocks above. No evidence however of human habitation. She had turned to go when she caught a sound.

A breath or a sigh?

And not her own.

'Inga,' she called softly. 'Inga, are you here? It's Rhona. Everyone's out searching for you. Your mum wants you to come home.'

She didn't expect an answer, but felt it important to say the words.

The sound of her voice died in the silence, and with it the vague hope that she might have been right.

Then a small voice said, 'Daddy's gone to get Mummy. He's going to bring her here and we'll all leave together on our boat.'

She was nestled in a crack in the far wall of the cave.

The torch beam found her face, making her blink. Wrapped in a dark blanket, she looked dry and unharmed. Rhona, keen not to spook the child, came slowly forward.

'Are you okay?'

The eyes that met hers were tired and a little afraid.

'Daddy told me not to show myself, if anyone found the cave. He told me he would be back soon with Mummy.'

To Rhona, Millar's instructions sounded more like a threat than a command.

'Did he tell your mummy he was coming for her?'

She shook her head.

'No, he said he wanted it to be a surprise.'

'The bastard,' McNab hissed under his breath when she told him.

'Magnus warned that he was a danger to the child's mother,' Rhona said.

'How long ago did he leave?'

'He brought Inga ashore last night. Told her to hide and wait for him.'

'How the hell does he get from here to the top of the island without being spotted?'

'He planned to walk through the night.'

'What?'

'It's three miles cross-country to Lady Village. All on the flat. From there to Lopness Bay, say another three miles. Two more and he's at the Sinclair place.'

'So he could be there by now?'

'Yes.'

'And I took PC Tulloch away from sentry duty. What a fucking idiot.'

'We need to get a message to Erling.'

'You stay here with Inga,' McNab said.

'We can't stay in the cave, the tide's coming in,' Rhona reminded him. 'I think we should all go together.'

The child had taken some persuading to abandon the cave. However her father had put it, she wasn't keen to cross him.

Rhona had explained about the tide and how she would be cut off, but it had taken McNab to convince the child. He'd reminded her of how she'd agreed to be a detective like him and that had helped lead them to the skull.

'You found it?' she'd said, and for the first time Rhona had seen a light in her eyes.

'Yes. And because of that, we think we know who it was.'

'Who?' she'd said.

'Your great-aunt.'

She hadn't been surprised by that. 'I knew it was something to do with me. I knew it. And the flower? Did Mr Flett find out about the flowers without my help?'

McNab had been at a loss to answer that one and had turned to Rhona for help. She'd decided to tell the truth. The child would hear it soon anyway.

'Sam was drowned on the causeway, when he went out looking for you.'

She looked stricken at this. 'Daddy didn't tell me that.'

'Your daddy didn't tell you a lot of things,' McNab said. 'How sad and worried your mum is. How everyone is searching for you. How much your friends miss you.'

'Daddy told me you all knew I was with him. That Sam had loaned him the jeep to pick me up.'

Rhona had suspected as much.

As they made their way back to the entrance, McNab had held the girl's hand, lifting her in his arms when they met standing water. Ivan was right, the tide was coming in. In the outer section of the cave it now reached as far as Rhona's knees.

Emerging, they found dusk falling.

Rhona looked up at the sea wall they'd climbed down earlier.

Could they get back up there in the dark, without Ivan to guide them?

56

He'd told Muir to go home not long after they'd begun the search. Watching him struggle against the wind, Erling had realized that the stuffing had been truly knocked out of the Ranger. Any sure-footedness was also missing, making him more of a liability than an asset.

Questioning Muir closely, map in hand, he'd had most of his questions answered before he let him go. Despite time spent here as a child, Erling wasn't as familiar with the western coast of Sanday as he was with the north. PC Tulloch, on the other hand, had professed to know this shoreline well, and they would meet up with his group soon enough.

Their own search had proved fruitless. Rough seas and deserted bays were all they'd found. They were less than halfway south when PC Tulloch had appeared out of the driving rain, striding towards them, his rosy cheeks belying the weather he'd come through.

His news that they'd located the *Antares* had been welcome. That there was no sign of the child, not so good. Every bone in Erling's body was screaming at him that she was already dead. And the blood McNab had apparently discovered in the cabin pointed that way.

Dusk was falling, and he knew that would bring an end to the search. The latest forecast suggested the weather would deteriorate overnight. It was time to get everyone inside. Whatever evidence lay on the *Antares* would have to wait until tomorrow.

Having delivered his message regarding the boat, PC Tulloch had made his way back to help guide DS McNab and Rhona up the cliff.

Bringing Ivan home to Sanday had proved to be the right decision, despite McNab's concern about familiarity between police officers and the public.

On Orkney we will always be close to those we serve. Neighbours, friends, relatives.

He marshalled his troops and set them walking back the way they had come. Drenched, and disappointed at their lack of success, they needed to dry off and get something to eat.

The call reached him at the campsite. Rhona's voice was broken in parts, but he picked up the gist of it. The girl was safe and well. Her report of Millar's probable location brought a chill to Erling's heart.

He had come here to be with her and tell of their search. Show Claire that they hadn't given up on her daughter. Weakened by his own guilt, he was losing any sense of himself. Any notion that he had been part of this community.

It seemed to him in that moment that the Sinclair house stood at the edge of their world. At the edge of their sanity. He approached with trepidation, aware he wasn't bringing hope, only an indication of their continued determination.

Through the window he saw her, sitting there, as still as death.

A trickle of blood ran down from her mouth. She was tied, as he had tied up Jamie Drever. The sight of it reminded him of his own cruelty. Even as he stood transfixed at the window, she turned her eyes slowly in his direction and, seeing him there, forbad him with a shake of her head to enter.

'Get help,' she mouthed, before a shadow crossed the path between them.

Millar was as big and powerful as Derek remembered. Claire was right. He couldn't take him on his own. Derek stepped back into the shadows.

The police were all on the western seaboard, out of range.

He thought of the girl. Where was she, if not with Millar?

He stood hesitant. Everything he'd learned as a Ranger seemed to melt into indecision. He couldn't go in there, and he couldn't stand out here and watch Claire taking the beating that had already begun.

He had hurt Jamie Drever in his anger. Twisting the rope tightly against the bony wrists, demanding to know the truth about his father. He had been capable of such cruelty, even found himself empowered by it.

Just like my father.

Just like Millar.

And what of Inga? What had Millar done with the child?

I can't let this happen.

There were three houses other than his own and Sam Flett's within sight of here, and he knew a place he could get a signal.

It was time for Sanday folk to look after their own.

The first to arrive was old Mrs Skea's grandson, Nele's father. Nele might be a timid wee thing, but Rognvald was anything but. It had been he, together with Millar, who'd given the

Glasgow policeman a ducking, something Derek had chosen not to reveal. The surprise arrival was Torvaig. The younger man wore a determined expression.

'This isn't your fight, son,' Derek said.

'It is. We told him where Inga was. We believed his lies about Jones.'

Next up was Lachlan Dunlop's dad, Fergus, and his younger brother, John.

Derek looked round the complete company.

'He has a knife,' he told them. 'He was playing with it, flicking the blade. We'll have to be careful.'

Creeping up on the building silently was a lot more difficult with five than one. Every step sounded loud in his head. The wind was on the rise. He could smell the impending gale, feel the crackle of energy in the air. The faces around him felt it too.

Whatever happened tonight would end in a storm.

Derek motioned the others to stay back and moved to the window. He dreaded seeing her there, more blood on her face, her arms tied, reliving in that sight his own viciousness.

But the room was empty.

The chair sat in the same place. On its arms hung the rope used to bind her. But she wasn't there.

The wind whipped his words away as he tried to tell them. Not believing him, they barged past and into the house. The kitchen where they'd met the night the child had gone missing was empty. The floor was bloodied and the air smelt of fear, but Claire was no longer there.

Bellowing with anger, the men split up and began to search the place.

Derek sent two of them outside to check for Claire's car.

If he's driven her away in it . . .

He cursed himself for taking so long to organize her rescue. She'd seen him at the window. Waited in fear for him to come back with help. And he'd let her down.

Panic seized him. He felt himself drowning in his own indecision again.

Then Torvaig caught his arm.

'Listen!'

The scream was grabbed by the wind, its impact splintered by its force.

'Did you hear that?' Tor demanded.

The others had gathered round them. Tense, listening.

The scream came again, high and piercing.

'Where the fuck did it come from?' Tor said.

'The beach. It came from the beach.'

They all turned in that direction. Tor took off, followed by the others. Derek struggled to keep up. It was pitch black and now blowing a gale. The wind on his chest felt like a punch.

Before them the waters of the bay heaved, the white of the sand already consumed. In the distance the lighthouse blinked its beam only to see it swallowed in the dense sheeting rain.

They halted at the water's edge, searching the dark mass of water for their prey.

Then he saw them. Two figures in the waves. Millar's hand in Claire's hair, jerking her head under the water, then out again. Derek imagined her holding her breath until the moment she might scream.

And scream she did, though the sound was weaker this time.

She was drowning.

They plunged in en masse, the younger Tor making the

biggest headway against the waves. Derek felt his boots fill, his clothes growing sodden, both becoming a weight to drag him down beneath the waves.

Sheet lightning lit up the sky with a crack.

In it he saw Millar's face, white, demonic even as he jerked Claire's head back, exposing her pale neck. In his other hand the knife glinted, two-pronged, blade and spike.

He's going to slit her throat.

The realization of this propelled him forward. Ahead of him, Tor lost his footing and Derek saw him disappear beneath the waves. They were beyond the sand now, in the place of the rocks. There was no guaranteeing a foothold.

Derek threw himself forward. The others were strung out, their progress dependent on where they'd entered the water, and where the current, stronger now, had pulled them.

I'm the closest. If I don't reach her in time no one will.

His fury and the undertow of an outgoing wave dragged him there.

Coming on Millar suddenly from behind, he hit his broad back with a thud.

Millar plunged Claire's head back under the water and turned to see what had met him, but Derek had sunk beneath the surface.

Claire's hair waved like tangle in his face and mouth.

As the next swell hit, Derek grabbed Millar's ankles and swept his feet from under him.

Unbalanced, he crashed forward into the waves, arms flailing. The knife dropped from his hand. Derek didn't let go of the upturned feet until he was encircled by the threshing arms and legs of the others.

What happened next, he would never be sure of.

What he did remember was pulling Claire's limp body

away. Lifting her head above the water, murmuring words of encouragement and pulling her towards the shore.

The body was travelling further out and east with every wave. It would soon pass the northern tip of Start Island. It would come to land somewhere, eventually. Maybe months or even years from now. After feeding a myriad of fish, what remained might appear on another shore.

But not here. Not on Sanday.

As a Ranger, Derek Muir knew that those swept away by the sea around Sanday were rarely returned there.

The others melted away, leaving him with Claire. Nothing was said. Nothing would ever be said. He helped Claire into the bathroom and heard her turn on the shower. He boiled a kettle and made a pot of tea. He stoked up the fire. He took the incoming call on the landline and heard Inga's excited voice. He carried the handset through to the bedroom and knocked on the door.

When Claire opened it, he handed her the phone without saying why.

Then he watched her face light up. Saw the joy in her eyes. As he turned away she took his arm, her hand shaking, and said a silent thank you.

The letter lay on the kitchen table. The letter Millar had made her write before dragging her down to the beach.

I cannot live without my daughter.

It was to be Claire's suicide note. The reason why she had given herself to the sea.

Derek screwed the note up and threw it on the fire. The dry paper blazed up briefly, then died.

McNab was the one to lead Inga inside, her hand in his. He noted Claire's bruised face, the cut at the corner of her mouth. Inga loosened her grip on him and ran to her mother, to be swept into her arms.

There were images that glued themselves to your brain. Images of death, but sometimes images such as the one before him now. McNab registered it, searing it into his memory, so that he might recall it in place of all the others.

'Thank you, Detective Sergeant McNab,' Claire said. 'Thank you.'

57

It was the silence that woke her. Rhona realized that on Sanday the absence of wind was as unique and compelling as the wind itself.

From the window, the beach, white and empty, was bordered by a sea that bore no resemblance to the frothing grey waters of the previous night. The sky arched above it, the palest of blues, a dawn tinge kissing the horizon.

The cottage slumbered on, as did McNab.

He lay crushed on the sofa, under the duvet he'd taken from Chrissy's room. Why he hadn't chosen the bed, she had no idea. Except perhaps that he hadn't expected to sleep. Not after the previous night's proceedings. When the adrenaline ran high, it was difficult to come down from it.

Despite his awkward pose, he looked peaceful. She studied the face that had gone through a gamut of emotions as they'd searched for the girl, from hope, through horror, to relief and joy.

He never gives up.

Rhona left him sleeping there, an idea having formed during her view of the sea from the bedroom window. Her wetsuit, packed and unused, she brought out now, donning it quickly in case she should change her mind.

Barefoot, she crossed the low grassy dunes that lay between the cottage and the beach.

Jumping down, she negotiated the dried seaweed that crunched beneath her soles before stepping into the softness of sand.

On Skye the water deepened swiftly, making submersion quicker. Here the approach took longer, the water creeping up your legs and thighs at a slower pace.

She'd reached the line of rocks that came together from east and west to form their own little bay. Stumbling a little as her feet met rock, Rhona dived below the surface and struck out.

The cold water that crept inside the wetsuit was gradually warmed by the heat of her body. She swam purposefully, until she felt the current begin to drag her eastwards towards the lighthouse. At that point she turned and, heading back into the shelter of the bay, bobbed in the flat calm and looked to shore.

From this location in the clear morning air, she could make out the grey stones of each of the dwellings in this northernmost part of the island.

Inga's house, Sam Flett's, Derek Muir's, the cottage and the schoolhouse. The wider circle took in Inga's little group of school friends. On land, this view hadn't been possible, but here, it was clear that, though not a village, what she looked on was a distinct community.

Feeling the cold start to penetrate, she struck out for shore. When she reached the shallow water, Rhona stood up and began to wade back.

Had it not been for the sun, she would have missed the knife. Glinting off the open blade, it acted like a mirror, the sparkle drawing her into the shallows to investigate.

As she reached for it, she instinctively stopped herself

and, drawing back, looked around for something she might use to grasp it, other than her bare fingers.

A fern of green seaweed provided the answer.

Rhona extracted the bone-handled knife and headed back with her find.

McNab was making coffee when she appeared at the door. Rhona ordered him to bring an evidence bag.

'What the fuck?' The stupid look he gave her suggested he was still half asleep.

'Go on,' she urged him as she dripped in the porch.

He registered her request and went to fulfil it.

The knife secured now inside the bag, she demanded a towel. A cheeky grin on his face, McNab fetched one as bid. Rhona shut the door and began to strip off the wetsuit.

'It's not as though I haven't seen you naked,' he reminded her, through the intervening door.

Rhona ignored the jibe and, wrapped in the towel, headed for the shower.

McNab, his interest now focussed on the exhibit she'd brought back, called through. 'Where the hell did you find this?'

'In the water, just off the beach,' Rhona answered.

When she returned, she found McNab busily taking photographs of the bone-handled knife.

'I'll send these to Hege. See if she can identify the knife as the one Millar was carrying.'

Last night, it hadn't seemed appropriate for McNab to interrogate Claire about a visit from her former partner, when she'd just been reunited with her daughter. At a nod from Erling, they'd bowed out, shortly after establishing that

'Daddy' had been there, but 'Mummy hadn't wanted to go to the boat because the weather was too bad'.

McNab had openly played along with the charade, despite Claire's cut lip and frightened eyes, realizing, as they all did, that she was shielding her daughter from the reality of what had happened there.

'Assuming the knife is his, how did it end up in the water?' McNab said as he refilled his coffee mug. 'And where's Millar now?'

This was the first time she'd visited the Ranger's home. Viewed from a distance, it looked very like the cottage. One-storey high, thick grey walls, flagstone roof, a small walled garden tucked in behind, with various outbuildings on the seaward side. In this case, the outbuildings were all in good repair, although at least one of them was obviously being used as a home for stray cats, which caused McNab to give it a wide berth.

The boat they'd used to cross to Start Island wasn't in evidence, and Rhona wondered initially whether the Ranger had gone out in it. But as she and McNab approached, the door was opened and Derek Muir stepped outside to greet them.

He looked much better than the man who'd addressed the assembled company at the strategy meeting, and he now seemed able to meet her gaze. He welcomed them inside, where a fire blazed in the hearth.

'Can I offer you tea or coffee, Dr MacLeod? Detective Sergeant?'

She thanked Muir, but declined the offer, as did McNab.

'I see your boat's gone?' McNab said.

The Ranger nodded. 'I didn't get a chance to secure it before the storm hit.'

'How are Claire and Inga this morning?' Rhona asked.

'I thought it better to give them some time alone together, so I haven't gone over yet.'

Eventually, McNab posed his question. 'Did you see Joe Millar last night?'

The Ranger met McNab's eye without hesitation. 'No, he'd left by the time I arrived.'

'And how was Claire?' Rhona said.

'Distressed.'

'He'd hit her?' McNab came in.

'You saw her face.'

'Did she say why he left in the middle of a storm?'

'He heard my pickup, and thought it was the police.'

It was a plausible enough explanation.

'Is there any chance he could have taken your boat?'

Rhona watched the Ranger's face as McNab posed the question. She thought he was surprised by it, then, as though it had caused a little spark of intuition, he gave a half-smile.

'I hadn't thought of that, but yes, I suppose it's a possibility.'

'Did Claire mention a knife?'

The Ranger's expression grew grave. 'No, why?'

'No reason,' McNab lied.

They spoke then of his transfer to Kirkwall.

'DI Flett gave me permission to attend the bonfire tonight. I'll be taken to Kirkwall tomorrow.' He appeared resigned to his fate, probably made more bearable by Inga's safe return.

McNab indicated they were about to leave. The Ranger rose to see them out, but McNab said it wasn't necessary.

At the door Rhona turned to find Derek Muir staring out of the window at the calm waters of the bay.

'What d'you think?' she asked as they made their way towards the Sinclair place.

'It's a minute's walk. Why did he drive there in the pickup?'

'It was blowing a gale, remember?'

'Something's not right,' McNab pronounced.

'You feel it in your waters, as Chrissy would say?'

He grinned at her then, his face lighting up. 'Christ, I miss Chrissy.'

Rhona agreed wholeheartedly.

The door of the Sinclair house stood open. Outside was a collection of vehicles, and from within came excited chatter and children's voices. It seemed all the neighbours had come to register their delight that Inga was back safe and well.

'It's too busy in there. You can't question Claire just now,' Rhona said. 'I don't think she'll talk about it anyway. She's got Inga back. That's all she cares about.'

'Let's go find something to eat,' he said. 'You can contact Chrissy from the hotel.'

The drive south bore no resemblance to the one that had brought them north the previous evening. High visibility and a clear sky gave spectacular views across the flat landscape to the calm sea beyond. It was difficult to believe, with no evidence of debris, that such a storm had ever happened. Had such a wind hit Glasgow, Rhona doubted whether it would have left the city unmarked.

As they approached Cata Sand, they saw a couple of pickups, and some men replenishing the bonfire.

'They don't give up, do they?' McNab said.

'You'll go tonight?'

He glanced round at her. 'You're fucking joking?'

'I'll be there,' Rhona declared.

'Why?'

'Because Inga will be, and everyone else who searched for her.'

'You're going soft,' McNab said in disbelief.

Rhona laughed. 'Unlike you, you mean?'

Tor was in the kitchen when they entered. He looked a little surprised by their sudden appearance, but immediately offered to cook them breakfast, which McNab accepted.

Rhona took herself into the bar and downloaded three messages from Chrissy, who'd also attempted to phone her three times.

Glancing at the contents of the texts, Rhona immediately called Chrissy back.

'He didn't die of a broken neck,' Chrissy said when she answered.

'I saw that. What killed him?'

'The pathologist found evidence of a wound to the brain, inflicted he believed by a long thin blade, via the right ear.'

Rhona quickly brought Chrissy up to date on Inga's safe return.

Her pleasure at the news was evidenced by the whooping sound at the other end of the line.

'Have you found the bastard?'

'No, but I have found what I believe is his knife,' Rhona said. 'A fisherman's blade with a spike attachment.'

She rang off as Tor appeared with two stacked plates and

a pot of coffee, which when tasted, proved to be extra strong. McNab obviously had him well trained.

Depositing the food, Tor scurried off, surprising Rhona, who thought he might have hung around to try and find out more about the previous night's proceedings.

She told McNab the latest news as he tucked into his breakfast.

'So we might have Millar on a murder charge?'

'If the spike on the knife's a match to the wound. And other forensic evidence from the schoolhouse places Millar there.' She paused. 'He might have been at the cottage.' She explained about the smell of diesel.

McNab looked thoughtful. 'I had the feeling someone had been in my room at the hotel.'

They finished up and headed for the community centre to meet Erling. McNab's mood was upbeat, a smile playing the corner of his mouth, and he was humming a tune that sounded like the theme of *Star Wars*. Rhona wasn't sure whether he was picturing himself as Darth Vader or Luke Skywalker.

'Why so happy?' she said.

'I'm heading home tomorrow. As are you. First flight out of here.'

'And the hunt for Millar?'

'That's DI Flett's job now.'

The community centre car park was busy. It seemed those who weren't visiting Claire at home had come here to get the news.

Hege was at the coffee machine and McNab headed straight for her, keen to establish whether she could identify Millar's knife from the photographs he'd sent.

Rhona made her way into the meeting room, where

Erling, Magnus and the remainder of the team were gathered.

The atmosphere was one of elation. For the officers gathered here, this would have been their first and hopefully their last search for a missing child.

PC Tulloch gave her a big grin.

'Dr MacLeod. You okay?'

'Thanks to you, yes.'

Erling, composed as always, called them to order, just as McNab appeared.

The knife was produced and McNab indicated that it had been identified by Hege Aater as the one shown to her by Joe Millar.

Rhona explained where she'd found it, and added the news regarding the results of the post-mortem on Mike Jones.

'So Millar is in the frame for his death and this knife could prove to be the murder weapon?' Erling said.

'Yes.'

Rhona recognized the assembled company's relief at the news. Jones had been badly dealt with by the local community, but the possibility that someone from Sanday had been involved in his death had obviously caused concern.

Erling then revealed that Derek Muir's boat had been discovered by the coastguard on the rocks north of Start Point.

'The boat was spotted by Rognvald Skea last night. He thought there was a man on board.'

McNab interrupted him 'You're suggesting that man may have been Joe Millar?'

'In view of the fact that Dr MacLeod found Millar's knife in the water, that must be viewed as a possibility.'

McNab looked bemused. 'Why would Millar take to the water in a storm?'

'Claire Sinclair confirmed this morning that Millar had been at her house, but had left when he heard Derek Muir arrive, assuming it was the police.'

McNab pondered this.

'Okay, I buy the fact he would have left if he thought we were arriving. I just don't buy why he'd take to the water, especially in high seas.'

Rhona saw McNab's point. Millar was an experienced fisherman and no doubt used to bad weather, but to launch a small boat in the seas they'd witnessed last night seemed unlikely.

'Maybe because it's the last place he thought we would look?' she tried.

McNab wasn't convinced. 'The guy evaded us for days and kept the girl hidden. Why would he do something so stupid?' He paused, a light in his eye. 'Unless?'

'Unless what, Sergeant?' Erling said.

'Unless someone *was* actually chasing him.'

58

One thing for certain, after today, he wouldn't be travelling this fucking road again. Ever.

Seeing an approaching car, McNab made no attempt to draw into the nearby passing place. The black pickup didn't look as though it planned to stop either, the result being that they just scraped past each other, thanks to the sandy verges.

The other driver, who stared straight ahead, was revealed to be Rognvald Skea, grandson of old Mrs Skea, who McNab had attempted to interview without success because of her strong Sanday accent. Rognvald Skea was also, he remembered, wee timid Nele Skea's dad.

And the man who'd spotted the Ranger's boat with its unidentified passenger on board.

'They're all fucking related,' McNab muttered under his breath, while aware that he was wrong, and that at least fifty per cent of the island's current inhabitants came from elsewhere.

Still, that knowledge didn't meet his current mood.

Despite Rhona's advice, he had every intention of speaking to Claire Sinclair and Inga. And he wasn't officially off the case until tomorrow. He'd left Rhona at the community centre (he still couldn't attempt the name Heilsa Fjold), without revealing his plan, aware that she would try and dissuade him from it.

And I promised Inga I would come.

Passing Cata Sand and the bonfire yet again, McNab felt he was in his own particular version of *Groundhog Day*.

But tomorrow I'll be back in normality.

The other vehicles had gone from the front of the house. McNab pulled up and cut the engine.

When he knocked, it was Inga who answered, her face lighting up at the sight of him.

'I thought you weren't coming,' she said in a whisper.

'I promised I would,' McNab said with a smile.

'Do you want to speak to Mum?'

'If that's okay?'

Claire was in the kitchen. There was a rich scent of meat cooking and she was chopping vegetables at the table. Seeing McNab, her expression moved from welcome to caution, then she mustered herself.

'Detective Sergeant. Can I make you some coffee?'

He nodded, because it would make things easier between them, and he didn't want to spook her. The bruising had coloured a little from last night, the cut to the side of her mouth crusted over. Seeing the injuries brought his anger back.

His main fear when he'd confronted DI Flett this morning was, if they assumed Millar had drowned, they wouldn't take account of the fact he might reappear to hurt Claire or Inga again.

'I thought they would have posted an officer here with you.'

'They offered,' she said quickly, 'but I don't think I need

one.' She looked as though she might explain why, then thought the better of it.

The kettle having boiled, she spooned coffee into the cafetière.

'I'm sorry I can't make you an espresso,' she said.

'It seems everyone on Sanday knows my likes and dislikes.'

'It's the price you pay for living on a small island.' She glanced at him. 'You hate it here, don't you?'

'I'm not good with open spaces,' he admitted. 'I prefer the city.'

'I did too, for a while.'

As she pressed down the plunger he noted the long thin cuts on her wrists. Seeing his concerned look, she shook her head, intimating she didn't want him to mention them in front of Inga.

They supped coffee for a bit, before she said, 'Inga says she's taking you to see her den?'

McNab nodded.

So that was the excuse Inga had given for his visit.

The girl was sent to feed the cats, prior to their outing. McNab declined an invitation to accompany her, explaining that most cats didn't like him.

Once the door had shut behind her daughter, Claire said swiftly, 'DI Flett interviewed me this morning. I told him everything that happened last night.' Her expression indicated she had no desire to do that again. 'I know I have you to thank for finding Inga. I can't tell you how grateful I am . . .'

If she'd been about to say more, she was cut short by Inga's voice calling for McNab from outside.

They left the car where it was and Inga led the way. Once

out of view of the kitchen window, she veered towards the schoolhouse. McNab followed on behind, knowing that what he was about to do had no rational explanation.

Yet he planned to do it anyway.

They crossed the intervening fields. In one a large flock of geese had settled and didn't take off despite their approach.

'When Nele's dad comes back from building the bonfire, he'll fire his gun at them,' Inga informed him.

Recalling Rognvald Skea's expression in the car, McNab was glad he wouldn't be around when that happened.

The schoolhouse, he decided, had already assumed an air of abandonment. Maybe it was because there was no smoke coming from the chimney. Three large cats paced around an empty dish set at the door of an outhouse. Inga promptly extracted a bag of dried food from her pocket and tipped it into the dish, and the cats fell upon it.

When they reached the back door, McNab discovered that the grave had been filled in, the marks of the digger tyres obvious.

So Hugh Clouston had returned after all.

He'd thought, when they reached the schoolhouse to discover it locked, Inga would accept that her plan wasn't possible, but he was wrong.

She immediately checked below a few nearby stones before eventually waving a key at him.

'Everyone keeps a spare key nearby, even Mr Jones.'

Stepping inside the big room with its arched ceiling, McNab felt the sense of abandonment even more strongly. The air was cold and, he realized, all the warmth generated by the stove had been lost from the stones.

Inga stood in the centre of the room, her small figure very still.

'Listen,' she said. 'Can you hear them?'

McNab listened, despite himself. Playing along. If this made the girl happy, he was willing to do it.

When she asked him a second time, he had to admit he heard nothing. It seemed to him that Sanday, since the wind had ceased, had become as silent as the grave.

Inga smiled as though she held a secret that he was yet to share.

He followed her to the bedroom, where the covered easel still stood. At this point, McNab did feel uneasy. He had no wish to look again on the drawing that had, he thought, brought about Mike Jones's death.

But Inga had no qualms about pulling up the sheet.

It's extraordinary. How Jones had fashioned this without seeing the child.

Inga seemed pleased. 'She looks exactly like me,' she said. 'Which is why we have to put the flower back.'

It was the story she'd told him, as he'd carried her from the cave. How she'd seen the girl, heard her singing, on the beach and among the ruins of the camp.

Mr Flett knew it was a warning. He told Mr Jones to put it back. But he didn't.

The flower still sat on the kitchen table in its clear plastic bag.

McNab found himself uncomfortable with the thought of picking it up. Inga had no such qualms. 'I'm not sure who she was, but I think she was trying to help me, and Ola.'

He brought the ladder, and climbing into the loft, McNab switched on the light. All was as it had been the last time he'd been up there, when Mike Jones had called to him from the hall not to touch the other flowers.

He'd been blasé then, but not now.

They eased their way between the beams. On either side, neatly spaced out, the flowers lay in their little graves of ash. When they reached the empty one, Inga indicated that McNab should be the one to do the deed.

McNab tipped the flower into the palm of his hand and placed it carefully back in place.

Seconds followed while Inga studied its return, her face serious and content at the same time.

Fanciful ideas, he thought, *but what's the harm, if it makes the child happy?*

He imagined what Rhona's response would be when she found out.

Now you're the one going soft, he heard.

There was no wind outside, yet it seemed to McNab that the eaves began to sing as though played by it.

The whining sound changed and became a voice. A child's high-pitched rhythmic chant. A playground song?

McNab felt Inga's hand creep into his, and she smiled up at him.

'See. She's happy now.'

Leaving the Sinclair house, McNab, rather than turning onto the road south, headed for the beach. Gazing out over the flat calm surface of the water, it was difficult to believe he was on the same island, or even the same planet, as the previous evening.

There was no doubt in his mind that the knife Rhona had found here did belong to Joe Millar. It was the part of the story that took Millar from the Sinclair place to the Ranger's section of beach to steal his boat, dropping the knife in the process, that didn't ring true.

If he had run for the beach in that weather, then what was behind him must have been pretty damn scary.

His final remark about Millar possibly being chased had fallen on deaf ears. DI Flett had swiftly brought the meeting to a close by assuring McNab they were searching both on land and at sea for Millar. Then he'd thanked him and Rhona for their help.

They'd been summarily dismissed.

It was what he wanted, and yet?

McNab didn't like things not to fit. He didn't like questions that had no answer.

If Millar was dead, drowned off this island, then that was justice of a kind, he reminded himself.

McNab went back to the car. One more run along that road, past the wreck of the German destroyer, past the cows and that bloody mortuary, and *thank Christ*, this would be over.

59

'So you decided to come?' Rhona said, glancing down at the wellie boots provided by Tor.

'I'm here for the food,' McNab told her. 'Tor said he wasn't cooking at the hotel tonight, because all the grub was here.'

'Well, there's plenty of it,' Rhona said, eyeing up the loaded trestle tables.

The edge of the sands were lined with cars, and others constantly arriving. It looked like the entire island was planning on turning out. A suitable distance away on the sands stood the community fire engine.

'Some items of Millar's outer clothing have been found on the rocks near the holed boat,' Rhona told him. 'The news came in when you were away.'

'So they've decided he drowned?'

'It looks likely.'

McNab shrugged, as though resigned to the fact he was no longer involved.

'Are you going to tell me where you went this afternoon?' she said.

'No.'

Rhona let it pass. She had ways of getting McNab to talk when she wanted him to.

Dusk already falling, it looked as though the decision had been made to light the fire. Four torches were in the process of being ignited. Rhona recognized the men holding them as the fathers of Inga's friends. Each man clasped his child's hand in his own. Next to Inga and her mother stood the Ranger. Derek Muir glanced in their direction, then bending down, said something to the girl, who came running over to McNab.

'Will you carry my torch?' she said.

Surprised by the offer, it appeared McNab might refuse, so Rhona pushed him forward and said, 'Of course he will.'

Now in the limelight, McNab tried to look willing, although Rhona suspected there was a great deal of silent cursing going on beneath that fixed smile.

She laughed, enjoying his discomfort.

The four men spread out round the base of the bonfire, Inga and McNab closest to Rhona.

Stepping forward together, they lit the wood near the base. A moment of silence as the crowd waited for the kindling to ignite, then a whoosh as it caught, and sparks and flames flew up into the air to a combined cheer.

Her eyes now drawn to the guy at the top, Rhona noted he was dressed in oilskins, similar to the ones worn by Joe Millar that night in the pub, and a sou'wester. Rhona wondered if it was symbolic.

Magnus had arrived, with Erling and another man Rhona didn't recognize.

Seeking her out, Erling introduced him simply as Rory, although it seemed to Rhona that there was something being left unsaid. When the two men went to check out the food, Magnus told her that Rory and Erling were an item.

Rhona smiled. 'That's a quaint way of putting it.'

'Well, I don't think they've reached the partner stage yet.'

McNab had returned, his job done. He acknowledged Magnus, then declared his need to eat.

Rhona followed the two men towards the heavily laden table, partly because she was hungry, but also because she was keen to observe the interchange, if any, between McNab and Erling.

It would be good if the hatchets were buried before McNab left Orkney. Erling, she was sure, would be open to that. McNab possibly not so much.

The moment didn't turn out as she expected.

Although the bonfire lit up the sky, visibility was poor outside the fire circle, despite the storm lanterns deposited on the tables. During the brief introduction, Rhona's first impression of Rory had been of a tall well-built bloke of Scouse origin. If she'd been asked to describe his face in detail, she would have found the task difficult. His laugh was definitely distinctive though.

It seemed the laugh had brought the presence of the two men to McNab's attention.

Spotting Erling first, he hesitated. Then his eyes found Rory. The two men were having a conversation which had an intimate look, as though the surrounding crowds weren't there at all.

McNab's reaction, she judged at first to be disapproving. What of, Rhona wasn't sure.

He swiftly selected some food and deserted the table, heading for one of the barrels of beer. Lifting a plastic glass, he began to fill it.

Perplexed, Rhona joined him. 'What is it?' she said.

'Who's the guy with the DI?'

'His first name's Rory. I didn't catch a surname. According

to Magnus they're a recent item.' Reading his expression, she added, 'Why?'

McNab shook his head. 'No reason. Are you drinking?'

'Since we're being driven back in the post bus, yes. But not beer. I'll have white wine instead.'

He filled a glass from one of the open bottles and handed it to her.

'To going home,' he offered.

'To home.'

60

The view from the tiny island hopper windows was restrictive, but impressive nonetheless. McNab had shown no interest in a window seat, and was now staring straight ahead of him, at the back of the pilot's head.

The weather had remained settled enough for both the plane and the police launch to make the trip. Magnus had opted to accompany Erling, Rory and Derek Muir on the ferry crossing, leaving herself and McNab to the perils of the tiny plane.

As it rose, buzzing like a giant bluebottle into a clear blue sky, Rhona was rewarded with a view of Cata Sand and the burnt-out remnants of the bonfire.

After his toast to home the previous night, McNab had eaten a plate of food, then declared his intention to leave the party. Rhona had chosen to stay on a little longer. Watching the spectacle of the fireworks, enjoying seeing Inga and Claire so happy.

She wondered what Claire had told her daughter regarding her father's visit. What story she'd spun to excuse her cuts and bruises. From the short period of time Rhona had spent with the girl, both in the cave and in the car on the way back, she'd come to the conclusion that Inga was well aware her father was bad news, although like all children in such circumstances, held out the hope that he might change.

McNab had been morose when he'd departed last night, and just as morose when he'd been picked up this morning. Rhona had hoped she might draw him on the reason for his mood during their journey south, but even the hour spent waiting at Kirkwall for their plane to Glasgow hadn't produced a conversation.

He'd deliberately, she thought, closed his eyes and feigned sleep on the main flight south, even going to the trouble of sitting in the line of single seats, rather than share a double with her.

Whatever it was, he didn't want to talk to her about it.

When Rhona suggested they share a taxi from the airport, he'd pointed out how silly that would be since they didn't live near one another.

At that, he'd wished her farewell.

McNab gave the driver his address and sat back in the seat, relieved at last to be alone and away from Rhona's questioning glance. Had she asked him outright, he might have told her, but the longer he'd remained silent, the more difficult it had become.

Besides, he could be wrong.

On entering the city, he made a decision, leaned forward and asked to get out here instead.

'Something up, mate?'

McNab shook his head. He could have said he didn't fancy going home to an empty flat, or that his girlfriend had dumped him and he needed to drown his sorrows. He did neither. Just paid up, grabbed his bag and got out.

Standing for a moment in the busy thoroughfare, he breathed in the noise and smell of the city. A bus rumbled past. A girl nearby, dressed to the nines, gave her boyfriend a piece of her mind.

Home sweet home.

McNab slung his bag over his shoulder.

On entering the bar, he ordered a double and sat himself in a corner. He took out his mobile and, bringing up the photograph he'd taken at the bonfire, fired it off to Ollie in the Tech department, adding a text message that said, 'Can you check this guy out against records.'

McNab lifted the glass, admired the amber nectar for a moment, then swallowed it down.

The Wi-Fi connection at Kirkwall had been abysmal. It was only on reaching Glasgow that Rhona became aware of how out of touch she had truly been. Glancing at the list of messages and emails missed, one name other than Chrissy's stood out in its frequency.

She scrolled straight to the final message from Sean and opened it.

It was brief, saying only, 'See you soon.'

Did that mean he knew she was on her way home?

Rhona had no idea. She thought of McNab returning to an empty flat and felt a little sorry.

He won't miss the cat though, she thought with a smile.

Reaching the front door, she searched in her bag for the key.

Climbing the stairs, she heard the low soft notes of a saxophone, and found her heart lift a little.

Notes and Acknowledgements

Sanday is a magical island in the Orkney archipelago. I chose to set *None but the Dead* on Sanday after I appeared there to promote *Paths of the Dead*. Paul Harrison, a true crime writer himself, showed me a magic flower he had found in his loft. He even offered me the chance to take it home with me. I didn't, because in truth the muslin flower in the evidence bag both frightened and fascinated me in equal measure. Hence the spark of an idea linking the distant past with the more recent past and the present on Sanday.

All the characters in the story are fictitious, as is the schoolhouse which plays a central role. Rhona's cottage is modelled on a delightful cottage I rented in the north of the island while doing my research. I, like Rhona, swam there, although I did so in June, not November.

I give thanks to everyone who answered my questions, including the fishermen who advised me on where a boat might be hidden. To Dr Jennifer Miller who, being an expert in buried and hidden bodies, answered my questions on grave excavation, especially in the wilds of Orkney, and to soil expert Professor Lorna Dawson who very kindly sent me a soil map of Sanday with her advice.

But the biggest thanks must go to the people of Sanday for their help and cooperation in the writing of this book.

extracts reading groups

competitions books new

discounts extracts

extracts

competitions

reading groups

discounts

books

new

extracts

events

reading groups

events

books

new extracts

books new titles reading groups

interviews

reading groups

events extracts extracts

new

books

discounts

events

new books events

events

interviews new books extracts

events new

discounts extracts discounts

books

www.panmacmillan.com

extracts events reading groups

competitions books extracts new